A Secret Scottish Christmas

D0873086

A SECRET SCOTTISH CHRISTMAS

Paperback ISBN: 978-0-9976567-2-5
Print Edition

Praise For Regan Walker's Work:

"Ms. Walker has the rare ability to make you forget you are reading a book. The characters become real, the modern world fades away, and all that is left is the intrigue, drama, and romance."

—Straight from the Library

"The writing is excellent, the research impeccable, and the love story is epic. You can't ask for more than that."

—The Book Review

"Regan Walker is a master of her craft. Her novels instantly draw you in, keep you reading and leave you with a smile on your face."

—Good Friends, Good Books

"...an example of 'how to' in good story building... a multilayered novel adding depth and yearning."

—InD'Tale Magazine

"Spellbinding and Expertly Crafted"... "The path to true love is never easy, yet Regan Walker leads the reader to an entertaining, realistic and worthy HEA. Walker's characters are complex and well-rounded and, in her hands, real historical figures merge seamlessly with those from her imagination."

—A Reader's Review

"Walker stuns with her gift for storytelling, magically entwining historic fact and fiction to create a thought-provoking, sensual romance, one that will stay with you."

—Chicks, Rogues & Scandals

"Walker's detailed historical research enhances the time and place of the story without losing sight of what is essential to a romance: chemistry between the leads and hope for the future."

—Publisher's Weekly

"… an enthralling story."

—RT Book Reviews

Acknowledgements

My gratitude goes to photographer Kenny Muir for allowing me to use his beautiful photograph of Dunnottar Castle, dressed in winter's splendor, for my cover. A special thank you also goes to those who helped me make this novel historically authentic: Simon Cruickshank, the proprietor of The Ship Inn in Stonehaven, built in 1771, who confirmed that the inn had sufficient rooms in 1819 to accommodate William Stephen's guests; and Paul at Big Game Indicating Dogs, who read my scene of the deer stalking with Ailie's setters and assured me it could well have happened that way.

In addition, I must thank my beta readers for their contributions, especially Liette Bougie and Dr. Chari Wessel, whose contributions were invaluable.

Characters of Note

(with their stories noted)

Aileen ("Ailie") Stephen

Nash Etienne Powell, twin brother of Robbie

Robert ("Robbie) Pierre Powell, twin brother of Nash

William Stephen, Scottish shipbuilder in Arbroath, and Lady Emily Stephen (from *The Holly & The Thistle*)

Claire Powell, mother of the Powell sons and wife to Captain Simon Powell (from *To Tame the Wind*)

Hugh, the Marquess of Ormond, and Mary, Lady Ormond (from *Racing with the Wind*)

Captain Nicholas Powell and Tara Powell (from *Wind Raven*)

Sir Martin Powell and Lady Katherine ("Kit") Powell (from *Against the Wind*)

Muriel, Dowager Countess of Claremont (who appears in many of my stories)

Captain Dougal Anderson of William Stephen and Sons, shipmaster

Mrs. Harriot Platt, Lady Claremont's cook from London

Martha McBride, William and Emily's cook in Arbroath

Rhona, Ailie's maid

Angus Ramsay, maternal grandfather to Ailie and William in Stonehaven

George Kinloch, the gentleman farmer from Dundee, dubbed the "Radical Laird"

There are no secrets that time does not reveal.
—Jean Racine

Prologue

St Peter's Field, Manchester, England
16 August 1819

The crowd surged around Nash like a living thing. Voices of children mingled with those of their parents anxiously awaiting the man they believed would give eloquent voice to their long-ignored cries for reform.

Unmindful of the smoke from the city's factories marring the blue of the midday sky, thousands had flocked to the vast green field. Mothers wore their Sunday best, some carried babes in arms. Their presence only added to Nash's fears.

The conversations he and his twin brother Robbie had overheard in Manchester's taverns had educated them to the people's hope that such a large gathering would rouse the government to act. They wanted representation in Parliament and relief from the heavy taxes that took bread from the mouths of their children.

Nash had seen for himself the hunger and sickness that stalked the overcrowded city like a destroying angel, claiming lives old and young.

Manchester's huge population lacked even a single Member of Parliament while some villages with a dozen people and a few cows had their own MP, a situation that kept votes in the hands of the landed few.

Jostled by the crowd, Nash took a step back, shaking his head. He doubted the workers in Manchester would see their hopes realized. The political climate in England turned a deaf ear to cries for reform. Fearful the lower classes would rise up like those across the Channel, the government's mood was one of suspicion, even fear.

The Home Secretary Lord Sidmouth had sent Nash and Robbie to Manchester to spy on those "fomenting rebellion". But in the days they'd been here, they'd uncovered no signs of revolt. As far as Nash could determine, none of the men in today's crowd bore arms. They carried only the meager food they had to sustain their families for the day.

What man brought his children to an armed rebellion?

Shifting his gaze to the right, Nash caught a glimpse of Robbie's head of nut-brown hair rising above the crowd some yards away. His brother's furrowed brow shouted the foreboding they both felt. As twins, they often shared emotions, a benefit to them as spies.

Nash's unease grew, his stomach twisting in knots, as he thought of the forces mustered a few streets away: six troops of the 15th Hussars cavalry and seven companies of infantry, to which had been added the Manchester Yeomanry.

Over one thousand armed men stood ready to subdue any violence offered by the unarmed crowd.

Convinced this would be an insurrection, Sidmouth wanted to make a point. But did the Home Secretary intend to do more? Nash feared Sidmouth wanted blood. Did his plan, undisclosed to Nash and Robbie, include teaching the people of Manchester a terrifying lesson?

Murmurs spread through the crowd as the man for whom they had patiently waited finally made his way to the wooden platform. Henry Hunt, with his distinguished head of gray hair, stood ready to address the people.

Nash glanced at his pocket watch, noting the time: half past one.

From the other side of the field, a band struck up a rousing "God Save the King" and, for respect owing their monarch, the men took off their hats. Nash, too, removed his cap, setting it back on his head when the music stopped.

With eager anticipation, the people surged forward, straining to hear Hunt's first words.

Suddenly, on the edge of the field, not far from where Nash stood, the Manchester Yeomanry appeared. Their blue uniforms and tall hats trimmed in gold made a flashy contrast to the common dress of the people.

Nash desperately wanted to believe the soldiers were there merely to assure order. The people must have believed it was so because they received the yeomen with shouts of goodwill. But the hard expressions on the soldiers' faces told Nash they were there for an entirely different purpose.

Without warning, the yeomen raised their sabers and galloped into the crowd.

Horrified, Nash watched as the cavalry, reeling in their saddles, hewed their way through the defenseless heads and naked hands of the people. Heedlessly, they chopped off limbs until their blades dripped blood, leaving gaping wounds and blood-spattered clothes in their wake.

The thronging masses panicked, shrieking in fear and protest. Eyes wild, men, women and children screamed and tried to run. Trapped by the crowd, there was nowhere to go.

Heart-rending cries from women and children filled the air, piercing Nash to his soul.

Ignoring the shrieks and groans, the uncaring cavalry plunged forward.

Catching Robbie's eye, Nash pushed his way through the fleeing crowd, heading toward the nearest yeoman to try to stop the *mêlée*. Before he could reach him, the soldier raised his saber and struck a woman in the head with the flat of his blade.

She plummeted to the ground. Her children fell to their knees beside her wailing, "Mama!"

Hot fury burned in Nash's chest, as he raced to the yeoman. "These people are unarmed!" he shouted above the din. "Drop your sword! Forbear!"

The yeoman, slurring his words beyond understanding, swung his blade at Nash.

The blow hit him on the side of the head. Stunned, he crumpled to the grass.

Blackness closed around him as he heard Robbie shout, "Leave off, you fool! He is Sidmouth's man!"

Chapter 1

Arbroath, Forfarshire, Scotland
December 1819

Aileen Stephen drew her blue tartan shawl tightly around her, burying her cold fingers in the soft wool as she stared out the window, watching snow fall in great lumps on the shipyard. In her mind, she saw the face that had come to her in a dream the night before. A dark-haired man of handsome visage who seemed to see into her very soul.

A man she did not know.

The stove in the shipyard office warmed her backside, but the air next to the large window carried winter's chill. "It's snowing again, Will. Soon, the entire yard will be buried."

As she watched, the snow covered the decks, rigging and masts of the schooners docked in front of the company's offices, making them appear like fairy ships. Beyond the snow-covered schooners, the North Sea showed its drab face, like an old sailor's, gray and sullen.

Behind her, she heard her brother scratching a line into his ledger. "Aye, no work outside today, but the lads are still working on the new schooner in the main shop and I've got others cutting sails. They'll have the week before Hogmanay and the New Year to spend with their families, so they'll not mind a bit of work before then. 'Sides, I've made sure the stove fires are stoked and fed with coal."

She turned away from the window and reached her hands toward the heat from the office stove, her ginger hair falling over one shoulder. Opening the door of the stove, she added a log and breathed in the sweet smell of the burning birch. "When are your guests arriving from London?"

Will looked up from his ledger. "They may be English, Ailie, but they're *our* guests and Emily's friends, so do be kind to them." He gave her one of his smiles that never failed to soften her ire. As older brothers went, he was more than tolerable.

"Haven't I been practicing the songs to play for them?"

"Aye, you have. They will love the music. I want Emily's first Christmas away from London to be a special time of celebration, one she will always remember." He leaned back in his chair and began to chew the end of his cedar wood pencil, seeming to contemplate the unknowable as only Will could. In truth, Ailie loved her English sister-in-law of one year and would be happy to please her, for Emily had made Will content.

"So, when do they arrive?"

Will twisted his pencil. "That depends on the weather, of course. I sent the *Albatross* a week ago. Allowing for time to load and take on provisions, they should be leaving London about now."

"Might I know who's coming?"

Her brother set his pencil down, crossed his arms over his chest and leaned back in his chair. His mouth quirked up in a grin. "Muriel, Lady Claremont, Emily's dearest friend. She's an older dowager and quite respected in London Society." He smiled as if remembering something. "Loves feathers and parties. You'll like her." Uncrossing his arms, he picked up his pencil. "I should probably warn you, though. Muriel dabbles in matchmaking. 'Twas the countess who picked me for Emily."

Ailie considered the possibility of an aging English countess who dabbled in matchmaking being one of their guests. Lady Claremont would be hard pressed to find candidates for her efforts in Arbroath. Ailie's younger brothers and unmarried cousins were all in Aberdeen, where her father and uncle ran the successful shipbuilding concern Alexander Stephen & Sons.

"Who is the countess bringing with her?" Someone for Ailie to talk to, she hoped.

"Ormond and his wife, Mary, of course."

Ailie had never met Lord Ormond, one of her brother's Cambridge friends, but Will had spoken often of him and his young wife, both English aristocrats. Emily, who knew the pair, reported they were great lovers of horseflesh and raised thoroughbreds for racing.

"The Ormonds attended our wedding in London last December. The marchioness is younger than you, yet she has already managed to give Ormond his heir and a spare."

"Is that a hint?" Will didn't need to tell her she had reached the age of twenty-four and was still unwed.

"Nay, Ailie. I know I sometimes tease you but if you desire to never wed, though Mother will be appalled, you will always have a home with Emily and me. It's just that…"

"What?"

"I would see you find the happiness I have found with Emily. Kindred souls and all that."

"'Tis rare, Will, especially for a woman who would not confine herself to the home."

"I know, but at least our guests will provide some interesting conversation that should appeal. Ormond wrote to say he's bringing his friends from Powell and Sons." At her puzzled expression, he added, "It's a London shipping company. Every man in the family is a shipmaster—and there are five of them." Will waggled his chestnut brows. "Ormond thinks we'll have much to talk about since the Powells buy ships and we build them."

She chuckled. "That *will* make for interesting discourse." Ailie's whole world revolved around shipbuilding. It would always be her preference to speak of ships rather than London gossip or Scotland's unhappy textile workers. She had just turned nineteen when Will returned from the war in France and urged her to leave Aberdeen to join him in his new venture in Arbroath.

She went back to her desk and picked up the drawing she'd been working on. "So, how many are coming?"

Her brother reached for the letter he had set aside. "According to Ormond, their children are spending Christmas with the grandparents. So, in addition to the Ormonds and the dowager countess, all four of the Powell brothers have accepted the invitation, the two who are married bringing their wives. Nine guests in all."

"Nine?" Her eyebrows rose. "'Tis fortunate you added that wing to the house after you married Emily." Will had already possessed a grand house on the hill overlooking the shipyard when he took his English bride. In the year that followed, it had become a sprawling estate, complete with an orangery for Emily, whose constitution favored a warmer clime.

Will grinned. "I had to enlarge the house. I did not change the company's name to William Stephen and Sons to remain childless. Emily and I expect to have many bairns. Come spring, Lord willing, we shall have the first one. Perhaps a braw lad with my auburn hair and brown eyes."

"Or a lass with Emily's black hair and thistle-colored eyes," Ailie teased.

Her brother paused, his face taking on a look of bliss that told her he was thinking about the children he expected to have. "Aye."

Resisting the temptation to roll her eyes, Ailie said, "Whatever the good Lord gives you, Will, I'm just glad we have the additional bedchambers for *our* visitors. Has Emily warned our cook?"

He shrugged his broad shoulders. "I believe so. She mentioned something about talking to Martha about the cook Muriel is bringing, but you can ask her at dinner."

"The countess is bringing her cook?" Ailie envisioned sparks flying in the kitchen as roast goose, boar's head and turkey replaced salmon, venison and steak pie.

"Emily thought Martha might need help with the English dishes for the Christmas feast."

"I just hope you ken what you're about. The Kirk does not abide Yule celebrations."

Will's expression took on the look of a determined Scot. "I have loved Christmas since my days at Cambridge and 'tis worth the risk of a frown from the parish minister to make Emily happy."

"As you wish. Are we still going to Grandfather Ramsay's for Hogmanay?"

"If the weather allows, aye. A short sail up the coast to Stonehaven could be great fun. Our guests might like to take a sledge through the snow to see the old castle. I'll ask Grandfather to book the Ship Inn. Now that I think of it, we'll need all their rooms. Perhaps Father will come from Aberdeen. What do you think?"

"Grandfather might not be pleased with so many Sassenachs descending on him, but he will expect us for Hogmanay. Once Father hears of our plans, he and Mother will be staying put in Aberdeen. Aside from the fact he doesn't like to travel at this time of year, he's still riled about what happened in Manchester. The last time I visited him, our uncle had just returned from Glasgow where the mood of the weavers is angry."

William frowned. "There's talk in the Arbroath taverns, too."

That night, after she retired to her bedchamber, Ailie took out her diary, drew her shawl around her and opened a new page. Replacing the candle that had burned to a stub, she dipped the quill in the ink and began.

15 December

I am preparing for a storm (not the current one that has brought so much snow, but one of a different kind). Will says we're to have guests from London to celebrate Christmas—in secret, of course, else Mr. Gleig, the parish minister, will have something to say about our celebrating a holiday banned by the Kirk for centuries. Bother. Father will be ever so displeased. And, after we sail our guests to Stonehaven for Hogmanay, Grandfather Ramsay might never speak to us again. Oh, did I mention the Countess of Claremont is bringing her English cook? Batten down the hatches.

Adelphi Terrace, London, 16 December

Robbie set his coffee on the table in front of the parlor sofa and turned his attention to the *Times* article. The correspondent, who'd been on St Peter's Field that sultry August afternoon when Robbie had nearly lost his brother to a drunken yeoman's saber, recalled in shocking detail the events of that day. The newspapers had dubbed the debacle "the Peterloo Massacre" in a parody of Waterloo. They were not far off.

It had been months since that terrible day, yet London still spoke of little else.

The names of the four hundred injured were printed along with the nature of their wounds in the hope sympathizers would contribute to the charity set up to support them.

Over one hundred of the injured were females, the mothers, wives, sisters and children of those attending the meeting. The fifteen dead were also named, including one Sarah Jones, mother of seven, fatally injured by a blow to the head.

How the Prince Regent, after all that, could congratulate the hussars, who had entered the fray after the yeomanry, inflicting more bloody wounds, Robbie could not fathom. But there it was, signed by

Sidmouth on behalf of the prince, clearing the hussars and magistrates of any wrongdoing.

No one in London believed a word of it.

Nash had recovered from his head wound, the scar buried under his thick brown hair, but Robbie shuddered each time he remembered the blood. He'd had to pull the drunken yeoman from his horse to keep him from taking another swing at Nash.

The newspapers had not exaggerated what followed that day. Sixty thousand people, peacefully gathered to hear about reform, attacked by saber-wielding yeomen and hussars. Like Nash, Robbie wondered if the result had been intended by Sidmouth all along.

Robbie took a drink of his coffee and read on, surprised to learn that a few days ago in the House of Lords, Sidmouth had openly spoken of a conspiracy and proposed coercive measures "to meet the evil". The new laws, dubbed the "Six Acts", would, among other egregious things, make any meeting to discuss radical reform an act of treason, the penalty death.

"Damn!" Robbie hissed under his breath. "Deuced stupid, if you ask me."

His gaze shifted to the page containing a poem by satirist William Hone titled "The Political House That Jack Built". Robbie thought it quite clever to sum up the reformers' grievances using a nursery rhyme in an irreverent manner.

"By God," he muttered. "He attacks lawyers, the Crown, the army, even the church. But he certainly has the massacre on St Peter's Field right."

"Who attacked all those folks, Nash?" came his mother's French-accented voice.

Robbie raised his eyes to see Claire Powell gliding into the parlor, her black hair neatly coiffed, the few strands of gray adding to her dignity but taking nothing from her beauty. She wore one of her French gowns, a confection in sapphire silk.

He allowed himself a brief smile for her confusion in her sons that had her addressing him by his twin's name. "'Tis the poet William Hone describing the grievances of the reformers and the blood spilled by the yeomanry in Manchester."

Her blue eyes flashed in anger. "*Sacrebleu.* I cannot think about that horrible—" She froze, turning to give Robbie an assessing gaze, then pursed her lips.

He laid aside the newspaper and tried to look innocent. "Is something amiss?"

"Robbie, you scoundrel! You have cut your hair to match your brother's. Even I cannot tell you apart when you do that. Well, not unless I hear you speak for a while. Why ever have you done it?"

"Nash and I believed it… necessary."

"I see." Likely she did, for their mother knew well that he and Nash had been on the Crown's business in Manchester. "The two of you have accepted another assignment, haven't you?"

He nodded, admitting the truth of her words but not providing any details.

"But why now when you are sailing to Scotland for Christmas?"

Robbie folded the newspaper and set it on the small table in front of the sofa, slowly rising to give his mother a knowing look, the message unspoken but clear nonetheless. She would not fail to note it.

Hands on her still slender hips, she scowled. "*Alors*, I begin to comprehend. Your next assignment is in Scotland, isn't it? No wonder you were so eager to join your older brothers when Lord Ormond extended his invitation."

Robbie cast his gaze toward the window looking out on the Thames, feeling only slightly guilty for not telling her he and Nash would be acting as spies once again. The family business, after all, was shipping, which served as a respectable cover for their more clandestine activities.

"Combining a holiday with friends and business for the Crown seems ill-advised, Son. I do hope Lord Sidmouth knows what he is doing." She dropped her hands from her hips and shook her head. "I've never been overly fond of that man, even when he was just Henry Addington."

"Believe me, I do understand and, as you might imagine, Nash is none too pleased with the Home Secretary either. But as this assignment is related to our last, I felt compelled to accept Prinny's summons."

She let out a sigh. "I can see there is no use arguing. I have long been aware that my four sons, like their father, do not require my help in making decisions. Are you and Nash packed? Mr. Stephen's ship is expected to sail within the hour. When Nick and Martin brought the children, they left immediately to join Tara and Kit who were already aboard."

Nick and Martin, Robbie's two older brothers, were married and had homes of their own. Robbie and Nash still lived in the family house on the Thames but, in recent years, their work for the government kept them away from London much of the time.

"You needn't worry, Mother. Nash and I sent our luggage to the ship with the footman when we came down. I only await Nash's appearance. He tarries over breakfast with some book on Scotland's plants, I believe."

"Well, if you hurry, you'll have time to say goodbye to your niece and nephews."

"Are you prepared for the three little hellions this Christmastide?"

His mother smiled. "*Oui.* Both their nannies came with them, so we'll have plenty of help. Your father and I are eager to spend Christmas with our grandchildren. One of these days, you and Nash—"

"Yes, yes. No time to discuss that now," he said, striding toward her. "I must find Nash if we're to sail with the tide." Inclining his cheek toward his mother as he passed her, he accepted her kiss.

Her forehead creased in a momentary frown. "Robbie, you will take care of your brother, *oui?*"

"Haven't I always?"

Chapter 2

Assured his luggage had been stowed below in the cabin he would share with Robbie, Nash left his brother chatting with Tara, Nick's American wife, and climbed the ladder.

A cold wind blew across the deck as the crew of the *Albatross* prepared to set sail. Watching them occupied with the familiar tasks, Nash wondered what the Scottish sailors and their captain thought of having so many experienced English shipmasters aboard. Nick and Martin had their own ships. Even Nash had been sailing for most of his thirty-two years.

He spotted the Marquess of Ormond standing alone at the rail and went to join him.

Ormond tugged the collar of his great coat up around his neck, nodding his greeting. "Do I speak with Robert or Nash?"

"Nash." His hands gripped the rail and, even though he had dressed for the frozen north with a many-caped greatcoat, beaver hat and leather gloves, he felt the cold to his bones. The brooding sky above them ominously threatened snow.

Ormond rubbed his gloved hands over his crossed arms. "If it's this cold in London, it must be damned awful in Scotland."

"I'm hoping for great heaps of snow," replied Nash, glad he had remembered to pack his woolen scarves.

"All those years I spent in France for Prinny must have thinned my blood," muttered Ormond, shivering beneath his greatcoat. "My family has lands in Scotland and, though I must visit from time to time, I have always tried to limit those occasions to the summer months." He turned to Nash with an amused smile. "Of course, William Stephen's invitation would have to be specific to Christmastide."

"I rather like the idea of snow at Christmas," Nash said thoughtfully. "Although I'd prefer to view it from inside a cozy room with a good book and a Yule log blazing in the fireplace."

"And a glass of fine French brandy in hand," added Ormond. He shot a glance at the aft hatch. "I assume the ladies have stayed below to see to the cabins." He turned back to Nash. "My good friend, William Stephen, went to a fair bit of trouble having this ship altered belowdecks to comfortably accommodate all of us for a few days' sail, even mustering a group of his men to act as servants. The ladies were pleased."

Remembering the flurry of female activity belowdecks and the seamen helping with chests, Nash nodded. "'Twas most considerate of him." He looked up and down the quay. "Are we all on board then?"

"All save the countess. I've been watching for her. I do wonder if, given her age, Lady Claremont is having second thoughts about making the trip. This is the worst winter in years."

As they were speaking, a handsome landau drawn by a pair of fine black horses pulled up at the foot of the gangplank.

"'Tis the countess," remarked Ormond, pushing back from the rail. "The crest on the door is hers."

"I know of her from my parents, of course," said Nash, "but I've not had the pleasure of meeting her. Robbie and I have not attended many balls this year."

"She is much loved in London. Her soirees are not to be missed."

"I seem to recall my brother Martin speaking of one he attended."

A footman, perched behind the carriage, stepped down and opened the door, handing down a silver-haired woman in a dark blue pelisse buttoned up against the cold. On her head she wore a stylish blue hat graced with white plumes. Given her obvious age, Nash was surprised at the agile way she alighted from the equipage.

Another woman of middle years followed the countess out of the carriage. Her mobcap and simple attire suggested she might be a servant.

Striding to the gangplank, Ormond said over his shoulder, "I see Muriel has indulged her fancy for feathers."

Nash fell into step behind him.

Reaching the countess, Ormond retrieved her hand from the footman helping her aboard just as Captain Anderson, a rather stern-looking Scot with dark curly hair and ruddy cheeks, strode across the deck to join them.

"Welcome, Lady Claremont," he said with a pronounced brogue, lifting his cap in greeting. "Allow me to introduce myself. I am Captain Dougal Anderson of William Stephen's shipbuilding. Your fellow passengers will be pleased to hear of your arrival." Then with a chiding tone, "They were afraid we might have to leave you behind."

"Stuff and nonsense!" the countess scolded in a commanding voice. Her back as straight as steel, her head held high, she confronted the captain nose to nose. A formidable woman, thought Nash. Definitely not one to be intimidated by the unsmiling captain. "I am an adventurer at heart, my good man, and I love to sail, this dashed cold weather notwithstanding."

Lady Claremont moved aside, allowing the captain to view the woman with light brown hair and white mobcap who had been waiting patiently behind her mistress. "I have brought my cook, Mrs. Platt."

"An English cook for my... *my* ship?" the captain sputtered.

Ormond turned to wink at Nash, clearly enjoying the exchange.

"No, no, my good man," the countess scolded as if addressing a schoolboy. "For our Christmas feast in Scotland." Then to her cook, she muttered, "One could not expect Mr. Stephen's cook to serve up a proper roast goose, minced pie and plum pudding."

The countess returned her attention to the captain. "Mrs. Platt's supplies are in a crate sitting on the quay. Please have it loaded promptly."

"Now see here—" The captain began, but stopping himself, he let out an exasperated huff and snapped his fingers at a waiting seaman, who hurried down the gangplank to retrieve the crate.

Ormond covered his mouth, stifling a laugh.

Nash pressed his lips together, holding in his own laughter, thankful Robbie chose that moment to emerge from the aft hatch to approach their small group.

The countess glanced from Robbie to Nash. "Another?"

"Twins," said Nash, managing a small bow. "Nash Etienne Powell, at your service, my lady." He gestured to Robbie. "This is Robert Pierre Powell, older than I by a mere five minutes yet he will not let me forget it."

The countess perused them. "Humph. I believe I may know one of your older brothers. Sir Martin. Yes, that's the one."

Nash had always been amazed at the power of his brother's charm over the ladies, but when Robbie bestowed his most brilliant smile upon the elegant countess and bowed over her hand, Lady Claremont had a very different reaction than Nash had expected.

She picked up a quizzing glass, dangling from a gold chain around her neck, and carefully examined Robbie through the lens. Dropping the glass, she said, "You must keep hearts in the *ton* all aflutter, Mr. Powell. I shall have to keep an eye on you." Then she turned to Nash. "You, too, I daresay. How confusing it will be if you have a smile like your brother's."

Nash thought to show her just how alike he and Robbie could appear but, just then, the captain pulled a pocket watch from his waistcoat, gave it an anxious glance and frowned. Narrowing his gaze at the Thames, in a tone that brooked no dissent, he said, "I would ask you and your servant to go below, Lady Claremont. We are about to sail."

Dinner in the captain's cabin that evening turned into an interesting one for Robbie, as he suspected it did for Nash.

A table from the crew's mess had been added to the captain's table and they all squeezed in for a meal of chicken, fried in the way of the Scots, roasted potatoes and a dark green vegetable the captain called "kale". Robbie thought it a sad cousin to cabbage. When sampled, it tasted sour, like he imagined old newspapers would taste if he ever had a mind to eat them.

The chicken and potatoes were quite good, however, and were soon consumed. Everyone, save the captain, pushed the kale around their plates as if too distracted by the engaging conversation to partake.

Robbie was not fooled. Neither was Nash, judging by the look they exchanged. But the company made up for the strange vegetable.

Joining the men was Ormond's wife, the former Lady Mary Campbell, a young aristocrat with pale blonde hair and eyes the color of green jade, whose features were as delicate as Dresden porcelain.

Next to the Ormonds sat Nick's wife, the former Tara McConnell of Baltimore, a darker blonde than Mary and with blue-green eyes Nick said were the color of a tropical lagoon. Tara was a beguiling creature who knew ships and sailing as well as Nick.

On the other side of the table sat Martin's wife, the redheaded Lady Katherine Powell, or "Kit" as she liked to be called. Her blue eyes, lighter than those of her husband's, always seemed to take in much. Robbie wondered if she had brought her sketchbook because she was rarely without it.

Martin was the only one of Robbie's brothers who had the blue eyes of their mother. He had met his wife Kit, the daughter of an earl, in an exclusive brothel, a meeting they claimed stemmed from a misunderstanding. Martin refused to discuss the affair, but Robbie had been in enough brothels to wonder what a lady like Kit would be doing there.

Since they were all close, unless in public, they addressed each other by their Christian names, except for Hugh, Lord Ormond, who had always been addressed by his courtesy title, or so Robbie had been told. Like the Powell men, Ormond had accepted special assignments from the Crown. And, if the tales were true, his wife, the rebellious Lady Mary Campbell had done a bit of spying herself in France.

Joining the young wives in their twenties was the Countess of Claremont, sitting to the captain's right, her feathers floating above her head like exotic plumage on a rare bird, so tall they threatened to brush the cabin's overhead beams. The flickering light from the lanterns only added to the illusion. Robbie had to admit she struck an elegant figure with her long strands of pearls over her silver brocade gown adorned with much lace.

The sobriquet The Grand Countess came instantly to mind.

Lady Claremont dropped her gaze briefly to the uneaten kale on her plate, a flicker of distaste crossing her face, then raised her eyes to the captain. "How is my dear friend Emily, Captain? I miss her greatly. It's been half a year since that husband of hers brought her to London for a visit."

"You will have to ask her, my lady," replied the captain. "But from all appearances, she is thriving. They are expecting their first child in the spring."

"Oh my! That is good news," said the countess. "I shall have to scold her for failing to tell me."

"Something to celebrate," chimed in Ormond, raising his glass of claret in toast. "I expect my friend Stephen has several bottles of champagne chilling in the snow even now."

The steward entered the cabin just then followed by two other men.

At the captain's nod, they began gathering up the plates and used tableware. From the relieved expressions on the faces of his fellow passengers, Robbie was not the only one glad to see the kale disappear.

A short while later, the steward returned carrying a large steamed pudding. The sweet scent of oranges wafted through the air amid exclamations of delight.

Robbie's mouth watered.

Kit, accepted a slice of pudding. "That smells wonderful."

"I love orange pudding," said Tara, taking a bite and groaning with pleasure.

"The fruit comes from Lady Emily's orangery in Arbroath," stated the captain. Looking around the table, his face set in a stony expression, he added, "As did the kale."

Robbie fought a grin.

Nash cleared his throat. "Ah… Captain, I am interested in orangeries and what can be grown in them. Has Mr. Stephen been long at it?"

Robbie was unsurprised at Nash's question. He would be the one to try and smooth an awkward moment, especially if he could do so while inquiring about a subject of genuine interest.

"Nay," returned the captain. "He built the orangery for the mistress when he added to the house. He shipped in mature orange trees from his father's orangery in Aberdeen so she would have fruit this winter. She also has a vegetable garden and flowers in pots and is experimenting with growing pineapples."

"I've read about growing pineapples in orangeries," offered Mary. Then to her husband, "I'd like to grow them at our country house. It would give me something to do, darling, while you are training that new crop of thoroughbreds. What say you to an orangery?"

"Our two boys do not keep you sufficiently occupied?" Ormond teased with a decidedly wicked grin. "Perhaps we should have another."

Mary swatted him on the shoulder. "Silly man. When I'm not teaching the boys to ride their ponies, think how much fun they will have in the winter months puttering in the orangery."

Ormond kissed his wife's cheek. "Very well, my love, you shall have one."

Robbie had seen the two tease each other before and admired the affection between them. But marriages like those of his two older brothers and the Ormonds were not the usual.

"There's more pudding, Captain, should anyone want some," offered the steward.

Nick held up his fork. "Over here, if you will."

The steward hastened to comply.

"Here, too," said Martin, catching the steward's eye.

Robbie met Nash's gaze. Both asked at the same time, "Brandy?"

The stern captain bestowed upon them a rare smile. "Aye, good French brandy. Mr. Stephen insists upon it."

Once the steward had poured the brandy, the conversation settled into the current topic on everyone's mind… politics.

Ormond leaned forward. "What's the mood in Scotland, Captain?"

"In Arbroath, 'tis quiet enough, but just south in Dundee and to the west in Glasgow there has been great discontent on the part of the weavers."

"The massacre in Manchester has not helped the situation," muttered Nash.

The captain nodded gravely. "'Tis stirred everyone up."

"And the Six Acts Lord Sidmouth has just introduced will make matters worse," Robbie tossed in.

Captain Anderson drew his dark brows together. "Six Acts?"

Robbie realized the news of the new legislation must not have reached Scotland and, from the looks on the faces of his brothers and their wives, some in London were not yet aware.

His fellow dinner companions turned to Robbie with expectant gazes, so he explained what he had read that morning in the *Times*.

"I don't see how that will help," said Martin.

The captain shook his head. "The government taxes a poor man's bread yet denies him a vote in Parliament. Even the Duke of Hamilton, Lord Lieutenant of Lanarkshire, which includes Glasgow, has spoken against the unfairness to the weavers."

Mary glanced at her husband. "It helps when a person of station advocates for justice."

"Well," said Ormond, running a hand through his dark hair, "I grant you there would certainly be less discontent if all who are excluded from voting were to be exempted from the payment of taxes."

"An unusual suggestion for a member of the nobility," Nick interjected. "But fair."

"As a Whig, I support reform," said Ormond, "but the great beast of government can be difficult to turn. My father, the Duke of Albany, is trying in the Lords."

Mary gave her husband an encouraging smile.

"Obviously, the English government has not changed since the days America and England parted ways," put in Tara, the look in her eyes intense. "We had the same problem."

Nick patted his wife's hand. "America is her own country now, sweetheart."

"Thank God," murmured Tara.

Martin leaned toward the captain. "Kit and I lived through the rebellion in the Midlands two years ago. I hope that does not happen to you in Scotland."

"Em..." The captain stared into his brandy as if unsure of what to say. "It might. There's been a wee bit of rioting in Paisley, put down by the cavalry. And last month in Dundee, south of Arbroath, George Kinloch, a respected man of the gentry, gave a stirring speech to ten thousand Scots, condemning the blood spilled in Manchester and urging reform."

Martin's brows rose. "Ten thousand, you say?"

"Aye. And the crowd listened, too. Still, for that wee speech, Kinloch is to be tried for sedition. I hear the poor man is now on the run."

Robbie met his brother's gaze across the table.

Kinloch, the very man we've been sent to Scotland to find.

Chapter 3

Arbroath, Scotland, 18 December

"Wait for me!" Ailie shouted, running to catch up with Emily who was trailing William as he strode toward the ship that had just arrived from London.

Emily paused and turned back. "You need not run. I'm happy to wait." In her blue woolen gown and MacTavish red and blue tartan pulled over her black hair, Emily looked more like a Scot than an English aristocrat. Only her proper English speech gave her away.

Ailie preferred to wear the Ramsay blue tartan of her mother's clan, but the Stephens were a sept of Clan MacTavish and William always wore that clan's red plaid, as did his new wife.

Slipping her arm through her sister-in-law's, Ailie strolled with Emily toward the dock, leaning in to say, "I wouldn't dare meet our guests from England without you."

Behind them, the sun had dipped low in the sky even though it was still afternoon. Winter days were short, cold and windy. While there had been no new snow, much of what remained on the ground and roofs from the last storm had not melted. The frigid wind out of the west made Ailie shiver.

"You must be anxious to see your friends," said Ailie.

"I am, especially Muriel and the Ormonds. The others I have yet to meet. Won't it be wonderful to have company for my first Christmas in Arbroath?" Her heather-colored eyes glistened. "I've not told Muriel of my good news."

They reached the dock just as the crew began lowering the gangplank. The passengers stood at the rail, a few waving to her brother.

Even from a distance, Ailie could see the women's fine coats, stylish hair and hats marked them women of quality. The older woman, whom she assumed to be the dowager countess, wore a hat with grand feathers.

Londoners, the lot of them.

"William says the Powells are in the shipping business," she said to Emily. "I do hope you aren't bored with all the talk of ships."

"Oh, do not worry about me, Ailie. I will be happy to visit with Muriel and hear the news from London. Besides, Lady Ormond and the other two wives are mothers of young children. I will enjoy hearing about their experiences."

Ailie squeezed Emily's arm and smiled at the woman she had come to consider a sister. "You'll have your own bairn in the spring."

They arrived at the gangplank and took their place beside Will.

Now that she was closer, Ailie studied the men and women standing at the rail. All the men had dark hair, making her think of the man she had seen in her dream. All were tall. Two appeared identical except for their clothes. Two of the women had blonde hair; the other was a redhead, whose hair color was somewhere between Ailie's ginger and Will's auburn.

The countess stood next to Captain Anderson, her age and feathers setting her apart from the other women. She pulled a white handkerchief from her reticule, flicking her wrist to swish the white cloth in the breeze.

"Oh, look!" exclaimed Emily. "Muriel is waving to me."

Captain Anderson descended the gangplank first, leading the countess. One of the tall dark-haired men followed, holding the hand of a pretty woman with fair hair confined in a knot at her nape beneath a small hat set at a jaunty angle.

Will offered his hand to the shipmaster. "Welcome back, Dougal. A good trip?"

"Aye, sir." Always polite, Captain Anderson tipped his cap to Ailie and Emily.

While Will spoke briefly with the captain, Emily greeted the countess and the tall dark-haired man and his beautiful wife, bestowing a huge grin upon the three of them. "Welcome to Scotland." Then she brushed the countess' cheek with a kiss. "Muriel, it is so good to see you."

"Too long is what it is," admonished Lady Claremont. "Took my venturing to this land of snow and ice to see this place where you live."

"Well, it's time you came," said Emily, hugging Lady Ormond and offering her hand to Lord Ormond, who bowed over it. All quite proper, Ailie noted. Rusty from disuse, she wondered how she would cope with all the bowing and formal address.

Not wishing them to think ill of her, she smiled at the attractive couple and the countess.

"Allow me to introduce my sister-in-law," said Emily, "Miss Aileen Stephen."

The countess reached for a small round glass hanging from a chain around her neck and peered through it at Ailie, examining her as if inspecting a bolt of new silk. Trying not to be put off by the odd gesture, Ailie returned the countess a small curtsey. "'Tis good to meet you, Lady Claremont. I have heard much about you from Emily."

"Humph," muttered the countess. "Don't believe half of it." She let her glass drop. "I can see you bear watching, pretty thing that you are. Unwed, Emily wrote me."

"Oh my," said Emily. "Muriel has you in her sights!"

Ailie felt her cheeks heat with embarrassment. She had no wish to be of special concern to the matchmaking countess.

The captain left Will and returned to the gangplank to see his other passengers off the ship. She could tell from the way they descended the gangplank the Powells and their wives were as at home on a ship as she was.

Will turned his attention to the Ormonds and Lady Claremont. "I see my wife has welcomed you." Drawing Emily close, he said, "'Tis time we met our other guests, *Leannan*."

Ailie's heart was in her throat as she took her place beside Emily and William, prepared to meet the Powell brothers and their wives. Edinburgh was home to a fair number of English and she had been there many times, but she had never entertained them in her home. Emily didn't count. She was English, aye, but she was also family.

Wrapping his arms around his greatcoat to hold in his body's heat, Nash waited with Robbie on the deck, watching the Ormonds and Lady Claremont embrace their friends in happy reunion.

In front of him lay a snow-covered shipyard with three ships tied up at the dock. Beyond the ships were several large buildings he assumed were the shops. The name "William Stephen and Sons" in tall blue letters stretched across the sign on the building directly ahead of him, suggested it was the company's headquarters. In the distance on the small hill, a sprawling estate was set against trees, smoke curling up from its many chimneys.

Nash had been told William Stephen was a successful shipbuilder, supplying the government and merchants with schooners and brigs. Here was the proof.

Robbie leaned in close. "I assume the tall man with the auburn hair is William and the woman with black hair next to him is his wife, Lady

Emily, but who is that beauty with the fiery red hair standing next to Lady Emily?"

The girl had caught Nash's eye, too, her flame-colored hair blowing free from her blue plaid shawl draped loosely over her head. "She might be William's sister," he surmised. "I see a resemblance." Taller than William's wife and slender, the young woman had a proud look about her. He wondered if she resented so many English descending upon her to celebrate Christmas.

Their eldest brother Nick crossed the deck to where Nash stood with Robbie. "Time to meet our hosts."

Nick returned to his wife and guided Tara toward the opening in the rail where the gangplank stood waiting. Martin and Kit fell into step behind them.

Tucking his woolen scarf up around his neck, Nash shared a glance with Robbie. "Let's hope the brandy they serve is warm."

Robbie grinned. "I'll pour."

At the end of the gangway, Nash waited behind his older brothers and their wives until it was his and Robbie's turn to meet their host. With Robbie at his side, he shook William Stephen's hand and bowed to Stephen's wife Emily.

Nash was the first to arrive in front of the redhead Emily had introduced as William's sister Aileen. She was more than a little attractive. Her copper-colored hair framed fair skin and eyes that were deep pools of cinnamon, sparks shining from their depths. She had a stubborn chin, but any thought of her being a troublesome lass ended when he glimpsed the sprinkling of freckles on her upturned nose. Finding his voice, he doffed his hat. "Miss Stephen, I'm pleased to meet you."

"And I," Robbie said, bumping Nash as he tipped his hat, his smile wide. "Are all women in Scotland so... beautiful?"

Nash wanted to kick his brother when the girl raised her brows and turned her head to her sister-in-law. Growing up around the shipbuilding industry and rough men, she had probably heard such flattery many times before. He was certain the impression left by Robbie's words was not what he had intended.

Emily smiled. "Of course not, Mr. Powell. Ailie is special."

Robbie glanced at the girl, an avid gleam in his eye. "I can see that."

"I'm not speaking only about her appearance," said Emily. "But you will discover for yourself my meaning during your stay with us."

Nash and his twin had often competed as children and, once they were in their twenties, the competition had expanded to include women. Their methods might vary but they shared the same goal of winning the ladies' affections. Now in their thirties, the rivalry could, at times, be intense.

William slipped his arm around his wife's shoulders. "Shall we return to the house and the fire, *Leannan?*"

"Oh yes, let's. There's just enough time for our guests to have a warm brandy or a cup of hot tea and get settled in their bedchambers before we are called to dinner."

Nash shot Robbie a satisfied smile at the thought of a warm brandy, then watched with dismay as the lovely Aileen Stephen flounced off with Lord Ormond and his wife, leaving Nash and Robbie to fall into step behind the others as they trudged up the path to the great house above the shipyard.

Halfway there, William turned to address them. "While we share a warm drink in the parlor, the servants will see your chests to your chambers. No need to change for dinner unless you wish it. In Arbroath, we often dine informally."

Ailie stood in the entry hall, waiting for Emily to descend the stairs having just returned from seeing her friend settled.

"Is the countess pleased with her bedchamber?"

"Oh yes, Muriel is quite content. I told her a cup of hot tea and shortbread would soon be delivered."

Earlier, the other guests had warmed themselves in the parlor and then followed Will and their housekeeper, Mrs. Banks, up the stairs to their bedchambers. The time spent in the parlor had allowed Ailie to get a better look at the twin Powell brothers. She was now certain one of them was the man from her dream.

'Tis the same face.

They were different in appearance from their other brothers. All the Powell men had dark hair, but the twins' hair was curlier and more streaked by the sun. Their eyes were hazel, rimmed with green and pierced with shards of gold.

Each the identical image of the other.

Which one had appeared to her? And why? The second sight the Ramsay women possessed could often be vague, but the elusive images were always significant, portenders of the future, harbingers of danger, or both.

It had been a dream that warned her of Will's capture by the French and another that gave her hope for his release. The dream she treasured most had given her the design of a schooner she hoped one day to see built in Arbroath.

"Come with me, Ailie," Emily urged as she hurried toward the countess' cook, who had been patiently waiting to one side. "I'm about to introduce Mrs. Platt to Martha. Since Mrs. Banks is occupied with our guests and the new maids, I may need your help to smooth ruffled feathers."

"I am happy to help if I can." She followed her sister-in-law and the English cook to the large kitchen at the back of the house. Beyond the kitchen garden was the orangery William had added.

With a trembling voice, Mrs. Platt said to Emily, "I understand my presence in your cook's kitchen may be unwelcome, my lady, but Lady Claremont thought I could assist with the Christmas dinner."

"And you shall," Emily assured her, linking the cook's arm with her own. "It just might take a bit of persuading." Glancing at Ailie, she added, "I've asked my sister-in-law to come with us. Our cook likes her."

Ailie mentally prepared herself for the encounter with Martha McBride. In her late thirties, Martha was a good cook but cantankerous as the day was long. In the kitchen, she reigned supreme, supervising assistants and scullery maids. Martha had no love for the English, much less an English cook who might ken more than she did about cooking for the Stephen household.

It had taken years for Ailie to gain the woman's trust. Emily, on the other hand, had been accorded the respect due the master's wife when she arrived. Even so, when Emily had suggested a few English dishes be served, Martha had been reluctant to agree. She only acceded to her new mistress' requests when Emily enlarged the kitchen garden and later began growing herbs and vegetables in the orangery.

Emily let go of Mrs. Platt's arm to enter the kitchen first. "Martha," she addressed the cook, who was facing away from them, stirring the contents of a pot over the hearth fire.

Two kitchen maids, busy chopping vegetables, looked up from their work.

Save for the orangery, on a cold winter's day the kitchen was the warmest room in the house, the fire kept going at all times and the stove nearly so. Ailie could often be found there in afternoons pinching a freshly baked tart.

The cook turned, tucking stray dark hairs into her mobcap as she faced her mistress. "Aye, Mistress?"

"Martha, I want you to meet someone." Emily stepped cautiously toward the cook, as one might approach a dog known to bite. "Do you remember me telling you that, along with our friends from London, Lady Claremont would be bringing her cook?"

"Aye." Martha slowly nodded as if trying to postpone the inevitable. Turning to one of her assistants, she gestured to the pot she'd been stirring and, wiping her hands on her apron, walked toward them.

"Well, she is here," said Emily. "Ailie and I want you to meet Mrs. Platt, who has sailed from London at Lady Claremont's request to help with the Christmas feast. I asked that she bring her recipes and all she would need. The crew should bring the crate in soon."

Ailie held her breath, waiting to see if Martha would object. The scrutinizing gaze Martha gave Mrs. Platt did not bespeak a welcome.

Emily made the introductions. To support her, Ailie chimed in, "Everyone is looking forward to the traditional English feast."

Martha's face took on a surprised expression. She knew Ailie didn't give a whit about the English observance of Christmas, but Ailie paid her no mind. She remembered William's reminder that the English were their invited guests. In Scotland, hospitality was everything.

Undaunted, Emily faced the cook. "Mr. Stephen and I enjoyed our Christmas with some of these same friends last year and he quite liked the roast goose and Christmas pudding."

Hands on her ample hips, Martha frowned. "What about the dishes the master likes at the holidays?"

Emily smiled sweetly. "Oh, we shall have those, too. William tells me there will be cock-a-leekie soup, haggis with tatties, steak pie, roast game and salmon. And the Scottish desserts, too."

"The master's favorite treat is cranachan," put in Martha.

"Yes, well, I look forward to that myself," said Emily. "You shall preside over the menus as always, Martha, but for the Christmas dinner, I ask you to consult with Mrs. Platt."

Tension hung in the room like a schoolteacher's rebuke.

Casting her gaze about the kitchen, Mrs. Platt offered a compliment Ailie thought quite diplomatic. "I can see you run an efficient kitchen, Miss McBride."

That was certainly true, thought Ailie. On the side of the kitchen opposite the windows looking out on the garden, William had one of the carpenters build cabinets painted a light gray. Open shelves held plates, pans and copperware, everything neatly in its place.

Martha smiled despite herself. She did manage well her kingdom.

The smile must have encouraged Mrs. Platt. "It will be my pleasure to assist you in any way I can." The compliment from an experienced cook years older than Martha could only be termed gracious.

Feathers smoothed, Martha inquired as to whether Mrs. Platt would like to have a chat and stay for tea. Ailie and Emily shared a look of relief.

The kitchen was large enough to accommodate Martha's invitation. In the center of the room, a long oak worktable with bench seats provided ample room for the servants to dine.

Martha glanced at Emily. "With your permission, Mistress, after our tea, I can show Mrs. Platt to her room."

"That would be lovely, Martha," said Emily, pleased. "And would you also have one of the servants take tea and shortbread up to Lady Claremont? She is in the chamber across from Ailie's."

"Aye, Mistress. Immediately."

"Wonderful," said Emily turning toward Ailie, "Now, I must consult Mrs. Banks about our guests."

"And I must see to the dogs."

Chapter 4

Robbie relaxed on his bed, idly watching his brother set out the books he had brought from London, wondering why Nash had done so. "You might have left the books behind. I'm certain William Stephen keeps a good library for Scotland's long winters."

"Perhaps, but he may not have these." Nash turned from his books to face Robbie. "Now that you mention it, we will need William's library for the times when one of us hies off to the village for news of Kinloch while the other remains behind. How's your Scottish brogue?"

"Miserable," returned Robbie. "Yours has always been better."

"'Tis merely a matter of practice. Tonight might be a good time for you to do just that since we're in the home of Scots."

Robbie thought of the voices he had heard since their arrival. "Emily's speech is as English as our own and William has only a faint brogue. Captain Anderson has a deep accent, but he may not be at dinner. Besides, I'd rather talk to William's pretty sister even if her brogue is not so pronounced." He gave Nash a sidelong glance, making a mental note of his brother's frown at Robbie's interest in Aileen Stephen.

Hearing no response from Nash, Robbie said, "Are you ready to join the others? We don't want to be late."

"Almost ready." Nash crossed the chamber to the chest at the foot of the bed he had claimed as his. "William told us not to change, but I want to wear a different tailcoat. As you have on a brown one, I'll wear dark green."

"We'll need to switch coats in the days to come if we're to assume each other's identity," Robbie reminded him. This they had done many times. Coupled with their ability to ape each other's gestures and expressions, they could be virtually interchangeable.

Nash pulled on the green tailcoat. "Whichever of us is in the village will have to don the locals' attire."

"I wonder how Kinloch might be dressed," Robbie mused. "He's a gentleman but he'll not be wearing a gentleman's clothing, will he?"

Nash straightened his cravat. "I doubt it. Wouldn't he be more likely to appear as a farmer, a sailor or a fisherman? All are plentiful in Arbroath, I would think."

They began to descend the stairs just as Aileen Stephen came through the front door, her cheeks rosy from the cold. She let her tartan scarf fall to her shoulders, revealing a bounty of bright red hair. A tempting picture to be sure.

Two great black and tan dogs bounded in after her.

"Why, hello," said Robbie, giving her one of his sincerest smiles. Beside him, Nash tensed, none too pleased at Robbie's initiative.

His brother smiled at the girl. "What dogs are these?"

She looked up at them, her dogs wagging their long tails, their paws on the steps sniffing at Robbie's feet. "Goodness and Mercy, a gift from the Duke of Gordon. He raises them on his estate in Moray to the north."

Robbie stepped down to the entry hall's stone floor and patted the head of the closest dog, a friendly sort, then returned his attention to the girl.

Nash alighted from the last stair to scratch one of the dogs behind the ear. "How ever did you come up with those names, Miss Stephen?"

"You may call me Ailie. Most everyone here does. You are Robbie and Nash?"

"I am Robbie and this is my brother, Nash," said Robbie, gesturing first to himself and then to his twin.

Her beautiful face lifted in a one-sided grin as she glanced between them. "'Twill be difficult telling you apart. As for the names of my dogs, do ye nae ken yer Scriptures?"

Robbie exchanged a look with his brother. Neither, he was certain, had a clue as to her meaning, yet she had spoken in the way of the Scots, intentionally deepening her accent. Perhaps she meant to suggest Englishmen might be ignorant of the Good Book's teachings.

"The twenty-third Psalm ends," she recited, "'Surely goodness and mercy will follow me all the days of my life...' aye?"

"Clever," said Nash. "I won't be forgetting their names any time soon." From the admiring look Nash gave the girl, Robbie surmised his twin wouldn't be forgetting her either.

Robbie returned his attention to the large lean dogs he decided were setters, but not the black and white speckled ones he was used to. These two were mostly black with small bits of copper and white trim. "I can scarce see a difference between them."

Her brows lifted. "This from two brothers who are made from the same mold? Really, 'tis easy to tell them apart. Goodness is the male and Mercy is the female."

"My brother's a bit slow," muttered Nash.

Robbie shot Nash a look of annoyance. "Seems I recall you accusing me of being too *fast*, Brother."

Nash coughed into his hand. "I was speaking of understanding just now, not your manner of living." Then to Ailie, "Please excuse my brother."

"I always make excuses for English rakes," she said matter-of-factly.

Robbie sputtered. Beside him, Nash appeared bemused.

"If you're looking for the others, I believe they are in the parlor. Just there." She gestured to a set of double doors. "I will join you shortly."

Robbie watched as she proceeded to a door to the right of the stairs, the dogs following on her heels, as the psalm suggested they would.

He turned toward the parlor. "I believe we have been dismissed." Then, in a low voice, "Now there's a tempting armful and, for a green girl, most interesting. A sharp tongue, perhaps, but interesting nonetheless."

"She's not one of your 'women on the town'," said Nash, looking over his shoulder as Aileen Stephen and her dogs disappeared through the door. "She's a spirited innocent. I find her… enchanting."

Ailie eyed the bottom of her dress, soiled from mucking about with the dogs. She hoped the Powell twins had been so interested in her setters they had failed to notice. Ah, well, she would make up for it by looking her best for dinner.

"Rhona, what do you think of this gown?" Ailie held up the blue silk gown she'd taken from the clothes press. It was one of her nicest gowns, one she had worn to visit her parents in Aberdeen to convince them she hadn't forgotten all they insisted she learn about being a lady.

When Ailie joined Will five years ago, he had insisted she have a lady's maid. A few years older than Ailie, Rhona came from a well thought of Arbroath family, and her older brother worked as a supervisor in the shipyard. Rhona had become more friend than servant. Ailie valued her opinion.

Rhona's brown eyes narrowed as she studied the gown. "'Tis a fine choice, Mistress. It reminds me of bluebell flowers. And if ye like, I can arrange yer hair with the sides pinned back."

"Aye, thank you. I prefer not to wear my hair on top of my head in the winter if I can, unless I'm in Aberdeen where Mother insists I appear the lady."

Once Ailie had donned the gown, she sat at her dressing table, watching her maid in the mirror deftly arranging her hair. Catching Rhona's eye, she said, "I saw Mrs. Banks as I was coming up. She says our English guests have settled in well. What do you think of them?"

"They seem easy to please and kind, like the mistress. And, except for the one American, they're all verra English."

"How are the new servants managing?"

"The ones yer brother hired for the holidays are mostly young ones from Arbroath. The maids above stairs are near useless for anything but gawking at those twin brothers."

Ailie could well understand the girls' fascination with the two men. "Aye, they're handsome enough. And the countess? How is she?"

Rhona paused, a faint smile on her face. "The young maids are terrified of her, I think. Lady Claremont shooed them out of her chamber when they asked to set out her gowns."

"I hate to ask, Rhona, but perhaps you'd best be the one to serve her. Would you mind terribly?"

"Nay, I wouldna mind. I am fond of older women of character."

Ailie thought about Will's description of the countess. "I haven't yet had the opportunity to speak with her. Will likes her very much. And she is Emily's good friend. I wonder how she will get on with Grandfather Ramsay."

Rhona, put the finishing touches on Ailie's hair. "They'd be a pair, 'tis certain."

"Aye. I just hope Grandfather doesn't tease her unmercifully."

"Dinna worry. Ye'll be there and can charm him." Ailie handed Rhona the pearl necklace with the sapphire pendant and Rhona fastened it around Ailie's neck.

Ailie centered the sapphire on her chest. "I did meet Mrs. Platt, the countess' English cook. She handled Martha rather well."

"That's a blessing."

Ailie nodded her agreement. "All we need is Martha in high doh."

Their eyes met in the mirror and they burst out laughing at the shared thought of the cook all riled up. It would not be a pretty sight.

Ailie took a last look at herself in the mirror. "Won't Will be surprised to see me dressed as if I were dining with Father in Aberdeen?"

"Aye, and 'twill make Lady Emily happy," said Rhona, smiling.

Ailie justified her extraordinary measures by reminding herself she was to dine with a marquess, his marchioness, a dowager countess and the daughters of two earls, one of which was her sister-in-law. "Perhaps I should do it more often."

Lifting her small blue tartan shawl from the bed where Rhona had laid it, she draped it over her shoulders. With a wave to her maid, she left her chamber, more excited than she had been in months.

Nash counted nine men and women gathered in the spacious parlor when he and Robbie entered. Sadly missing was the redheaded sister of their host.

Two footmen glided among the guests offering them drinks, as the conversations became lively. In one corner, Lady Claremont held court with their hostess and Martin's wife, Kit.

A footman approached with a tray of drinks. The choice of brandy was an easy one for both he and Robbie.

Nash sipped the fine cognac and glanced about the room. The walls were papered in gold above cream-colored wainscoting. Persian carpets in deep shades of red and blue were strewn about the dark wooden plank floors. Two wing chairs upholstered in gold velvet flanked a huge stone fireplace in which burned a well-tended fire. In addition to other chairs and occasional tables set around the perimeter of the room, there were two sofas and a low oval table between them.

Above the fireplace hung a tall gold-framed mirror lighted by candle sconces on each side.

The elegantly appointed parlor was as fine as any in London, but with a touch of the Scots' preference for a more comfortable room, where a man could bring his hunting dogs and his guns as well as his guests.

Still, it wasn't the Scottish drawing room he had expected.

There were no mounted elk heads, no crossed swords and no family crests. Instead, the walls held an array of what appeared to be family portraits. Nash made a mental note to ask Ailie who they were.

In one corner, there was a polished mahogany pianoforte. He wondered if Emily played. William Stephen had attended Cambridge and then married the widow of a knight, who was also the daughter of an earl. Perhaps the room had been decorated with Emily in mind.

"As subtly as I can," said Robbie, glancing at their host, who was speaking with Ormond, "I'm going to ask William what he knows of the town and the political views of its citizens."

"All right. And, while you're at it, I'll greet our hostess. I want to ask Emily about her orangery."

Robbie returned him an incredulous look. "Don't tell me you're still fascinated by her pineapples?"

"And why not? 'Tis an achievement to grow them in Scotland, particularly in winter. Really, Robbie, you should read more." Determined to learn what he could, Nash left his brother and strode off to speak with their hostess.

"You must visit the orangery," Emily encouraged him when Nash told her of his interest in horticulture. "After breakfast would be a good time; if there is sun, the light then is most favorable."

Nash thanked her and meandered among his brothers and their wives, who seemed to be enjoying themselves.

Despite William's words they need not change for dinner, their host had declined to follow his own advice, donning a black velvet coat with gold buttons and trousers in a red, blue and black plaid.

When Nash remarked on them, William looked down at his trousers. "We Scots call them trews. And this," he said, pointing to the woolen cloth of his trews, "is the MacTavish tartan, the Stephens' clan."

Sensing someone had entered the parlor, Nash shifted his gaze to glimpse the woman he'd been waiting for. Ailie stood just inside the doorway, the light from the candles dancing in the shimmering waves of her copper-colored hair.

She glanced from one end of the room to the other and accepted a glass of sherry from a footman before saying to no one in particular, "I trust I'm not late."

Nash walked the short distance to meet her. "Not at all," he said, thinking she had made a splendid entrance in her blue gown and tartan wrap. "Now *everyone* is here and we are an even dozen."

She sipped her sherry, looking up at him from beneath long dark lashes. Her eyes were the same golden color as the liquid in her glass. "Which Powell twin might you be?"

He smiled. "Nash." Trying not to drown in her stunning eyes, he said, "Just remember I'm the one with the green tailcoat. Robbie is wearing brown."

"Well, that will help, at least for tonight, but whatever shall I do after that?"

"You have only to ask and I will tell you." Her sweet scent wafted to his nostrils, making him want to draw her close, to imprint upon her lips a memory that would endure forever, to give her something to distinguish him from his twin apart from tiresome explanations. Instead, he let out a remorseful sigh and resorted to small talk. "Have you always lived in Arbroath?"

"Nay. William and I are from Aberdeen where our father Alexander Stephen and our two younger brothers rule over a shipbuilding enterprise larger than William's. I came here five years ago to join William when he returned from France."

"Your brother fought in France?"

"Aye, and was taken prisoner. We were relieved to get him back in one piece with only a few minor wounds." She took a sip of her sherry.

He stared at her lips and her upturned nose sprinkled with freckles. He had never seen a more winsome creature.

"How about you?" she asked, bringing his gaze back to her eyes.

"Me?" He blinked, trying to think what she could mean.

She laughed. "You are from London, aye? Did you fight Boney in France?"

Nash had to handle the question carefully so as to say nothing of their spying. "Ah, yes. I am from London. My family owns Powell and Sons Shipping. We're all involved in the business in one way or another. And our business supported the war." Before she could ask in what manner they had served, he said, "My two older brothers, Nick and Martin, are masters of their own ships. On occasion, Robbie and I sail but, recently, we have been on the land side of the business. I do a bit of design work now and then."

"You design ships?"

Detecting an interest on her part and, thinking to impress her, he said, "I do. Brigs, schooners, sloops. Should you come to London, it would be my pleasure to show them to you."

"I see you are monopolizing our host's delightful sister," said Robbie, suddenly appearing at Nash's elbow.

"The man in the brown tailcoat," quipped Ailie. "You must be Robbie."

Robbie gave Nash a look of feigned dismay. "You divulged our evening code?"

Nash had no intention of apologizing. "I did. The fair damsel required assistance and I was only too happy to provide it."

On the far side of the room, the butler, a tall man with thinning brown hair, impeccably dressed in formal attire, appeared in the doorway. "Dinner is served," he droned.

"That's Lamont," Ailie explained. "Our new butler from Aberdeen. Before he came, Mrs. Banks would just throw open the front door and welcome our guests. But William thought more help was needed what with Mrs. Banks being occupied with the new servants. I'll be interested to see if William decides to keep Lamont once all of you return to London."

Nash detected wry amusement in her eyes. "How does Mrs. Banks feel about it?"

"She's not certain but, for the now, he is useful."

Still conversing, the others ambled toward the open double doors.

Nash offered his arm to Ailie. So did Robbie. She accepted both with a smile. Arms linked together, the three of them set off for the dining room.

Ailie decided that Robbie's charm could rival that of any Scot she knew. Nash was by no means less appealing than his twin, just more reserved. Robbie's easy laughter appealed to her, but his flirtatious ways suggested he might not be constant. She had called him a rake and, upon reflection, she rather thought that had been a correct assessment. Still, he was a very charming rake.

Both dressed like gentlemen, fastidious in their attire and seemingly as at home in a drawing room as on the deck of a ship. And, since their arrival, both had flirted with her, which was not too surprising since she was the only unattached younger female.

Were they to change coats, she doubted she could tell them apart. In appearance at least, they were very alike and very British, their speech quite proper. Most of the men she knew spoke with a brogue, occasionally adding in a Doric expression of the Lowland Scots. Well, except for her father and brothers, gentry who had long engaged in business with London merchants. She had become used to Emily's aristocratic speech, but having a house full of upper class English would be a new experience.

As the three of them entered the dining room, Ailie saw that Emily was seated at one end of the table with Lord Ormond and Captain Nick Powell on either side of her, and Will was at the other end between the dowager countess and Lady Ormond.

"A beautiful room," Nash remarked.

"My brother had it refurbished when he added onto the house. The blue walls beneath a ceiling of white were Emily's idea. I quite like them."

When Ailie realized the twelve of them would require every chair, she thought perhaps Will had envisioned just such a dinner when he ordered the long mahogany table, now covered with white linen, Emily's fine porcelain dishes and silver candlesticks.

The crystal chandelier hanging above the table, its candles causing the crystals to flicker as if lit from within, was a thing of beauty. "Will acquired the chandelier in Edinburgh."

"It's magnificent," said Robbie. "French?"

"Aye." Under the chandelier in the center of the table, Ailie recognized the arrangement of deep pink camellias as being from the orangery.

At Will's insistence, Ailie took her place between the Powell twins, Muriel on their left and Nick Powell on their right. 'Twas no surprise her brother had placed her where she would be hemmed in by the only unmarried men at the table. Ailie was not opposed to marriage, but he would have to be an unusual man. One who loved her, yes, but one who would also allow her to pursue the work that was her passion.

Across from her, Martin Powell sat between his redheaded wife and Nick's American wife, the honey-blonde Tara, the only other woman who wore her hair like Ailie, most of it left long.

Because of where Will had placed Ailie, a husband would dine next to his wife, not exactly the thing in aristocratic circles, but this was Arbroath. No one seemed to mind, certainly not the husband and wife, who were casting sheep's eyes at each other.

To help her remember who was who, Ailie noted Martin was the only blue-eyed Powell brother. The eldest brother Nick, whose face had the rugged appearance of a man who'd spent years at sea, had amber eyes. But, to her mind, the most glorious of the brothers' eyes were those of the two handsome twins, gold disks etched in brown and ringed in dark green, the color of Scotland's moors on a sun-filled day.

Unfortunately, their eyes, like their faces, were identical. *Bother that.*

As the footmen served the carrot and orange soup, Kit must have become aware of Ailie's watchful gaze. "'Tis our first holiday without our daughter since she was born a year and a half ago," explained Kit. "We are enjoying the time together."

"You have a daughter," Ailie remarked. "How lovely. What's her name?"

"Anne Claire."

Ailie inclined her head, wanting to hear more.

Kit obliged. "Anne was my sister's name and Claire is Martin's mother's name."

Not wishing to inquire as to what happened to Kit's sister, Ailie said, "Anne Claire is a bonnie name."

"Annie is the light of our lives," said Martin, his smile wide as the proud papa.

"Given our family's propensity to have sons," interjected Nick, "she may be the only female grandchild our parents will see, so Martin did well to add Claire to her name after our mother."

The footmen poured the wine and took up the empty soup bowls.

Declaring they should proceed as they meant to go on, Will announced, "Since Emily tells me the ladies insist, and we cannot very well call every man 'Powell', given names will be used for all save Ormond, who has been the Marquess of Ormond since birth."

Will smiled broadly, apparently satisfied with himself, and added, "Even Lady Claremont has expressed a desire for us to address her as 'Muriel' during her stay. 'Tis the name Emily calls her."

The countess' mouth formed a faint smile. "Indeed."

Ailie thought the dignified woman might be enjoying her respite from London's more formal life.

"I don't see why I should be left out of all this happy bonhomie," complained Ormond. "After all, Hugh is a perfectly acceptable given name."

"Hear, hear," said his wife Mary. "Away with 'lord' and 'lady' for our sojourn in Scotland."

"Oh, very well," chimed in Will. "If you can adjust to losing your lordly title for the weeks you are here, I see no reason why we cannot oblige you, though you will have to excuse me should I slip now and then."

Martin raised his wine glass in toast. "To Hugh, formerly known as Lord Ormond!"

Ailie and the rest of the happy company lifted their glasses. "To Hugh!"

"And I don't want to hear a single 'Sir Martin' the entire time I am here," threw in Martin.

Everyone laughed, even the very proper countess.

The footmen served the fish course, fresh trout baked with butter and herbs from Emily's garden.

"Salmon and trout are often on the menu," said Emily in response to their guests' first bites. "I hope you like the seasoning. The herbs are fresh from the orangery."

"'Tis very good," said Tara, "as was the soup."

Hugh, formerly Ormond, returned to their prior conversation, saying to Will, "For the benefit of those who don't know, you might as well hear of all our children, or as you would say in Scotland, our 'bairns'. Mary and I have two sons, Henry and Philip, both still in leading-strings."

"Tara and I have two boys as well," put in Nick. "Both babes. Sean is the eldest, born a few months after Martin and Kit's daughter. He's named for my wife's father, who owns Stag Shipping in Baltimore. Since he was not keen on our marriage, we thought to make him a happy grandfather. Our youngest, Simon, was born this last summer. We named him for my father."

"A prolific group," offered the countess.

"They are," agreed Will, "and Emily and I will soon be joining them." Emily blushed and dropped her gaze but a half-smile played about her mouth. They had shared many a conversation in which her sister-in-law had confided how much she looked forward to her first child.

"A cause for champagne," said Hugh.

"I had planned to have it for our Christmas feast," returned Will.

"Are the children spending Christmas with their grandparents?" inquired Muriel.

"Mine are," replied Hugh. "And most happily if you ask my parents. Mary's mother will be joining them for the holiday."

Martin exchanged a look with his older brother. "Ours, too, are spending Christmas with our parents in London."

Ailie began to squirm in her seat as everyone turned their eyes on her and the twin Powell brothers. She read, "What about you?" on their faces and tried to find an interest in her fish. Married people, she had learned, expected those still unwed to join their shackled state like a disease they hoped everyone caught.

The arrival of the next course, roast venison, filled the room with smells of juniper berries, bay leaves and thyme simmering in a red wine sauce. Accompanying the venison were side dishes of potatoes, peas and sautéed kale.

Ailie's stomach rumbled.

Their English guests were effusive in their praise of the venison, potatoes and peas, but to a person declined the kale.

On Will's right, Muriel spoke in a hushed tone to Ailie's brother. "We had the opportunity to sample the kale on the ship. I daresay Captain Anderson was disappointed with our reaction."

From the other end of the table, Emily chuckled. "I concede it takes time to get used to that vegetable, but the Scots love it. They even call their kitchen gardens 'kaleyards'."

Muriel accepted a helping of peas from the footman. Ailie thought she heard a muffled "Humph."

Looking amused, Will took a sip of his claret. "While we eat, I should like to know what activities you favor on the morrow."

Nick was the first to speak. "What have you in mind?"

"I thought to hunt the pink-footed geese," replied Will. "We should have a good supply for your visit, especially for Christmas dinner. I can equip all those who want to join me. But those who would hunt the geese need to be prepared to leave no later than eight." With a look around the table, he added, "That's before the sun is up."

Nick held up a hand. "Count me in."

Martin exchanged a word with Kit and she nodded. "Me as well," he said. "I've never hunted your pink-footed geese. Might like the novelty, as long as I'm back in time to spend the afternoon with Kit. We've had too little time together of late."

"We'll return by the afternoon," said Will.

"Thousands of the geese winter here from Iceland," explained Ailie. "They're smaller than your average goose, so you'll find them a more challenging target."

"Ailie is right," agreed Will. "And because they are smaller, we'll need twice as many for Christmas dinner than we would for ordinary geese. But I assure you, they are quite tasty." He turned to Ailie. "Mind if I borrow Goodness and Mercy?"

"Not at all. You have trained them to hunt geese and they love it."

Nick's brows rose. "Goodness and Mercy?"

"My sister's setters," said Will, glancing at Ailie. "She'll be happy to tell you how she named them. For those of you not joining the hunt, we have other pursuits. There's a Yule log to find in the forest. That can wait till the afternoon. We have a sledge, or as Tara would call it, a sleigh, and horses for any who prefer to ride."

"The orangery is open, too," offered Emily. "'Tis always warm there."

"My brother keeps a fine library should you want to read," offered Ailie. "We have the Waverley novels."

Leaning forward and looking across Ailie to Nash, Robbie shot his brother a knowing look, making Ailie wonder if Nash had read the novels. "Are you a reader?"

Nash's hazel eyes twinkled. "Voracious. Robbie teases me unmercifully about my penchant for books, particularly those related to horticulture."

Robbie cast her a winning smile. "I do."

Ailie glanced from one brother to the other. One twin smiling at her was charming; two was a bit overwhelming.

"Might we do more than one thing?" asked Tara. "I'd like to see the orangery in the morning but then go with the others for the Yule log in the afternoon."

"Of course," said Will. "Just remember our winter days are short. Daylight ends mid-afternoon."

On Ailie's right, Robbie spoke up. "A walk in the woods appeals." Then with another brilliant smile, "Felling a Yule log seems more civilized after the noon meal."

"I intend to stay around the shipyard," said Nash, "at least for the morning. Perhaps you could give me a tour, Ailie? I'd like to see the shops if that is permissible."

Ailie nodded, thinking she might enjoy showing the Englishman the shipyard. "That can be arranged."

"I'll let my foreman know," Will offered. "He'd be delighted to tell you about the schooner the lads are building."

Kit leaned forward. "While Martin is hunting the geese, I plan to have some time with Emily and Lady Claremont and do some sketches."

"Sketches?" asked Will.

"My wife is an accomplished artist," Martin offered, a look of pride in his blue eyes.

"She is," agreed Tara. "My sister-in-law's ability to capture the personality behind the face is uncanny."

"In that case, my dear," said Muriel, speaking for the others, "we humbly submit our faces to your inspired sketchbook." No one objected.

Will turned to Mary. "Have you decided what you'd like to do?"

The elegant young blonde paused to consider. Ailie couldn't help but admire her beauty, like the Greek heroine, Helen of Troy, in the flesh. "Well," she began, "as long as Hugh is going geese hunting, I'd like to visit the stables. Hugh tells me you have a fondness for horses."

"Certainly," said Will. "And you can ride if you like. My groom would be happy to accompany you."

Mary smiled. "That sounds just the thing."

Will turned to the countess. "Now, how about you, Muriel? I don't suppose you want to join the hunt?"

Muriel grimaced. "Absolutely deplore all that blood." Then, with a twinkle in her eye, "But I'm happy to eat the roast goose! As for the morrow, nothing would please me more than a leisurely breakfast and some time with my friend, Emily, and Kit if she would join us." To Emily, she said, "We should check with Mrs. Pratt and your cook about the plans for Christmas dinner. I don't believe my cook has ever roasted a pink-footed goose."

"A good idea," said Emily, casting a glance at Ailie. "When Ailie and I left them earlier, Mrs. Platt and Martha were getting along famously. But it is wise to ask what the two of them have decided about the menus. We may encounter some disagreements there."

With dinner concluded, Will suggested they retire as a group to the library. Typically, the women would leave the men to their port and brandy and take tea in the parlor. "But for tonight," he told them, "Let's get to know each other better."

Ailie did not disagree, for she was coming to enjoy their English guests.

In the library, Robbie accepted a glass of cognac and watched with amusement as his twin brother stared in rapture at the tall wooden shelves lining the walls filled with leather-bound books. The smell of leather and wood, to which was added the faint scent of birch burning in the fireplace, would delight a man such as Nash, who was always looking for a comfortable nest where he could get lost in his books.

"This room is Nash's idea of Heaven," Robbie remarked to Ailie who had accompanied them into the room with the other guests.

"Mine, too," she replied with a smile directed at Nash. Robbie silently admonished himself. He would have to be careful not to throw too many bones to his twin or he would soon lose the girl's affection to his brother.

Several members of their company had gathered to admire the painting that hung above the fireplace. It depicted a statuesque auburn-haired woman in a flowing amber gown. Robbie was struck by the serene expression on her face.

"Our mother," William informed the others when they inquired.

"A beautiful woman," Nash said, turning to look at Ailie. "I note the resemblance."

Robbie had to credit Nash for claiming early ground with the girl. Nash's compliment had caused the girl to blush, roses suffusing her cheeks. Indeed, Ailie Stephen looked very much like her mother, save the older woman's hair was darker and the artist had not included any freckles he could see.

"A kind thing to say, Mr. Powell, and I thank you." Ailie dropped her gaze, bid them a good eve and went to join the women sitting on one of the blue leather settees.

Robbie watched the girl walk away, intrigued. "My congratulations, Brother, you have managed to stake the first claim."

Nash merely shrugged.

In the center of the room, a mahogany table surrounded by six chairs provided a place for study. Robbie envisioned it spread with maps. Nash's passion was his books, but Robbie loved maps and nautical charts.

"I expect I will find you here often," he said to Nash.

Nash sipped his brandy. "Only the shipyard and orangery hold more interest for me. Well, and the Mistress of the Setters, as you call Ailie."

Robbie didn't miss the wistful look that appeared on Nash's face at the mention of the redhead's name. On the occasions they had competed for the affection of London ladies, Robbie could not recall seeing that look.

Opposite the fireplace on the other side of the room, a painting of a ship in a sculpted gold frame drew Nash away from Robbie's side. Interested, Robbie followed.

It wasn't as if the walls in their London home weren't covered with paintings of ships. Still, Nash was the designer in the family, or at least he had been before they'd accepted the recent assignments from the Crown. He would be drawn to one of unusual design.

The schooner's sleek hull and raked masts were not unknown to Robbie since his family had acquired a few of the Baltimore clippers from Nick's father-in-law. This design had the clipper bow, but the stern appeared quite different.

"Most unusual," murmured Nash. "The stern has a reverse rake, angling forward toward the bow." Robbie sipped his brandy, sensing his brother's rising passion for what he was seeing.

Brandy in hand, William strolled over to where Robbie and Nash stood admiring the painting illuminated by candle sconces on either side.

"Is that one of your ships?" Nash inquired of their host.

"It will be one day. That's the *Ossian*, named by her designer for the narrator of myths in the volume published by the Scottish poet James Macpherson."

Nash examined the painting. "She's a fine-looking schooner. Designed for speed, I wager."

William took a drink of his brandy and smiled. "'Tis an advanced design. None have been built like it in Scotland. I had a local artist do this painting from the designer's sketches."

"I'd like to speak with your designer," said Nash. "Would it be possible?"

A slow smile spread across William's face. "Aye, I expect so. She's sitting just there with the other ladies."

Robbie and Nash turned to see Ailie Stephen perched on the settee with Emily, the countess and the wives of their brothers, sipping tea. Ailie had to be the one William referred to.

The look on Nash's face was one of wonder. "Your sister is a draftsman?"

Robbie well understood. No women they knew engaged in ship design, not even in the American company owned by Tara's father where Tara had been allowed to sail with her brothers.

William nodded. "She is indeed."

Robbie's curiosity got the better of him. "How ever did that happen?"

William brought his hand to his chin. "I'd have to explain a bit about our family to tell you that."

Robbie and Nash stared at their host expectantly.

"Very well, if you insist. For ten years, I was the only child of our parents. They despaired of ever having another despite my father having named the business Alexander Stephen & Sons. When Ailie arrived, they were delighted, notwithstanding her sex. They took her everywhere and encouraged her love of ships. Eventually, she tagged behind me to my father's shops. That is, when she wasn't cajoling our father's men into showing her the new ship designs."

Nash's brows furrowed. "She picked up the skill just watching?"

"Not exactly. My father's men considered her an adorable gamin, treating her like a pet. Unbeknownst to us, she was asking questions and learning. By the time our younger brothers arrived years later, Ailie had become a fixture in the shops, already sketching her own designs."

Robbie examined the painting. "Lord knows she has talent."

"And vision," said Nash. "That design takes the schooner another step into the future."

William set down his glass, now empty, and crossed his arms, gazing at the painting. "Aye, it does. When our father discovered he had three sons, none of whom cared to design ships and a daughter who did, he patted Ailie on the head and chided our mother for failing to instruct her in the finer attributes of being a lady.

"As a result, my sister was given lessons in deportment, dancing and French. When not engaged in those activities, she was confined to the drawing room where she poured tea and learned embroidery. But at night in her bedchamber, the little rebel designed some of what became my father's best ships."

Robbie liked the sound of that. A woman with spirit and a will of her own always appealed.

Nash shifted his attention to the gamin in question. "I see. Stubborn, she won in the end."

William gave a small laugh. "Aye, she did. When I returned from the war in France, I was quick to steal her away to Arbroath."

Robbie wondered if a rebel could be so easily tamed. "So, she now works for you?"

"Aye and no. She's my partner and oversees the draftsmen. When she is at the concept stage, you'll find her in the office at the desk next to mine." Then looking at Nash, "Tomorrow when she shows you around, ask her about the *Ossian*. It's her favorite subject."

Robbie carefully scrutinized his brother's face. He was certain Nash eagerly anticipated the opportunity to be alone with Ailie Stephen. But Robbie, too, intended to seek some time with her. Perhaps the afternoon's hunt for the Yule log would afford him the chance he needed.

When William took his leave and ambled over to the others, Robbie faced his brother. "I told you she was interesting."

"And I seem to recall saying she is enchanting."

"Ho!" quipped Robbie. "The game is afoot."

Chapter 5

Ailie woke with a start, her dream rapidly fading, the images slipping away like rabbits into the brush. She raised her head from the pillow, listening to the sound of boots retreating in the corridor. Her brother and the men must be departing for their hunting jaunt.

She dropped her head to her pillow and tried to call back the dream.

The face belonged to the same man as before, one of the Powell twins, but this time he wore a grin. She couldn't tell if it was from pleasure, triumph or something else. And she had no idea whether the man was Robbie or Nash.

She was beginning to detect small differences in their natures, not apparent when she'd first met them. She had to observe them for a while to be certain she had it right. It seemed to her that Robbie's smile sometimes took on the appearance of a smirk. Nash, on the other hand, smiled less, but when he did, his eyes twinkled with mirth.

The bits and pieces of her dream that she could remember included the inside of a dim, hazy tavern, then the sound of men fighting, chairs being knocked over and voices expelling curses.

What could it mean? On the rare occasion she had been inside a tavern, she'd been looking for Will and she remembered none of that.

She shivered as a feeling of disquiet came over her. Sliding out of bed, she lit a candle and padded to her small desk, her fingers brushing across the pages of her diary sitting open. She'd written the last entry just before she'd blown out the candle the night before.

18 December

The English have arrived in Arbroath and still, we remain, giving me reason to believe we will survive the onslaught. After all, 'tis only the holidays we share with them. At dinner, they turned up their noses at the kale, just like Emily did at first. What is wrong with the English palate? They did enjoy the venison and, like Will, the men savored the French brandy. In that, they remind me of Grandfather Ramsay and his ale. Speaking of which, I do believe he is in for a Hogmanay such as he has never known. Our guests are a lively bunch of Sassenachs, the women no less than the men. Mary and Tara seem rather independent, which endeared them to me. The countess is the picture of English nobility, but with a dry sense of humor. Father would approve.

She went to the fireplace and added a log to the crackling fire, watching the flames and listening to the muted sounds. The thought of having a full house appealed to her, even if it meant many more servants and maids scurrying about the place. The young maids' giggles, she presumed, were for the handsome Powell men and Ormond.

Dawn brought light to her chamber that faced the shipyard. She glanced out her window and then set about brushing her teeth. She had just finished when Rhona came to help her dress.

"A linen dress for the morning would be best as I'll be making my usual jaunt in the orangery. I will return to change into a woolen gown for the rest of the day. If the weather allows, today we'll search for the Yule log."

Rhona took the green linen dress from the clothes press. "Will ye be going to the shipyard?"

"Oh, you remind me. One of the Powell twins asked me to give him a tour this morning."

Rhona slipped the gown over Ailie's shift and corset. "Which one?"

"I think he is Nash. Does it matter? I can hardly tell them apart."

"A handsome pair, to be sure. And unwed, Mistress."

"As Will would have me be aware. Is the countess up yet?"

Rhona buttoned the back of Ailie's dress. "I checked before I came here. The fire in her chamber is now burning well, so I expect her to be up soon. I will go there after I leave ye. From my tending to her needs last night, I can see she is a woman who knows what she wants. She likes efficient service and is truly grateful when she gets it."

"She will be pleased with you, Rhona. Perfection is difficult to duplicate, even in London."

Rhona picked up the brush but Ailie thought to let her maid attend Muriel. "You go on. The countess will be up by now. Tell her if I finish my morning walk early, I will look for her at breakfast."

Nash loved nothing so much as waking to the smell of freshly baked bread and coffee. Sniffing the air as he laid in bed, he detected spices and cinnamon threaded among the enticing smells. Fruit scones, perhaps?

His nose, peeking above the cover, was cold, a sure sign the fire had died during the night. One of those silly maids he frightened last night in his state of undress was probably too timid to set foot in their chamber to stir the fire to life.

Only the delicious smells stirred him to rise from his nest in the warm bed. Throwing off the cover, he braced himself against the chilled air and cast a glance at his still sleeping brother in the next bed. Apparently, Robbie had concluded a trip into town to visit the local taverns did not require an early rise. Too, Robbie was never one to be ambitious for the morning. He preferred nightly pursuits. In that, they were truly different, and it had served them well when it came to their work for the Crown.

Glimpsing the pale shafts of sunlight filtering through the curtains, it occurred to him the men going to hunt the geese must have left some time ago. He did not regret his choice to stay behind. Besides, his older brothers would surely elaborate on their morning excursion when they returned.

For his first morning in Arbroath, he had something entirely different in mind. He intended to sample the wonderful breakfast he suspected was, even now, being set out on the sideboard. Then he planned to visit Emily's orangery to glimpse her achievement with pineapples in the early sun, as she had suggested.

But after that, he would have a tour of the shipyard by the beautiful Ailie Stephen. He had never been so captivated by a woman and learning they had in common a fondness for designing ships only made her more intriguing. Her tenacity reminded him a bit of Nick's wife Tara, who, as a young girl, had insisted on going to sea with her brothers.

Nash rubbed the stubble on his face and decided he could avoid shaving until evening. Robbie disdained shaving as well so their appearance would not be different. Besides, it suited Robbie's destination this morning for him to show a bit of beard.

Placing the unopened razor horizontally beside the bowl of water would be his signal to Robbie not to shave. Then Nash washed with the same sandalwood soap Robbie would use and splashed water on his face, drying it with the towel one of the timid maids had left.

Dressed, he tied his cravat simply as he and Robbie had agreed and lifted the brown tailcoat from where Robbie had left it on a peg the night before. He had only to run a comb through his hair before slipping from the room.

In the dining room, the servants were just changing the linens from those who had eaten earlier. "Breakfast will be ready shortly," said the young footman.

Nash nodded. "I shall return then."

Emily had told him where the orangery was the night before so he hurried to the corridor between the kitchen and the library across from William's study. At the end, he found a door. The moment he opened it, he was surrounded by warm sweet-smelling air. He closed the door, drinking in the scented air, as enticing as the smells that had awakened him.

The structure he had entered was separate from the house. He did not see the stoves he knew must be the source of heat, nor did he smell any fumes. For some years, hot water had been piped into homes in London from stoves located outside, so perhaps the stoves were in a separate structure.

The orangery had to be thirty feet in length. On one end, backed against a wall of brick, stood a virtual forest of orange trees in rows of large wooden boxes, their brightly colored fruit peeking through green leaves. Emily had certainly been busy in the year she'd been here.

In the middle of the orangery were a variety of plants, some in pots and others in large raised platforms framed in wood. Included among them was the dreaded kale.

One side of the orangery featured wide glass doors, the kind that folded open, allowing the plants to be moved outside in the summer. But even on this winter day, pale sunlight flowed through the angled windows to bring light into the large space.

Outside, the world was covered in winter's snow but, inside, the scent of the orange trees and flowers dominated, reminding him of his trips to the West Indies.

Several pots of flowers stood on one side. He recognized the yellow hibiscus and brightly colored camellias. More clay pots containing flowers lined the windows. He bent to smell the delicate flowers of the lily of the valley, recognizing the sweet smell as Ailie's from their dinner the night before. Nearby, the white Christmas rose was just beginning to flower.

As he made his way to the far end, he saw a smaller glassed area. Carefully, he opened the glass door and stepped inside where he encountered even warmer air.

So this is where Emily is growing her pineapples.

Six leafy plants growing in clay pots had been sunk into a rectangular pit strewn with chips of oak bark. Some of the pineapples, their spiny leaves rising in the air, were already yellow ripe. He was impressed.

William had told him the Scots had been growing pineapples for a hundred years, yet Nash had never seen it done before.

Returning to the somewhat cooler main part of the orangery, Nash walked among the orange trees, occasionally glancing toward the windows and the snow-covered ground outside just to remind him where he was in Scotland in December.

When the invitation had first come, Nash had questioned Ormond's thinking stuffing his friends into a ship in the dead of winter and sailing them to the far edge of the North Sea. But the assignment from Sidmouth that Robbie had accepted for them changed his wonder into a fortuitous opportunity. Now that Nash had met Ailie Stephen, he wondered if it were fate.

Suddenly, between branches of green leaves, a flash of vivid red hair caught his eye. He eased around a tree for a better view. Dashing barefoot through the fruit trees, her long hair flying behind her, was Ailie.

"Can it be the Mistress of the Setters loose in the orangery?"

She gasped and whirled around, blinking, her hand over her mouth.

Slowly, he emerged from the trees. "I have caught you!"

She dropped her hand to her chest. "So you have. And scared me to death in the doing of it. I had no idea anyone was here."

He came closer, noticing her flushed cheeks. Looking down at her bare toes, he thought of the ladies in London who would be horrified for a man to glimpse a bare ankle, much less bare feet. "Do you often run barefoot in the orangery?"

She let out an exasperated huff. "Every day as a matter of truth. I cannot very well run in deep drifts of snow, now can I?"

He smiled, delighted to have her alone. "I suppose not. I am glad to find you here, though our being alone is not quite proper, is it?"

"You're a houseguest and you're in Scotland. 'Tis different."

"Then I shall look forward to more moments alone with you." He imagined running with her not through the orangery but through heather on Scotland's sun-bathed hills. He could imagine lying with her in that same heather. Shaking off his wild imaginings, he asked, "May I escort you to breakfast, Miss Stephen?"

"You may, Robbie. But first, I must find my shoes and stockings. I left them just inside the door."

"'Tis not Robbie who would escort you, but Nash." He was used to people mistaking him for his brother, at times he and Robbie even encouraged their confusion, but he did not want this woman to be confused.

"You are wearing the brown coat Robbie wore last evening!" she protested. "'Tis most unfair." She turned abruptly and headed to the door. He fell into step behind her. When she arrived at her shoes and stockings, unceremoniously dumped in a pile on the stone floor, she turned. "Em… you must turn around while I recompose myself. The task requires a wee bit of time."

"How can I refuse the Head Draftsman?" He turned his back to her and heard the muffled sounds of stockings and shoes being drawn onto what he imagined were gracefully arched feet, slender ankles and shapely legs. He fought the temptation to turn. "How is it, Ailie, that you never mentioned your skill at designing ships when I told you I did some designing myself?"

"I would have done, but we were interrupted by the call to dinner. And once you asked for a tour of the shipyard, it seemed best to save that discussion for today."

Nash considered a woman who did not blather on about all she knew. Such a female was rare. That Ailie held something back she knew would interest him for a time when they would be alone appealed greatly. She was unlike the women whose favors he had sought in London. *She is all that is fresh and innocent yet entirely direct.*

"Then I shall not be disappointed." Hearing no sounds, he said, "May I turn around now?"

"Aye."

When he swung around, the woman who faced him was neatly composed, her previously unruly hair tied back at her nape, her stockings and shoes restored to their proper places. Though her cheeks were still flushed, the gamin was now clothed like a lady. Like a Scots lady anyway. He preferred her simple way of dressing to the lace, petticoats and frippery of the women in London.

"Shall we go?" He offered his arm and she placed her hand upon his sleeve. The small gesture felt so natural. In the brief time he had known her, she had managed to win his affection. What would she think if she knew he was a spy for Lord Sidmouth out to capture a Scot? He never planned to tell her.

They walked through the doorway back to the main part of the house. "How is it you speak the King's English with only a wee bit of brogue when you did not spend years in London as William did?"

"Like my brothers, I have been blessed with a good education. By my father's order, my governess was a Scot who had been educated in England. She drilled me near every day in the proper way to speak. Even so, you might still hear me utter a word or two you'll not recognize. And when you meet Grandfather Ramsay in Stonehaven, you may need me or Will to translate."

"Stonehaven?"

"Aye, just up the coast. We are sailing there for Hogmanay." At his raised brows, she said, "Hogmanay is what the English call New Year's Eve, I believe. 'Tis a very big affair in Scotland, even more so in

Stonehaven. The tradition goes back to the times of the Norsemen. Did William not tell you?"

A New Year's Eve celebration with the lovely Aileen Stephen. The very thought raised images of walks through the snow and a kiss under the moon. "No, he said nothing. Now, I will look forward to it."

A kissing bough had always a part of the Powell family's celebrations of Christmas. Perhaps Emily would have one for their celebration in Arbroath. The thought of kissing Ailie beneath the bough brought a smile to his face. Robbie might compete for her affections but Nash had plans, which did not include his brother.

She glanced up at him, her sherry-colored eyes glistening. "But first breakfast and a tour of the shipyard, aye?"

Robbie didn't need a horse for the half-mile walk to the village of Arbroath, which was convenient since he'd announced he'd be taking a walk in the woods.

As he traversed the snow-covered road, the sun's light was bright but gave little warmth. Some of the snow had melted only to freeze again, causing his boots to make a crunching sound as they broke through the thin crust of ice.

Arbroath's countryside had a beauty of its own even a Londoner like Robbie could appreciate. Some of the trees were evergreens but others had lost their autumn foliage and now held on to the snow, the branches making a lacy pattern against the pale sky. The quiet, save for the occasional scurrying of a rabbit or the sound of a wintering bird, took some getting used to.

Robbie missed the bustle of London and the noisy parade of carriages and cries of street vendors. He even saw good in the city's constant rain, for a deluge always washed the streets of their stench. And Christmastide brought foods and friends he rather enjoyed.

He pulled the woolen scarf he'd borrowed from Nash over his ears and stuffed his gloved hands in the pockets of his woolen jacket, the kind a farmer or storekeeper might wear. Tugging the same cap he'd worn in Manchester down on his head, he turned his thoughts to the last intelligence they had received.

George Kinloch, scheduled to be tried at the end of December for sedition, had fled. The information they were given before leaving London indicated Kinloch had a cousin near Arbroath who might help him sail from Scotland. According to Sidmouth, the "Radical Laird", as he'd been dubbed, had spent time in France, becoming absorbed in the frenzy for change.

Reform was one thing, revolution quite another. It was the one thing Sidmouth's government feared most.

Robbie raised his gaze from the path to see the snow-covered stone buildings of Arbroath looming in the distance.

He planned to frequent the harbor's taverns and see what he could learn. Knowing they would be suspicious of strangers, he had developed a story about visiting a friend who worked for the Stephen shipyard. If pressed, he would say he had lived in London for a time.

In truth, he was determined to say very little. Men everywhere understood grunts, didn't they?

Coming out of the woods, he entered the town, strolling along the seafront, listening to the familiar cry of gulls swarming in the blue sky as they vied for fishermen's scraps. A group of fishing boats was tied up at the quay, the fishermen sorting their nets. Women, Robbie assumed to be the fishermen's wives and daughters, loaded the morning's catch into baskets.

Ignoring the shrieking gulls, they sat in their plain wincey dresses and tartan headscarves, talking to each other as they worked. Children played at their feet, reminding Robbie of the street urchins in London.

Water lapped against the quay where several ships were tied up, their bare masts rising above the decks like a forest of winter trees stripped of their leaves. Snow clung to the decks of the ships that must have been in port during the last storm.

He continued down the quay, passing a gun battery of six twelve-pounders facing seaward, likely a remnant of the town's defense against Napoleon's threat, now reduced to an idle curiosity with the Frenchman's exile to St. Helena.

In pursuit of the nearby taverns, Robbie turned up one street that looked promising. The town certainly didn't lack for public houses. Nearly every third door led to such an establishment.

He chose one that appeared larger, judging by its three tall windows facing the street and the cluster of men standing out front. Above the door, painted in black letters, was the sign, "The Plow and Harrow".

He touched the brim of his cap to the men lingering just outside the door. Ignoring their questioning gazes, he plunged into the dimly lit tavern. Immediately, his senses were assaulted by the smell of sour ale and smoke curling up from the pipes several men smoked as they sat at a large table talking.

He crossed the stone floor to the bar and asked for ale. As he waited, he cast a furtive look on either side of him. Wooden tables held several groups of men. At the largest, what looked to be merchants, wearing proper waistcoats and jackets, were having a heated discussion.

Like Robbie, they wore half boots, except the odorous brown substance clinging to the heel of their boots suggested they'd stepped in something other than snow. Though he knew Kinloch to be a farmer, he could not imagine Kinloch doing that even for a disguise.

Thanking the proprietor, Robbie slid a coin over the counter and carried his ale to a small table adjacent to the large one, listening to the local farmers who drank ale while talking and chewing on the ends of their pipes.

The argument the men had been engaged in when he'd first entered the tavern must have ended, for now they speculated on the arrival of the next storm. When they'd exhausted that topic, they laughed about one of their fellow farmers who had managed to misplace some cows in the snow. All very boring and nothing of politics.

He was about to leave when the conversation turned to the clearances happening in the West.

A bald man with sideburns and ruddy cheeks addressed the others. "Word is Lord Stafford's factor, a man named Sellar, has been torching crofters' roofs to empty the glens for his lordship's sheep."

"Them English swells care naught fer the puir folks whose verra lives lay in that soil," said an older man with gray hair and a wizened face.

"I hear Stafford doesna even visit his lands," said the first man. "My uncle told me Sellar forced one auld man and his wife from their home in the cauld night where they died."

"He's tearin' the heart outta the Highlands, all for Stafford's sheep."

Sinking into a dour mood, the men shouted to the proprietor for another round of ale.

On his other side, Robbie heard murmurs of disagreement. Finally, one man slid his chair back and stood to address those at the large table. "Ye have it all wrong. Stafford's givin' notice but some cottars ignore it. Sellar's jus' doin' his job."

Rising from his chair, a young farmer at the large table took offense. "Ye be Stafford's man, too?"

"Can ye talk mair slow?" slurred the first man, pretending not to understand.

The young man, egged on by his dour companions, threw a fist.

A hullabaloo ensued as fists flew in all directions, ale splashed onto the stone floor and chairs were upturned. Men from both sides strained to get at each other.

The proprietor yelled. "Och! Ye fools!" and waded into the fray. "See what comes of yer bleetin'?"

Robbie had no desire to become a part of their fight. Not that he didn't enjoy a stimulating round of fisticuffs now and then, but he could not risk his identity or his mission being compromised.

Pressing himself against the nearest wall, he inched his way to the door. Avoiding tankards sailing through the air and stepping over groaning bodies, he at last gained the exit.

He opened the door to the street and the men standing outside, hearing the noise, rushed past him to join the fight.

Robbie pulled his scarf up around his neck against the brisk wind. He found it surprising that men so easily given to violence had never mentioned the events in Manchester or Kinloch's speech in Dundee. He would have thought such events would have united them and been the subject of great debate.

He headed toward the waterfront, hoping to hear of ships that might be sailing in the next few weeks. On the street called Horner's Wynd, he entered The Lorne Tavern.

Relieved to see a smattering of men dressed as sailors and a few fishermen in the blue knitted shirts they favored, he claimed the one free stool at the wooden bar. As he waited for the proprietor, he stared at the painting of a ship hanging on the wall facing him.

A fully rigged black-hulled schooner. He could just make out the name *Panmure* on the starboard bow.

"Ye ken somethin' of ships, do ye?" the proprietor asked, coming to take his order. The burly man's curly gray hair and muscular arms reminded Robbie of a ship's carpenter he once knew.

"Aye, a wee bit," Robbie replied, pulling off his cap. "Sailed a few times."

"What ye efter?"

Hoping the inquiry spoke to the drink Robbie wanted, he grunted. "Ale."

The burly man nodded. "Ye're a stranger in toun. Visitin'?"

"Aye, fer Hogmanay. I've a mate up at Stephen's shipyard." He spoke truth but the proprietor did not need to know his "mate" was the shipyard's owner.

"Some guid men work fer that yard."

Robbie attempted a grunt of agreement, relieved the man did not ask for a name.

The proprietor poured the ale, then looked over his shoulder at the ship. "That'd be the *Panmure*, built right 'ere in Arbroath by Alex Fernie. Named fer the Earl of Panmure, who lost his title efter the Fifteen. She's in the harbor now if'n ye want tae get a look at 'er. She sails fer France end of the month."

"She's a bonnie ship." Robbie speculated this could be the ship on which George Kinloch intended to sail were he holed up in Arbroath and looking for escape. "She tak' passengers?"

"'Tis a merchantman, but, aye, sometimes the master'll tak' a few. Lookin' tae sail south?"

"Mebbe." Robbie downed the rest of his ale.

"Cap'n Gower's a former mate o' mine," he offered. "Ye might ask if'n he has room in the crew's quarters."

Robbie made a mental note of the shipmaster's name, thanked the proprietor and, with as few words as possible, indicated he might return in a day or two.

Anxious to see the *Panmure* for himself, Robbie tugged his cap down on his head and launched into the cold wind blowing onshore. He set a brisk pace as he strode to the quay, setting in his mind the two taverns he'd visited, the men he'd encountered and conversations he'd had so he could report all to Nash. To act for each other, they had to possess the same information.

Several ships were in the harbor. He had passed them before without much notice since his focus had been on the taverns. Now he carefully scrutinized them.

The three-masted *Panmure*, the largest, was tied up at her moorings, her sails harbor-furled, rolled up tight and tidy as he would expect in a squared-away ship. The few sailors on deck stood out of the wind in huddled conversation, not busy with repairs or loading. The ship would not be sailing anytime soon. Most of the crew were likely in town or with their families.

Taking the gangway in a few long strides, he looked to the officer of the watch. "Cap'n Gower around?"

"No, he's gone into town, but he should return tonight."

Robbie couldn't wait that long. The noon meal might be in process at the Stephens and he intended to return for the afternoon. "I dinna suppose Cap'n Gower takes passengers?"

"Aye, he does, but the passenger cabins have been booked for the next sailin'." He lifted his gaze to the ships lined up at the quay. "You might try one of the others in the harbor."

Robbie tipped his cap. "Much obliged."

As he headed back to Stephen's shipyard, he wondered if the cabins were reserved for George Kinloch and whoever might be traveling with him. The coincidence of the ship's destination and Kinloch's former association with that country were too great to ignore.

Chapter 6

Breakfast with Nash Powell turned out to be an amusing experience for Ailie. She had gone to her room to change her gown and, when she entered the dining room, she found him standing in front of the sideboard, staring at the dishes offered.

"Confused?"

He scratched his head, holding his empty plate. "A bit. I scarce know where to begin."

She looked around. "They've left you all alone?"

"The countess and Emily were leaving just as I was coming in. They told me Kit, Tara and Mary ate early with their husbands before they left for the geese hunt."

Ailie watched Nash pile eggs, biscuits and butter onto his plate, turning up his nose at the more Scottish fare.

He pointed to a pale substance in a round dish. "Do you actually eat that?"

She resisted a laugh. "'Tis gruitheam, or to the uninitiated Englishman like yerself, curds and butter. And, aye, we do." She spread some on a girdle scone and placed it next to the strong-smelling cheese she had just added to her plate.

Drawing his attention to the triangular scones, she said, "Don't you want to try a scone?"

"*Those* are scones? They seem a bit… flat."

"Do not be insulting Martha's girdle scones or she will be denying you supper. Try one."

"Very well, because you asked," he said with a brilliant smile, looking very much like his twin. She didn't have to ask if he was Nash since he wore the same coat he'd had on when she'd encountered him in the orangery.

Ignoring the curds mixture, he added a scone to his plate and carried it to the table. With a few adds to her own plate, she took the seat across from him.

He picked up a scone and lathered it with marmalade and butter. "I will content myself with this, a biscuit and the eggs." He looked at her with a hopeful expression. "I don't suppose there is bacon?"

She chuckled. "We Scots do not favor pork as do the English. Did ye nae ken the Scots call the English 'pork-eaters'?"

"What?"

Ailie gave him a sidelong glance. "You need take no offense. 'Tis just one of those curious things, like the French calling the English '*rosbifs*'. Some Scots do raise pigs, but most often they send the carcasses to Aberdeen where they are salted for export." She went to the sideboard to bring a dish to the table and placed it before him. "Don't you want to try the smoked haddies?"

"The *what*?" He pursed his lips as he stared at the plate of haddock, their skins bronzed from the smoking process. Ailie was highly entertained. "Perhaps later," he said, clenching his teeth.

It was all Ailie could do not to laugh. "'Tis a shame," she said, forcing her expression to remain serious. "They're a specialty of this part of Scotland, you know." She shook her head and reverted to a Scot's way of speaking. "If ye'll nae try the haddies or the gruitheam, we ha' verra guid chocolate and tae."

He stared at her openmouthed for a moment. "Tea, please."

She fought a fit of laughter, but there was something about his honesty, much like that of a small boy, that charmed her. Having dismissed the footman when she first entered the room, Ailie poured Nash his tea.

With a nod of thanks, he happily settled into his breakfast.

From beneath her lashes, she watched him eating his eggs and marmalade-lathered scone and had to admit he and his brother were attractive men, broad-shouldered and well featured. And those hazel eyes. *Right.*

She speared a bit of haddie on her fork. "What kind of ships do you design?"

"Schooners and sloops mostly but, unlike you, I only dabble in the design of the merchant ships we sail. I give my drawings to Tara who sends the ones she likes to her family in Baltimore. Stag Shipping, her family's business, has used a few. From what I saw, you are an expert. I'm still amazed at the *Ossian.*"

"Is that because the designer is a woman?"

He sighed heavily. "You needn't be prickly. I was amazed because I have never seen such a schooner. Once I considered the effect of the changes you made, I could see they would increase the ship's speed. You must show me your drawings and tell me what led to your design."

"All right," she said, wondering how much she would tell him. "I keep the drawings in the office. After I show you around the yard, we'll go there."

When they were finished eating, he helped her put on her cloak and donned his greatcoat before she led him out into the frigid morning air.

She stared up at the sky. In the distance, gray clouds hovered. "I do hope the snow holds off till tomorrow."

"Me as well. Today is the day we're going to select the Yule log," he said cheerily. The look in his hazel eyes reminded her of a small boy out for an adventure.

He might be adorable, but he was no boy. Like his twin, Nash was tall, lithe and muscular, with a strong manly jaw. His dark hair, tinged with gold from the sun, curled around his nape. She wondered what it would feel like to run her hands through those curls. She let out a sigh. His coming to Arbroath made her want things she had not thought of in a long time.

"Knowing my brother," she said, "he will hunt for the log to please Emily even if it snows."

Nash stepped into the cavernous main shop of the shipyard, the air warmed by stoves placed about the room. Light spilled into the large space from windows high in the timbered walls. The noise in the shop echoed off the high walls.

He counted twenty men working. Some, with long-handled mallets, pounded the inside of the hull that stood open to the room, the weather deck not yet in place. The youth of a few suggested they might be apprentices. Two sawyers were bent to the task of cutting wood. Other men concentrated on joining timbers.

"We can leave our outer garments here," Ailie shouted.

He helped her to shed her cloak, sliding the back of his fingers over the tops of her arms. The gesture had been innocent but the contact with her, even with her wool gown between them, set his pulse racing. Her faint sweet scent drifted to his nostrils causing him to inhale deeply.

She had changed clothing since the orangery and now wore a sensible woolen gown, but its simple lines did not detract from her loveliness. As before, she wore her fiery hair long and tied back with a ribbon.

He placed her cloak on a peg where the workers' coats hung in a long line. Doffing his greatcoat, he added it to the collection.

"Come," said Ailie, "I'll introduce you to the foreman."

She walked briskly toward a man who stood to one side, arms crossed, observing the progress of the work. Nash fell into step beside her.

The foreman must have sensed their approach. As they neared, he turned and smiled at Ailie. He was somewhere in his forties, Nash judged, with thick red-blond hair and striking blue eyes. His manner was congenial, particularly toward Ailie. Obviously, he liked his job and the boss' sister.

"Good morning, Miss Stephen. Yer brother told me ye'd be comin' by with a visitor."

"Mr. Ferguson," she said, her voice rising over the din of the shop, "this is Mr. Powell, one of our guests from London. He and his brothers are here on holiday. They're interested in the yard as they are in the shipping business in London."

Ferguson extended his hand and Nash took it. "I've heard of Powell and Sons. We make fine ships here, Mr. Powell, should ye be wantin' one."

Nash grinned. "I would agree. My brothers and I had the pleasure of sailing on the *Albatross* from London."

Ferguson smiled. "Aye, that would be the one we modified to carry more passengers."

"If it's agreeable with you," Ailie said to the foreman, raising her voice, "Mr. Powell would like to look around."

The foreman glanced at Nash and nodded. "Of course. Ye know our yard as well as anyone, Miss Stephen. But I'm happy to answer any questions ye might have, Mr. Powell."

Nash was eager to hear what Ailie had to say but, as a matter of courtesy, he would allow the foreman to speak first. "Could you tell me about the schooner you are working on now? Then we'll just look around."

"Be glad to." He turned to face the ship under construction. "This one's a merchantman for Glasgow, larger than most we build. The men are just finishin' the hull before they start on the captain's cabin, galley and crew quarters." He went on to explain in some detail the configuration that would be constructed below decks. It was not unusual but the foreman did have an eye for detail.

When the foreman finished, Nash thanked him and then strolled with Ailie around the ship's hull. Ailie pointed out things Nash might have missed.

"The keel is of tropical purpleheart wood from Tobago. The hanging knees in the bow are made from American live oak."

Nash eyed the hull fasteners of pure gleaming copper. He gave a low whistle. "Such fine materials come at a dear cost."

"Aye, but then the best usually does." Running her fingers over the hull, she added, "We sometimes use English oak, shipping it up from the Thames. I just like the American oak better."

As they passed the workers, the men looked up from their tasks and waved to her. She knew each one of them, calling them by name. Despite the appearance of a beautiful redhead in their midst, not one of the men leered at her. In their eyes, Nash saw only respect.

Perhaps it was her skill at designing ships but, reconsidering, he rather believed she and William knew their craft and treated their workers well.

His conclusion was confirmed when she said, "They will have time off for Hogmanay to spend with their families, so they work hard to finish what they can before they leave."

"That's generous of you and William."

"There's more. When they leave for the holiday, Will gives each a drink of brandy. His way of thanking them."

"No wonder they like working here."

"In the summer," she added, "Will has casks of ale delivered to the shops on hot days."

"Again, I am impressed."

"Will and I learned the importance of treating our workers well from Father."

She took him to the blacksmith's and then to the joiners' shops. Like the main shop, each was clean and neatly kept. He couldn't help thinking that was at least in part due to her influence.

"Shall we go to the office so you can see the drawings of the *Ossian?*"

"I was hoping you might suggest that," he said, returning her smile.

With Nash at her side, Ailie drew her cloak tightly around her and took the path to the office. As they entered, she was surprised to find the iron stove well stoked and the room warm.

"Will must have asked the servants to keep the stove going."

"So this is where you created the *Ossian,*" he said, taking off his greatcoat to reveal his dark blue tailcoat and buff breeches. Any woman would think him handsome. "And where you work?"

"Much of the time." She slipped her cloak from her shoulders, laid it over her chair and reached down to open the drawer that held her most favored drawings. "I am sometimes in the shop with Mr. Ferguson. But it was here I first began the *Ossian's* design." She lifted the drawings to the top of her desk. "It's been some time since I looked at my design. Our orders are for more ordinary ships."

Would she ever see the *Ossian* in the water?

Nash took a pair of spectacles from his pocket and came to stand beside her, his shoulders mere inches from hers. She could feel the heat of him as he leaned over the drawings and detected the faint scent of sandalwood.

He took off his spectacles and turned to speak to her.

She was already facing him when their gazes met. Neither looked away.

In the moments that passed, Ailie felt the room grow overwarm and she began to feel awkward so close to a man she did not really know.

She stepped away from his intense gaze, her heart thudding in her chest.

"Tell me about the *Ossian*," he said a husky voice.

Without looking at him, she traced the lines of the schooner on the drawing and began to explain something she had never told anyone. "I saw the ship in a dream, its sleek black hull and its billowing white sails against a blue sky, as its bow cut through a wind-tossed sea. 'Tis stamped on my mind like a part of me."

Emotion gathering in her voice, she raised her gaze from her desk to the ships outside the window and the North Sea beyond, seeing again what she had first experienced in the dream. "I could feel the schooner rolling through the waves and the salty spray whipping my hair across my face as my heart raced in my chest." Then turning to face him with tear-filled eyes, she said, "I was there, Nash. On the ship. And somehow, I knew one day it would be real."

For a few seconds, he said nothing, just stared into her eyes. Had she revealed too much to a man she barely knew?

He nodded slowly. "I believe it, too, Ailie. One day, you will sail on her and I would dearly love to be with you when you do."

She cleared her throat, blinking back tears as she glanced down at the drawings. "You are kind to humor me."

"I'm not humoring you." In his voice she detected only sincerity and maybe, just maybe, admiration. "I believe you will see your ship built one day."

"'Tis a pleasant thought." Forcing her eyes away from his penetrating gaze, she glanced out the window. "If we want to be in on the Yule log hunt, we'd best be going."

On the way back to the house, she realized she had identified a difference between Nash and Robbie. Nash wore spectacles but she'd not seen them on his twin.

Robbie managed to reach his chamber without being seen. There, he changed back into the breeches and dark green tailcoat he had worn before setting off to the town. He pulled on his polished tall boots and tied a simple cravat before joining the ladies in the parlor, where he hoped to find a warm brandy and a warmer fire.

Both were soon forthcoming.

He relaxed into one of the gold wing chairs set before the fireplace, nursing the glass of brandy cradled in his hand. Time passed as he pondered what he had learned.

In the other wing chair, sat Martin's wife Kit busy drawing. To be precise, she was sketching him. She had told Robbie he must submit since his older brothers had been quick to give their consent.

"I drew Emily and the countess before you arrived in the parlor. It's my thought to sketch everyone before we return to London and give the sketches to William and Emily as a remembrance of our visit."

"A thoughtful gift," said Robbie. Considering Kit's talent, known to everyone in the family, it was an exceptional gift.

Her pencil made faint scratching noises as she worked, her blue eyes darting between the sketchbook and him.

"You have an interesting face, Robbie."

"You have guessed right."

"I did not guess." Her upturned nose rose a bit higher. "You must remember, I have observed you and Nash on other occasions, enough to be pretty certain it was you. There is much more to you than appears at first glance. Your face speaks to me of your own character, different than Nash's."

"But Nash and I are just alike," he protested, hoping Martin's talented wife did not see too much. "Even our mother has trouble telling us apart."

"Perhaps under some circumstances, I, too, would have difficulty." She paused to incline her head while carefully regarding him, then resumed her sketching. "An artist notices small differences others might miss. I often see people as animals."

"Do you?"

"For example, I see you as a playful otter, while Nash, to me, is the silent jungle cat, more dangerous than he might appear at first."

"Perhaps beneath the otter is a lion."

She laughed. "Oh yes, I see that, too."

Robbie hoped others did not observe all his sister-in-law saw. He and Nash staked their lives upon the fact people could not tell them apart.

An aged hand rested on his shoulder. Robbie looked up to see the silver-haired Lady Claremont, peering at him through her quizzing glass. On her face was a sober expression. He felt like an insect under a magnifying glass.

She straightened, dropping her glass. "You do wear a mask, young man. A charming one, I grant you, but still a mask."

"See?" said Kit. "I am not the only one who sees the otter before the lion."

Robbie held his tongue, afraid anything he might say would speak of hidden truths.

"Mark my words," the countess went on, "I know your type well. You will be snatched from your bachelor state in the wink of an eye." Then she gave out a "Humph" and muttered, "A rogue seldom sees his fate coming."

He grinned and tried to make light of it. "Who am I to argue with The Grand Countess?"

She patted him on the shoulder. "Very wise, Mr. Powell."

"Would you care to sit down? I would happily give you my chair."

"No, thank you. I am tired of sitting." Her head swiveled toward the door. Robbie's gaze followed. "Ah, the mighty hunters return," she announced.

Kit set her sketchbook and pencils on the table where her glass of sherry rested and stood. "I'll finish this later."

Robbie got to his feet to welcome the hunters back. They came toward the fireplace, reaching their hands toward the flames. "How was it?" he asked Ormond.

Hugh rubbed his hands together. "Cold enough to freeze fire."

"Not for a Scot," replied William, looking askance at his friend. "I can see the comforts of London have made you soft."

"We shall see about that, my friend," Hugh tossed back. "Our time together has only begun."

Kit kissed Martin on his cheek. "Welcome home."

"I missed you, Kitten." He drew her into his arms. "You're warm."

Robbie watched the pair for a moment and then turned to see Mary embracing her husband. 'Twas not surprising Hugh had fallen for her.

Tara appeared in front of their oldest brother Nick and planted a kiss on his lips.

Robbie envied Hugh and his brothers their wives. Sharing common pursuits with a woman as well as a bed appealed but, even more, he envied them the loyalty and affection their wives showed them. Perhaps it was time he considered marrying. The countess might have the right of it. Perhaps his fate was already before him. Could the alluring Mistress of the Setters be a candidate for his wife?

"You smell of pond, Husband," Tara chided Nick as she nuzzled his neck. "Did you bag many birds?"

"Dozens, my love," he replied, slipping his arm around her waist.

William draped his arm over Emily's shoulder. "We've enough for soups, stews and roast goose aplenty."

"Now I'm jealous," said Tara, her blue-green eyes solemn beneath her frown. "I should have borrowed a stable boy's breeches and tagged along."

Robbie chuckled remembering his sisters-in-law knew how to shoot. And this particular one had donned breeches many times to climb the rigging of Nick's ship. Their two young sons would surely grow up to be ship captains. With parents like that, how could they not?

A footman entered the room and poured brandy for the returning hunters, asking if the countess wanted another glass of sherry.

"That would be lovely, my good man," she replied.

Seeing a movement in the doorway, Robbie lifted his gaze just as Nash appeared with Ailie. His twin had a strange look on his face, as if his mind were elsewhere, and Ailie's cheeks were flushed. Was it the cold or something else? Robbie wondered what had transpired between them to produce such a result.

He crossed the room to meet them. "You two missed the noon meal. The soup was delicious."

Ailie smiled. "Did you like it?"

Robbie smiled back at the lovely girl. It was impossible to do otherwise. "I did."

"Ailie and I had a late breakfast together," interjected Nash, "before she gave me a tour of the shipyard."

"Your brother refused to try the smoked haddies," she told Robbie.

Nash shrugged.

"His loss, I fear." Robbie sensed a familiarity between the two he had not observed before. Dismayed to realize his trip into town had set him back in the race to win the affections of the lovely Aileen Stephen, he vowed to make up for it when he had an opportunity.

With Emily by his side, William came to join them, pausing in front of Nash. "What did you think of the shipyard?"

The look on Nash's face spoke of his admiration. "'Tis a busy place."

"We'll be even busier once spring is here," said William.

Nash gave Robbie a pointed look. "You should find time to tour the shops. William has a fine enterprise here."

"Coming from one of the Powells, that's a high compliment," said William. "Did Ailie show you her drawings of the *Ossian*?"

"She did and I am more impressed than ever."

William smiled at his sister. "I thought you might be." Scanning the assembled group, he said, "If we are to find the Yule log before we lose the light, we should leave now. The sledge will hold six and the rest can ride."

The men finished their brandy as William asked, "How many are going?"

When Nash said, "Me," Robbie followed suit.

Ailie and Tara both said they were going.

Hugh exchanged a look with his wife. "Mary and I would like to ride."

Martin drew his wife close. "Kit and I will stay here by the fire. I shall regale my wife with tales of my hunting prowess. By the bye, Ailie, your setters are marvelous retrievers."

Ailie smiled. "Thanks, but 'tis Will who deserves your praise. He trained them to hunt."

"I, too, will remain," said the countess. "I have yet to see Emily's orangery."

Emily kissed William on his cheek. "Enjoy yourself. I will escort Muriel to see my plants and trees. Since I imagine you and the hunters will be famished, I'll ask Martha to have dinner ready when you return."

"William brought meat pies to the geese shoot to tide us over," said Nick. No wonder Nick had not mentioned being hungry. Every member of the Powell family knew that their eldest brother took his meals seriously.

"I would not let them starve," Will assured his wife. "Now, if I have it right, Hugh and Mary will ride, and the rest of us going will take the sledge. When we return, the bathhouse off the kitchen is at the disposal of the men needing to bathe. For the women, just let the upstairs maids know and a bath can be brought to your chamber."

Robbie and the rest of them accepted their coats and cloaks from the waiting footmen.

"Then let us away," said William, striding toward the front door.

Robbie kept his eye on Ailie Stephen. Though he would have enjoyed a ride on one of William's fine horses, he had intentionally not asked to do so, intending instead to sit beside the Mistress of the Setters in the sledge. But as they headed toward the sledge, it became clear that Nash, still beside her, had the same idea.

Chapter 7

Ailie loved gliding over the snow in the open carriage, the sound of the harness bells echoing through the woods.

The wind blowing off the snow was cold on her face, but Will had given them lap blankets to keep their legs warm. The rest of her was wedged between the broad-shouldered bodies of Nash and Robbie Powell. The seating arrangement had been suggested by Will when he climbed up to the driver's seat to join the groom, leaving Nick and Tara a seat of their own, facing Ailie and the Powell twins.

At least she was warm but, in truth, the nearness of the handsome Powell brothers was disconcerting, particularly after her time spent with Nash in the shipyard. She had to remind herself they were only here on holiday and would sail to London in a matter of weeks.

Maintaining a calm appearance, she focused her attention on Nick and Tara in front of her.

Tara took in the three of them and smiled. "Is William your only sibling?" she asked Ailie.

"I have two other brothers in Aberdeen, but I am the only daughter."

"It's the same with me," said Tara, apparently happy to encounter one like herself.

"That is how my wife came to crew like one of my men," said Nick. "She went to sea with her father and brothers after her mother died. She's a monkey in the rigging."

Tara tossed her husband an impudent look just before the sledge hit a bump and the groom made a sharp turn, jostling them like raw peas in a pan.

"I have never had the pleasure of traveling this way through the woods," said Robbie, pressing his leg into hers on the sudden turn. With a wink at her, he added, "I shall have to do so more often."

Ailie could have sworn Nash rolled his eyes, as he slipped his arm over the top of the seat in what she took as a proprietary gesture. She felt like a mouse between two cats. At least they had not changed clothes from the morning so she could tell them apart.

"In Maryland," Tara informed them, "sleigh rides in the countryside are a tradition. The bells the horses wear are a part of the sounds of our Christmas."

Riding behind the sledge, dark-haired Hugh and his fair wife Mary laughed. When the road was wide enough, they came alongside, adding to the conversation.

Mary had told Ailie the pair of black horses pulling the sledge reminded her of the Friesian she kept at the family estate. "We don't have room for Midnight in London but we often visit Hugh's parents so they can see the boys, and I ride him there."

After traveling for a while, Will had the groom stop in a wooded area where there was a stand of mature birch trees, the bark partially covered by snow. "Will's been scouting the best trees for the Yule log," Ailie explained.

Nick and Tara alighted from the sledge first. Nash climbed down and helped Ailie to the ground, Robbie right behind her.

They all gathered around Will, who pointed to the trees behind him. "There are some good choices for your Yule log behind me, but to save a lot of labor, I've spotted a few we can root out of the ground where they fell. The older ones are better for burning, too, the more knotted the better." The groom handed Will a rope. "We've brought a sled to haul the log back when you've found the one you want."

With that, Will released them to hunt for the log.

Ailie gazed into the forest. The carpet of snow made the woods appear lighter. She surveyed the birch trees within easy range, almost certain her brother had identified a log he liked. But Will would not deprive their guests of having a hand in selecting the one that would burn during the celebration of the English Christmastide.

Plunging into the woods, Nash cried, "Come on, Ailie, let's find a good one."

"Not without me," said Robbie, taking her elbow and urging her forward.

Though it was low in the sky, the sun had not yet set as they entered the woods, their boots crunching on the ice-crusted snow.

A snowy owl, disturbed by the invaders, launched from its perch. Their English guests gasped as the huge bird with its five-foot wingspan flew over their heads.

"Never seen one of those before," remarked Nick.

"Magnificent bird," said Nash. "I've read about snowy owls."

When the owl had gone, Hugh leaned up against the thick trunk of one birch, crossing his arms over his chest. Fixing his eyes on Will, he grinned. "Are you certain you don't want to cut down this one?"

Before Will could respond, Mary pelted her husband with a snowball.

Hugh's searching gaze found her, a teasing smile on her face. Looking highly offended, he said, "We'll see about that!" Ailie could tell by his expression as he reached for the snow he was not offended at all, but excited. Forming his own snowball, he launched it into the air to hit Mary's back just as she turned to run.

The fight was on.

Ailie joined up with Tara, who led the ladies in a battle of great proportions as snow flew all around them. "We shall bury you in snow," Tara shouted to the men.

Nick tossed a snowball, hitting his wife's head, thankfully covered with the hood of her cloak. "Not likely!"

Ailie threw a snowball at one twin and then the other. Everyone was so covered in snow she couldn't tell one Powell twin from the other. She, too, was covered in white, panting for the effort at returning the many snowballs aimed at her. It was great fun.

After a blizzard of snowballs whizzing everywhere, Will called a halt to their battle. "My hands are frozen. Time to hunt the log before 'tis full dark." At his instruction, the groom lit torches and handed them to the men. "These will help," offered Will.

It wasn't long before a shout of "Over here" had them all moving toward a fallen log of considerable girth.

Will gave the log an assessing look. "Well, now. It just might fit the fireplace if we use this end." He pointed to the end where the huge log narrowed. "We'll know more once we haul it back and dry it out in the shop."

By the time the men had towed the log to the sled, lifted it into place and tied the sled to the back of the sledge, the sun had set and it was beginning to snow.

"Everyone in!" shouted Will.

Mary and Hugh remounted their horses and, once again, rode beside the fully loaded sledge the groom had turned around to head back.

Will held a torch to help guide their way, slower now for the huge log they towed.

"I have not had so much fun in a long while," said Nick, sitting across from Ailie and the Powell twins.

"Only because some of your well-aimed snowballs hit me," teased Tara.

On Ailie's right, Robbie swept his hand toward the woods. "Here in Scotland, one can forget the work left undone, the crush of London's crowds and the obligations awaiting us. I quite needed this."

Ailie glanced at the silent Nash, his forehead furrowed, and wondered, which of those things Robbie had mentioned had caused him to frown.

From her perch in the parlor, Muriel watched the snow falling outside, worrying about the young men and women who had ventured into the woods and not yet returned. She had begun to think of them as her charges, just as she had Emily years ago.

The ones who were wed concerned her less, but the Powell twins and the Stephen girl were old enough to be wed and have children of their own. A situation she would soon remedy if she could. A few weeks might be sufficient. She had done it in less time with others.

Surely the young Aileen Stephen could choose between the two Powell brothers. Muriel was not unmindful of the way the two men had looked at the girl. No, a match was definitely possible.

She smiled with warm affection at Emily sitting across from her in the wing chair and remembered Christmastide a year ago when she had introduced the tall auburn-haired Scottish shipbuilder from Arbroath to her friend. It had been love for him from the start, or nearly so, but Emily had required some convincing.

Now, Muriel's dear friend sat reading on a cold winter's night in the far northwest of Scotland, expecting her first child.

Muriel's only regret was that Emily had ended up so far from London. At least she was happy, which had been Muriel's intent when she first conceived the match.

After their visit to the orangery, she and Emily had claimed the two wing chairs on either side of the fire and enjoyed their tea. When the last of Mrs. Platt's teacakes had been eaten, Emily had taken up her book.

Muriel stared out the window across the room, watching the snow that had begun to fall. Her mind drifted back to the past, her fingers playing with the long strand of pearls.

Of all the matches she had made, perhaps her own was the best. Like Robbie Powell, the Earl of Claremont had been a very charming man, and though she would confess it to only a few, he'd had a reputation as a rogue. Now that he was gone, she missed him terribly.

As for the Powell twins, they might appear the same, but she was certain they were very different men. Nash, the quieter one, had a dry sense of humor. He might appreciate the fiercely independent Aileen Stephen, who could benefit from a man who would make her laugh. But then, she might also find humor in the teasing of Nash's brother, Robbie. Muriel had no doubt the rogue could be brought up to scratch.

Through the open doorway, Muriel heard the front door open. The group of young people rushed inside, brushing snow from their coats and laughing as they bemoaned the effort required to haul the log into the shipyard.

A few minutes later, William strode through the doorway and approached Emily. "We found a good one, *Leannan*," he said, kissing her forehead.

The look in Emily's heather eyes suggested pride in her husband's achievement in bringing home the Yule log for his English wife.

William greeted Muriel and then dropped his gaze to the book in Emily's lap. "Did you read all afternoon?"

"No, only a short while. After I showed Muriel around the orangery, we had a lovely English tea."

Amid much laughter, the others flowed into the parlor. Muriel rose from her chair to allow them access to the fire. Emily, too, got to her feet to stand next to William.

First to reach them was Hugh. She still thought of him as Ormond, having known him by that name since he was a youth. His parents, the Duke and Duchess of Albany, were among her closest friends. "Muriel, you will be gratified to learn we have secured a birch log of sufficient size to burn for days."

"Yule logs are one tradition I approve of," she told him.

"This fire is delightful," remarked Hugh's wife Mary as she reached her palms toward the flames. "My fingers were frozen around the reins of my horse by the time we got back."

William said to Muriel and Emily, "We left the log in the shop where the stoves will dry it out. By Christmas Eve, it will be stripped and ready to drag into the house."

"Oh, good," said Nick, the eldest Powell brother, bringing his wife Tara with him to warm themselves by the fire. "Another chance to heave a load. 'Tis more work than hauling up one of my anchors."

Tara poked him in the ribs, which earned her a kiss on her nose. "The exercise will do you much good."

"I thought I got enough exercise chasing you around our chamber," Nick teased.

Muriel had scant experience with Americans, but she rather thought this young woman had been just what the arrogant Captain Nicholas Powell had needed. Tara would not let him get away with anything.

"I'm surrounded by rogues," Muriel muttered.

"Did someone call for me?" asked Robbie in a cheery tone as he stepped up to the group, joined by his twin and Aileen Stephen.

"You're not the only one of your kind among our guests," said Aileen. "What about your twin brother?"

Muriel observed the two brothers exchanging a glance that spoke of shared pursuits. Was she wrong in thinking the two men were so very different? She had just begun to ponder how she might sort them out when Aileen spoke up. "You must see the Yule log, Muriel. 'Tis enormous."

"All in good time, my dear. Doubtless I shall be here to welcome it into the parlor."

"Did anyone think to gather greenery?" asked Emily of the group now gathered in front of the fire.

"Sorry, no," said William. "When it began to snow, I thought we had better return. There is always tomorrow."

Emily gave him a look of approval. "It was wise not to tarry in the woods. Not with the way the snow is coming down."

Muriel looked out the window, frosted around the edges. The snow descended like a white curtain.

A footman swept into the room carrying a tray of small mugs.

Aileen lifted one from the tray. "Hot cider, anyone?"

Chapter 8

20 December

Nash slipped out of bed, immediately noticing the warmth of the bedchamber. His eyes darted toward the crackling fire. Some worthy servant had stirred the fire banked the night before, bless him.

In the bed next to his, Robbie slept on.

Crossing the room to the window facing the back of the house, he wiped the steam from the glass and gazed out at the snow-covered landscape. Shafts of light from the rising sun glistened in the branches of the snow-laden evergreen trees. He stared contentedly at the magical scene, so far from the hurried pace of London, and felt his soul take a deep breath.

Suddenly, across his vision streaked the two black setters, leaping to stay above the snow. Laughter sounded as a snowball flew toward the dogs that barked loudly when the snowball found its target. Nash turned his head to glimpse their intrepid mistress in a man's breeches, boots and jacket, a blue tartan scarf around her neck.

She stood on a rock rising above the snow, her bright red hair hanging to her shoulders. Had he not seen Tara wearing breeches on Nick's ship, he might have been surprised, but the bold decision to wear a man's clothing seemed consistent with Ailie's character. She wore them very well, her long shapely legs catching his eye.

The dogs barked as they dashed toward her, creating furrows in the snow with their bodies. When they reached Ailie, they tried to jump onto the rock but only sank deeper, their muzzles coated with snow-flakes.

She laughed all the harder, bending over, hands on her knees.

Nash could not recall the last time he'd engaged in such lighthearted frivolity. He envied Ailie's playmates the fun they were having with their mistress.

The sight of her copper hair and her beautiful laughing face brought an excitement to the day as he anticipated seeing her again. Perhaps he would ask her to go with him in search of greenery this morning. He could put off the trip to Arbroath's taverns till the afternoon, or possibly postpone the Crown's business until tomorrow. Surely he and Robbie had time.

Last night, Nash had learned of Robbie's trip to the town and the altercation in one of the taverns. Robbie had an excellent memory, which made him especially good at cards. From his one visit to Arbroath, he'd drawn a detailed plan of the town, including the harbor, the main streets, the taverns and the ships tied up at the quay. The detail of the streets and tavern names had been very fine, requiring them to don their spectacles to capture it all.

From his brother's drawing, it became clear there were more tav-erns to investigate than they had time. "We'll have to get lucky if we're to find Kinloch," he had told Robbie. "And we've a ship's passenger list to confirm." If Kinloch were in Arbroath, as they believed he was, he would inevitably come to town to while away the hours with his fellow rebels as he waited for the ship to sail. What else had he to occupy his time?

It made sense the man from Dundee would have booked cabins on the *Panmure* if his destination, like Captain Gower's, was France. After all, there Kinloch would find his views welcomed.

All the pieces fit.

Nash watched Ailie frolicking in the snow with her dogs, thinking of how his own views had changed since Manchester. After the poverty and despair he had witnessed, he had begun to question whether those advocating reform were the radicals the government claimed them to be.

Sidmouth feared a revolution like the one that had forever changed France: the loss of the monarchy, the murder of nobility and radicals taking over the government. That he was prepared—with the support of the prince regent—to do violence to prevent such an outcome had been well demonstrated.

Two years before, their brother Martin had been in Derbyshire to witness the violent end of the uprising there. And Nash had not forgotten the madness in Manchester that had almost claimed his life.

A gentleman Scot who could draw ten thousand to his cause had to be dealt with or so Sidmouth had told them when he ordered them north. Nash had hesitated, but Robbie did not. In the end, Nash had decided to go to Scotland, for he would not let his brother undertake such a task alone. Robbie relied upon him as a designer of plans.

Ailie and her dogs suddenly disappeared from his view. Not wishing to delay, he turned to face Robbie, still abed. "The day is upon us, Brother."

Robbie stirred, groaned and rolled over, turning his back to Nash.

"Very well. I shall see you whenever you manage to rise."

Eager to see Ailie, Nash slipped on his coat and left the chamber.

He reached the top of the stairs just as she was ascending, her head down, her man's clothing covered with snow. Anticipating the inevitable collision, he reached out and held her arms to steady her lest she lose her footing.

"Oh!" She started, lifting her eyes to him.

He gave her a grin that would have done Robbie proud. "Is this what the stylish young Scottish miss is wearing this winter?"

Hand over her heart, she said, "Really, Robbie, you scared me to death."

"It's Nash you have nearly sent flying in your haste, but I shall forgive you the error. Have you had breakfast yet?"

She paused to study his face for a moment. "Oh, sorry, Nash. No, I've not eaten. I was hoping to change before anyone saw me. The snow's too thick for me to exercise the dogs wearing skirts."

"Personally, I like you clothed in this manner." He dropped his hands from her arms to look down at her close-fitting breeches. "Tara would call you a kindred spirit."

Her face was close to his as she looked up at him from the stair below. Her freckles, scattered over her nose like fairy dust, caused him to lean in. It would be so easy to bend his head and kiss her. He wondered if he should attempt it, but he never got the chance.

She climbed the last stair and walked past him, then looked back. "Wait for me and I will join you for breakfast." Laughing, she added, "Save me some haddies."

"The whole plate," he replied with a smirk.

He watched her as she made her way to her chamber, her long hair hanging down her back like a waterfall of molten copper. A beauty, indeed, with a spirit to match her red hair. A woman he wouldn't mind waking up to for the rest of his life.

As he descended the stairs he decided he must find a way to distinguish himself from his twin, else she would continue to get them confused. He wanted her to see him for the man he was, to recognize him at first sight. More, he wanted her to believe he was the man who could win her heart. A kiss might do it, confirming for them both what lay between them.

In his plans, he would find a way.

Rising with the sun, Ailie had thought to avoid being seen by their English guests. It *would* have to be Nash she encountered, who she had mistakenly believed to be Robbie only because of that impertinent grin he'd given her. Once she had looked deeply into his hazel eyes and felt the effect of his presence, the force of his gaze, she recognized him.

She enjoyed the company of both twins, but only Nash turned her legs to jelly. When he'd placed his hands on her arms to keep her from falling, she had felt his strength anchoring her to the stair. With any other man, she would have brushed away his hands, but she had not wanted him to let go of her. Perhaps that is why she had told him about her dream of the *Ossian*. It had seemed perfectly natural to share with him what she had shared with no other.

In her chamber, Rhona was waiting for her. "Good day, Mistress. Did ye enjoy yer morning walk?"

"More like a romp. Goodness and Mercy are especially frisky this morning with the new snow. I ran them till they were panting from navigating the deep drifts. They lie fagged out in the kitchen."

Rhona chuckled and helped her peel off the soaked clothes. "Ye do more for those dogs than ye would a man."

Ailie toweled off her damp skin in front of the fire and put on a clean shift and corset, showing her back to her maid. "Oh, I don't know about that. You have yet to see what I would do for a man I loved."

Rhona pulled the laces tight. "Ye're right in that, Mistress. Will ye be going outside again this morning?"

"To gather greens with the whole lot of them, I expect. I look forward to seeing the house decorated for the season and smelling Martha's shortbread." In truth, Ailie loved this time of year. Spending it with Nash Powell, his brothers and their wives and their friends had turned out to be more than a little diverting. She was actually enjoying herself.

"Shall ye wear the bottle green woolen gown?" Rhona asked, sorting through Ailie's gowns.

"Aye, and the dark green cloak." Rhona slipped the gown over her head and fastened the buttons.

"How is the countess?" Ailie inquired, taking a seat at her dressing table, aghast to see her hair had become tangled from the morning's activity.

Rhona patiently combed through the tangles. "She is verra well. I am coming to like her and her ways. She can sound cross sometimes, but I think 'tis just an act."

"I thought the same. I am glad she decided to come. Emily is so happy to have her here."

Rhona gathered Ailie's hair and tied it at her nape with a ribbon. "If you do not require more, I'll be off to tend her."

"Go."

When Rhona quit the chamber, Ailie took out her quill and ink and jotted a short note in her diary.

20 December

I am to meet Nash Powell (the twin I took to the shipyard) for break-fast, so this will be short. The snow that fell last night is so deep I fear none of the workers will make it into the shipyard today. However, Goodness and Mercy are pleased and enjoyed their morning romp. As for the rest of us, we've plenty of food in the larder and the Yule log has been acquired so 'twill be a day of gathering greenery to decorate the house and perhaps card games in the parlor. Emily says Mrs. Platt will make wassail.

She decided not to record in her diary her growing attraction for Nash Powell. Besides, she had yet to determine if he was the man in her dream. It could be either Nash or his twin brother. And why had she seen a tavern? None of their guests had yet to go to Arbroath town. Could it have been a scene in London?

By the time she got to the dining room, it was filled with their guests. She paused in the doorway, listening. At one end of the table,

Muriel was opining on the importance of a London season for a young lady.

The countess garnered many arguments to the contrary, the most strident from Nick's wife Tara, who had found her brief time in London's social whirl disappointing.

Mary agreed, glad her season had been cut short by her trip to France where she'd fallen in love with the marquess who became her husband.

Emily and Kit sided with the countess, saying they enjoyed their time of parties, balls and dinners. "The year was all too short," said Kit.

Ailie took a plate from the sideboard and added to it some haddies, eggs and girdle scones before taking the chair next to the Powell twin she thought had to be Nash. She was rewarded when he leaned in to whisper, "You clean up well, Mistress Stephen."

"Thanks, I do try." She hadn't noticed his clothing when she had narrowly avoided colliding with him on the stairs. Now she could see his cinnamon-colored coat fit his shoulders to perfection. His cravat, like the other men's, was white and simply tied.

"How about you, Ailie?" Will asked from the other end of the table.

She stopped eating and looked up with raised brows. She had been so occupied with thoughts of Nash, she had lost the thread of the conversation.

Will persisted. "Are you still glad you rejected the idea of a season when Father first proposed sending you to London?"

Embarrassed that all their guests should know of it, Ailie nevertheless admitted the reason she had declined. "I could not imagine the *haut ton* accepting a Scot in their midst."

Loud protests sounded around the table.

"Now there you would be wrong," the countess stated emphatically. Everyone quieted, leaning in to hear what Muriel had to say. "You would be a novelty, Aileen, and there is nothing the aristocracy likes so much as a novelty. That said, you have no need for a season." The countess fixed her eyes on Ailie, who expected the silver-haired woman to peer at her through her quizzing glass at any moment.

The focus of everyone's attention, Ailie fought the urge to squirm.

"I can take you under my wing and show you all around London," the countess continued. "Of course, you would have to allow me to remake you in the image of the *débutante* with silk and satin gowns and your hair done up in curls, perhaps with a feather or two." Muriel's mouth twitched up, hinting at a smile. "At my side, no one would challenge your right to enter London Society. And I daresay the young men would follow you around like puppies."

Ailie felt Nash stiffen at her side. She wasn't sure she wanted men, especially English men, following her about like puppies.

Robbie suddenly appeared at the door as handsome as his twin and wearing his usual grin. "Indeed, they would. Good morning all," he greeted them, receiving nods from the men before striding to the side table.

"What say you to Muriel's offer?" asked Emily. Ailie could see by her eager expression, her sister-in-law approved of the idea.

All eyes on her, Ailie felt her cheeks flood with heat. Did she want to do such an outrageous thing? Go to London to be surrounded by the English? It was what her parents would want but Ailie had always preferred to stay in Scotland immersed in building ships.

"The Countess of Claremont is known by all of London to be a grand lady," Hugh encouraged. "And much loved, I might add. Her parties are the hit of the season."

"There's not a person of worth who would risk missing one of her balls," put in Martin. "The countess can be a formidable ally or, should one cross her, a formidable enemy. None would dare offend her or anyone in her favor."

Ailie considered the elegant older woman with new eyes. "Truly?"

"They exaggerate, my dear," said Muriel, "but I do not. You have only to ask Emily, whom I tutored along. The invitation is yours to accept."

From across the table, Emily set down her teacup and gave Ailie an encouraging smile.

Her breakfast forgotten, Ailie asked, "Might I think on it?"

Will winked at the countess. "I suspect Muriel will give you until she sails for London to decide."

Ailie shifted her gaze to the countess at the end of the table.

Muriel smiled. "Just so."

Robbie had observed Nash's reaction to the countess' prediction that men would follow Ailie Stephen about London. A beautiful redhead gowned in silk and satin would be most welcome, at least by the men. The slight Scots brogue in her voice would make her unique among the young women on the marriage mart. As the guest of The Grand Countess, men would be intrigued.

He understood why Nash did not want Ailie going to London. Robbie wasn't at all certain *he* liked the idea of the lass being paraded about in front of the ravenous rogues, even though, at times, he acted the rogue himself.

Here in Scotland, Ailie was a rare jewel, ripe for wooing yet isolated. In London, escorted through rooms crowded with bachelors seeking a wife, the competition for her hand would be fierce.

Though it mattered little to him and, he was certain it mattered not at all to Nash, as the only daughter of a shipbuilding magnate, Ailie Stephen would have a good dowry. She'd be one of The Golden Girls, as Robbie thought of them, the daughters of rich gentry who came not with lands, but with large portions.

Faced with a choice of a simpering ingénue just out of the schoolroom or an intelligent woman of uncommon beauty and wealth, the men looking for wives would consider Miss Aileen Stephen a most delectable choice. To Robbie's mind, she was too great a prize to be offered up to the swains in London.

He brought his plate to the table and took the only available seat across from Nash. He winked at Ailie. "I recommend staying in Scotland."

At his words, Nash visibly relaxed.

"'Sides," Robbie tossed in, "Almack's serves up tepid lemonade and weak tea. You'd not like it."

"Balderdash!" roared Muriel. "At my parties, I serve only the finest champagne. Why, there's also brandy and other spirits in the card room."

Emily frowned. "Do not discourage my sister-in-law, Robbie. 'Tis a great opportunity Muriel has extended to her. I am confident my friend would see Ailie has a wonderful time."

"In the meantime," interjected Will, saving them all from another debate, "we have greenery to gather if we're to dress the house on Christmas Eve. The snow is deep but the winter sun is with us. If you are willing to brave the weather, we can venture into the woods once again."

Voices around the table echoed words of agreement.

Mary and Hugh exchanged a glance. "We still prefer to ride," said Hugh.

"I, too, would like to ride," said Nash. Then to Ailie, "Might you be my guide?"

Robbie kept his expression calm, but he was taken aback. This was Nash's day to go to town. The deep snow he had seen upon rising might suggest a delay, but surely not a long one. He could easily cover the ground if he were to ride.

Ailie nodded to Nash. "I would be happy to show you the way to some greenery perfect for the house."

For once in his life, Robbie had been too slow, missing the opportunity to extend the invitation to the lovely girl. He let out a sigh of frustration. He would have to be patient; there would be other opportunities.

Emily spoke up. "I've asked the servants to set up tables for cards in the library. And Mrs. Platt has promised to make wassail. Perhaps we might have a game of loo, Muriel?"

Muriel took a sip of her chocolate. "Well, it's not whist, my favorite, but a game of loo will do."

Emily laughed. "I recall that 'tis true of you."

The countess laughed at their rhyming, making Robbie think the two shared some private memory. Since he enjoyed cards and Nash had usurped his place with Ailie, rather than make a nuisance of himself in the woods, he decided to be useful by contributing to the game's participants. "Whist or loo, I can play either," he ventured. "We just need two more."

"We'll play," offered Martin. "Loo is one of Kit's favorite games." Kit nodded enthusiastically.

"If it's all right with you, William," suggested Nick, "Tara and I would like to see the shipyard."

"I don't know how many of my men will make it in today, but if you will allow me to be your guide, I'd be happy to give you a tour and tell you about the work we have underway."

"Nothing could be better," said Tara. "I've only seen my father's shipbuilding enterprise in Baltimore. I would look forward to seeing yours and, with you as our guide, we'd miss nothing."

"In addition to our repair work," said William, "we built three schooners last year and have one under construction now I can show you."

"Powell and Sons *buys* schooners," said Nick with a wry smile, "but then I am certain Hugh mentioned that."

William chuckled. "Aye, he did. Perhaps before you depart for London, we can do a bit of business." He turned to Robbie and the rest of them. "Now that we are all agreed, I'll leave the arrangements for the horses to Ailie and the cards to my lovely wife, while I take Nick and Tara to the shipyard."

As the others rose and filed out of the dining room, Robbie caught Nash as he made to leave. "A word, Brother?"

Nash waved Ailie on and turned to Robbie. "What is it?"

"We've work to do in Arbroath, or have you forgotten why we are here?" If Robbie were being honest, his irritation with his brother stemmed more from his monopolizing the beautiful girl than from shirking his responsibility.

"I have not forgotten."

Robbie took account of his brother's guilty expression. "Our enjoyment of the Stephens' hospitality cannot come before our obligation to the Crown. I sense Kinloch is here and I'd rather catch him before he boards the *Panmure*."

"If I get back early, I can still go to town today. Otherwise, tomorrow. If the ship isn't sailing until the end of the month, we have time."

"Not so much that you can be constantly seeking out Miss Stephen."

Nash raised his brows. "Jealous?"

Robbie huffed. Nothing irritated him more than being called out on a weakness.

Nash stared at him for a moment, seeing more than Robbie cared for him to. "Don't worry," he said, "I'll go tomorrow at the latest." Then he turned and walked away.

Robbie considered his brother's choices. He had never before pursued a woman to the detriment of their duty. Was it the assignment that was so distasteful? Or, perhaps Nash's feelings for the girl were more serious than Robbie had believed. Was this desire he was witnessing, or could it be more?

Chapter 9

"Mind the holly thorns!" Ailie shouted to the others riding behind her as they ventured deeper into the woods. She had given them cloth sacks in which to put the greenery they found and, just as they left, Will had given Hugh and Nash each a new tool.

Captain Anderson had brought the pruning shears he called "sécateurs" back from France for Emily, telling her they would make short work of cutting woody stems.

Now all they needed was the greenery they hunted: holly, red hawthorn berries and branches of Scots pine. Planning for the house to be well decorated for the English Christmastide, Emily had been growing rosemary, ivy and the hellebore she called Christmas rose in the orangery.

Ailie had left Goodness and Mercy back at the house knowing the snow would be deep in the woods.

She led the others along the road, now covered with snow up to the horses' fetlocks. No ice had formed and the horses, unshod for the winter, soon found their footing. The horses showed great enthusiasm for the venture, snorting and shaking their heads when snow from high branches fell upon them.

Being outdoors in the cold air enlivened Ailie's spirit. That she rode with Nash only raised her enthusiasm for their outing.

"I see some holly bushes over there," cried Mary excitedly. Ailie turned in the saddle to see Hugh's wife riding off to the left. Hugh reined his horse to follow.

Ailie urged her mare on. She remembered a hawthorn tree in this part of the woods and was determined to find it. The birds often ate the berries, but if she could find some they had left, the red berries would make an attractive decoration along with the Scots pine branches she hoped to gather.

Nash pulled up next to her. "What are you searching for?"

"A hawthorn tree."

"Not just any greenery, then."

"No, a tree I remembered being in this part of the woods." She took the path to the right. The horses plodded more slowly, the snow now to their knees. "The deeper snow will make the going slower," she told Nash, "but I'm hoping we'll be rewarded with some berries."

"Very well, lead on."

Farther ahead, Ailie heard the sound of running water. The sound grew louder as they neared the small burn where water rushed over rocks. She spotted the hawthorn tree just beyond the water. "We're in luck! The branches are laden with berries."

"Those small red dots beneath the snow on the branches?" Nash asked.

"Aye."

Nash dismounted and waded through the snow to where she sat her horse, watching him. He took hold of her waist and lowered her to the ground.

Her hands on his shoulders, Ailie slid down the front of his greatcoat until her feet touched ground beneath the snow. He didn't let go but fixed her with his green and gold eyes.

She could not tear her eyes from his handsome face and the longing she saw in his eyes. Her heart sped as he said her name and bent his head, drawing closer.

He closed his eyes and, when his lips touched hers, she closed her eyes, shutting out all but him and his kiss.

His lips were surprisingly soft and his touch tender, causing her to welcome the kiss. Around them stood the cold snow-covered woods but, in his arms, she was warm, his lips moving over hers igniting a flame within her.

He raised his head. "I've been wanting to do that since that first evening in your parlor."

It was the only time in her life Ailie had been rendered dizzy by a man's kiss. With her hands still on his shoulders, she looked into his beautiful eyes, hoping he would kiss her again.

He smiled and so did she, like two children sharing a secret.

Acceding to her unspoken wish, he kissed her again. This time, when their lips touched, she wrapped her hands around his neck and held him close.

The kiss, less gentle than the first, stirred a response deep within her. He put his hands on her hips and drew her against his body. Their coats between them did not prevent her from feeling the heat of him. She delighted in his masculine smell tinged with the scent of sandalwood.

Tentatively at first, she returned his kiss. Despite the intimate nature of his tongue entwining with hers, it was not at all unpleasant. She had heard her brothers speak of such kisses but this was her first experience. With Nash, what had been described as something she never thought to enjoy became an exchange of passionate ardor such as she had never known.

He pulled away first, leaving her breathless. "Forgive me, Ailie. I shouldn't—"

She put her gloved finger to his mouth. "Don't say it. I'm glad you did. I liked your kissing me or couldn't you tell?"

He gave her another of his winning smiles. "I could tell." Then taking one of her hands, he led her toward the hawthorn tree. "We had best gather those berries before we forget why we came."

"Aye." She laughed. "I had nearly forgotten myself."

His smile was subtle as he shook his head. "You are always surprising me, Ailie. Innocent you may be but with enough passion to require all my self-control."

Bending his head toward the smaller branches, he began to cut. Since he had the shears, she directed him to those branches that were heavy with berries.

They worked side by side, Nash cutting and Ailie putting the branches in the bag. In her mind she relived his kisses. What could they mean? He was an Englishman, she a Scot. Most likely, he was an Anglican; she was a Presbyterian. She had only known him for a matter of days. In a matter of weeks, he would return to London and she would never see him again. Perhaps, to him, the kiss meant little.

They filled the sack. "What next?" he asked.

She looked around them, fighting the urge to return to his arms. A stand of small Scots pine trees stood nearby. "Some pine branches would go well with the berries and they will make the house smell like the woods. Let's cut some of those."

"I live to serve," he teased. Working his way around the hawthorn tree to the young Scots pines, he asked, "How many?"

"Enough to fill another sack." She took one from her saddlebag and brought it to where he stood. "Don't you gather greenery in England for your Christmastide?"

"We do, but not Scots pines. I don't suppose you have mistletoe in Arbroath?"

"Mistletoe… the Druid's herb? Not much of it in Scotland, none that I know of in Arbroath unless a ship brings it, but even if one did, the Kirk would not approve."

"'Tis what the English use in their kissing boughs." His smile made her think of a small boy who had a frog secreted away in his pocket. "My mother always hangs the balls of holly, ivy and mistletoe from the entry hall chandelier. 'Tis allowed for a gentleman to kiss a lady caught beneath the bough."

"Ah," she said, "I see. But in Scotland, the Parish Kirk frowns on celebrations of what it considers to be the Yule, which is why we don't celebrate Christmas, at least not openly, even though we do recognize the birth of the Christ Child. But with Emily a part of the family, I expect that will change. When word gets around that the Stephens have brought the English Christmastide into their home, our parish minister will think the whole lot of us have become Anglicans."

He laughed. "Would that be so bad?"

From his expression, Ailie sensed the question might be important. "Perhaps not, but most everyone in Scotland is Presbyterian. In truth, 'tis the same God whose praises we sing, whether Anglican or Presbyterian, no?"

His smile told her he liked her answer. "I would certainly look forward to having a kissing bough to catch you under this Christmas."

Her cheeks grew warm. Silently, she cursed her sensitive skin. "Now you remind me of Robbie," she said in a teasing manner. "I will ask Emily about a kissing bough since I can see it means much to the English." Ailie wouldn't mind him catching her under such a bough.

"Ho there!" came the cry from the woods.

Ailie looked up to see Hugh and Mary making their way toward them. "Seems we've been found."

Hugh arrived first and leaned down to pat the large sack tied to his saddle. "We have two great bags of holly and some other evergreen branches that Mary found to decorate your many rooms. Are you two almost finished?"

Ailie met Nash's eyes. It had grown colder since they had arrived in the woods and now she no longer had his arms around her. "Aye," she replied. "We're done here as well and I, for one, would not turn away a cup of hot wassail."

Robbie looked up from his cards to see Muriel pondering her next move. Not far away, the fire burned steadily, occasionally giving out with a loud pop. He liked the library and its rich smell of leather, wood burning and a faint remnant of pipe smoke. It reminded him of White's, his favorite club in London where doubtless he would be this very moment were it not for Lord Sidmouth.

Through the windows, he glimpsed the pale sun casting its rays onto a white world. His thoughts drifted to Nash, who was somewhere out there enjoying the morning with the Mistress of the Setters. He envied his brother the time alone with the spirited girl. Nash had always been one to seize an opportunity. But since he did not have Robbie's luck at cards, if one of them was to remain behind and play, it had best be him. Let Nash gather the Christmas foliage.

Muriel raised her head. "Emily, dear, might I have a glass of Madeira?"

"Of course," said their hostess. The footman having left the library a short while ago, Emily rose to fetch the wine Robbie had learned the countess favored.

Very soon into their play, it had become apparent loo was a game the five of them knew well. They were now into Double Pool rounds and Muriel, who had yet to declare if she would play the hand Emily had dealt her, was stalling.

The Grand Countess was a clever woman and an adroit card player, thus Robbie was certain she was making use of the delay to consider her next move. His suspicious nature wondered if she'd even wanted the wine. After all, it was early in the day and breakfast not long finished.

Martin narrowed his eyes on Muriel. "An underhanded move, calculated, I suspect to gain time."

"When one has much on one's mind," said the countess, "additional time is required and a glass of Madeira helps me think."

Robbie couldn't imagine what might occupy the thoughts of The Grand Countess if not her cards. *Her next ball?*

Emily set the glass of the dark honey-colored wine before her friend. "After luncheon, wassail will be served in the parlor."

"Thank you, dear," said Muriel. "A cup of wassail always brings back pleasant memories." She gazed toward the window, a wistful expression on her face.

Martin fiddled with his cards. "Ah yes... memories. I recall once playing loo when the stakes were very high."

Muriel gave Martin an assessing look. "Are you thinking of your past pursuits, Sir Martin?"

"Possibly," he drawled, avoiding Muriel's piercing gray eyes.

Did Muriel know that Martin, like Hugh, had spied for the Crown in France? Perhaps in addressing him as Sir Martin, she was letting him know she was aware Martin's knighthood had been conferred upon him for just that work.

"That's all behind him now," Kit put in. She glanced around the table. "Perhaps I shall do a sketch of our card game. It will make a nice addition to my collection."

"I have decided to trade my cards for the miss," Muriel announced, reaching for the extra hand to exchange for the one she had.

The play continued, becoming spirited at times. Robbie took most of the tricks, which surprised Emily and Muriel, but not his brother, Martin, or Kit, who were aware of his reputation.

They were just finishing their game when the four who had ventured into the snow returned. At the door to the library, Ailie announced, "We're back with the greenery. Luncheon will be served shortly in the dining room," then disappeared as quickly as she had come.

Was he imagining things or did she appear overly happy, her face lit with some unexplained joy? *Faith!* What had transpired in the woods?

George Kinloch set his tankard on the marred table and peered through the smoke hanging in the air of St Thomas Tavern to glimpse the hideous picture hanging above the bar. The face of the old saint was twisted into a grimace but whether it was in distaste or horror George could not say.

Would he meet his end like Thomas à Becket, the Archbishop of Canterbury, martyred for his defiance of the English Crown? The charge of sedition hanging over his head suggested as much. Still, he did not regret accepting the invitation to speak in Dundee when it had come. The Crown's actions in Manchester and the wrongs against the poor workers had to be redressed.

A well-organized, self-disciplined man, the father of seven grown children, George had always tried to live a calm, orderly life. When he received the shocking news he had been charged with sedition, he had hurried to Edinburgh to meet with his solicitor. There, they worked up a list of relevant details for the advocates who would conduct the defense.

All to no avail.

From his friends, he had learned that no defense would be successful, that the government in London had decided he would be convicted and sentenced to transportation to Botany Bay. It was then George had written his dear wife Helen telling her he must flee. And France was the natural choice of destinations.

The men sitting around George grumbled about the weavers' discontent and talked of the uprising that would surely come to Glasgow. George wanted no part of it. God knew the weavers had cause, but he feared any grand display would merely provide an excuse for another massacre by the Crown's soldiers.

He wanted more for the people of Scotland. He sought reform, not revolution. He was, after all, the Justice of the Peace for the County of

Perth. Still, he could not forget his time in France that had made him aware of the plight of the poor who had no voice and often no bread.

With conditions as bad as they were in Britain, why continue a tax that supported the war against Napoleon? It was not unlike the American colonists' complaints that had led to their rebellion: taxation without representation.

George was confident someday the needed reform would come to his own country, but he would have to leave now if he were to live to see that day.

He reflected again on the archbishop who had defied a king. Fearing for his life, Becket, too, had sought refuge in France. His mistake had been returning to England to be murdered at the king's pleasure. Hopefully, George could avoid such a fate. That he had to place himself in the hands of brutal men he considered ruffians to assure his escape could not be avoided. The men who guarded him got things done and protected his life.

"Did you procure passage for me and my cousin?" he asked the gruff man whom he had to thank for helping him escape to Arbroath.

"Aye, ye're sailin' on the *Panmure* on the twenty-sixth."

George nodded. *The twenty-sixth, after the trial in Edinburgh.* By then, he would have forfeited bail and been declared an outlaw.

Until he sailed, he would have to bide his time with St Thomas' good ale and be thankful for the rough men who guarded his person. It wasn't as if he had a choice.

Called to luncheon, everyone found a seat at the dining table. Nash pulled out a chair for Ailie and she gracefully subsided into it. To his chagrin, Robbie claimed the chair on her other side. Nash comforted himself in the knowledge she had earlier returned his kiss and had stopped him when he would have begged her forgiveness for the

115

liberties he'd taken.

He was, he trusted, on the way to winning her heart.

The footman ladled soup into his bowl. Nash stared down at the thick white broth. The steam rising from the surface had a decidedly fishy smell but the appearance of the soup was not unappetizing. Pieces of what looked like fish, small chunks of potato and bits of dark green floated in the broth. Tentatively, he dipped in his spoon, then thought to inquire, "Is there a name for this soup?"

Ailie turned from her own bowl. "'Tis another of our dishes. Cullen Skink."

He paused, his spoon halfway to his mouth. "What?"

Ailie shook her head. "Really, Nash, 'tis just haddie stew."

"Is that the smoked fish you eat at breakfast?" he asked, appalled.

Muriel, sitting beside Emily, narrowed her eyes on her bowl. "Are those pieces of green I detect by any chance *kale*?"

William laughed. "No kale. Shallot tops."

Muriel dipped her spoon into the fish stew. "I am greatly relieved."

Robbie, obviously proud of his just finished bowl, urged Nash on. "Try it. It's very good. We might have to take some of the smoked haddock back to London. You know how Mother loves to dabble in Father's galley and it would keep well at sea."

"In Baltimore," said Tara, "we would call this fish chowder, but our fish would not be smoked and we'd add salt pork and parsley, sweet marjoram, savory and thyme. I agree with Robbie, Nick. It's good. We should take some back to London, too."

Nash, thinking himself quite brave, brought the spoon to his mouth and tasted, surprised to find he liked the salty fish combined with the sweet milk, potatoes and shallots. "Actually, I find it rather tasty, perfect for warming one's insides on a cold day." He smiled at Ailie. "You see? I can learn to like your food."

For some odd reason, that caused Ailie to blush, which made the freckles scattered over her nose stand out. He thought the effect quite charming.

Across the table, Muriel made a noise that sounded suspiciously like "Humph".

After luncheon, they retired to the parlor to sample Mrs. Platt's wassail. Nash had a fondness for the drink that tasted of apples, cinnamon and cloves. It reminded him that Christmas was a little less than a week away.

Remembering Robbie's admonition, he thought perhaps he should go to town but, later, when the temperature dropped, he decided against it. Thus, he was in the parlor with the others, gathered for dinner, when the unexpected visitor arrived.

Chapter 10

"Guid eve'nin' tae ye!"

At the sound of the familiar voice, Ailie turned. "Grandfather!"

Making her excuses to Muriel, Ailie hastened to meet him at the parlor door. The footman must have taken his coat and cap, leaving him in his dark blue woolen jacket, knitted vest and trousers. A scarf of the same blue was tied around his neck almost, but not quite, like a cravat. Beneath his silver hair, strong features and blue eyes, he sported a well-trimmed beard.

She kissed his leathery cheek that smelled of the sea and smoke, reminding her of his days at sea as a fisherman and of his current occupation. "You must come warm yourself by the fire, Grandfather, and then I will introduce you to our guests."

She ushered him to the fireplace, proudly announcing to the others, "Grandfather Ramsay has paid us an impromptu visit. Once he warms up a bit, I will properly introduce you."

Their guests parted to allow them to pass, curious gazes and smiles following them across the room. When they reached the countess, Ailie's grandfather paused to give Muriel a long studying perusal before continuing on.

They reached the fireplace just as one of the footmen came to add a log to the fire.

"Would you like something to drink?" Ailie knew the answer before asking. Most of their guests were drinking wassail, but her grandfather would want a fisherman's drink.

"Ale'd be guid."

The footman nodded to Ailie and went to fetch the drink.

Her grandfather stretched his weathered hands toward the flames. "It's fair jeelit outside. Cauld enough tae freeze kelpies."

Ailie was amused at his mention of the mythical water spirit. "'Tis been freezing cold all day, Grandfather, and it's worse now that the sun has set. I'm delighted to see you but why ever did you come out in such weather?"

Ailie's brother appeared beside her. "Aye, is all well?"

The footman returned, handing her grandfather the ale.

"Weel," began her grandfather, taking a long draw on his drink, "when ye sent word a band o' Sassenachs were comin' tae Stonehaven fer Hogmanay, I had tae see 'em fer meself. A mate o' mine was sailin' this way so I hopped aboard."

Wondering where they would put him, Ailie asked, "How long will you be able to stay?"

"I hae tae leave in the mornin' when my mate returns."

"One night," she murmured under her breath, exchanging a glance with Will.

"All the bedchambers are taken," explained Will. "Even the servants have had to double up. But you can have my study. You remember, it's the room on the other side of the entry hall just before you reach the library. The large sofa will make for a comfortable bed and you'll not be disturbed."

"'Twill do me jus' fine. I've slept on fishin' boats fer most o' me life, ye ken."

Angus Ramsay, now a widower, once owned his own fishing boats, but when he gave up the sea, he sold them and went into business in

Stonehaven smoke-drying haddock. He was the reason they never lacked for smoked haddies. Now in his sixties, Ailie thought him quite distinguished looking, his weathered face, tanned and lined from so many years in the sun, speaking of his character.

"Well then," said Ailie, "if you're sufficiently warmed, you'd best meet our guests and join us for dinner."

Her grandfather eyed Muriel. "I'd like tae meet *her* first."

Will rolled his eyes. "I leave that to you, Ailie. I'll see about preparing the study. And, Grandfather, after you've met the others, you must greet Emily."

"Aye, I'm fond o' the heather-eyed lass, soon tae be the mother o' me new gran'bairn."

Resigned to her role as interpreter, when Will left them for Emily, Ailie looped her arm through her grandfather's and sallied forth to introduce him. "Now behave," she said, leaning close to his ear. "You're about to meet a countess of great renown of whom Will and I are quite fond, a marquess and his marchioness, the daughter of an earl and four shipmasters."

"Unless one o' them is Robert the Bruce, I'll nae be swept off me feet."

Ailie grinned, unsurprised that her grandfather would not be impressed by titles of British nobility. He saved his ardent passion for Scotland's heroes. She stopped in front of the countess. "Muriel, may I introduce you to Angus Ramsay of Stonehaven, my maternal grandfather?"

Muriel nodded and graciously offered her hand.

Having frequently been a guest in their father's home in Aberdeen, Angus Ramsay was not unmindful of the ways of the gentry. With more polish than Ailie might have expected given his station, her grandfather smiled at Muriel and bowed over her hand.

"Muriel is the Countess of Claremont, Grandfather, but our guests have decided to use given names for their stay with us, so I suspect she will allow you, for the now, to address her as 'Muriel'."

"Here's tae ye, a grand fair lady, Muriel."

Muriel's hand went to her quizzing glass but she did not raise it, perhaps sensing that Ailie's grandfather would have found it highly amusing and very English. But, as a lady, she did not fail to show her gratitude. "Most kind of you, sir."

After that, the introductions proceeded smoothly.

According to Will, Hugh, while a marquess, had friends in many walks of life and could be unassuming. Mary, his gracious wife, accepted Ailie's grandfather and he her. After making the introduction, as they walked away, Ailie's grandfather said, "She has the look o' a green-eyed sea witch. I 'spect her husband's under her spell."

Ailie was bemused by her grandfather's ready acceptance of the fishermen's folklore. "From what I have seen, you're not far from the truth."

Her grandfather took to Tara as soon as he discovered Nick's wife was an American of Scots-Irish blood. "One o' us!"

Nick told him that Tara sailed as often as she could. "My Irish cook is a great keeper of the fairy lore, Mr. Ramsay, and believes my wife is the *leanan sídhe*, a fairy of terrible power." Nick added a grimace to go with the description.

Nick and Tara shared a chuckle, but Ailie's grandfather just smiled, accepting fully Tara's mythical origin. In Scotland, the glens had always produced legends of fairies, old clan tales, forebodings and superstitions. They were as much believed as the Scriptures.

When Ailie introduced her grandfather to Martin's wife, Kit expressed a desire to sketch him. "I'm doing sketches of everyone this holiday, Mr. Ramsay," she told him. "You have such an interesting face, I hope you will allow me to draw a likeness of you."

"I shall put meself at yer disposal," he said with a wink at Martin, who obviously knew the effect his wife had on older men.

They arrived in front of the twin Powell brothers and Ailie's grandfather paused. "My oath! 'Tis two fish from the same barrel."

Nash and Robbie smiled good-naturedly. Ailie knew they had heard such remarks many times, yet they were kind to her grandfather, which pleased her.

Ailie introduced them, putting the correct name to each twin, not only because of the clothes Nash wore but because of the unseen connection that now existed between them. When she met his penetrating gaze, she recognized him.

Her grandfather looked up at Robbie. "Rabbie," he said, pronouncing Robbie's name in the Scots fashion. "'Tis the name o' the Bard o' Ayrshire. Ye're unwed, aye?"

"Both of us," put in Nash, shooting Ailie a surprisingly bold look.

Before her grandfather could say more and embarrass her completely, Ailie excused herself and rushed him away. "Really, Grandfather."

"Weel, 'tis time ye find a man, and that one's named Rabbie." To that, Ailie had no intention of replying. Her grandfather was worse than Will.

She led her grandfather to where Emily and Will stood talking with a footman.

"Guid tae see ye, dear Emily."

"You, too, Angus." Emily kissed him on his cheek. "I have requested another chair be added to the dining table. It will be a snug fit but I'm sure we will all do just fine."

"I don't think our guests will mind, *Leannan*," said Will. "They are getting along splendidly."

"As long as ye put me next tae Muriel," said Grandfather Ramsay, "sittin' close will nae fash me."

Will gave Ailie a side-glance, his brows drawing together.

"Don't ask," she said.

At dinner, her grandfather—now addressed as "Angus" by all their guests—was quick to claim the chair next to Muriel who sat in her usual place adjacent to Will. Since the rest of them took the seats they'd had at their first dinner, that left Ailie between Nash and Robbie but with Angus squeezed in next to Muriel. Snug indeed.

After the barley soup and a fish course of baked cod in cream sauce with leeks, Will announced, "In honor of our English guests, we're having roast beef tonight."

Exclamations of delight sounded around the table.

"We English do like our roast beef," said Robbie. He winked at Ailie. "And I wouldn't turn away a slice of cheddar cheese."

"I do believe there is cheddar cheese for you," Emily assured him. "We can thank Muriel for her cook's good services."

"Mrs. Platt is a jewel," said Muriel.

As the footmen served the roast beef, Ailie's grandfather turned to the countess. "Ye brought yer cook?"

"Of course, my good man. If we're to have a fine Christmas dinner it was necessary."

Ailie's grandfather shot a look of incredulity at Will. "Ye're celebratin' the Sassenach Yule?"

Will leaned toward him. "Grandfather, we have *English* guests who have come to celebrate Christmastide. We're not telling the Parish Kirk minister. I learned to love Christmas when I was in England and I promised Emily we could celebrate the holiday as she always did before she married me."

"Aye, weel if 'tis Emily's wish, I willna object," he said sheepishly.

Ailie had always known a lady could turn her grandfather from his intended course. Her own grandmother had managed to wrap him about her pinkie.

"William," said Angus, "I fergot tae tell ye, I brought some o' today's smoked haddies and left them with yer man at the door." Ailie smiled to herself. "Yer man at the door" was their grandfather's name for their new butler.

"Very generous, Grandfather," said Will.

Ailie darted a look at Nash. "Just think, smoked haddies for breakfast."

"Eggs and scones for me," he muttered under his breath.

Ailie jabbed him in the ribs. As close as they were, it was easily done.

"I look forward to the haddies, myself," said Robbie, loud enough for Angus to hear. "How good of you to bring them."

"Aye, 'tis me business, ye ken."

A conversation then ensued among their guests about the business of smoking fish, her grandfather explaining he followed the Norse tradition of smoking the fish over an open fire.

"The Norse left their imprint on this part of Scotland," she said. "We keep many of their traditions."

Loving her grandfather as she did, the smell of the smoked fish brought back wonderful memories of Ailie's summers spent in Stonehaven as a young girl, when she'd spent hours talking to her grandfather as he carefully tended his smoking fish.

Their guests were probably being kind not to remark on the faint odor of fish and smoke that lingered about her grandfather, as much a part of him as the pungent shag tobacco he smoked in his pipe. She had never stopped to consider him from someone else's viewpoint—from that of London aristocrats and gentry, who were more accustomed to a drawing room than a fishing boat. But as she looked around the table at their guests, she saw only attentive interest and approval as he described his work. Inside, she relaxed. *They like him for himself*, she realized, *just as I do*. And she liked their guests all the better for it.

"I dinna suppose ye have any neeps an' tatties?" her grandfather asked Emily, as he slipped a bite of beef into his mouth.

Nash raised his brows. "Neeps and tatties?"

"Turnips and potatoes," said Will. Then to their grandfather, "Tatties aye, neeps no. But there are carrots." Angus accepted some carrots and potatoes onto his plate as he pulled a rolled newspaper from inside his jacket and thrust it at Will. "The weekly. Thot ye might like tae see it."

Ailie recognized their weekly newspaper the *Montrose, Arbroath and Brechin Review*. Robbie and Nash leaned forward, trying, she supposed, to get a look at it. Perhaps, being so far from London, they were starved for news. "Would you like to see the paper when Will's done with it?"

"I would," said Nash.

"Here," Will handed him the newspaper, "just leave it in the library when you're finished. It's mostly local news, but occasionally there might be something that would be of interest to you and the others."

From across the table, Martin said, "Shipping news?"

"Often," said Will, "in the back of each issue, especially now that we have three shipbuilders in Arbroath and more than twenty ships operating from the harbor."

"Weel," began Ailie's grandfather, "there's talk o' the clearances in the West, such as ye'd niver see here. No MacTavish ever put a puir man off his land." He paused as if trying to recall more from what he had read. "An' the laird from Dundee is still missin', bless 'im."

Mary addressed her husband. "Is that the one Captain Anderson told us about?"

"I believe so, sweetheart," said Hugh. "The captain was unhappy about a man from Dundee charged with sedition for some speech he gave."

"The verra one," said Angus. "Admired in these parts. A man o' quality who speaks fer the puir."

Robbie and Nash exchanged a look. Ailie, sitting between them, wondered what was behind it. Why would they find George Kinloch of interest?

"I am happy for Kinloch to have escaped the authorities," she said, speaking her mind. "The man only wants what's fair for the people of Scotland. How is that sedition?"

Nash turned his wine glass in his hand, staring at the red liquid. "Perhaps it was not him but the worrisome crowd that came to hear him."

"It might not have been sedition in November when he gave the speech," Robbie interjected, "but, since then, the government has adopted a series of acts, one of which requires a magistrate's permission to convene any public meeting of more than fifty people if they are discussing matters of state."

"Ridiculous!" exclaimed Muriel. "Why the men's clubs of London would have to close their doors. Most nights, that is all they talk about."

Emily turned to look at her friend. "How might you know what men discuss at their clubs, dear Muriel?"

Muriel's back went rigid, her nose lifting. "Many a night the Earl of Claremont would return all riled up about some argument a gaggle of men got into at White's. The subject was always politics."

"Doubtless, 'tis not the nobility the government is worried about," offered Nash.

Her grandfather ruefully shook his head. "'Tis a sad day when a man canna gather his friends tae speak o' what's important tae him. If 'tis reform the Dundee laird seeks, ah'm sorry tae say he will nae be gettin' his wish any time soon."

The meal having concluded, the ladies retired to the parlor for tea, while Robbie and the six other men lingered around the table drinking brandy and port and smoking cigars. In the case of Angus Ramsay, a pipe.

With a glass of fine cognac in hand, Robbie listened to the conversation between Will and Angus on the political climate in Scotland, hoping to hear more about Kinloch.

"The problem," explained William, "is too much power in the hands of too few. For Aberdeen, Arbroath and three other boroughs, there is only one representative in Parliament. For all of Scotland there are only fifteen."

"Manchester has none," mumbled Nash.

"That is a travesty," put in Martin. "The massacre there reminded me of what happened in Derbyshire."

Robbie shared a look with Nash. William's words had echoed what they had heard in the taverns in Manchester. They had never told Nick and Martin of their spying for Sidmouth but their parents knew.

"Weel," put in Angus, leaning back to send a puff of smoke into the air, "at least we hiv Joseph Hume in Parliament."

"I have heard my father speak of him," said Hugh. "Elected last year?"

"Aye," said William. "After a long absence. Like as not you've also heard he's a radical, as all those who seek reform are labeled these days."

Angus pulled his pipe from his mouth. "Hume comes from guid stock. I knew his fathir, maister o' a fine fishin' boat in Montrose."

"Montrose?" asked Nick.

"Halfway between Arbroath and Stonehaven to the north," said William.

Robbie wanted to ask about Kinloch and he was certain Nash had the same urge, but it might give away too much for either one of them to mention the man. The thought occurred that no man here knew more about Kinloch's whereabouts at the moment than he and Nash.

Muriel set down her teacup and inclined her head to better consider Aileen Stephen sitting beside her on the parlor sofa. She intended to take up her conversation with the girl, interrupted earlier with the entrance of her grandfather. London could provide many opportunities for a young woman like Aileen. If she did not make a match with one of the Powell twins, Muriel was confident a future husband awaited the girl in London, perhaps even a man possessed of a good title.

Aileen appeared to be anxious as she asked, "Did it go well at dinner?"

"Whatever do you mean, Child?"

"My grandfather. He is very dear to me, you understand, but I worried he might say something… well, something that might disturb you, something inappropriate."

"Nonsense!" Muriel inwardly smiled, remembering Angus Ramsay's words to her. "Actually, I found him rather charming. The genuine article. As you may have noticed, I appreciate directness and honesty."

Aileen pressed her palm to her chest. "I am so relieved. It was my hope you and he would get along." Moving in closer, she smiled. "I believe he likes you."

Muriel thought of Angus Ramsay's intense blue eyes and the lines around them that suggested, at least at one time, he had laughed much. "I think he misses his wife. How long has she been gone?"

"Grandmother Ramsay died five years ago, the same year I came to live in Arbroath."

A sudden thought occurred to Muriel. "Do I perchance look anything like her?"

Aileen pursed her lips, giving Muriel an assessing look. "Aye, a bit. She had your silver hair and gray eyes, but her face bore more lines. And she wore the linen-wincey of a fisherman's wife, not silk, pearls and feathers of a titled lady."

Unable to resist, Muriel flicked the feather in her hair ornament. "I do enjoy my pearls and feathers."

"But like you," Aileen added, "Grandmother Ramsay had a quiet dignity about her."

"If you find in me a hint of the dignity possessed by your much-loved grandmother, I stand highly complimented."

Aileen smiled. "You are such a dear."

"That is my secret, but you must tell no one." There was something about this young woman that intrigued Muriel. Emily had told her the girl designed ships, a most unusual pursuit for a young lady. Yet, her manner indicated she possessed the breeding and intelligence of a young woman raised to marry a man born to wealth and position.

Not every man would want such a challenge. But for the right man, no other woman would do.

"Enough about us old folks," said Muriel. "We must see about you, my dear." She patted Aileen's hand. "And I shall help you. If no man is to your liking here in Scotland, then a year in London at my side will find you the perfect match. I am a very good judge of character, you know."

Aileen laughed. "Oh I don't doubt it for a minute, Muriel. William told me you matched him with Emily. But London? And marriage?" She shook her head. "I don't know."

Muriel fingered her pearls, thinking of all the matches she had made over the years. "What say you we forsake the tea for a glass of Madeira? And while we drink our wine, I shall tell you all about what lies in store for you should you accept my invitation to come to London."

Exhausted from the long day, Ailie was nevertheless determined to pen a note in her diary before retiring for the night. So, with quill in hand, she scratched out a few lines.

20 December, second entry

Today I was kissed for the very first time. Oh, not the kiss of my brothers or another man in my family. Or even the kiss of Donald Innes after that dance in Aberdeen when I was sixteen. This was different. Nash Etienne Powell kissed me in the woods in a most passionate manner and I liked it. But what did it mean to him? He and his brother are older, more experienced. I hesitate to think how many women they have known. Perhaps Nash sees me only as a diversion for his holiday in Scotland. And now Muriel, Countess of Claremont, wants to take me to London to show me about. My thoughts are in a jumble. How could I leave Scotland? Might a year with Muriel be, as she says, "quite diverting"?

130

Chapter 11

Nash had hoped to see Ailie at breakfast but Emily informed him both William and his sister were occupied with some issue at the shipyard. Angus Ramsay had departed early, apparently leaving word he would see them all at Hogmanay. So, Nash breakfasted with his brothers, their wives and their hostess, which turned out to be a noisy affair.

After that, he wanted only a moment of quiet before going to town. Retreating to the library, he found the book Emily had recommended to him. The book's author, John Abercrombie, was a horticulturist, knowledgeable in the use of greenhouses to grow exotics.

The library was well organized and he easily found the book, settling onto one of the blue leather settees where there was good light from an adjacent window. Putting on his spectacles, he became absorbed in *Abercrombie's Practical Gardener* and the description of the new ornamental style of greenhouse that afforded the plants more light.

He had only been reading a short while when Martin's wife flitted into the room, petticoats rustling, sketchbook and pencils in hand. "Would you mind if I draw your likeness while you read? I promise to be as silent as a mouse in the corner."

"All right," he said, peering at her over his spectacles. He knew Kit to be a woman of her word and not given to unnecessary chatter.

She took a seat at the wooden table in the center of the room and went to work; he went back to his book, trying to ignore the faint scratching of her pencil on the paper.

After what seemed like an hour, he closed the book and looked up to see Kit smiling. "I am almost done and I can add the last touches later."

"May I see?"

"Yes, of course." She reversed her sketchbook and Nash blinked in astonishment. The image was the spit of that in his shaving mirror and without the spectacles.

"An amazing likeness. Am I the last or have you more to do?"

"Oh, I have more. I want each of the couples to have their own page. I have yet to add William to the sketch I did of Emily. I've only begun the sketch of Angus from seeing him at dinner. Then there is Ailie. I might do hers last."

"What about you? Who will draw your likeness?"

"Oh, I did mine first. The mirror in our bedchamber is most accommodating. Self-portrait is the artist's first subject so I know well my own imperfect countenance."

"A remarkable talent. As I think on it, the women in the Powell family are all quite remarkable. You are an accomplished artist; Tara sails Nick's ships as well as any man; and our mother, well, she fell in love with her kidnapper, didn't she?"

Kit laughed. "When you put it like that, yes, I suppose we are an unusual group. Keep that in mind when you add to our number." She picked up her sketchbook and pencils, waved goodbye and left.

Nash stared at the smoldering fire, thinking about Kit's advice. Ailie would fit right in with the Powell wives, but could she be made to want to join them? Would she ever agree to come to London?

He set the book down on the settee so Robbie could find it easily and rose, more determined than ever to finish their work in Arbroath so he could devote himself to winning the Scottish lass.

In his bedchamber, Nash donned the clothes Robbie had worn when in Arbroath and covered them with a plain woolen scarf and a dark greatcoat. His knife was secured at his waist and he carried a small flintlock pistol in the pocket of his coat. He didn't expect trouble but, ever since Manchester, he vowed to never again leave on a mission unprepared for the worst.

Shortly after Nash finished dressing, Robbie entered their chamber. "Are you finally leaving for town?"

"I am. After luncheon, don't forget you need to go the library and take up the book I left on one of the settees."

Robbie patted his coat pocket. "I've got my spectacles. By the bye, what book is it? One of the Waverley novels Ailie mentioned?"

"No. It is a book by an esteemed horticulturist."

"Horticulture? *Plants* again? It sounds dull beyond belief."

"To you, perhaps. I found it most interesting. Besides, Emily recommended it to me at breakfast. At one point, Kit wandered into the library to observe me reading. There's another on the shelf on the geography of Scotland that looked to be a worthy choice, too. As long as we're here, it might be good to learn something of the local geography."

"Which, I remind you, is under several feet of snow."

"Don't quibble. It will melt in due season. Perhaps I will return to see the heather bloom." Nash thought of that heather and Ailie lying on a hill overlooking a loch with him beside her. "Yes, I just might."

Robbie sighed loudly. "Very well. Perhaps I can nod off for a nap. Are you sure you want to miss luncheon?"

"I'll get a meat pie at one of the taverns. I want as much time in the town as daylight allows."

"You have the map in mind?"

Nash tapped his temple. "I do."

As he did most afternoons, George Kinloch followed his protectors into the dimly lit St Thomas Tavern where they would spend a few hours. He doubted Thomas à Becket would find the atmosphere of sour ale and smoke appealing. No wonder his face in the picture above the bar displayed a grimace.

George sighed, knowing he must be accepting of his guards' choice of establishments. His cousin Grant had hired the men and, though the tavern's atmosphere was a far cry from his farm near Dundee, it provided a respite from his small rooms at the boarding house and a refuge from Arbroath's icy winds.

George had quickly learned the names of the men his cousin had hired, who were just now ordering ale. The tallest was the beefy Hamish whose name George easily remembered because his fists were like large hams. Hamish's brother, Iain, a man of smaller stature, seemed content to stand in his brother's shadow. The brains of the group appeared to be Derek, a fast-talking man with dark, intense eyes, who delighted in the rhetoric of reform which, all things considered, George never tired of hearing.

The man who caused George's stomach to tie in knots was the hot-headed Lachlan, a Highlander from Argyll, and the only blond among them. Lachy, as his companions called him, would have been one of those men who had come to hear George's speech carrying banners shouting, "Bread or Blood!"

Remembering those signs, George cringed. He was proud of the fact the meeting in Dundee had been conducted in an orderly manner and that there had been no disturbance of the peace of any kind.

Today, as always, he sat at the round table, the rough fabric of the brown wincey jacket and trousers, so foreign to his usual attire, chafing his skin. The ridiculous too-large brown top hat he wore, crumpled from years of abuse, had been given him to hide his distinctive baldpate, leaving only his fringe of dark hair to be seen. Regrettably, the effect rendered him a comical figure.

Soon, he hoped to return to a gentleman's clothing. In France, where he could resume his role as a member of the gentry, he would find a better suit of clothes.

Lifting the ale that was placed before him, he took a long swallow, remembering the speech that led him to this day. He had been surprised at the thousands who had gathered that day in November to hear him speak about what could be done to alleviate the distress of the working classes.

Only later did he learn that special constables had been sworn to keep the peace as they had in Manchester. Thankfully, they had not intervened, but the government had its vengeance all the same. Guilty only of denouncing the massacre in Manchester and calling for much-needed reform, George had been charged with sedition. *Sedition!*

He did not have to think long before forfeiting his bail and fleeing north.

In France, he would be safe from the oppressive hand of the British government and Sidmouth's fearmongering among the Members of Parliament, who never ventured north to witness the plight of the workers.

All George had was one man's voice. Yet what good could he do if that voice were silenced, trapped inside the stone cage of prison walls? Or, dispatched to Botany Bay? No, he would flee now and hope to return one day when reform was no longer a dreaded word.

The conversations around him grew louder as the customers raised their voices to be heard in the crowded tavern.

Hamish raised his tankard in the semblance of a toast. "Willna be long now, Georgie lad. Ye'll be on that ship afore ye ken it."

"The name is Mr. Oliphant, Hamish. You must address me as Mr. Oliphant."

Having been to the *Panmure* to speak to Captain Gower, Nash went to The Foundry, a tavern on Mary Street where he'd found a hearty meat pie, washing it down with ale.

As he watched the other men in the tavern, he thought about Ailie. Finding time alone with her in this dashed cold weather was proving a challenge. Either they were surrounded by people or alone in the freezing woods. Being with her without being able to touch her was proving tortuous. He had only to be near her to stir thoughts of his lips on hers.

Reminding himself he was supposed to be gathering information, he listened more attentively to the men's conversations around him, but learned nothing substantial. Having finished his ale, he decided to brave the cold and seek another tavern.

He supposed he picked the St Thomas Tavern because the irony of the name appealed, a tavern in Presbyterian Scotland named for the Archbishop of Canterbury.

Becket might have been low-born and the rumored companion of King Henry in their earthly pursuits, but he became a martyr venerated by both Catholics and Anglicans.

No matter its namesake, the smoke-filled tavern was clearly one favored by the locals. Men of all sorts crowded up to the bar and most of the tables were filled. Nash slid into a chair at a small table against the far wall to nurse his ale while going over his conversation with the *Panmure*'s master in his mind.

Captain Gower had graciously allowed Nash to see his ship, his first mate remembering his prior appearance—which had actually been Robbie's visit to the ship a few days before.

"Aye, we've two cabins sometimes booked by passengers, but they are both reserved for our sailing the afternoon of the twenty-sixth. We'll return in a month's time, weather permitting, and you can book passage then."

The captain did not mention the passengers' names and Nash did not ask for fear of rousing suspicion. If the shipmaster had knowingly promised one of his cabins to a fugitive from the law, he might warn Kinloch.

Nash returned his attention to the tavern's customers, catching bits of conversation.

Five men came through the door. The proprietor waved them to the large round table that he must have been saving for them, as it was the only one unoccupied.

Once they had their ale, the men began to speak in low tones. All had dark hair save one whose eyes flashed fury beneath his fair hair. Had they but known a spy lurked in their midst, they might have spoken in a regular voice. Men who lowered their voices as if to hide their words when all around them raised theirs were, to Nash, like a tasty lure to a hungry fish.

The word "ship" coupled with the name "Georgie" rang in Nash's ears like a ship's bell. The man who had spoken them was a rough character, a great burly fellow in a stevedore's plain clothing. His scarred face, thick chest and huge fists made Nash think he had seen many fights. But the man to whom he had spoken, the man he had called "Georgie", who insisted he be called "Mr. Oliphant", presented a puzzling figure. Nash scrutinized his common worker's clothing and the odd hat that seemed to dwarf his fine-boned head. Despite being dressed as a commoner, his manner and speech shouted he was a gentleman.

Putting together the information Captain Gower had given him with the words spoken to "Georgie" in the tavern, Nash concluded the man he was looking at might well be George Kinloch, who could be sailing for France on the twenty-sixth as Mr. Oliphant.

Nash ruminated about this, thinking that when George and his companions left, he would follow them. His thoughts were interrupted when a skirmish erupted next to the round table.

One man, who had been sitting at a small table next to the wall, abruptly stood, sloshing his ale onto the floor. "I say ye're wrong!"

His companion pounded the table. "Them weavers deserved better than tae end up deid." His words were slurred but Nash instantly grasped their meaning.

"Haud yer tongue fer yer owin sake," said his companion, furtively looking about the tavern. Nash judged him the more sober of the two.

By this time, every man's attention had turned to them.

The man who had remained seated tugged on his friend's jacket. "Sit ye doon. I hae no intention…"

From the round table, the blond man with the angry eyes rose and stepped toward the two arguing. "The two of ye need tae quit yer bletherin!"

The man seated, who'd clearly imbibed too much ale, awkwardly got to his feet and pushed his finger into the blond's chest. "Dinna tell me what tae do, ye scunner!"

Nash might not understand all their words but the men's expressions spoke loudly.

The blond narrowed his gaze, drew back his fist and rammed it into the drunken man's face, sending him crashing into his chair, both collapsing to the floor.

His companion's eyes narrowed as a scowl formed on his face. "Ye nickum loon!" He reared back and took a swing at the blond.

The blond ducked and laughed. "Away an bile yer heid!" Then, with a smile on his face, he hit the man, sending him flying into another table, causing ale to spill on its occupants.

"Now see here!" a man splashed with ale protested. He stood, brushing the liquid from his jacket.

Chairs scraped across the stone floor as other men rose and moved to source of the argument like fish to bait.

Nash rose and moved aside, staying clear of the worst of it.

More tankards of ale hit the floor. Shouts echoed off the walls as the fight widened. The men at the bar left their tankards to jump into the fray. Soon the entire tavern was involved in the tumult.

The man "Georgie" was suddenly escorted from the tavern by one of the men at his table. As the two of them slipped through the door, the one escorting George yelled, "Hamish, ye and Lachy finish this."

"Aye, Derek. 'Twill be me pleasure." The big man turned to drive his fist into his opponent's jaw.

Nash decided it was time to leave. He had no intention of using his pistol or knife on a bunch of drunken Scots, not unless they threatened his life. His greater task was to follow the man he believed could be Kinloch.

Rising, he headed toward the door. A few feet from his goal, a fist plowed into his shoulder. He stumbled for a moment, then turned, confronted by a man holding up his fists in challenge.

"Not today, ye muckle haddie," he said, remembering to speak with a brogue, as he slammed his fist into the man's face. With his nose bleeding, the challenger fell to the floor and Nash made his escape.

Back on the street, he was greeted by a blast of freezing cold air. The sun's light was dim as he looked down the street one way and then the other. There was no sign of George or the man who had swept him to safety.

He muttered an oath, unhappy at losing Kinloch. But if he lingered any longer, he'd be missed back at the Stephens' and Robbie would come searching for him. He had no choice but to return.

After a few tortured hours trying to decipher Nash's horticulture book, Robbie's head began to nod, the words blurring on the page. Warmed by the smoldering fire and embraced by the settee, he soon drifted into a dream of a becalmed ship on a glassy sea waiting for wind.

The touch of a hand on his head brought him instantly awake.

"Nash!" said Ailie excitedly, dropping onto the settee next to him, "I might have known I'd find you here. What are you reading?"

Coming out of his stupor, Robbie shoved his spectacles back onto his nose and blinked. Ailie Stephen had the most alluring eyes. Surrounded as they were with her fiery hair, she was a most fetching creature. "Ah…" he breathed, gathering his thoughts. "'Tis a book on horticulture and greenhouses." He showed her the cover.

She grinned. "Not a surprising choice after our morning in Emily's orangery." She tilted her head and gave him a beguiling smirk. "You did seem to enjoy our excursion into the woods to gather hawthorn berries." There was something about her easy familiarity and sly smile that told Robbie more had happened in the woods than gathering hawthorn berries.

He decided to try an experiment. "Would you like to do it again?"

"What? Kiss me here?" She looked toward the door. "Someone might see."

Why that wily brother of mine. He kissed the girl! Robbie smiled at the pretty redhead. "That makes it all the more exciting."

He leaned toward her.

She did not move.

He inclined his head and closed his eyes as he gently kissed her soft lips. He did not wish to frighten her. Apparently, he did not. He opened his eyes to see hers sparkling with happiness as she slid her hands to his nape and pulled him to her.

He kissed her again. This time, she joined in with greater abandon than he would have imagined coming from a green girl. Her lips were warm and oh, so inviting. How could he resist? When she opened her mouth to his tongue, he decided to indulge fully in what she offered.

The book slid to the floor and he wrapped his arms around her, lifting her onto his lap.

She tasted sweet, reminding him of summer and honey.

As the kiss ended, she said, "Oh Nash, that was wonderful, different than the first one, but still very nice."

"I rather enjoyed it myself. However, you were right. The difference might be accounted for by the fear of discovery." So, he and Nash kissed differently. Well, thank God for that. Robbie had no intention of spending his excellent kissing skills to improve the girl's opinion of his brother.

Smiling sweetly, a slight blush on her pale skin, she leaned in to say, "I told you I liked it."

"So you did." Having taken his disguise this far, Robbie had to carry it through. Tempted to kiss her again, he thought better of it. "Still, perhaps we should go before someone sees us."

She dropped her arms from his shoulders and he slid her from his lap, commanding his body to relax.

"But Nash, next time, can you kiss me without your spectacles? I cannot see you clearly when you wear them."

"And next time," he suggested, suddenly glad for his spectacles, steamed as they were, "let's find a more private location."

"I'll think of somewhere we can be alone," she said.

He got to his feet, picked up the book and placed it on the settee. When she rose to stand next to him, he removed his spectacles but did not meet her gaze. "The others will soon be coming back from their afternoon pursuits. Might I suggest we retire to the parlor for a glass of claret?"

"Aye, I would like that. But first, I must change for dinner. I'll meet you there. By the way, where is your brother, Robbie?"

"Robbie?" he asked innocently, throwing in a shrug for good measure. "Oh, I think he went for a walk. He cannot have gone far. I'm certain he's around here somewhere."

Chapter 12

Twilight had descended by the time Nash arrived back at the Stephens' though his pocket watch, identical to Robbie's, told him it was only late afternoon. Still freezing from his long trudge through the snow, he opened his bedchamber door and pulled up short.

Robbie lay on his bed, his hands clasped behind his head, his stockinged legs crossed at the ankles and a wicked grin on his face. "You devil," Robbie drawled, a smirk replacing his grin.

Nash took off his greatcoat and gloves and stretched his hands toward the fire. "Whatever are you talking about?"

"You might have told me you kissed the Mistress of the Setters."

Nash whipped around, shooting a glare at his twin. "That is none of your concern!" He was about to turn back to the fire when another thought occurred. "How did you learn of it?"

Robbie crossed his arms over his chest. "Ailie, of course. Who else? She came looking for you and found me in the library, whereupon she assumed I was you. I don't think she is aware we both require spectacles to read. After some meaningless trivialities about plants, she informed me she enjoyed your kiss."

Nash stared at his brother. "You didn't—"

"I did," said Robbie blithely, getting to his feet. "'Tis the nature of the game, is it not? Should not I take advantage of her error as you took advantage of the woods to kiss her in the first place?"

Nash's anger boiled over, a sudden need for satisfaction consuming him. His fist flew to his brother's jaw.

Robbie stumbled back and shook his head. Rubbing his jaw, he said, "Can't recall you ever doing that before."

"Damn you, Robbie!" Nash spit out. "The game, as you call it, has changed!" His aching knuckles were a small price to pay for the satisfaction he gained in sending Robbie a clear message. "This competition must cease."

"Ah ha," Robbie said, fixing Nash with an assessing gaze. "I begin to understand. You are more taken with this girl than the others whose charms we have vied to possess."

"What if I am?" It didn't seem right discussing Ailie with his brother, but he could see it was unavoidable. He had to know. "Just what kind of kiss was it?"

Robbie averted his gaze. "Hardly one to brag about." Picking up one of his tall boots, he sat on his bed and began to polish the black leather with fervor. It was one of Robbie's quirks that, when he traveled, he preferred to see to his own boots, whereas Nash would leave it to the servants.

Nash narrowed his eyes on his twin. "Ailie is not a mouse to be fought over by two tomcats. I don't want you kissing her disguised as me."

Robbie glanced up. "All right, if you insist."

Nash heard a note of amusement in his twin's voice. Did Robbie think him insincere? "You doubt my intentions? I assure you they are most honorable."

Robbie paused in his boot polishing. "You must admit this is new. I cannot recall an instance in our previous contests involving women when you were so... possessive, nor so violent when I made an advance."

"Blast it, Robbie, this one is different! *She* is different!"

"Very well, if you're bent on having the girl, perhaps I can help."

"I don't need your help," Nash insisted. "I don't want it." Robbie had a way with women, an ease with seduction. Nash was not prepared to risk Ailie being attracted to Robbie's more overt charm. Nor did he want her to be confused as to which of them was kissing her. "I think 'tis best if you just avoid her."

Robbie snorted. "How can I do that when she mistakes me for you *as we intend*?" Nash was about to object when Robbie held up a hand. "However, for the sake of our brotherly affection, I will endeavor to be more circumspect."

The anger that had exploded before welled again in Nash's chest. "Exactly what does that mean?"

In a solicitous tone, Robbie said, "Unless she throws herself at me with full knowledge of who I am, I will be pleasant but take no liberties. That way, she will think well of you, and you need not worry I will unfairly gain ground. But I warn you, I am open to resuming my pursuit of the lass should she shift her affections. The Mistress of the Setters is a fetching creature."

Nash frowned, returning his brother a skeptical look. He did not trust Robbie with Ailie. She was too tempting. "I would ask you be no more than 'merely pleasant' toward her."

"Have you considered that when I am pretending to be you, should I fail to be warm toward the girl, she will think your affection has cooled?"

"Warm does not include kissing her," Nash said, stuffing his legs into the same buff-colored breeches and ivory waistcoat his brother wore. Robbie had yet to put on a coat, so Nash asked, "What coat did you wear when you were with Ailie?"

"The black velvet."

"Then I must wear that one tonight."

"Indeed you must," agreed Robbie. "Ailie is expecting me—or rather, you—to join her in the parlor for a glass of claret."

"What? Why didn't you tell me she was waiting?" More frustrated with his twin than he'd been in a long time, Nash hurriedly pulled on his boots.

"Oh, you have plenty of time. She intended to change first, as I knew she would. Ladies take an awfully long time to put on what we so quickly remove."

Nash sighed in exasperation. "Don't remind me of your skills in that area."

"So tell me," Robbie urged, "how did the visit to Arbroath go?"

Still angry with his brother, Nash forced himself to concentrate on their work. Robbie had to know what he'd learned. "Better than expected. I need that map of the town to show you."

"Of course. I have it right here." Robbie went to his chest, pulled out the map they had both memorized the day before and smoothed it out on his bed. Rubbing his jaw, which was now red, he said, "Your right hook has improved."

Ignoring his brother's comment, Nash lit another candle and brought it to the small table between their beds, determined to brief his brother and then leave. "I went to the *Panmure* first." He pointed to the harbor. "The captain told me he plans to sail for France on the afternoon of the twenty-sixth. I imagine at high tide. Then I went to a local tavern called The Foundry." He pointed to its location on Mary Street and took a seat on the end of Robbie's bed, the map between them. "The customers were a mixed lot whose conversations led me to believe they are mere weathercocks, changing their political views with the direction of the wind."

"Not worth a return visit to that one," said Robbie.

"But here," Nash said, pointing to the St Thomas Tavern, "I encountered a bit of luck."

Robbie looked up from the map. "Luck?"

In his mind, Nash saw again the crowded smoke-filled tavern. "A group of men came in shortly after I arrived. They took the only available table, which the proprietor must have been holding for them. Fortunately, I was sitting close enough to overhear their conversation."

Nash paused for a moment, recalling the men's words. "One of them, a large man with huge hands, spoke to a smaller one dressed in odd clothing. The large man called the other one 'Georgie' and told him he would be on the ship. The oddly dressed man seemed alarmed that his given name had been used and commanded the other to address him as 'Mr. Oliphant'. It struck me that this 'Georgie' who masquerades as Mr. Oliphant could be Kinloch. When a fight broke out, he was hurriedly ushered out of the tavern by one of his companions."

"Did you follow them?"

"I would have done, but a fist in my shoulder delayed me at the door." Nash rubbed his shoulder, still sore from the man's punch.

"No wonder you're in a foul mood." A look of concern crossed Robbie's face "Are you hurt?"

"No, and you can stop your worrying. I do not need you to rescue me from every fight that comes my way. I can well defend myself."

Robbie glanced at him with raised brows. They were both thinking of that day at St Peter's Field, but there had been other times as well. At Eton, Robbie had once stepped in to take the punch of a swaggering bully that had been meant for Nash. And last year when their work for Sidmouth took them to the cotton spinners' strike in Lancashire, Robbie had pulled him from an angry mob.

Ignoring his brother's look of disbelief, Nash continued. "When I was finally able to extricate myself, which, I might add, I did with little trouble, George and his companion were nowhere to be seen. With the sun nearly down, I had to return."

"You'll need to describe them for me so I'll know what to look for when I venture into town again."

"Not only can I describe them, but I can tell you some of their names."

Ailie watched in the mirror as Rhona attempted to arrange her hair in a new style.

Twisting a long strand into a curl, she said, "'Tis how the ladies wear their hair in London, or so Lady Emily tells me."

"It takes more time and requires more pins," Ailie complained, wanting to hurry to meet Nash.

"Aye, but ye'll like how ye look when I'm done. Yer hair will be curled on top of yer head and the rest long over yer shoulder."

Ailie wondered if Nash would like it. She thought of his kisses in the library, a bit different than the first in the woods. She hoped it signified she was more to him than a passing fancy. But what if she were? Would she take an Englishman for a husband? Muriel might urge it upon her and William would accept such a match given his own choice. But what did she want?

There were times when Nash had been endearing, like when he encouraged her to believe the *Ossian* would be built one day, and when he accepted her wearing breeches. He was even tolerant of her teasing him about kale and haddies. She smiled, remembering him in spectacles, like a professor buried in his horticulture book. Though she knew shipmasters who read when at sea, their books were not about growing things on land. But then, Nash didn't speak much of sailing. Perhaps, like her, he spent his days ashore.

"I like this blue gown on ye, Mistress," said her maid.

Ailie thought the blue velvet edging around the bodice, cut lower than her other gowns, and short puffy sleeves would go well with her small tartan shawl. "I like it, too. It's the same indigo color as Grandfather Ramsay's knitted Ganseys."

When Rhona set down the brush, Ailie eagerly asked, "Are you finished?"

Rhona chuckled. "Aye. Whoever ye're so eager to meet will be pleased at the sight of ye. Ye're a bonnie lass."

"Thank you." Her cheeks flushed at the thought of being so transparent.

"I'll get yer shawl."

Ailie rose and Rhona slipped the blue tartan shawl over her shoulders. "No need to wait up for me tonight, Rhona. I'll ready myself for bed."

By the time Ailie entered the parlor, Nash was surrounded by their guests engaged in lively conversation. All were present, save Nash's brother Robbie. Her work at the shipyard that morning had kept her from joining them in their pursuits. She had been so consumed by Nash's kiss in the library, she had forgotten to ask him if he'd been reading all morning.

She looked toward Nash, the only man in the room she wanted to see. He must have been waiting for her, as he smiled and crossed the room with two glasses of wine in hand.

"The claret I promised you," he said, passing her one of the glasses.

"You don't mind everyone else is drinking wassail?" She had noticed the distinctive smell of apples and cinnamon when she'd first arrived.

"Not at all." His gaze shifted to her hair. "You've fixed your hair differently. Most becoming." He lifted a long strand, curled at the end, touching her skin at the base of her neck in the process. "Very pretty."

A shiver ran through her. "It was my maid's creation," Ailie said, trying to recover from the touch of his fingers. "I did not mean for it to take so long."

"No matter. The effect is splendid and worth the wait. Shall we join the others?"

"Aye. But where is Robbie? When we were in the library, you mentioned he had not gone far."

Nash hesitated. "Oh, I'm sure he'll be down in a bit. He is changing for dinner."

"He's probably freezing if he's been outside. Was he gone long?"

Nash appeared to hesitate. "I didn't ask."

"Next time, he might try the orangery."

"Robbie? I don't think so. He'd prefer the woods, cold though they may be."

She gave him a lopsided grin. "So would I if I were with you."

"I shall remember that," he said, gently taking her elbow. He led her toward the cluster of people gathered in front of the fire, the dancing flames casting a warm glow over their faces.

Emily was the first to greet them. "Why Ailie, you look lovely."

"Doesn't she?" agreed Will.

Ailie felt herself blushing at the compliments.

Smiling at Nash, Emily said, "Good evening."

Since Emily had not added a name, Ailie felt the need to say, "He is Nash, Emily; Robbie has yet to appear."

"I do apologize, Nash, for not recognizing you."

"Worry not," Nash quipped. "It happens quite often, I can assure you."

Emily gazed up at Will. "I do hope you and Ailie won't have to spend the whole of tomorrow at the shipyard. I was hoping we might go skating on the pond. I'm certain it's frozen by now."

"A most excellent idea, *Leannan*. With hot wassail and warm brandy to follow."

Ailie took a sip of her claret. "I might have to check on matters at the yard in the morning, but, after that, I would look forward to skating."

"Me as well," Nash agreed.

A lock of his dark hair had curled onto his forehead and Ailie wanted to reach up and brush it aside, a wifely gesture to be sure and one that had her looking at her hands holding her glass. She must not give in to such thoughts based on a few kisses. They must find a place to be alone so he didn't feel the need to cut short their time. She remembered with particular fondness their first kiss even though it had been in the snow-covered woods.

They were almost finished drinking their wine when Lamont summoned them to dinner.

Robbie arrived a bit later and took the seat next to Muriel.

Dinner began with oysters and Madeira handed about in tall glasses on a tray.

"The Madeira is for Muriel," said Emily. "It's her favorite."

Then came the fish course, baked salmon in cream sauce, which was followed by roast chicken and a ragout with vegetables. And more wine. Dessert was a pudding, for which Ailie had no appetite.

"I thought we might have coffee and tea in the parlor as a group tonight if it pleases you," offered Will. "And there will be games of chess for those interested. But before you go, since we all went our separate ways today, Emily has suggested for the morrow, we might ice skate on the pond. What say you?"

"So that's why you told us to bring skates," said Mary.

"'Tis a grand idea," said Tara. "When I was younger, my family in Baltimore always skated on the pond near our house."

"I've not skated for an age," said Kit, "and I really want to do some sketches of the rest of you demonstrating your skill on the ice."

Martin inclined his head toward his wife. "I insist you join me on the ice. Christmas in the country with snow wouldn't be Christmas without ice skating."

"Do you skate, Muriel?" asked Robbie.

"Definitely not. But I will watch the rest of you and keep Kit company when she takes up her sketching."

Nash turned to Ailie. "I look forward to sharing the ice with you."

"Are you a very good skater?"

He winked at her. "That's one of the things I can do better than Robbie."

She thought of their kisses in the woods. If they had been alone, she might have told him she was sure he was better at kissing than Robbie.

Robbie was anxious to know where Kinloch lodged. Catching him there might save them a tavern brawl. He had thought to go to Arbroath town the next day and see if he could find the man's lodgings. But upon reflection, the better course just now would be for both he and Nash to participate in the ice skating. Since everyone was attending, his absence would be noted, concluding he was either ill or being unsociable.

Having decided to participate, when he and Nash retired to their chamber after a game of chess, Robbie made his intention known. "I think we should both attend tomorrow's ice skating."

"Probably wise. Even Muriel means to attend."

"The day after, assuming it's not snowing again, I will go to Arbroath while you and the others can engage in whatever William has planned. Hopefully, I can find Kinloch and follow him to wherever he is staying. It may mean I'll be late and you'll have to cover for me. Say I went to see William's ships or some such excuse."

"I doubt if any will suspect you have gone to town," said Nash. "Upon your return, you can always say you were in the orangery where you became fascinated watching pineapples grow."

Robbie sailed his boot through the air nearly colliding with Nash's head.

22 December

Ailie shot up in bed, the dream still clear in her mind, vivid images of scenes she had experienced deep in the night.

What had begun with gruff men sitting around tables quaffing ale had changed to men running toward a ship docked at the harbor as shots were fired. She could still hear the loud crack of the pistol as it belched fire and smoke.

Breathing heavily, she dropped her legs over the side of the bed and brought her palm to her chest, trying to calm her racing heart. Once, she had experienced a cannon being tested and it had been very loud. But she had never lived through the chaos of men firing pistols and muskets at each other. The war with Napoleon had raged for years, yet she had never witnessed a battle. How horrible it must have been for Will, who had endured many before he was captured.

The light coming through her window told Ailie the sun was just rising, which meant it was late. Goodness and Mercy would be waiting for her. Undoing her plait, she ran her fingers through her long thick hair, thinking the dream must have been the result of too much wine last night. First she'd had claret with Nash, then the Madeira with the oysters and then more wine at dinner. The coffee served in the parlor with their games of chess had helped her stay alert. By the time she found her bed, many thoughts swirled in her head, not the least of which was her exchange with Nash.

"Do you really believe the man from Dundee is in the right?"

His question seemed to come out of nowhere. Just a minute before they'd been sitting by the fire, calmly discussing the new ideas for greenhouses he'd read about that morning.

"The laird from Dundee," Nash repeated, as if to jog her memory. "The one who gave the speech and has been charged with sedition. Do you believe he is in the right?"

"Why, of course! Did I not say that? He speaks for his fellow Scots demanding only fairness. I read his speech, reprinted in the weekly, and what I read urged reform, not rebellion. He did criticize the government for the massacre at Manchester, but I thought the criticism fair."

Nash frowned at his coffee. "London fears the large crowds speaking against the government will lead to a revolution like the one in France."

Anger rose in her chest. "If those in the government do not treat the workers more fairly, they will certainly have another rising on their hands—one led by Scots. Only this time, the Scots will not be seeking their freedom but, led by the weavers, they'll be after fair pay and equal representation."

She had watched him closely as he nodded, but it seemed to her he displayed little enthusiasm. His expression spoke only of resignation.

"Do the gentry in London agree with the government?" she had asked, hardly believing anyone could.

"The Crown approved of the yeomen's harsh actions in Manchester and supports Lord Sidmouth's new legislation. Many in the upper classes do as well. But perhaps not all."

"Aye, one of our own, Alexander, the Duke of Hamilton, has given money to the relief being raised for the Manchester victims. Will told me the duke has written to your Sidmouth to warn him that using force like they did in Manchester could lead to insurrection in Scotland."

"That is precisely what worries the government," said Nash with a look of regret. "But still, you would have the man Kinloch go free?"

"I would. Can you not see, Nash? If Kinloch were thrown into prison, or worse, it would only give the weavers another reason to revolt."

The whole discourse had reminded Ailie of the gulf that existed between them. Not just the place of their birth and their faith, but their politics. That being the case, it might be wise for her to remember that he would soon sail back to London and it would be as if he never came. Or would it? He had awakened her to passion and perhaps more. Could she ever forget him?

Before meeting her dogs and seeing to breakfast, Ailie wrote again in her diary.

22 December

A most troubling conversation with Nash Powell last eve has made me see the difficulty of any relationship with an Englishman. Or, perhaps 'tis just a relationship with a member of the gentry who believes the British Crown can do no wrong. But how can anyone believe that with the events in Manchester so fresh in everyone's mind? The gov-

ernment still pursues the laird from Dundee, George Kinloch, in whom Nash and his brother Robbie appear to have an interest. I must ask them about that.

Another disturbing dream troubled my sleep last night. This time, I heard pistols being fired and saw men running through the streets of Arbroath. It was so real. What can it mean?

Chapter 13

Muriel relaxed onto the bench facing the frozen pond, warmed by the fire William had built for those retreating from the ice. Bundled up in her blue pelisse and hat, her hands warm in her large fox muff, she watched as her charges skated over the ice, laughing at near disasters averted only by quick action at the last moment.

The two black setters came to sit by the bench, their eyes fixed upon Aileen, turning their heads with their mistress' every move. Muriel slipped one hand from her muff to pat their dutiful heads. She did so love a faithful dog.

Muriel patted the front of her coat, feeling beneath it the long strands of pearls she was never without. Into her mind came the memory of another day long ago. It was her first—and only—season and the man skating beside her was the young Earl of Claremont she'd only known a short while. The watchful gaze of her chaperone, a maiden aunt, had never left them as they glided over the ice.

"With your soft gray eyes, Muriel, you should wear pearls," he had said, taking her hand. "Marry me and I will see that you have a strand fit for the most beautiful girl in all of London."

She had laughed at his flattery, but she thrilled to his decisive candor. At the end of their skating, captivated by his sincerity, his intelligence and his determination to forsake all others for her, she had agreed to marry him. To this day, she was never without the pearls he had given her when they were wed. Their time together had been a joyous celebration of their love, his early death a torture. But she had no regrets, for the memories were sweet ones.

In the years that had passed, she had devoted herself to helping others find the same love she had known. If the Lord had granted her an eye for a good match, well then, Muriel would use it. She could credit several matches to her efforts.

Dismissing the memories, she looked toward Aileen, skating over the frozen pond with one of the Powell twins. From this distance, she could not discern which one, but recalling the way Nash Powell had looked at the girl the evening before, Muriel guessed it might be him.

Sir Martin's wife, the young woman everyone called "Kit", glided to a graceful stop in front of Muriel. "May I share your bench?"

"Please do and take me away from my reminiscing."

"We can't have that, Muriel, not with so much life going on around you."

She offered Kit a hand as she stepped from the ice. Once seated, Kit unbuckled her skates and greeted the dogs. Gazing at the skaters circling around the pond, she said, "I want to do a bit of sketching before they tire of the ice."

"How are your sketches coming?"

Kit picked up her sketchbook and pencils she had left on the bench when she took to the ice. "Quite well. I've only a few left and then I'll add some at Christmas and Hogmanay." She turned to a new page. "I'd like to do one of all of them skating on the pond. It's so picturesque with the tall evergreens on one side and the sun low in the horizon silhouetting the skaters."

"It is lovely here," Muriel remarked, "but they do lose the light awfully early this far north."

"'Tis worse than London," said Kit, "but the light on the ice just now is truly magical."

The dogs ran off just then, circling to where their mistress drew close to the edge of the pond.

Muriel considered her mood. "I find myself content to be in Arbroath. The company is good, the fires are warming and the orangery like the tropics. I think it will be a Christmas long remembered."

"I agree. Martin has said so as well." Kit took off her right glove and began to draw, glancing between the skaters and her sketchbook. "I do believe my husband is enjoying all the male company. It's rare when he and his brothers are together in one place anymore. Nick's often at sea and the twins are hardly ever in London."

"Oh? And why is that? Do they sail frequently, too?"

"They used to, but this last year has kept them in England on some government business or other."

"Hmm…" Muriel mused. "Does it have anything to do with ships, I wonder?"

"I don't think so. At least Martin has not mentioned that. I hesitate to think they are involved in some dangerous business."

"Surely nothing is more dangerous than sailing the Atlantic," quipped Muriel.

Kit paused in her sketching. "You wouldn't say that if you'd been with Martin and me two years ago. In Pentridge, you may recall, there was a rebellion put down by the hussars."

"Ah yes, I remember. A nasty business that."

"It was, but you are right to say that sailing the Atlantic is also dangerous. Tara and I worry whenever our husbands go to sea without us. And I know Mrs. Powell worries whenever her Simon is on a long voyage. When we can, we sail with them."

"But the children…"

"Yes," said Kit. "Nowadays, the little ones keep us women at home. But it will not always be so. Too, when the men return and the families get together, we have a marvelous time."

As Muriel had come to know them, she believed the Powells a fine family. "Only two more of the brothers to see to the altar," she muttered.

Kit laughed. "And those two may present the greatest challenge."

Muriel tapped her chin. "I've a keen fondness for a challenge. Both the twins are gentlemen and would make admirable husbands. Robbie's a rogue, of course, but I rather fancy rogues. When they fall in love, they do it so ungracefully, so irreparably. 'Tis quite a thing to see. Nash is the more scholarly of the two, slower to action perhaps, but no less determined to succeed."

Kit lifted her eyes from her sketchbook to study the skaters. "I think that is Nash skating with Ailie now."

"I do believe you are right. I've been watching them. They seem to get on well together. Last evening they were arguing about politics, yet here they are today taking command of the ice together. I must ask Emily what she thinks of such a match, though I'd be sorry to lose the girl's company in London. She could be the toast of the *ton*."

Kit laughed. "She very well could. Your gracious invitation is still open then?"

"Indeed it is and I do hope she will accept."

Slowly picking himself up off the ice, Robbie reached for his hat that had tumbled from his head in the fall. He rubbed his throbbing hip. *Damn ice is hard on a man's constitution.*

Aboard ship, Robbie stayed out of the rigging. Amazingly, he had no trouble walking on a rolling deck. He was a fairly good shipmaster and an adroit navigator. His talent lay with charts and steering clear of rocks and shoals.

In London, he favored the gentlemen's clubs where his game was brag, at which he succeeded more often than not. Ice-skating, on the other hand, he considered a trial by freezing cold and slippery terrain. That his younger brother, as he liked to think of Nash, was at this very moment adroitly skimming over the ice with the Mistress of the Setters came as a mortifying set down.

His sister-in-law, Tara, came to a perfectly executed stop in front of him. "Can I help?" In her scarlet pelisse and hat, she was a lovely sight for a wounded man.

"Ah, the Queen of the Rigging." He rose to his full height, placing his top hat back on his head. "I might have known 'twould be you who offered a hand. Very gracious. May I propose we skate together to that bench over there at the edge of the pond where sits the countess and Kit?" After meeting Ailie, Robbie had begun to think of Martin's wife as The Other Redhead.

Tara laughed. "I'd be happy to escort you." She took his arm, for which he was most grateful, and they began to skate together. "In Baltimore, I practically grew up on the ice in our cold winters. Deep in the woods there were many ponds like this one. If you hadn't been seeking to be the fastest man on the ice, Robbie, you would have done just fine."

"You recognize me?"

"Nash does not move nearly so fast. But like the tortoise, he generally gets where he wants to go in the end."

"Hmm..." he muttered, for the first time thinking of Ailie as the place Nash intended to go. Unsurprisingly, Robbie's skating improved mightily in Tara's company. Glancing at her blue-green eyes, he said, "'Tis hard for some of us hares to slow down, you know."

"I do understand since I am married to one. But no matter. You will change with the right woman, just as Nick did."

"Slow down, you mean?"

She laughed. "Hardly. That would be asking too much. But the right woman will make you less reckless. It will be important for you to survive for her, for your children."

"Ah," he murmured, as they arrived at the bench. To the countess and her companion, he asked, "Might I join you?"

"Yes, please do," said The Grand Countess. Muriel smiled, reminding Robbie that while she might have the demeanor of a queen, she had the heart of a grandmother. "A charming rogue is just what we need to entertain us, isn't it, Kit?"

Kit moved over to allow Robbie room to take the space between them. "Indeed. Robbie will most definitely liven us up."

He thanked Tara for her assistance. She waved goodbye and skated off with elegant grace to where Nick waited for her.

Robbie unbuckled his skates from his boots. "How did you know it was me?"

"More like I knew it *had* to be you," said Muriel in her dignified voice. "I believe it is Nash skating with Aileen, is it not?"

"It is." Robbie let out a sigh as he watched his twin sharing laughter with the girl. The two appeared to be enjoying themselves. "He is much better on the ice than I am."

"And you are better at flirtation and charm," said Muriel. "I suspect the mothers in the *ton* hide their daughters when you enter the ballroom."

"Why, Muriel," said Kit, pausing in her sketching, "how ever did you guess?"

"I recognize a rogue because I married one." The countess patted Robbie's knee. "Reformed, they make wonderful husbands."

"I do hope you are right, Countess," said Robbie, "as I have recently thought of taking a wife."

"Oh how the mighty fall!" exclaimed Kit. "Do your brothers know?"

Thinking the idea was now firm in his mind, Robbie replied, "I have only recently decided."

"I see you watching William's sister," observed Muriel. "Is she in your sights?"

"If she were to show an interest, she certainly would be. However, at least for the moment, Nash seems to be occupying the field."

Robbie watched the nine skaters gliding around the ice: Nick and Tara, now that she was restored to her husband, Mary and Hugh, as athletic on the ice as on horseback, William and Emily, absorbed in each other, and Nash and Ailie. All skated as couples. Martin, skating alone, was taking on some fancy jumps.

"Martin has an aptitude for the ice," he said. "I must have forgotten. Do you also like to skate, Kit?"

"Not so much as Martin." Her pencil moved in quick jerks over the sketchbook.

Robbie leaned over to look at her drawing. In the middle of the large pad, Kit had sketched the pond and the skaters, not so you could discern their features, but the figures were clearly drawn so that he could make out who they were. At the four corners of the drawing, she had added smaller individual pictures: the countess on the bench, Martin in a leap, the two setters running and Robbie taking a fall.

"Did you have to include my disastrous fall from grace?"

Kit chuckled. "I thought to round out our afternoon of skating. Things do not always go well and you so rarely fall, Robbie. Besides, I would have my sketches reflect real life."

"That is to your credit, my dear," said the countess.

William skated over to them, Emily in tow. "Are you finished?" he asked. "I think the group is ready for some hot wassail."

"Wassail sounds delightful," said Kit. "I can add what details remain when I am back in my chamber."

"Bless you, dear man," said Muriel. "A hot cup of wassail is just the ticket."

Robbie smiled to himself. *Or, perhaps a warm brandy and a few moments with the Mistress of the Setters.* Surely, "circumspect" did not mean he could not enjoy her company.

"Allow me," offered Nash, taking two cups of wassail from the footman's tray and passing one to Ailie. "This will warm you up." They had returned with the others from the pond just as the sun had dropped behind the hills. Still feeling the chill off the ice, they had gathered in the parlor, clustered around the fire to get warm.

"Did you enjoy yourself?" Ailie inquired, taking a sip of the hot spiced cider that smelled of cinnamon and oranges.

Unable to hide the joy of being with her, he grinned. "Tremendously, but for the most part, that was due to the company." They had talked of their childhoods and laughed over their foibles. She had not mentioned George Kinloch so Nash hoped she did not hold against him his views. They had enjoyed themselves so much they were the last to leave the ice.

Ailie's sherry-colored eyes glistened as she looked at him over the rim of her cup. "You are a very good skater, you know."

"One of my few talents."

"I suspect you have many, Nash Powell. Were you athletic as a child? I neglected to ask."

"Robbie and I played cricket at Eton but, after that, Father insisted we learn the family business and sail with him. Not that we hadn't been on ships as small boys but, from that time on, the lessons were of a more serious nature. My athletics were mostly climbing the rigging and swabbing decks. Eventually, as we gained experience and Father trusted us, we learned to sail as shipmasters."

"Were you happy for the change?"

"Oh yes. Being with our father is always an amazing adventure. Captain Simon Powell," he said, "the very name is like magic to the men of Powell and Sons. You would have to see him on the deck of his ship firing orders in a storm to understand. Only Nick has achieved our father's skill as a shipmaster."

"Ships have been in my blood since I was a wee lass, though I have not sailed far."

"With my father, I have sailed to the West Indies, America, France and much farther." Nash remembered how William had described his sister. Regarding her with admiration, he said, "Your brother described for Robbie and me your determination to become a designer of ships."

A pretty blush pinked her cheeks. "Aye, I made a right keen nuisance of myself in Father's shops in Aberdeen."

"I admire you, Ailie. One day you will be known for the *Ossian's* unique design, I've no doubt." What he didn't say was that he planned to be with her when that day arrived.

Behind him, Emily drew everyone's attention. "Our cook tells me dinner will be in a half-hour's time, so plan accordingly!"

The footman collected their cups and Nash escorted Ailie to the top of the stairs where he told her he would see her at dinner. She turned one way and he the other.

Dinner was a jolly affair as they recounted the day's adventures on the frozen pond. The meal, after the usual soup and fish, consisted of a braised leg of mutton. When he inquired of Ailie about the bacon he would have expected to taste along with the sheep's meat, she told him, "Martha would never use bacon."

"One can always hope," he said. With a deep sigh, Nash resigned himself to living without bacon, perhaps for the rest of his life, unless he could persuade Ailie to come to London. Could he ever live in Scotland? An intriguing thought.

For dessert they had fresh pineapple from Emily's orangery, which Nash considered a great treat. He was just in the middle of taking a bite when William began to speak.

"Tomorrow, depending on the weather," he said, "I thought to offer those who are interested a chance to hunt."

Nash looked up expectantly "Geese again? I missed my chance the last time."

"No. This time, we'll be going to moors to hunt the red deer hinds. The herds are culled each year at this time to keep them and the land healthy."

Kit's brows furrowed. "What do you mean by culled?"

"Without natural predators, the herds grow too large for the vegetation they have to survive upon," replied William. "The last wild wolf was killed three-quarters of a century ago. We will be looking for the stragglers, the weaker ones. Still, with the weather as it is, the short hours of daylight and the canny deer, we'll have a challenge on our hands."

"If we're successful, we can look forward to a fine saddle of venison. I must warn you, it means another departure before daybreak and we'll be gone until late afternoon."

Despite William's admonitions, Nick shared a glance with his wife, then eagerly spoke up. "We're for the hunt."

Kit gave Nick's wife a look of surprise. "You, Tara?"

"I used to hunt the white-tailed deer and wild turkeys with my brothers," she replied. "It would be a grand thing to be able to tell them about deer stalking in Scotland."

"If you are going," said Ailie, "so will I, but just be aware deer stalking involves much wandering and waiting. 'Tis not so exciting as shooting at hundreds of geese taking flight."

With that, Nash chimed in, "'Twill give me time to ponder. Count me in." There was no possibility Ailie was setting off for the moors without him. A whole day with her stalking the deer even if he never got a shot would be something to remember.

Kit spoke up. "I'd like to go to sketch the hunt, if it would be permissible."

"Aye," said William, "no one is required to shoot. I'll have guns and spyglasses for those who do. The ride will be long, ladies, and once on the moors, 'twill be windy and cold. Dress accordingly. I have jackets and hats more fitting to deer stalking should you have none."

Nash detected a gleam in Ailie's eyes, making him wonder just what she would wear.

When William's words of caution did not dissuade the women from going, Martin said, "If my wife goes, so do I."

Hugh conferred with his wife. "Mary and I have decided to stay here and have a late morning ride."

William turned to Robbie. "And you?"

"I'm not much for hunting." Nash knew the words to be false, but he was also aware of why Robbie had spoken them. Robbie glanced at the countess. "Perhaps a game of piquet with Muriel might serve."

"I should like to see *that* game," said Emily.

"Well," said Robbie, "if I am late, you two can start without me."

"Humph," mumbled Muriel.

Nash believed for much of the day, the two ladies would be playing alone. Any card game involving Robbie would not take place till late afternoon.

After the women left for the parlor and their tea, Nash enjoyed a glass of port with the men. When they rejoined the ladies, Robbie invited Ailie to play a game of chess, which she accepted.

"Be warned," she said with a twinkle in her eyes, "I am quite good at the game growing up with Father and Will and long winter nights to perfect my skill."

Robbie smirked and set up the board. "We shall see."

Nash talked with William about ship designs while shooting glances at his twin, who was enjoying his game with Ailie. Robbie had always been more proficient at chess than he was.

Even before the first of the chess games had concluded, the couples going on the hunt began drifting toward the parlor door, intent upon seeking their beds for the early morning.

"I'll have the servants knock on the doors of any going on the hunt," said William. "We'll have a short breakfast and lots of hot coffee before we set out. Dress warmly."

As Tara and Kit were leaving, Ailie rose from her game with Robbie and asked to speak with them. What the women conferred about, Nash had no idea, but after their heads nodded in agreement, Ailie went back to her game.

With no early commitment, Mary and Hugh lingered over their conversation with Muriel and Emily. Nash waited until Ailie and Robbie finished their game and then walked with them and the others up the stairs. At the head of the stairs, he wished Ailie a good night.

In his chamber, Nash found Robbie pulling out the map he had made upon his first visit to Arbroath town.

"Did you win the game?"

Without looking up, Robbie shook his head. "I let the lady win."

"That was gracious of you. Was it also 'circumspect'?"

"Of course." Robbie looked up from the map. "Now, as for the morrow, I'm for town and tracking Kinloch to his hiding place. It may not be far from the tavern you visited if they go there every day."

"Then 'tis just as well Ailie and I are both going on the hunt."

Robbie folded up the map. "It will certainly make it easier for me to slip away for my own hunt."

That night, Nash lay in his bed listening to rain pelting the window, wondering with the downpour if there would even be a hunt tomorrow.

Chapter 14

23 December

Ailie peered out her window into the darkness and saw stars glistening from the sky. Sometime during the night, the rain had stopped and, from what she could see, much of the snow had been swept away. Of course, the puddles that remained would soon freeze. On the moors and in the glens where they would stalk the deer, the snow would remain and more of it than on the coast.

Since the promised knock had sounded on her door, she assumed the hunt was still on and silently thanked the servant who had stirred the fire in her chamber to life. At least she would not have to shiver as she dressed.

Lighting a candle, she reached for her clothes she had laid out, knowing she would not want to search for them in the dark.

The evening before, she had spoken with the two other women planning to stalk the deer. Kit, who would go along only to sketch, initially told Ailie she would wear a riding habit. Tara dismissed that as impractical.

"I wear breeches on Nick's ship," she said. "Not knowing what I might encounter here in Scotland, I brought a pair with me."

Ailie nodded her approval. "Then I shall wear the same. If we're to make our way over the moors, stalking deer and splashing through mud with the men, we'd best dress the part. A lady's gown will only slow us down." She shot a glance at Kit. "Are you certain you do not want to borrow some breeches and boots from me? Or some trousers? I have both. It might be best to ride astride if you are able."

"Oh, very well," Kit said, her blue eyes flashing. "I cannot argue with reason. Martin will just have to accept me in the scandalous garb. Some trousers will do, Ailie. I can wear them with my half boots. And, yes, I can ride astride, or at least I could as a girl."

Concerned they would be warm enough, Ailie offered to provide woolen scarves for them if they had failed to bring some. She had many. As it turned out, Tara had brought one and Kit had not.

Before getting ready for bed, Ailie had Rhona deliver the promised clothing to Kit's chamber, including the woolen scarf and a jacket for good measure. Martin's wife would not regret her decision. The three of them would be united in their determination to be practical. After all, it wasn't as if they were heading for the streets of Edinburgh where the world would see their shameful attire.

Clothed in her breeches and heavy woolen jacket, along with a tartan scarf and her boots, Ailie entered the dining room. The footman took no notice of her unusual clothing. Having worked for them for some time, he wouldn't be surprised.

Alone, as of yet, she perused the offerings on the sideboard lit with branched candlesticks: rumbled eggs, slices of smoked beef, salted herring and biscuits with butter and currant jelly. Her stomach growled.

For hot drinks, they could choose from chocolate, tea and coffee. They would need the strong drinks if they were to face the pitch-black morning.

"No haddies?" asked Nash, coming up behind her where she stood holding her plate.

"Disappointed?" His warm chest against her back gave rise to an irrational desire to turn into his arms. After his kiss in the library, she could hardly look at him without blushing.

He chuckled. "Elated, more like."

"You jest." She turned to face him so he could see her smirk.

"I do." He reached for a plate and stared at the offerings.

"'Tis too early to jest, Nash. My eyes are barely open."

He came to stand beside her, inclining his head to give her breeches a quick look. "I approve your choice of hunting attire."

"Thank you," she said shortly, adding eggs, herring and a biscuit to her plate. "I cannot imagine stalking deer in a gown."

"No, though I imagine some women do."

"Not in Scotland in the winter. But then not many are likely to hunt deer either. My attire will not shock Will and Emily. And today, I will not be alone."

Before long, the others going on the hunt trailed in and joined them. At first, everyone sat quietly, heads bent to their plates, as if talk was beyond them this early.

Ailie finished eating and sipped her chocolate. Nash, sitting next to her, was on his second serving of eggs and biscuits.

Fortified with two cups of coffee, Will looked up from his plate. "I see the ladies have decided to match our clothing, gentlemen. Knowing where we are going, I applaud their choice."

Martin gave Kit a brief look before saying, "I was persuaded by my wife's choice when she told me both Tara and Ailie would be similarly attired."

Tara grinned at her husband. "Told you."

Nick lifted his eyes to the ceiling. "Incorrigible."

Amused at their antics, Ailie shot Nash a glance. "Kindred spirits, aye?"

Nash gave her a wink.

"Ah," sighed Will, patting his stomach after his second helping of eggs. "I am finally ready to face the moors." He rose from his chair. "To the stables, lads and lasses!" He marched from the room, shouting over his shoulder. "Ailie, bring the setters!"

The front door slammed as the rest of them got to their feet. Ailie glanced toward Kit and Tara. "The adventure begins."

Robbie ate breakfast with Muriel, Emily and the Ormonds before setting out for Arbroath. He made a point of tasting the smoked haddies, a sweet smoky flavor, which, once sampled, would long be remembered. Like Nash, he preferred bacon with his eggs.

He had thought to take a horse to Arbroath but, at breakfast, Hugh and Mary spoke about venturing farther afield in their morning ride, so Robbie thought it best he walk. If he encountered them in the woods, he could always dash behind a tree. Walking might be messy after the rain, but it would obviate the need to see to his horse once he arrived.

As he set out, a gray sky hovered above the trees. Beneath their branches, the snow lingered in the shadows, stubbornly refusing to give up its ground. He supposed when one lived with snow and ice most winters, one got used to such weather. In London, snow was rare and, for the most part, insignificant, though it could leave a pretty mess when mingled with the soot.

By the time Robbie reached Arbroath, the townspeople were going about their business. The ships docked in the harbor were now washed of snow and the streets clear.

Since Nash had observed the man "Georgie", with the map in mind, Robbie headed toward High Street and the tavern named for a saint. Being the middle of the day, he was unsurprised to find St Thomas Tavern crowded with men looking for both food and drink.

A plump tavern wench Nash had not mentioned bustled between the tables serving tankards of ale and meat pies while trying to avoid the pats on her bum.

The round table Nash had spoken of was occupied with what appeared to be the same men as before, including the giant-fisted Hamish, Derek and Lachy and one other who sat beside the man he presumed was "Georgie". The man's odd hat didn't quite seem to go with the rest of his clothing. In truth, he didn't seem to fit with his companions either. He did not partake in their conversation, but stared into his ale, his forehead creased in worry.

Robbie bided his time, intending to follow the men whenever they departed, no matter how late. He ordered ale from the wench, who appeared in some distress for all she had to do.

"Yer ale, sir," she said, setting the tankard in front of him. He smiled and looked into her kind but haggard face ringed in dark curls beneath the mobcap sitting askew on her head.

"Thank ye. A guid job ye do, miss, with so many tae serve." Robbie hoped his terrible accent was hidden in the din of the tavern's many conversations.

"Aye, 'tis a dreich day an' the puir withir has the fellows doon aboot the mou."

Not having a clue as to her meaning, he placed an extra coin on the table. "Fer ye."

She dropped a brief curtsey and smiled broadly, showing him her imperfect teeth. "Thank ye."

As long as she was here, Robbie thought to learn something. He looked about. "All yer usual customers?"

She scanned the room before returning her attention to him. "Aye, most." Shooting a glance at the round table, she added, "Them comes in every day and stays fer 'ours. The one w' fair hair, Lachy they calls 'im, 'as a tairrable tempir."

If Robbie remembered correctly, Lachy had started the fight that Nash had become involved in.

"That be all, sir?"

He nodded and followed it with a smile of encouragement.

An hour passed and Robbie gained no new information, but when a spy spends hours in a tavern, he notices many things. Like how closely Hamish and the man with ferret eyes guarded George, wedged between them. From the way Nash had described Derek, the man who had hustled George to safety, Robbie deduced the ferret eyes belonged to him. Frequently, Derek patted his jacket pocket as if assuring himself the weapon he carried remained with him. If Lachy was the man the tavern wench described as having a terrible temper, then the only one Robbie could not name was a younger, thinner version of Hamish.

The other customers paid the five men scant attention, another hour passing as customers came and went.

Derek finished his ale and stood. "Enough fer the now, lads."

Robbie feigned a look of disinterest as the five men got to their feet and shuffled past him toward the door. When they'd gone, he rose, pulled his cap down farther on his head and followed, glad to leave the tavern behind.

Outside, he paused, watching the five men walk toward the harbor. He followed but kept at a distance. When they turned right on Bridge Street, so did he.

The blast from a shotgun made Ailie turn in the direction that Will, Nick and Tara had gone when they went in search of a red hind they'd spotted some distance away. At Ailie's feet, Goodness and Mercy whimpered, waiting for her command. The dogs had sniffed the deer tracks she and her companions had been following till they disappeared at the edge of a small burn winding its way between two hills on either side of the glen.

"Get on!" she commanded. The dogs bounded ahead. "Let's see what they've found," she said to Nash and Martin. Kit, too, was with them, sketching from her seat on a nearby rock that Martin had cleared of snow and covered with a blanket.

Extending the spyglass, Martin peered through the lens. "Looks like they got one."

He handed the glass to Ailie and she held it to her eye. The setters were approaching Will, who was bending over the deer's carcass gutting the animal for the drag back to the horses. "Aye, first kill of the day." She gave the glass to Nash and they set off toward her brother.

Many things had prevented them from taking a deer in the preceding hours. The hinds had been wily, to be sure, but the one time Nash had spied one, he could not get a clear shot. Martin had been tracking another, but as he went to shoot, a hind stepped behind the one he had looked to cull. Ailie herself had spotted a deer on a crag, but it was a healthy specimen, worth keeping to spawn future generations.

Such was the beauty of the snow-covered moors that she had not minded. She considered them fortunate to have encountered any hinds at all. One could stalk deer for days and see none. Besides, they had witnessed the sun rise over the vast winter landscape, the pale light glistening on the snow, a sight so dramatic, so magnificent, their guests from London had stared open-mouthed at the wonder of it.

Martin went to help Kit off the rock as Ailie and Nash proceeded ahead, walking side by side.

"Deer stalking is not for the impatient, is it?" he asked.

She laughed. "Nay. But it provides much time to contemplate."

"So it does." He gave her an intense look that made her blush. Was she the object of his contemplation? She hoped so, but still she worried. She had fallen for the Englishman, but had he fallen for her?

They caught up to their companions and Goodness and Mercy came at her call. Will and Nick were dragging the hind's carcass from the other side of the small burn where it had fallen to where Ailie and Nash waited with Tara.

The setters, scenting the deer, strained toward the kill but remained by her side. "Your shot, Will?"

"Tara's," he answered, looking chagrined. "I'm just helping retrieve it."

Ailie turned to see a broad smile on Tara's face beneath the slouch hat Will had given her. The breeze blew her dark golden hair. With her brown woolen jacket, breeches and boots, she appeared every bit the deer-stalker she was. Ailie had grown to like Nick's wife. Perhaps it was as Nash had told her. They were kindred spirits.

"Congratulations," she said to Tara.

Nick smirked. "There'll be no living with her now."

"Nick," Tara gleefully replied, "just think how jealous my brothers will be."

"A lucky shot," Nick teased.

"Of course, it was," admitted Tara, "but don't be telling them that."

Martin and Kit, trailing behind, now joined them. "At least one of us has taken a deer," said Martin.

Goodness and Mercy lifted their noses into the air, then froze, their tails up. Following their line of sight, Ailie spotted two hinds setting off on a slant up the steepest part of the hill on the other side of the burn. "Will!" she said just loud enough for him to hear.

He acknowledged her words by slowly raising his shotgun to his shoulder and taking aim. Nash, standing between Ailie and Will, poised his gun for the second shot.

As they watched, the deer climbed ever higher, displacing snow. Suddenly, the snow higher up gave way, tumbling down in a great rush, overwhelming the two hinds.

With a thunderous roar, mounds of snow cascaded down the hill in an avalanche, carrying the hinds with it. Great clouds of snow, like the white foam on waves, billowed up to blot out the sky.

Will and Nash dropped their shotguns from their shoulders.

"Everyone back!" shouted Will, his steps receding from the burn as he handed his shotgun to Nick and dragged the hind carcass with him.

Nick and Tara moved with Will. Martin, his arm around Kit, ushered his wife to safety.

Ailie had been so fascinated by the sight she had failed to move. Goodness and Mercy barked a warning. She was just about to follow her companions when Nash grabbed hold of her arms and drew her away from the tumbling snow, spraying them with a white mist as it came closer.

"You can gawk from a safe distance but not here!"

His words were harsh but the concern she detected in his voice warmed her heart. Admittedly, she had been slow to move. She allowed him to pull her from danger back to the base of the hill behind them. Then he took a stance in front of her as if to guard her from any assault. Not even Will would be so daring in his move to protect her. He might shout at her, compelling her to act, but escort her to safety and guard her person? Only Nash had done that.

Will assured them they would be safe standing on the lee side of the burn up against the hill.

Ailie watched as the avalanche of snow thundered to the bottom of the hill, dumping the last of its frozen cargo into the burn and just beyond it. Her companions stared in wonder.

When the avalanche ended, the glen turned eerily silent, the absence of sound no less dramatic than the thundering Ailie had felt in her bones a moment before.

When the cloud of snow cleared, one hind had disappeared, completely buried, but the other hind's legs stuck out of a large mound.

"We might as well have this one, too," said Will, gesturing to the hind whose legs rose above the snow. "Nick, I'll need you and Nash to help lift the hind out of the snow." He hadn't asked Martin and perhaps it was due to Kit's fearful expression as she clung to her husband.

Calling her dogs to her, Ailie approached Kit. "Are you all right?"

"She's fine," Martin answered for her as Kit nodded, "just a bit shaken."

"Aye, even I have not seen an avalanche before. But I've heard of them trapping people beneath dozens of feet of snow. We were lucky."

Midway down Bridge Street, Robbie darted into the recessed area in front of a door as Hamish turned to look back over his shoulder. The big Scot might not remember him from the tavern but Ferret Eyes would. It would be disastrous for Robbie to be caught now.

His heart pounded in his chest as he stole glances at the retreating men. A minute later, they turned right onto Marketgate.

As soon as they were past the corner, Robbie left his hiding place to follow. Were they leading him on a fool's errand, aware he followed? Or, was this the way to their lodgings? It occurred to him that they might take a different route each day. Were he guarding Kinloch, that would be his strategy. Keeping to the same routes made finding one's prey easier.

Robbie peeked around the corner to see the five men disappear through a door halfway down the street. He did not pause as he passed the door but turned his head to note the address: 7 Marketgate.

The building looked to be a boarding house, two stories high. Clean and presentable from all appearances, yet not a place the gentry would stay. However, sitting less than two streets from the harbor, it provided a good place to hide if one waited for a ship.

Satisfied he had what he needed, Robbie walked on, his boots echoing on the stones beneath his feet. From behind him, he heard another set of footfalls where previously there had been none. It could be just another passerby, but his senses immediately went on alert, the spy in him rising to the fore. Was he being followed?

That night at dinner, the only thing anyone wanted to talk about was the avalanche. Nash listened to his fellow hunters recount their fearful exploit in the glen that could have left them buried in snow like the hinds. Hearing them speak of it, a knot formed in his chest as he relived the horror he had experienced when Ailie had failed to move from the path of the thundering snow rushing toward them.

All day, stalking the deer, he had been acutely aware of her presence. As they rode to the moors, she sat her horse like a lady on a jaunt in Hyde Park, her back straight, her head held high. But once they left the horses with the groom and set out across the moors, Ailie became the stealthy hunter, her eyes searching the landscape for prey, her commands controlling her dogs. When the hill began to violently shed its snow, his only thought had been to get her to safety.

"I'm sorry I snapped at you," he confessed to her on the way back.

Her reply had come with a small smile. "You were right to do so. I was dawdling. Besides, how can I complain when you might have saved my life?"

He shuddered when he remembered how close the snow had come to the very spot on which she'd been standing. Having been concerned for Ailie, he sympathized with the anxious look Emily had given William upon their return. As they were called to dinner, their hostess had not taken her usual seat, but sat adjacent to her husband, reaching out for his hand.

William made light of what had befallen them, telling his wife not to worry, that they were never in danger. But watching Emily, Nash thought she remained unconvinced.

Sharing a look of exasperation with Muriel, sitting across from her, Emily said, "You see how it is, Muriel. William does not understand how I worry whenever he goes hunting, now more than ever."

Muriel muttered, "In my experience, one cannot call the hunter back from the hill if he has a mind to go, my dear. 'Tis a waste of time."

"The good news," William interjected, putting a stop to his wife's fretting, "is that we shall have venison for dinner tomorrow and on other occasions as well. And tonight we celebrate the huntress among us." Raising his glass, he said, "To Tara, the only one of us to get off a successful shot all day!"

Nash cast a glance at Tara who, along with Ailie and Kit, had changed back into a lady's attire for the evening. She appeared quite pleased with herself. "As Nick reminds me, it was a lucky shot. My fellow hunters also had deer in their sights but the hinds failed to cooperate."

Everyone raised their glass. "To Tara!"

"I'm glad I had time to sketch the beauty of the glen before the avalanche," said Kit. "Afterward, all was under snow."

"Do you intend to sketch the avalanche?" asked Emily. "Since I was not there, I'd be interested to see it."

"I might, though it would be from memory."

"It's not something one could easily forget," suggested Tara. "The closest thing is the crashing of a towering wave on a ship's deck, threatening to sweep you into the sea."

Robbie gave Ailie one of his winning smiles. "How did the Mistress of the Setters fare today?"

Jealously rose within Nash when he glimpsed the attraction in his brother's eyes for the girl Nash had begun to think of as his.

"I enjoyed the moors and the dogs had a good time. The avalanche was terribly exciting, of course." She gave no indication of how close she had come to getting buried in snow. "How went your game of piquet?"

When they had returned from the hunt, Robbie was in the library with Muriel and Emily, but Nash had no idea when he had returned. They had not had a chance to speak. Robbie's time in Arbroath must have taken up much of the morning. He wondered how creative Robbie had been in covering his absence from the game.

"I took a long walk," he told Ailie. "When I returned, I felt in need of a nap, so I was late to piquet. I'm afraid it really came down to a game between Emily and the countess."

"You did manage to win a round once you finally arrived," said the countess, "snatching victory from my hand."

"Humph." The twinkle Nash glimpsed in her eye gave away her enjoyment of the game no matter Robbie had won.

Emily laughed. "Don't forget the round you won, Muriel."

"You should have come on the hunt, Robbie," said Nick. "Tara is right; only a storm at sea can beat an avalanche for excitement."

"Unless you were one of the hinds," put in Ailie.

"Aye," said William, "we never did find that second one buried under the snow."

"Our ride along the shore, while perhaps not as exciting as the deer stalking, was breathtaking," offered Mary.

Hugh's smile, directed at his wife, made Nash suspect the Ormonds had spent the afternoon in their chamber. *Ah, the joy of having a devoted wife.* And, just that fast, his thoughts turned to Ailie, who rose from her chair with the other women and departed for the parlor for tea.

Nash leaned in to William. "Might I have a word with you before you retire tonight?"

Robbie paced in his chamber waiting for Nash, who had apparently chosen to linger with the ladies. He, on the other hand, wanted their business done and behind them, so they could enjoy the rest of the holiday. He'd seen far more of Arbroath's taverns than he desired and far too little of William's delightful sister. He had even begun to relish the company of the dowager countess, finding her dry wit refreshing.

The door opened and Nash entered, looking, Robbie thought, a bit too pleased with himself. "I had begun to think you would stay in the parlor till dawn."

Nash took off his coat and hung it on a peg. "I had to speak to William. So, tell me, what happened in Arbroath today?"

Robbie unbuttoned his waistcoat and sat on his bed to pull off his boots. "While you were chasing deer on the moors and avoiding falling snow with the Mistress of the Setters, I managed to locate George Kinloch's lodgings."

Nash's brows rose with a look of surprise. "You followed them?"

"I did."

"You were not spotted, I hope."

"Not by George or his companions but, as I was leaving their street, I might have been followed by someone else. I did not turn to look at him but, by the sound of his boots, he is not a small man. Perhaps I only imagined there was someone on my heels, but the hair on the back of my neck prickled. Fortunately, I lost him after crossing the bridge back to the harbor."

"Who else but one of Kinloch's guards could possibly be following you?"

"They have friends, I'm sure. We have cornered the fox in his den, Nash. 'Tis time to move."

Robbie waited as Nash stared into the fire, one hand on his hip. It was like Nash to be pensive before a major undertaking. He had acted that same way before they had gone to St Peter's Field. "Well?"

"I wonder if we are doing the right thing."

Robbie gave Nash's back a puzzled look. "How could returning a fugitive to gaol be wrong?"

Nash whipped around. "Have you heard nothing since we left London? Kinloch is only a fugitive because it was convenient for the government to charge him with a crime he didn't commit. Together with Henry Hunt, who rots in prison for a speech he never gave, the people here consider Kinloch a hero of sorts, a man who—as Ailie put it—wants only what's fair for the people of Scotland. Even you concede Kinloch's speech in November was not an act of sedition."

"But Sidmouth—"

"Is often wrong, as the scar beneath my hair reminds me."

Robbie and Nash had never before questioned an assignment, yet now Nash did. Something had brought about a change in his thinking. *Or someone.* "It's Ailie, isn't it? You cannot bear for her to know. Are you sure you haven't let your infatuation with the girl cloud your judgment?"

"My feelings for Ailie are not a mere infatuation. I don't like keeping secrets from her, especially one she would not approve of."

"You are making too much of this. We can slip into Arbroath, see Kinloch back in custody and return, all in a few hours. Ailie will be none the wiser. After all, that is the reason we are here."

"*One* of the reasons we are here. Don't forget, the purpose of our sailing to Scotland, as our brothers and our friends believe, was to celebrate Christmastide with all of them."

Too tired to argue with his brother, Robbie pulled off his breeches and shirt and crawled into bed. "Perhaps a night's sleep will clear your mind."

Nash lifted his coat from the peg. "I'm going for a walk. As tomorrow is Christmas Eve and Christmas Day follows, Kinloch will have to wait. We owe it to our friends and family to be here."

The door closed and Robbie turned over, stuffing his pillow under his head. Nash would see reason. He always did.

Ailie was too wound up to sleep. The avalanche and the memory of Nash pulling her from its path had left her unsettled. Did a man act like that toward a woman he considered only a holiday fling? Pacing in her room brought her no respite. Perhaps a walk would do her good. She often walked to the shipyard at night to look at the stars.

Taking up her blue tartan scarf and dark blue cloak, she decided to stop at the kennel to get Goodness and Mercy.

When she arrived, they whimpered, wagging their tails, eager to go with her, despite their excursion over the moors.

With the dogs trotting beside her, she took the path down to the shipyard, burying her hands in the wool of her tartan scarf as she'd forgotten her gloves. At the dock, she stopped to inhale the salty air blowing onshore from the North Sea. Closing her eyes, she listened to the familiar sounds of the night, the water slapping against the ships moored at the dock, an owl hooting from a tree in the distance and the hisses and yowls of the shipyard cats fighting over some rat.

She opened her eyes as the dogs wandered off, sniffing for something of interest.

Gazing up at the night sky. Absent a moon, the stars were on brilliant display. She recognized Orion the hunter from his belt, marked by three stars in an angled row, and the Milky Way that swept across the sky in a great swath of stars as if God had cast them from his great hand.

She stared upward for a long moment, letting her soul grow peaceful in the chilled night air. The sounds around her were soon absorbed by silence.

"She walks in beauty, like the night of cloudless climes and starry skies…"

Her heart leaped at the familiar voice. Before she could turn, Nash pulled her into his warmth and crossed his arms over her chest. She leaned against him, content in the nest of his arms. "You would quote Lord Byron to me?"

"Oh, so you are familiar with our poet?"

"As I am of Rabbie Burns, the Bard of Ayrshire. Byron's mother was a Scot, you know, a Gordon, in fact. He was raised in Aberdeenshire. My governess favored both poets."

Nash pressed a kiss to her temple, his breath warm on her face. "I was not aware of Byron's Scottish origins, but I thought his poem particularly apt for this night… and a fitting description of you. Are you out here admiring the stars all alone?"

His lips ticked her skin, causing her to shiver. "I couldn't sleep."

"My brave lass for whom the night holds no terrors, you rest uneasily?"

He called her his lass. How she loved that. For a passing moment, she wondered if she should tell him about her dreams, but she allowed the moment to pass. "Aye, sometimes."

He nuzzled the side of her head. "As do I."

Turning her to face him, he said, "I am gratified you recognized me from only my voice."

She couldn't see his eyes in the darkness but she felt the intensity of his gaze. "I know *you*, Nash. Not just your voice, but your touch. Only you speak to me in verse and tender words. And, if that weren't enough, I have kissed no other man as I have kissed you."

He pressed his forehead to hers. "As I would have it, sweet Ailie."

Inclining his head, he pressed his lips once, twice and yet a third time to hers, each time pulling away before she could fully enter into the kiss. His teasing lips were more enticing than if he'd kissed her full on the mouth. The soft touch of his lips, their warmth so quickly withdrawn, enticed her. His scent of sandalwood and wool, blended with his own smell, enveloped her.

When his lips lifted from hers, she opened her eyes. "You would tease me?"

"Nay, I would but tempt you to more."

Her eyes had grown accustomed to the dim light, allowing her to see more of his features beneath his dark brows. A lock of his hair had fallen onto his forehead. She brushed it aside. "I would gladly succumb."

This time he did not tempt, but claimed her mouth in a stirring kiss, full of passionate intent. This kiss was different than their first kisses in the woods and the others in the library. It was deeper, more demanding. When his tongue slipped inside her mouth, she yielded, threading her fingers in his hair, holding him to her.

Ripples of pleasure radiated from her lips to her breasts, even to her woman's center, shocking her with the force of it. She had never felt the like of it before. The night around her faded away. Her feet were no longer anchored to the dock, but sailing with him high above it.

There was only Nash and his kiss.

When he lifted his lips from hers, she experienced the same quiet she had on the moors when the avalanche stopped, as if the entire world held its breath. She was glad for the darkness that hid the flush in her cheeks, the burning heat she could feel despite the cold air all around them. But her ragged breathing could not be hidden. Neither could his.

With one arm around her waist, he slid his other hand to her neck, his thumb stroking her jaw. "I cannot seem to stop at one kiss with you, Ailie. 'Tis just as well we are standing on the dock and not sitting on a parlor sofa or I might do something we'd both regret."

"I'll not be regretting that kiss, Nash, not ever. And I'll not be forgetting it either."

"I don't want you to forget. I want you to remember it always."

Her heart soared at his words. If he wanted her to remember his kiss, surely he wanted to be with her beyond his time in Arbroath.

He dropped his hand from her neck to join his other one at her waist. "Have you thought more about going to London, Ailie?"

"Do you mean Muriel's offer to take me under her wing and sponsor me in the *ton*?"

He let his hands fall from her waist and reached for her hand. With determined steps, he began to walk along the dock, taking her with him.

The dogs returned, sniffed at Nash's heels, then ran ahead. The ships, tethered to their moorings, rocked on the water like brooding ghosts.

"Well, that's one way of getting you to London, I suppose. Does it appeal?"

She wondered what thoughts were going through his mind. She detected impatience in his voice. Was he angry as well? Did he want her to come to London?

"I have come to like Muriel very much and would enjoy her company." In a rush of words, she said, "Part of me thinks I should stay to help Emily with the baby, but I could be back by then, couldn't I? Too, our housekeeper, Mrs. Banks, is very good with babies, so perhaps there is no reason not to go. Is that what you meant?"

He was just ahead of her but she heard his sigh, his warm breath a cloud in the cold night air. "You might have more choices before we set sail for London."

She pulled back on his hand and stopped. He turned to face her. "You're being cryptic, Nash Powell."

"I am... for the now, as you would say." Even in the darkness, she could see his white teeth as he smiled.

Perhaps he was not angry, after all. "Oh, very well, be mysterious."

He tilted his head to the sky. "Look, Ailie, there's a shooting star!"

A bright star streaked across the black velvet canvas above them, making all the other stars seem dim by comparison. "They do come at this time of year."

He squeezed her hand. "I shall remember this one as coming for us."

A wave of joy washed over her. The thought that the star might mark more than the time of the year pleased her immensely. He had recited poetry to her, told her to remember his kiss and now he chose a shooting star to mark their time together. Could he come to love a Scot? Could she love an Englishman? The realization that she might already love him made her pause. If she weren't careful, if he just sailed away come the New Year, she could be left alone and hurt. But it was too late to guard her heart.

They made their way back to the house. He waited while she returned the dogs to their kennel and then escorted her to her chamber. Like the gentleman he was, he bowed, kissed her hand and wished her a good night before disappearing down the dark corridor to his own room.

Ailie floated into her chamber, certain she traveled on an invisible cloud.

Before she blew out the candle, she opened her diary, dipped the quill in the ink and thought long before she wrote.

23 December

Today's stalking for the red hind led us into the path of a terrible avalanche. I have never seen one before, but I knew enough of them to recognize the great mass of snow rushing toward us for what it was. Nash pulled me from danger as I stood paralyzed before the onrushing snow. He was quite cross with me. At first I was angry, but then I wondered, did his being cross mean he cares? Or, might he have merely acted the gallant? But that was before tonight's kiss in the shipyard beneath the stars.

I will never forget that kiss as long as I live.

As I consider my future, I pray he will be in it. I would like to see his face every day, to always know only his kiss. Nash asked me about Muriel's invitation to go to London, which looms ahead. I am inclined to go.

Yet the strange dreams still trouble my sleep. I feel like I am hurtling toward something, but what?

Chapter 15

24 December, Christmas Eve

The next morning Nash did not wake with a changed mind. Instead, he was more resolved than ever to try and persuade Robbie to allow Kinloch to sail. Besides, what harm could the man do in France? He would be gone from Scotland and unable to inspire those who might be inclined to rebellion.

Nash had just finished shaving when Robbie began to stir. Patting his face dry, Nash turned to his brother. "I've lost all taste for Sidmouth's assignment."

Robbie opened one eye and then closed it. "You would have me go to Arbroath alone?"

The words echoed in Nash's mind, more unsettling than a blow. With them, Robbie played his trump card, leaving Nash torn between his loyalty to his twin and love for Ailie.

Love is what he felt for her, plain and simple, and she would have Kinloch go free. Yet Robbie had been his constant companion since they were toddlers.

The irony of was not lost on him. Robbie had always envisioned himself Nash's protector, yet Nash could not allow Robbie to go to

Arbroath alone to face the ruffians guarding Kinloch.

He let out an exasperated sigh. There was no help for it. He would go to town with Robbie and hope he could turn his brother from his intended course.

"All right. I will go with you to Arbroath the day the *Panmure* is to sail, but I still have reservations about your cause concerning Kinloch. The more I think on it, the more I wonder, just why was the man charged with sedition in the first place?"

Robbie sat up. "I remind you, Brother, Kinloch might have been arrested in Dundee, but the charge against him came from London. Our lot has never been to question Sidmouth."

"Manchester changed that for me, Robbie. None but the basest of cowards would attack unarmed men, women and children. I cannot justify the deaths on St Peter's Field, nor can I excuse the government's failure to dispense justice after." Fury rose in his chest as he remembered that day. He shook his head. "No, I cannot."

Robbie cast him a worrisome glance. "I can see you mean to be stubborn. Very well, we shall celebrate Christmas and deal with Kinloch on Boxing Day."

Good Lord. Nash had forgotten entirely the *Panmure* would sail on that holiday, unobserved by the Scots.

"You do recall that the twenty-sixth is Boxing Day?"

"I didn't until you mentioned it, but now that I think of it, when I first learned the *Panmure*'s captain meant to sail on the twenty-sixth, the date sounded familiar. 'Tis the day when Mother gives gifts to the servants."

Ailie woke from the dream, her chest heaving. This time, she did not have to call back the images, for they were terrifying and indelibly stamped in her mind. One of the Powell twins lay on the ground, his eyes closed and his skin pale as a ghost, as blood gushed from his head.

Was the gruesome specter a prophetic sign foretelling of one twin's death? Her mind shouted, "No!" If the man were Nash, she could not bear his loss. And, if Robbie, Nash would never be the same, having lost part of himself.

She sprang from her bed, determined to banish her rising dread. Perhaps the dream merely reflected an irrational fear after the avalanche. But she knew it was not so.

Lighting a candle to add to that of the fire burning steadily, she went about her morning toilette, dabbing a bit of lily of the valley scent on her neck and wrists before donning her blue velvet wrapper.

Taking a seat at her dressing table, she combed the tangles from her hair she had forgotten to plait the night before.

A pale young woman looked back at her from the mirror, her brows drawn together in worry. She could not very well greet their guests looking like this. She set down her comb and pinched her cheeks. Then she thought of Nash kissing her under the stars and a blush arose on her sensitive skin.

A soft knock sounded on the door and Rhona peeked her head in. "Ye're up?"

"Aye, I woke early."

"Just as well." Rhona opened the door wide and entered. "Yer guests are all awake, too. Lord Ormond and his wife are having an early breakfast before going fer an early morning ride. The countess is up, too, and reminded me that today is the English Christmas Eve. She seemed verra excited about it, saying her Mrs. Platt is to make special pies."

Ailie started. "I completely forgot! That means the men will be dragging in the Yule log and Emily will need help with decorating."

"Ye ken," said Rhona, picking up Ailie's brush and taking over the job of her hair, "I rather like the English celebration of the Christ Child's birth. 'Tis proper to have a festive celebration."

Rhona's long strokes with the brush were soothing. Ailie closed her eyes, feeling the tension leave her shoulders. "It would not be difficult to welcome the Savior's birth each year as they do. I just realized that tomorrow is Saturday and the first day of their Christmastide. I expect our friends will want to attend an Anglican church. It will have to be St Mary's."

"And then ye'll all be off to the Parish Kirk the next day?"

Ailie opened her eyes, as she considered the possibility. "Two days of church might be a bit much. Perhaps Will won't mind if we do not attend this Sunday."

"He'll be wanting to please the mistress, so St Mary's on the morrow seems fitting."

"Aye, you are right. After all, if Emily were in London, she'd be attending the Anglican church service on Christmas Day."

George Kinloch stood before the window in the largest of his rooms in Miss Grahame's boarding house, staring at the stone buildings across the street, as drab as the sky above them. Behind him, the men's voices faded as his thoughts turned to his family.

Were they getting ready to celebrate Christmas? Would they be in church tomorrow?

His last letter to Helen had been written from Edinburgh on the fifteenth of December, telling her he was leaving the country. If all went well, his next one would be sent from France, encouraging her to come and bring their girls. His sons would remain in Scotland to see to his affairs.

With only two days before his departure, plans were well advanced. Taking his father's middle name as his surname, he would travel as Mr. Oliphant. His cousin Grant would arrive the night before they sailed, bringing with him a wig. George had agreed to wear it until they were free of Britain.

His conscience did not accuse him of any crime, but he would still be uneasy until they sailed. At least he'd be sailing to a country that had once welcomed him.

The angst he felt was that brought on by the distance that separated him from his loved ones about which he could do nothing.

As he turned to face the room, the voices resumed their normal volume.

Hamish was making inquiry of his brother Iain. "Ye followed 'im?"

"Aye, after he passed the boardin' house, I slipped oot tae see where the mon went. He were the same one that were in the tavern, ye ken?"

"And?" Derek said. "What'd ye learn?"

"Not much. He crossed Shambles Bridge so I cum back."

Hamish cuffed his brother on the side of the head. "Ye dolt. Ye should've followed 'im tae see where he went."

Muriel was in her element at this time of year. The earl had always insisted on helping her decorate Claremont House, the impressive four-story edifice in London that he had purchased for her, which was still her home.

The moment the kissing bough dangled from the entry hall chandelier, he would sweep her into his arms and kiss her soundly. "We must christen it properly, my love."

She remembered the tradition with great fondness. That they had never had children of their own was a source of deep sadness, particularly at Christmas, but the earl made up for it by inviting all their nieces, nephews and cousins for the holidays. It was one of those cousins who now had the title and lived in the family's country estate.

Rhona bustled about Muriel's chamber, folding her nightclothes and straightening the bed. "There's a fine breakfast waiting fer ye this morning, my lady. Ye'll need yer strength if ye want to participate in everything the mistress has planned."

"I don't wonder there will be much to do since Emily tells me she has been busy planning for Christmas for quite some time."

"Aye, she has. Fer the now, the greenery sits in piles in nearly every room of the house just waiting to be hung. Three footmen stand ready to assist. Early this morning, the mistress went to the orangery to cut the flowers she wants fer the table. Even the kitchen's to be decorated."

"I'm certain Mrs. Platt won't mind helping. She always decorates our kitchen at Claremont House with a great deal of aplomb."

"Martha will be grateful. She has never done it afore and she has taken a liking to your Mrs. Platt." The maid paused in her work and turned to face Muriel. "I fergot to tell ye the master has arranged for sleds so all of ye can slide down the snowiest hill."

Muriel smiled to herself. "My charges will certainly look forward to that. They're an adventurous lot."

Rhona laughed. "Aye, my lady, and Mistress Ailie is surely one of them."

In the dining room, Muriel wished everyone a good morning, noting, for the first time, Aileen was not sitting between the Powell twins.

Did this break from their happy threesome reflect some change in their relationship?

She took the seat adjacent to Emily and was about to ask for coffee when a footman approached and inquired if he might assist with her choices. "Thank you, my good man. Indeed, you may. Eggs and biscuits would serve. And some hot coffee post-haste." The footman dipped his head, poured her coffee and went to the sideboard.

Muriel reached out to pat Emily's hand. "How are you this Christmas Eve morning, my dear?"

Emily placed her other hand on her slightly rounded belly, her eyes sparkling with excitement. "I am splendid, Muriel. This morning, I felt the baby quicken for the first time!"

From the other end of the table, William lifted his coffee in toast. "The bairn is a braw lad."

"Or lass," said Emily with a teasing smile directed at her husband.

"Lass, definitely," insisted Aileen, winking at her sister-in-law. The good-humored exchange between the three of them brought a smile to Muriel's face. Her friend had found a good man and a good home.

The footman returned, setting a plate before her. The smell of hot biscuits wafted to her nostrils. "Excellent."

From across the table, whichever Powell twin it was gave her a broad grin, his straight white teeth on display. "And how fares the countess this morning?"

Surely that smile had to be Robbie's. "I am quite well, thank you, but don't be expecting me to go sledding with you, young man."

"No matter that, Muriel," came his reply, accompanied by a smirk. "As soon as the kissing bough is up, I'm claiming a kiss."

Muriel took a sip of her coffee. "I expect that will be the pinnacle of my day."

"Speaking of our day," said William, "once we have dragged in the Yule log from the shed and helped Emily to decorate the house, those of you who wish may adjourn to a nearby hill to try our skill with a sled, Muriel and Emily excluded, of course."

"Thanks to our deer-stalkers," Emily said, "we'll have a special Christmas Eve dinner tonight of roast venison. And my sister-in-law has graciously agreed to play the pianoforte for us in the parlor afterward."

"English Christmas carols and hymns of the season," put in Ailie, adding with enthusiasm, "I've been practicing!"

Both Powell twins grinned at the pretty girl, but it was Nash who said, "I shall look forward to that."

Robbie took hold of the heavy birch log. Together with Nash, William and Nick, he heaved it onto the sled where it landed with a loud thud. Tara and Ailie, who had come to lend their encouragement, clapped their hands.

Nick stood back, wiping his forehead with the back of his hand. "That log's as heavy as my best bower anchor."

"Ain't light," observed Robbie.

William picked up the large loop of rope at the head of the sled and glanced at Robbie and Nash. "How about if Nick and I pull while you two push from the sides?"

Robbie and the others agreed.

William said, "There's enough snow on the ground to help us, but 'tis all uphill."

Nick laughed. "You would have to remind us of the hill."

Robbie stared down at the giant birch log William's men had dried, stripped of bark and cut to fit the fireplace. Now, they had only to get it there. He and Nash took the sides of the log and began to push. Tara and Ailie stood to the side urging them onward.

Nick and William took hold of the rope at the front of the sled and began to pull. "My men could have brought in the log," said William, "but where is the fun in that?"

"Indeed," said Nick, "I always thought hauling in anchors to be 'fun', too."

From the side, Tara laughed. "'Twill do you good."

Robbie gave the log a shove. "This might be my only chance to add 'dragging in a Yule log' to my list of skills."

Ailie rolled her eyes.

"A list that is doubtless in desperate need of additions," tossed in Nash. Robbie was glad his brother could jest given the serious nature of their recent conversations. Until this assignment for Sidmouth, they had always enjoyed doing things together.

"Put your backs into it men!" William shouted.

With many grunts and groans, they pulled and pushed the heavy log up the hill. Once, it had threatened to slip away on a patch of ice, but they recovered it and pushed on. Though he might have chosen another activity for Christmas Eve morning, Robbie enjoyed the camaraderie of his brothers and Will spurred on by the cheers of Tara and Ailie.

Eventually, they reached the top of the hill. By that time, Robbie was wiping his brow. His cravat had begun to feel like a constricting snake around his throat.

"Make way for the Yule log!" William shouted when they arrived in front of the house. Like the rest of them, their host was breathing hard.

The front door opened and Emily stepped out with the butler, who appeared quite beside himself to see his master and some of his guests sweating as they lifted the birch log from the sled and placed it on the long runner Emily had provided for them.

"It's a magnificent log!" exclaimed Emily, welcoming them into the house. "Come see, Muriel!"

Robbie and his companions grunted as they lugged the log into the parlor and lifted it onto the grate. Basking in the smiles of their hostess and the countess, Robbie and the others stood before the great log, admiring their achievement.

A surge of pride coursed through Robbie. "By God, we have done it!"

The rest of their group gathered around, applauding. Hugh slapped William on the back. "Great job, my friend!"

"No thanks to you," William teased.

"You wound me," said Hugh. "I would have offered to pull the sled behind the worthy mount you gave me, had you but asked. However, I can see you meant to do without such help."

William smiled. "I did, didn't I?"

Now that the log was in place, Robbie thought it was time to light it. "Shall you put flame to the Yule log, William?"

"Aye." With a look of regret, he told Emily, "We don't have the bit of last year's log to use, as tradition requires, but next year we will." He turned to the butler. "Lamont, can you take it from here?"

The butler bowed. "I will see it done, sir."

Robbie stifled a laugh at the serious tone of the butler when everyone else was in a jovial mood. "Do we next hang greenery?" he asked.

"Oh yes," said Emily. "That is just what we should do. The ladies and I will supervise. Pick a room, Ladies! The parlor where we stand is not the only room to be decorated. We have the dining room, the library, the study and even the kitchen. Whatever greenery is left over will go into your chambers. That way, the whole house will smell of the woods and Christmastide."

Robbie gave The Grand Countess a lopsided grin. "Be sure they hang a kissing bough, Muriel."

"Humph," came her reply, but he could see a faint smile on her face.

"I have an idea for a kissing bough, Muriel," said Emily. "And since you have more experience with decorating than the rest of us, why don't you take this room?"

"As you wish, my dear." The countess took up her quizzing glass to examine the pile of greens laid to one side. "Dashed lot of plants, Emily, but where is the mistletoe?"

"We don't have mistletoe in Arbroath, Muriel, but we can still make a kissing bough out of other greenery and some red and white flowers I cut from the orangery just this morning. Thanks to Ailie, we've lovely red berries. I'll leave you a footman to help you."

"Very good," said Muriel.

"I'm going to get Mrs. Banks and tackle the kitchen," said Emily. "I just hope Martha is in a mood to cooperate. Join me when you're done here, Muriel, and we can have a meeting with our cooks."

"Excellent idea," said Muriel. "Else there will be kale in the stuffing."

Robbie chuckled. He was certain the countess' dislike for the vegetable was not as great as she made out. He remained in the parlor to see how the ladies parceled out the rooms. Mary chose the library and Tara the study. Kit wanted to be able to go from room to room, sketching, so she chose none.

When Ailie headed to the dining room, Robbie followed with Nash. Best to keep their friends guessing.

"Wonderful," chimed in Emily as they departed. "Just ask a footman if you require assistance."

The three of them stepped into the dining room and Ailie paused, her gaze shifting from the side table to the dining table. "Where do we hang the greens?"

Robbie laughed. "That's right, 'tis an English tradition." Hands on his hips, he said, "Well, let's see. Almost any surface will do, but certainly on the sideboard, down the center of the table and on top of that painting."

Mirth danced in her lovely eyes. "Do show some respect. You speak of my father."

Nash went to stand beneath the large portrait. "*That* is your father? All this time, I've been looking at it thinking it was some distant relation. I don't see a resemblance."

From where Robbie stood next to Ailie, he could see her father was a formidable man. "It's there in the chin," he said with a smirk aimed at Ailie. "Both are stubborn."

She swatted his shoulder. "Behave, Robbie!"

"You must admit," Robbie said, "you do have his chin."

"Aye, I suppose I do, but for all that, my father is a good man and has built some fine ships."

Nash crossed the room to ask Ailie, "Is there a ladder, per chance?"

Ailie glanced at the footman, standing just inside the large doorway like a statue. With a nod, he departed, saying he'd bring one straight away.

Soon, they were covered in greenery, red berries and white flowers. It was a new activity for Robbie. In London, their mother had always seen to decorating the house on Christmas Eve.

Ailie handed up a hawthorn branch to Nash, who stood on the ladder in front of her father's portrait. "Ouch!" she shrieked and stuck her finger in her mouth. Robbie thought it a tempting sight. "Mind the thorns," she warned Nash.

Nash added the hawthorn branch to the pine branches he had already placed on top of the gilded frame. "Thanks for the warning."

Robbie entwined greenery around the candelabra on the dining room table and thought of his other Christmas holidays. About now, he would be sinking into a comfortable leather chair at his club, brandy in hand, with nothing more on his mind than a lady's face and that evening's card game. Instead, here he was in the frozen north decorating a table.

Since Nash had claimed the only available lady in sight, Robbie would concentrate on their current assignment for Sidmouth. And, for that, he needed Nash.

"I'm going to see if Emily has some velvet ribbon for bows," said Ailie. "I think they would look nice on the chandelier."

As she flounced out of the room, taking the footman with her, Nash looked down at him from the ladder. "I don't even want to think about tying bows on that hanging tower of crystal."

Robbie regarded his brother. "I expect you will if Ailie wishes it."

Nash breathed out a sigh Robbie took as significant. "You're right, of course,"

"By the bye, Brother, have you thought more on your reservations about our apprehending Kinloch? Might I hope for a change of mind?"

Nash peered down from his perch. "I told you I would go, and I will. But as for a change of mind? Not a chance."

Chapter 16

By late afternoon, tired from the sledding they had indulged in, Nash bathed and went to his chamber to dress for dinner. Boughs of holly now framed the mirror and fragrant pine branches circled the candlestick on the small table next to his bed. Appetizing smells of apples baking with cinnamon, spicy mince pie and plum pudding wafted through the air.

"Christmas has definitely arrived at the Stephens' house," he said as donned his clothes.

Robbie looked at him from the edge of his bed where he sat pulling on his newly shined boots. "It has indeed."

"There is something about Christmastide that brings new dishes to the table and new smells to my nose. They remind me of the season and home."

Robbie stood and reached for his jacket. "London awaits us. Do not be so captured by William's lovely sister you forget all we have waiting for us once we complete our task for Lord Sidmouth."

Nash donned the clothing he had set out earlier. "I have not forgotten; I've been planning. In fact, I have been giving some thought to what we might tell Sidmouth should the Radical Laird slip through our fingers."

Robbie shot him a sharp glance. "Lord Sidmouth considers us to be better at our work than to let that happen."

"Does he? We delivered no revolutionaries to him in Manchester."

His attention fixed on the mirror, Robbie tied his cravat for the second time. "The Home Secretary well knows that bit of work got out of hand for no misstep of ours. Besides, after his soldiers plucked Henry Hunt from the speaker's platform, there were no revolutionaries to be had."

Nash returned his brother the smile of a saint. "You make my point."

Late that afternoon, Muriel stood in the parlor admiring the greenery scattered about. "Oh, Muriel," Emily said breathlessly, as she entered the parlor, "you have done a marvelous job here. It is beyond lovely! Why, it's the equal of your decorations in London I have long admired!"

Muriel was quite pleased with the way the large room had turned out. Every painting's gilded frame was adorned with boughs of pine and holly. A garland of holly, ivy and rosemary, intertwined with white Christmas roses, spanned the length of the fireplace mantel and draped down each side. "It does look rather like Christmas, if I do say so myself."

"Oh yes, it does. The scent of all the greenery, the Yule log fire and the smell of wassail has quite put me in the mood."

William peeked his head in the doorway. "The kissing bough has just been hung in the entry hall. Want to partake in the historic event?"

"Come," urged Emily, taking her arm. "You must see it. William made the frame and Ailie and I filled it with greenery. No mistletoe, of course, but the holly, rosemary, and other evergreens make for a nice arrangement. We'll just pretend there is mistletoe."

"Given your guests," said Muriel, "I'm quite certain they need pretend nothing to make good use of the bough."

They stood in the entry admiring the green and red bough hanging from the chandelier.

"The apples add a nice touch, don't you think?" asked Emily.

"I do," said Muriel. "And the red velvet bows are just the right embellishment."

"Ailie thought to add them. They also grace the dining room chandelier, though I cannot imagine how she and the Powell twins managed to do it."

"They are very clever young men," said Muriel. "I imagine they can accomplish most anything they set their minds to."

"The house has never looked so grand, *Leannan*," said William. "You and Muriel and the other ladies are to be congratulated for bringing Christmas to Arbroath." He pulled Emily under the bough and into his arms. "Let us be the first to christen the bough."

While William and Emily managed that, Muriel returned to the parlor where a footman was just ladling out the wassail. "I'll have one of those, my good man."

Ailie had been late to dress for dinner. While she had not engaged in the sledding, she had helped Mrs. Banks and Emily put the finishing touches on the kitchen decorations. Unable to resist, she had snatched a piece of warm shortbread, cooling on the worktable and was just leaving the kitchen when Emily asked her to help finish the kissing bough. Only after that had she gone to her chamber to bathe.

"'Tis an unusual gown Lady Emily had made fer ye," said Rhona. "'Tis silk, no?"

Ailie ran her hand down the front of the high-waisted gown, the silk a tartan of red, green and gold that rustled as she walked. She might not have chosen the particular plaid, but it went remarkably well with her hair. "Aye, 'tis silk. Perhaps I should wear my hair up tonight, it being Christmas Eve."

"'Twould be pretty that way." Ailie took a seat and Rhona went to work, fashioning Ailie's hair into a long looping knot on the back of her head. A few curls were left out to frame her face and dangle down her nape.

When her maid had finished, Ailie stared into the mirror, seeing a remarkable change.

"You're a wonder, Rhona. I look positively... elegant."

"'Tis the truth, ye do. Just remember to take yer cloak should ye go out into the night air, or yer neck will freeze."

Ailie laughed. "That and the rest of me. Perhaps, I'll confine any walks to the orangery."

When she entered the parlor, filled with their guests, Ailie was glad she had taken care with her appearance.

"A lovely change," said Emily, coming to her side. Her sister-in-law wore an ivory silk gown with a red shawl. Her ebony hair was curled around her face, a contrast to her alabaster skin. "I'm delighted the gown fits you so well."

Emily ushered her to the other ladies standing to one side as Ailie thanked her for the gown.

"I will do a sketch of all the ladies," remarked Kit, her dark red tresses the color of Ailie's mother's hair before it began turning gray. Ailie was surprised at Kit's choice of gown, but the scarlet silk brocade was quite striking on her.

Mary left Hugh's arm to come to join them. "I have never seen silk tartan before. It's exquisite on you, Ailie." Dressed like a young queen, Mary's gown had been fashioned from pale green satin to which had been added a gold sash. Her fair hair was sleeked back and confined to her crown.

"You would pay me compliments," Ailie said to the other women, "yet your gowns and hair are stunning." Truly, Ailie was overwhelmed.

Even the ladies in Aberdeen were not more elegantly attired than these.

Tara, Ailie's kindred spirit, had set her informal clothing aside to don a silk gown the same color as her blue-green eyes. "I see we are all dressed in similar fashion for the evening," she remarked. "The maids must have been busy."

"I think it fitting we dress like this for your English Christmas," said Ailie, "but for Hogmanay, which you call New Year's Eve, you need not dress so elegantly. If the weather cooperates, we'll be in Stonehaven."

"Another adventure!" exclaimed Tara. "How exciting."

Muriel left the men standing at the fireplace to join Ailie and the other women. "Why, you ladies all look like you are attending one of my balls."

Emily gave Muriel's gown a long perusal. "Are you certain you do not speak of yourself?"

The women fixed their gazes on Muriel's golden gown. The bodice was trimmed in jet beads and the golden overskirt ended in stylish Vandyke points trimmed in the same beads and black silk tassels. Around her neck, she wore her customary pearls, only wound double to fall higher. Circling her silver hair was a band of crystals and, soaring above all, a large ivory feather.

"Oh, my," said Mary. "You have quite outdone yourself, Countess."

"*This?*" Muriel looked down at her gown. "Pshaw. It's at least ten years old though, as I recall, it was unique at the time. My dressmaker copied the gown from one of those dolls she managed to sneak out of Paris."

"It's timeless," remarked Kit, "as are you, dear Muriel."

"Humph," Muriel murmured, but Ailie could tell she was pleased. Ailie only wished Grandfather Ramsay could be here to admire her.

"Shall we join the men?" inquired Emily. "I do believe they are staring at us. Clustered together as we are, they might be reticent to approach, thinking we are engaged in some discussion fit only for feminine ears."

"Childbirth, you mean," said Mary. "You are right. We'd best go rescue them."

With that, Ailie and Emily ventured forth to greet the men and the other ladies followed.

Nash greeted Ailie with an approving smile, his hazel eyes sparkling. "You are lovely." In his eyes, Ailie saw more than just the compliment and fought her rising flush.

"I must agree with my brother," said Robbie. "The Mistress of the Setters outshines all the ladies tonight."

She accepted a cup of wassail from a footman. "Why thank you, Robbie, but I have seen them and I know you lie." She shifted her gaze from Robbie to Nash, taking in their identical attire. Both wore green velvet tailcoats, ivory waistcoats and black trousers. "Did you dress this way to confuse us all?"

"'Tis a Christmas tradition," said Nash, taking a drink of the cup he held. "We defy our family to try and tell us apart."

"When we intentionally ape each other, not just in our clothing but in our speech," added Robbie, "few can do it."

Ailie was curious to know how alike the twins could appear. "What about your parents? Don't they know their sons?"

Robbie exchanged his empty glass for another brandy from a passing tray. "Eventually they come to it after a bit of conversation."

"Well, promise you will never try and confuse me. It would be most disconcerting."

The twins hesitated, exchanging a look, and then said together, "We promise."

The dinner that followed was a worthy feast. They ate the succulent roast venison with roast vegetables and potatoes while Will told stories of his first Christmas in London. He had celebrated the holiday with his chum, Ormond, who took him to his country home to meet his family.

"We did a lot of riding as I recall," said Hugh.

"Aye, and a lot of eating and drinking," added William. "If you think our home is large, Ailie, you should see the Duke of Albany's estate in Ruislip outside of London."

"That's my parents' home," explained Hugh. "Most of the time, Mary and I live in our townhouse in London."

Mary smiled at Ailie. "If you accept Muriel's invitation, you must visit us in Mayfair. I will invite the ladies for tea."

"That is most kind of you." Ailie snuck a glance at Nash, seeing an invitation in his eyes.

For dessert, they had Will's favorite, cranachan, a Scottish tradition their English guests had not sampled before.

"Anything in it we should know about?" asked Hugh, his spoon suspended above the layered confection.

"Not unless you are averse to toasted oatmeal, cream, honey, raspberries and a dash of brandy," replied Ailie. "I assure you, no kale is hiding beneath the layers."

Everyone laughed and picked up their spoons.

"Our cook bottled the raspberries herself last summer," offered Emily.

Will licked some of the honeyed confection from his bottom lip. "If you don't want yours, Ormond, old chum, I'd be happy to take it from you." He made as if to reach his spoon toward Hugh's cranachan.

Hugh raised his spoon like a sword poised to repel an attack. "You're not getting mine 'old chum'. I do believe I will like the dessert."

Many chuckles echoed around the table.

"I like both the cranachan and the shortbread," said Nash with a grin aimed at Ailie.

Ailie tossed him a teasing glance. "I'm relieved we have finally found a Scottish dish or two you like."

When dinner was concluded, they retired as a group to the parlor for tea, port and brandy. Ailie played the songs on the pianoforte she had practiced for their guests: *The Twelve Days of Christmas*, *While Shepherds Watched Their Flocks at Night* and *Joy to the World*.

Everyone gathered around to sing.

Will's strong tenor voice, at times, rose above the others. The Powell men sang with vigor, joining the ladies to make wonderful music, at times jolly and at other times reverent. Tara, it turned out, sang beautifully, so Ailie encouraged her to sing a solo from *Joy to the World*.

When Ailie finished playing, the faces around her all bore smiles.

As she rose from the bench, Mary encouraged her husband to take a turn at the pianoforte. "My husband is a remarkable talent," said Mary. "His mother taught him to play as a boy."

Ailie went to stand with the others as Hugh agreed to play for them. Nash made room for her, taking her hand, hidden in the folds of her skirt.

Hugh flipped the tails of his coat behind him and spread his long fingers over the keys. He began to play Handel's Hallelujah chorus from the *Messiah*, filling the room with the glorious sounds. Ailie listened with rapt attention, transported by the spirited music.

When Hugh's fingers lifted from the keys, there was silence for a moment. Then everyone burst into applause, even their dour butler standing at the parlor door, praising, Ailie thought, not just Hugh's considerable talent, but also the Messiah for whom Handel had written the piece.

Christmas Day

At dawn, Ailie padded downstairs and set out into the cold morning. Knowing it would be a busy day, she wanted to give the dogs a run before they were fed. Like the day before, gray clouds hung low overhead. She sniffed the air, recognizing the scent of snow on the wind.

When she let Goodness and Mercy out of their kennel, they greeted her enthusiastically but were silent when normally they would have barked. They always acted that way just before a snowfall.

Heading toward the dock, she spotted a lone figure in a greatcoat and top hat walking ahead of her. The setters bounded ahead, wagging their tails.

"Ho! What have we here?" said Nash, bending to pet their dark heads. "A Happy Christmas to you, Goodness and Mercy."

"You're up early," said Ailie, coming up to him. She could not hide the joy she felt at seeing him. Beneath his hat, his cheeks were red from the cold. He'd wrapped a green woolen scarf around his neck. Even in the dull light, his green and gold eyes sparkled.

"I thought to watch for the impending snow," he said. "Want to join me?"

"I would like that." She turned to walk beside him.

He offered his gloved hand and she took it. "In London, I like to watch it when it first comes down. I like the feel of snowflakes on my face."

Ailie inwardly smiled, seeing the small boy in him emerge as he turned his face to the sky expectantly.

They walked down the hill, the dogs running ahead. A short ways on, he said, "I like this time of morning when all is still, though typically, I'd be looking for the sun to be rising over the sea."

A line from Burns came to her. *"We two have paddled in the stream, from morning sun till dine; But seas between us broad have roared since days of long ago."*

"Another of Burns' poems?" he said, giving her a lopsided grin.

"Aye, one that reminds me of us."

Nash's brows drew together beneath the brim of his hat. "What seas roar between us, Ailie?"

"The timeless ones between Scots and Sassenachs, I suppose. But I sense there is more I cannot see."

They had come halfway down the path and he paused, turning to face her. "Not between us, Ailie. Any distance between us can soon be erased by time together." The chilled air around them grew heavy with the anticipated snow. "Do you worry about *us*?"

She dropped her gaze, pondering what to say, then looked up. "You have not known me long enough to be aware of the Ramsay women's second sight but, aye, I worry. My dreams speak a warning of danger." She could not bring herself to tell him all that her dreams revealed.

He pulled her close. "Ailie, see only what is in my eyes." He took her head in his hands and kissed her. When their lips met, her heavy heart lifted.

As he raised his head, she opened her eyes to meet his steady gaze. In the depths of his hazel eyes, she saw his longing, his desire and what might even be love.

"Can you see my feelings for you?"

"Aye."

"Then come." He took her hand and pulled her along toward the dock just as the snow began to fall. "Let us not worry. Instead, let us celebrate Christmas by greeting the new snow together."

After a light breakfast, Nash again ventured into the gently falling snow, this time with Ailie and the others for the walk to Arbroath town and the Christmas service at St Mary's.

Christmas had always been special to him, this one even more so with Ailie beside him. William and his sister had graciously agreed to attend church with their Anglican friends where, he assured them, Reverend Bruce would undoubtedly welcome them all, "even the Scots Presbyterians."

"After all," quipped William as he struck off down the same road Nash had traveled before, "we're all Jock Tamson's bairns."

Nash raised a brow to Ailie. "Jock Tamson?"

"'Tis a Lowland Scots' expression. 'Jock Tamson' is our way of referring to John Thomson, the minister of Duddingston Kirk in Edinburgh. He refers to his congregation as his bairns. Because he is well loved and well connected, the expression has spread to other parts of Scotland. It just means we are all one in the sight of God."

"Ah," said Robbie, "I like that. No reason we can't observe the day together as long as we begin in one church or the other, hmm?"

Ailie directed a winning smile at Robbie. Nash experienced a pang of jealousy, as he always did when she gave her attention to his twin. He had hoped Robbie had given up his quest for the Mistress of the Setters, as he called her, but with Robbie, one never knew.

Nash did not want to disturb the mood by advising William that even though the Powell family attended an Anglican church, they were also Methodists. Their French mother, formerly a Catholic, had accepted the teachings of John Wesley and passed them along to her then growing family.

"Will you mind missing your own service tomorrow?" Nash asked Ailie. William had told them since tomorrow was Boxing Day, they would keep the English tradition of giving gifts to servants and baskets for Arbroath's poor, and not attend the Parish Kirk's Sunday service.

She shook her head. "One day of the week for worship together is good. Besides, no kirk will be celebrating Christmas tomorrow."

The town, now familiar to Nash, somehow looked different with the snow falling. They walked on, passing the harbor, and a cold shudder of alarm coursed through him when he realized St Mary's was located at the bottom of High Street, one street away from Marketgate where Kinloch lodged and a short distance from the harbor and the *Panmure*.

All too close in proximity for his comfort.

He exchanged a look with Robbie, seeing the discomfit on his twin's face. What if Kinloch was walking the street with his guards and happened to see them? Would they be recognized in a gentleman's clothing? He wondered, too, if anyone attending the service would remember him or Robbie from their afternoons spent in the taverns. He comforted himself in the knowledge that the vast majority of Scots were Presbyterians, like Ailie and William. Thus, it was logical to suppose that Kinloch's religious affiliation would be as well.

But, as they entered the church, Nash realized he had been wrong.

Brushing snow from his greatcoat, he happened to look over his shoulder and glimpsed Kinloch sitting in the last pew flanked by his guards. He wore the same commoner's garb, however, the hat was gone. Apparently, when the men in the church removed their hats, Kinloch did as well. The baldpate Nash had always assumed was covered by the too large hat was now on full display. Kinloch's gesture of respect had to make his guards nervous. Their furtive glances around them suggested as much.

With their two older brothers and Hugh, who was also dark-haired, Nash and Robbie would not go unnoticed. William, too, was tall. So it was not surprising the five tall men and their ladies drew many interested glances as they moved toward the vacant front pews.

When he was halfway down the aisle, Nash removed his hat. As he waited for their group to file into the pews, he spoke into Robbie's ear. "Kinloch is here. Last row on the right."

Robbie nodded but didn't turn.

All through the service, Nash tried to focus on the hymns they were singing and the Christmas message, but the feeling he was being watched, that eyes bored into the back of his head, made that impossible. A glance across Ailie to Robbie told him his twin was experiencing the same unease.

Ailie sat close so that Nash could feel the heat of her through her cloak. A sudden desire to protect her seized him. He didn't want her mixed up in this; he didn't want Kinloch's rough guards aware of the Stephens or their shipyard, yet they had only to ask to learn the shipyard's location. At least tomorrow Kinloch would be gone. Nash prayed the man from Dundee would slip out of Arbroath's harbor with nary a word said, but a niggling doubt suggested it would not be that simple.

Once the service ended, they rose to leave. A quick look toward the rear of the sanctuary told him that Kinloch and the men with him had departed, doubtless in haste.

Outside the church, the snow had stopped falling, leaving the air damp and chill. Kinloch was nowhere to be seen.

For a few minutes, their group lingered with the other parishioners. The minister, glad to have drawn so large a company of visitors, welcomed them in a hearty manner, wishing them a blessed Christmas.

Emily introduced her female guests to the ladies of the church, using the proper forms of address. Suddenly they were Lady Ormond, Lady Claremont, Lady Katherine Powell, Mrs. Nicholas Powell and Miss Stephen. Nash and Robbie drew aside as the women of St Mary's expressed their delight at having so many illustrious visitors from London.

Nash cast his gaze over the crowded churchyard. "Kinloch and his guards might have gone, but I daresay they noticed us."

Robbie scowled. "I am certain of it. Worse, they have observed our friends."

"It would take very little effort for them to learn where we are staying. I am concerned our friends are now in danger." He did not mention Ailie by name, but his stomach tied in knots fearing she could be threatened by one of the rough men guarding Kinloch.

Robbie nodded. "It troubles me as well."

On the walk back to the Stephens' estate, William said the words Nash had been expecting. "By the bye, one of the men attending the service told me George Kinloch has been proclaimed an outlaw for failing to appear at his trial."

With that, Nash despaired of being able to persuade Robbie to let Kinloch go free, for he was now officially a fugitive.

Chapter 17

Ailie followed the others through the front door, breathing in the wonderful aroma of the wassail heating on the stove and their dinner cooking. Her stomach growled. "What delicious smells."

Footmen stood ready to accept their coats. Nash helped Ailie out of her cloak. She could tell from his distant look he was preoccupied. A glance at Robbie suggested his mind, too, was somewhere else.

They had spoken little on the walk back from town, making her wonder at the cause. Was it something in the minister's sermon? "I'm not Anglican, but I thought the service was lovely. Don't you agree?"

"What? Oh, yes..." muttered Nash. "St Mary's is smaller than St Martin-in-the-Fields in London where we attend, but the smaller church made the service more intimate."

Certainly it had been an intimate experience for Ailie sitting so close to Nash. For once, she minded not at all a crowded service with bodies pressed close.

Emily drew everyone's attention. "In the parlor you will find sherry, brandy and hot wassail to warm you. Dinner should be served in an hour."

A footman opened the double doors and, with grateful nods, the couples headed into the parlor.

Muriel made as if to join them, but took only a few steps before turning back to Emily. "I much enjoyed the walk, my dear, however, a blazing fire and a cup of hot wassail are just what I need at the moment."

"You shall have it, Madeira, too, if you like," offered Will.

Muriel's eyes lit up as she sallied forth to join the others.

Still in the entry hall, Ailie told Emily and Will, "I am glad we are to dine early. I didn't eat much breakfast, knowing a feast was coming."

"Have you ever attended an English Christmas feast?" Nash asked Ailie.

"Not precisely, but we have roast pink-footed goose quite often during the winter."

Emily smiled at Will. "I will join you in the parlor as soon as I check on the feast." She had only taken a step when Will looked up at the kissing bough hanging from the chandelier above them and pulled Emily under it.

"Before you go, I must have a kiss. Setting the example for the others, don't you know?" Emily laughed but submitted willingly, bringing a smile to Ailie's face.

"Happy Christmas, *Leannan*."

Emily was radiant as she left him to join their plump housekeeper, who appeared in her lace mobcap at the base of the stairs.

And why shouldn't Emily be radiant? Thought Ailie. She had a loving husband, a bairn on the way and a house full of happy friends. Ailie wondered if she would ever have those things. She had knowingly chosen a path rare for a woman, becoming part of her family's ship-building enterprise. While she delighted in her work, there were times—and this was one of them—when she wanted more, when she wanted all that a woman who had chosen wisely could have.

Will motioned toward the parlor. "Shall we?"

Ailie and the twins followed her brother into the parlor where the Yule log burned brightly and their guests sipped cups of the warm spiced apple drink. A helpful footman held out a tray. Nash took two cups and handed one to Ailie.

Robbie went off in search of brandy. "I prefer it untainted by honey and fruit juice."

Ailie sipped the warm spicy drink. "I do like your wassail," she told Nash, "but all that dancing around apple trees that went with the drink would have been frowned upon by the Kirk."

Nash laughed. "Well, that might have been true at one time but, like the Yule log, the drink has become just another sign of the season."

"Today, we'll dine on your English dishes," she told Nash, "but on Hogmanay, you'll dine on those favored by us Scots."

"More haddies and kale?"

His expression was decidedly bleak, but she believed he was only teasing her. "Aye. And cock-a-leekie soup, steak pie, roast salmon and haggis with tatties."

"Haggis?"

"Practically our national dish, 'tis sheep's intestine, oatmeal and spices cooked in a sheep's stomach."

A grimace of epic proportions emerged on Nash's face.

Ailie gave him an indulgent smile. "Do not look so disgusted at our beloved haggis. Rabbie Burns himself thought the dish worthy of an ode. He called those who looked down upon the humble haggis 'poor devils', while those who delight in the rare taste he called 'warriors'." She began to quote from the poem she had learned as a young girl, *"But mark the Rustic, haggis-fed, the trembling earth resounds his tread."*

"I would be willing to try it," Nash said, bravely she thought. "For you."

She laughed. "If you could see the look on your face, Nash, you'd see how unconvinced you appear. You might want to confine your celebration of the New Year to salmon and dessert."

His countenance brightened at the word dessert. Teasing him about food had become great fun, but she didn't want him to dislike anything about Scotland. Perhaps she might encourage him with talk of sweets. "For dessert we'll have shortbread, Dundee cake and clootie dumpling."

"I have had your shortbread and it's very good, and cake I understand, but I have no idea what a clootie is."

"That's just the cloth in which we cook the sweet dumpling. Emily tells me the dumpling is a little like your Christmas pudding, but not as rich. The one Martha makes is her mother's recipe made with treacle and served with custard."

"I do know what treacle is," he said proudly, "and I approve."

"At last we find common ground," she teased. "You will like the dumpling. Oh, and sometimes the cook stirs in charms that speak of the future." She pursed her lips, concentrating. "Let's see... Finding a coin means wealth; a ring signifies marriage; and a wishbone promises the finder his heart's desire."

He took a sip of his wassail and winked. "Some of those possibilities appeal."

"Some are not so popular. A man who finds a button and a woman who gets a thimble are destined to remain unwed."

Nash frowned. "I wouldn't want a button, not since I met you, Ailie."

Her cheeks flushed at his words and the intense gaze that went with them. Did he hint at a future together? She took a sip of her wassail. "Nor do I desire a thimble since meeting you."

Fortified by the wassail and warmed by Nash's presence, Ailie was ready for the English Christmas dinner. When their butler announced, "Dinner is served," Nash offered his arm and the two of them strolled into the dining room with the others.

On the way Nash, explained that after the Christmas feast they would typically play games, which, if one lost, one had to pay a forfeit. "Such as a kiss under the kissing bough."

His seductive smile reminded her of their walk in the snow early that morning. She might have to let him win. It would be the first time she looked forward to losing at anything.

Nash pulled out a chair for her, whispering in her ear, "I'm just not sure I want to kiss you while others are watching. It would have to be a very proper kiss, which, all things considered, would require great restraint on my part."

Having observed Nash in conversation with the Mistress of the Setters, oblivious to all around them, Robbie had taken his leave from the parlor to undertake a reconnaissance of the Stephens' property. He wanted to see if any of Kinloch's protectors might be lurking about. Though he couldn't be positive that he had been followed that day on Marketgate, there was still the matter of that morning when he and Nash had been clearly observed in church.

Only one of the guards he had seen in St Thomas Tavern impressed Robbie as being astute enough to take note of those sitting around him. That man was the one called Derek whose penetrating gaze Robbie had felt more than once.

Careful to take cover under an eave or behind a tree, Robbie made two slow circles of the house and shipyard before returning. While he hadn't noticed anyone, save a stable boy tending the horses, that didn't mean someone hadn't been there, silently lurking, making note of the fine estate that hinted at connections to London. Then, too, there were landed Scots who supported the government. Kinloch's guards might assume the Stephens were among them. Derek would consider all of them a threat to the fugitive he guarded.

Robbie only hoped that with the *Panmure* sailing tomorrow, Kinloch's guards had more important things to consider.

He entered the house, handed the footman his coat and went first to the parlor to warm himself by the fire, lest he signal to the others he'd been outside. Explanations were bothersome.

When he finally arrived in the dining room, everyone was already seated.

Ailie waved to him. "Nash told me you had been detained, so I saved you the place next to me."

Robbie slipped into the chair, nodding a greeting to Nash, and gave the Mistress of the Setters a brilliant smile. "There is nowhere else I'd rather sit."

Ailie smiled with her beautiful eyes. "A rake's supreme compliment."

"You missed the soup," said Nash shortly from Ailie's other side.

"But here's the fish, now," Ailie encouraged. She peered at the silver platter the footman carried. "Cod, I think."

"Better late than never, Mr. Powell," chided Muriel.

Robbie returned the countess a grin bordering on a smirk. "Do not forget, dear Muriel, we have an appointment beneath the kissing bough."

"Humph," came her reply. "By the bye, Ailie, lovely velvet bows on the chandelier."

"Do you like them? Nash and Robbie had the devil of a time getting them up there."

Robbie remembered the bow-tying effort. Before it was done, he and Nash had uttered their complete repertoire of oaths. But, for the Mistress of the Setters, no task was too difficult.

When the roasted goose—of the pink-footed variety—was served, there were many "Oohs" and "Aahs". Four birds, roasted to perfection, arrived on silver platters, and were carried to the sideboard where two footmen began carving.

Robbie's mouth watered. Reconnaissance always gave him an appetite.

Across the table, Nick's gaze fixed on the roast goose set before him, a goose surrounded by slices neatly carved. "William, your cook has made our geese a glory to behold."

"Even better to eat," said William. "But I believe it is Muriel's cook, Mrs. Platt, who is responsible for much of this dinner. Am I correct, *Leannan?*"

"Mrs. Platt and Martha worked together on our feast. I have asked them to come to us when dessert is served so that we may properly thank them."

"An excellent idea," said William. "And now that you each have a glass of champagne in front of you, let's all toast to a Happy Christmas."

Robbie raised his glass along with the others. "Happy Christmas!"

When they had lifted their glasses to the babe, the marquess interjected yet another toast. "Let us drink to the new bairn Emily and William are expecting next spring!" When they had drunk to that, Hugh added, "And to our host and hostesses for a most memorable holiday in Scotland!"

Robbie raised his glass with the others and Muriel proclaimed, "Hear, hear!"

For the moment, Robbie wouldn't think of Lord Sidmouth.

Oyster stuffing, carrots glazed in orange sauce, asparagus and a winter salad of lamb's lettuce, watercress and mustard greens accompanied the roast goose. Robbie was in heaven.

"A splendid Christmas feast, Emily," pronounced The Grand Countess. "As fine as any I ever had in London."

Murmurs of agreement echoed around the table.

"I could become accustomed to this," said Ailie.

It occurred to Robbie that if she went to London with Muriel, she might be there for next Christmas. Robbie had been reluctant to give up the game, but it was now apparent Nash had serious intentions toward the girl.

Lacking Nash's proclivity for plants, Robbie had not yet been to see the orangery, so he had to ask, "Did you grow all these vegetables and salad greens in the orangery?"

"All save the apples surrounding the roast geese," replied Emily.

"Those, Captain Anderson brought me from London."

"Emily's a wonder with growing things," put in Ailie. "You should pay the orangery a visit, Robbie. You will be astounded."

"'Twas the first place I went the morning after we arrived," said Nash, now working on a second helping of roast goose.

Robbie thought his twin too self-satisfied in his pursuit of plants and Ailie Stephen for that matter. After all, Robbie had interests, though his tended more toward the dangerous variety, like racing down Rotten Row or bare-knuckle boxing at Jackson's.

While not needed on this trip, Robbie also possessed decent navigational skills. If Ailie designed ships, he could sail them, assuring they would arrive at their destination. "I would be happy to have a tour of the orangery if you were to escort me, Ailie." *So there, dear Brother.*

Nash frowned into his carrots. Muriel looked at Robbie askance, raising one of her silver brows. He ignored them both.

"I'd be pleased to show it to you," offered Ailie.

"I have a sketch of it if you'd like to see it," put in Kit. "By the bye, Emily, the stuffing is quite tasty." Then to Muriel, "Do you think Mrs. Platt might share her recipe?"

"She'd be flattered you asked," returned the countess. "It is a family recipe of which she is quite proud."

At that moment, in walked Mrs. Platt and the Stephens' dark-haired cook with Christmas pudding, mince pies and English gingerbread cake. Robbie's eyes followed the parade of desserts; he was quite fond of gingerbread.

"Oh, what lovely desserts!" exclaimed Mary. "Where shall I find the room?"

"I fear we shall manage all too well," said Muriel, eyeing the confections.

"Our thanks to the two cooks who have brought us this grand feast!" proclaimed William.

They rose as one from their seats to praise the two women. "To the cooks!"

Nash wondered what Robbie was about. First, he had left the parlor and—Nash was quite certain—the house, and then, all during dinner, he had flirted outrageously with Ailie. After dinner, there had been games in the parlor. Not satisfied to have kissed Muriel under the bough, when Robbie guessed Ailie's riddle in a game of rhyming charades, he had dared to claim a kiss from her as forfeit. *Rogue indeed!*

Back in their chamber, Nash confronted his twin. "Good Lord. Did you have to kiss her?"

"It was a circumspect kiss," Robbie insisted. "Mark that I also kissed Muriel, who seemed to enjoy the attention. I do like the dowager countess. She has a quick mind."

"I daresay it was not Ailie's mind that made you want to kiss her, intelligent though she is. And how could it be circumspect when you made Ailie blush?"

"That blush did not result from my kiss, Brother, but what I said after."

Nash fumed. "Just what was *that*?"

"I told her there were more kisses where that one came from. She had only to ask."

Nash snorted. "Hardly circumspect. More like provocative."

"I was merely teasing the lass. Now, do you want to know why I was late to dinner?"

Nash took off his coat and sat on his bed, pulling off his boots, still miffed. "Do tell."

Robbie loosened his cravat and let out a sigh. "Seeing as you were occupied with the Mistress of the Setters, I thought to determine if anyone was watching the house or the shipyard. After this morning's encounter at St Mary's, it occurred to me they might have followed us home and posted a watch. Our direction could be easily ascertained."

Somewhat mollified, Nash said, "I'm grateful you thought of that. I would not want our business in Arbroath to bring harm to our family or friends. Learn anything?"

"No. All was quiet. But, of course, they might have been here and gone. The *Panmure* sails tomorrow afternoon so perhaps they are unconcerned about any interference at this point."

Nash experienced a foreboding, much like the one he'd had that terrible day on St Peter's Field. "I don't suppose I can dissuade you from your intended course?"

In a parody of Nash's own words, Robbie tossed back, "Not a chance. And you'd best develop a plan. Recall that Emily said after presenting boxes to the servants, she intends to take baskets to Arbroath's poor. The ladies, including Ailie, are going with her, which puts them in town when we'll be on Marketgate waiting for Kinloch to depart for the ship."

Nash stared into the fire. He had a plan, but it might not be one Robbie would approve.

Ailie sat at her dressing table, brushing her hair, the blue tartan shawl warming her shoulders. Underneath it, she wore only her shift. The girl looking back at her from the mirror glowed with happiness, her eyes filled with tears of joy.

The cause wasn't the evening, which had been most pleasant, or the English food, which she had quite liked, or even the games played with her new friends. No, the reason for the tears of joy filling her eyes could be explained only by Nash Powell.

She could tell him apart from his twin now, even when they wore the same clothes. It was not just his unique mannerisms, his dry humor—so different than Robbie's overt charm—or the lock of dark hair that often fell onto his forehead, teasing her to touch it. Rather, it was the way Nash looked at her, his thoughtfulness toward her and his kisses.

They shared glances only they understood, and they shared their love of ships and simple pleasures. Her heart had become inexorably intertwined with his. Was it so important that he was English and she a Scot? That he was an Anglican and she Presbyterian? Or that they had different views on the current politics?

Other than a few bouts of calf-love as a young girl, Ailie had never been in love, but she was certain what she felt for Nash was the stuff of which Rabbie Burns wrote in *A Red, Red Rose*. Nash had become a sweet melody to her, playing in her mind. Was it too much to think her love for him would endure "till all the seas ran dry"?

She remembered his laughter, his face set aglow by the firelight, his glorious hazel eyes shining with mirth. When he kissed her, her blood sang in her veins. She wanted to see his face every day. She wanted to share a bed with him every night.

Knowing she must record her thoughts this Christmas, she took a seat at her writing desk, dipping her quill in the ink.

25 December

A Happy Christmas, as the English say, made more so because I spent the day with Nash Powell. To please Emily and her friends—who are now my friends, too—we attended St Mary's. It felt so right to be sitting in church with Nash. Afterward, we shared wassail and the Christmas feast. Yes, he is English, but he understands me and believes in my dream of one day seeing the Ossian sail. His very touch has me tingling in places I have never tingled before. I long for his kisses. It is hard to say goodnight when I must part from him. His words make me think he, too, has such thoughts.

We have a week before he sails for London. Will he ask me to go as Muriel's companion, or possibly something more? I could not bear it if he asked not at all.

Chapter 18

26 December, Boxing Day

Nash's plan was not without risks. But he could bear his brother's wrath more readily than he could the idea of sending an innocent man to prison. Or looking into Ailie's accusing eyes if she were to learn he'd had Kinloch arrested.

He and Robbie had intentionally chosen to wear gentlemen's clothing, though of a plainer variety. Their jackets and breeches were made of ordinary wool, their waistcoats an indiscriminate color, and their hats shorter than the ones they wore in London. Today was not for visiting taverns but for watching those heading toward the harbor and a particular ship.

Nash had seen men in Arbroath dressed in similar fashion, so he and Robbie would blend in. Their greatcoats, worn over all, concealed their pistols which, at least in Nash's case, he had no intention of using.

Nash left Robbie pulling on his boots and went down to breakfast. He had intended to pass through the parlor on his way to the dining room, but when he reached the threshold, he paused, encountering an unexpected sight.

The ladies, chatting and laughing, stood in the midst of tables covered with baskets, baked goods, ribbons and fresh vegetables and flowers he recognized as having come from the orangery.

"If you linger there much longer, young man," quipped Muriel, "we shall put you to work!"

Ailie came to him, her cheeks flushed. He hoped it was for excitement at seeing him. She wore a simple blue day gown, her hair captured at her nape by a ribbon of the same color. The effect was enchanting. "Oh Nash, isn't it amazing what Emily and Muriel have done?"

He gave her a smile conveying his deep affection. "Good morning, Ailie. Yes, if you mean all that is before me, the effort appears... overwhelming."

She glanced toward the dining room. "The other men have gone into breakfast."

"Hiding behind closed doors?" he teased.

She swatted him on his arm. "We sent them away if you want the truth of it. They were a distraction, as are you!"

Nash looked behind her to take in the flurry of activity engaged in by the five other women laughing as they tied bows on the basket handles. "Have you ever done this before?"

"Aye, if you mean have I brought gifts to the shipyard families and to the church for the poor, but no, if you mean have I worked with so many women to assemble pretty baskets. Why don't you go in to breakfast?" In a flirtatious manner, she added, "I'm sure the men have saved you some haddies. There might even be an omelet with kale."

The smirk on her face told him she was in excellent humor. "Very funny, Miss Stephen."

"Go," she urged. Looking over her shoulder at the women, she said, "We will join you as soon as we have finished assembling the baskets. Will has arranged for a wagon with bench seats on the sides so the other ladies and I can ride with the baskets between us. Won't that be fun? Will has even agreed to take us himself."

"Brave man," said Nash as he proceeded into the dining room.

Stepping inside, Nash greeted the men and found his way to the sideboard.

"Did you run the gauntlet of skirts, bows and baskets?" asked Hugh.

"I did," he said, lifting a plate and perusing the offerings. "'Twas most impressive." Nash availed himself of a bowl of oatmeal and raspberries, but could not summon much hunger given what he knew lay ahead.

He took a seat adjacent to William who was in his usual place at the head of the table. "Ailie tells me you are to drive the wagon taking the ladies to town. I thought it quite brave of you."

"Aye, I'm determined to be the knight today."

The others chuckled.

"What stops will you make?" Nash hoped William did not find it an odd question. He had to know if they would be anywhere near him and Robbie.

"We'll visit the shipyard folks first, the ones with large families and small incomes who could use some help. And then we'll go to St Mary's to deliver the rest of the baskets to the minister there who knows the needy families in town. You are welcome to join us."

"Too many petticoats for me," Nash replied, taking a swallow of his coffee and forcing down his rising panic. William's schedule would put the women near the harbor just as the *Panmure* was to sail.

He lifted his head to consider Hugh and Nick sitting across from him. "What might the rest of you be doing while the ladies deliver their baskets?"

"I thought to ride along with them," said Hugh. "They might need another hand to carry baskets."

"It is perfectly all right to admit you want to spend the day with your wife," said William. "We require no excuse."

"Very well," offered the marquess, "I intend to spend the day with my wife, but I'm sure you could use the manly support, Will."

Aware of how often Hugh and Mary had kept to themselves since coming to Arbroath, Nash smiled.

"Martin and I plan to go over the orders Powell and Sons expects to place for ships this next year," said Nash's eldest brother Nick. He waggled his brows at their host. "We want to be prepared when we meet with William later today. How about you and Robbie?"

"We hope to sample some of the local taverns in town." There, he'd provided a reason for them to be in Arbroath.

William gave him a curious look, but said nothing. Nash averted his gaze, regretting that Ailie's brother might think he preferred getting foxed with Robbie to being with Ailie and the ladies, but he had to lay the groundwork should they be seen.

Robbie viewed Marketgate from where he and Nash stood at the corner of that street and Bridge Street, a short way from the harbor. It was the most likely path Kinloch's guards would take and the crossing allowed them a clear view of both streets.

The sky above was clear of clouds for the first time in days, but the air was bitter cold. He stuffed his hands into his coat pockets, wrapping his right hand around his pistol. He hoped the threat of force would render Kinloch cooperative, though he worried about the guards, particularly Hamish and Lachy. It was too late to ask for the magistrate's help and such men often complicated matters. He wanted no bloodbath on the streets of Arbroath.

At the moment, those streets were bare, save only for snow piled in the corners. The atmosphere was dreary, the tall buildings lining Marketgate standing like cold dark sentinels braced against the wind blowing offshore.

"I don't like it," he said in a hushed voice. "It's too quiet. Feels like the whole town has gone into hiding. I fear we waited too long. Kinloch might already be aboard the *Panmure*. Passengers often board early on the day of sailing."

"Not Kinloch," argued Nash. "His plan will be to board at the last minute, leaving no time to be seen or a magistrate to be summoned. Still, I doubt many of Arbroath's citizens would inform on him."

"We're not in Dundee," Robbie reminded him. "Many in Scotland oppose the kind of change Kinloch advocates. 'Tis why he is called the Radical Laird."

"Not all oppose his views," muttered Nash.

"No, not all," agreed Robbie, noting the brooding look on his brother's face. He recognized its source. "The Mistress of the Setters is one who supports him."

They had inquired about the tide and, using their own knowledge and the activities underway onboard, guessed at the *Panmure*'s expected sailing time, now a mere quarter of an hour away.

From where they stood, Robbie could see the masts of the ships in the harbor. They had passed the *Panmure* on the way to their current post, and he had observed the seamen working aloft, putting the sails in their gear and pushing them off the yards, leaving them hanging down ready to set. The captain and his officers had been walking the weather deck, likely checking in with the bos'n and carpenter to assure the supplies essential for repairs had been loaded. Robbie had overseen the same procedures many times.

Nash followed Robbie's gaze. "Captain Gower must be pleased with these westerlies blowing offshore. 'Twill make his departure from Arbroath a smooth one." Then with a stern look, he added, "It's not too late to turn back, Robbie. I wish you would. If we have to tell a lie, let it be to Sidmouth, not our family and friends."

Robbie never replied for, in the distance, he saw a group of men emerge from an alley close to the harbor. "Damn! They have taken a different route." To the five men, a sixth had been added, a gentleman by the look of him. Kinloch had foregone his odd hat for what looked to be a gentleman's wig. They moved toward the quay at a leisurely pace, perhaps so as not to draw attention. "We must be quick!"

Robbie took off at a run, Nash on his heels. Fifteen feet from the men, Robbie slowed.

The men turned at their approach.

"George Kinloch!" Robbie shouted, "Halt in the name of the Crown!"

The guards placed themselves in front of Kinloch and the other gentleman.

Robbie pulled his pistol, intending to fire a warning shot.

"Robbie, no!" Nash shouted. "Let him go!"

The blond they knew as Lachy raised a pistol and smirked. "I'll no be askin' agin, Englishmon. Drap yer pistol!"

Robbie held his pistol steady, focusing his eyes on the space a foot above Lachy's head. Before he could fire, Nash yanked his arm to the side. Robbie's pistol shot a burst of flame and smoke as the ball went wild.

Robbie bit out an oath. "I wasn't going to shoot him."

Ahead of them, Kinloch shouted, "No!"

Lachy fired his pistol, which spewed fire and smoke into the air.

Searing pain shot through Robbie's head as stars appeared before his eyes just before his vision went black.

Splattered with his brother's blood, Nash dropped to the pavement beside Robbie, staring at the fountain of red flowing from his head to pool on the ground. "Oh God, Robbie!"

The muffled sound of boots approaching made him look up, but the tears streaming from his eyes blurred the image. "Physician! I need a physician!"

"Ye'll miss yer boat Kinloch if ye dinna go now!" said a heavily-accented voice.

Nash wiped the tears from his eyes to see George Kinloch bending over him, his guards pulling on him, urging him away.

"I'll not leave a man to die on my account," Kinloch said, shaking off their hands and returning his attention to Robbie's still form.

"Go!" Nash shouted. "Go, while you can."

"I cannot leave you alone. Let me at least summon a physician."

"Go," said a familiar voice from behind Nash. *Ailie.* "I will get one for him."

"I am sorry," Kinloch lamented. "Truly I am. I will pray the wound is not fatal."

Prevailing over the objections of their charge, Kinloch's guards swept him across the street and to the waiting ship.

Ailie crouched beside Nash, her hand on his shoulder as she handed him a handkerchief. "Press this to the wound while I fetch the physician."

Nash nodded. "Oh, Ailie, please hurry."

As she ran back toward High Street, Nash took off his coat and made a pillow for Robbie's head. Then he pressed the cloth to the bloody wound.

From the deck of the *Panmure*, Nash heard a cry of orders and turned to see the sails of the big schooner bloom open and stretch taut. A minute later, the ship pulled away from her mooring, heading into the harbor, her spread of canvas rising higher and higher as she caught the wind and picked up speed.

His heart aching, Nash said a silent prayer for his brother, as he watched the *Panmure* slant away to the south toward France.

Ailie ran down the street toward Mr. Wilson's receiving room, her mind filled with images from the horrible scene she had just witnessed.

She had wandered off as the ladies finished handing out baskets and happened to glimpse Nash and Robbie talking to a group of men. Walking toward them, she heard the pistols fire and saw the smoke as one twin dropped to the ground. Terrified, she had run to them and heard Nash shout his brother's name.

That is how she knew the twin who lay bleeding on the ground was not the man she loved. Guilt assailed her for the joy she felt because Nash had been spared.

Her dreams—both portents of the future and harbingers of danger—had become reality.

Many questions swirled through her mind, but there had been no time to ask. Why had Robbie been shot? She had heard enough to know it was George Kinloch who stood over Robbie and Nash. Why had he come to Arbroath? Why did Nash urge him to go? And why did Kinloch think Robbie might die on his account? The Powell twins had to be more than mere passersby when the pistol was fired, for there was the matter of Robbie's pistol lying on the ground beside his open hand.

She raced up the stairs to the door, the sign above it announcing "W. Wilson, Physician". The bell on the door jingled as she entered the small waiting room, her chest heaving from exertion.

The waiting area was empty but the air against her cheek felt almost hot after the cold wind blowing outside. She knew the receiving room as well as she knew her own parlor, for she had been there more than once seeking help for injuries sustained by their workers.

The nurse opened the inner door and approached. "Why, Miss Stephen, what is it? Trouble at the shipyard?"

"No," she said breathlessly, shaking her head. "One of our guests has been shot down by the harbor and lies bleeding. Can Mr. Wilson come?"

"Aye, I'll fetch him straight away."

The nurse disappeared through the door that led to the examining room and returned almost immediately with the middle-aged Mr. Wilson, his brown leather satchel in hand.

The nurse held his bag while he slipped on his coat. "Good day, Miss Stephen. I understand we have a patient lying in the street."

"We do and I thank you for coming in haste to tend him."

Mr. Wilson grabbed his hat and accepted back his satchel. "As we go, you can tell me what happened."

She told him the few things she knew as he ventured down Bridge Street and then onto Lady Loan Shore that ran by the harbor.

"Is the wounded man conscious?"

Hurrying to keep up with his long stride, she said, "He wasn't when I left him with his twin brother." Remembering what she had seen, she added, "There was a lot of blood."

"It happens with head wounds."

She tried to draw hope from his words but the scene she had left was too terrible for her to believe Robbie wasn't in grave danger.

They arrived at the place where Nash hunched over Robbie's prone form. Mr. Wilson crouched next to them. "I am Walter Wilson, the physician. Let me see the wound, please."

Nash lifted the cloth Ailie had given him, his tear-streaked face and dire expression conveying his desperation to know Robbie would live.

The surgeon opened his case and took out a bottle marked "Spirit of Lavender". Dousing a fresh cloth with the liquid, he dabbed at the blood flowing from Robbie's left temple.

"Lavender?"

"Aye, oil of lavender is useful for digestive ailments but also good for cleansing wounds and soothing headaches and 'tis kind to the skin. I just want to wipe the blood away to see how deep is the wound." Lifting the lavender-soaked cloth, now crimson with Robbie's blood, Mr. Wilson appeared relieved. "He's fortunate 'tis only a flesh wound, but he'll have a wicked headache and a nasty scar."

Nash let out a sigh. "Thank God he will be all right."

Ailie reached her hand to cover Nash's, trying to comfort him. "Mr. Wilson is an excellent physician, trained at Edinburgh University. You can trust him with Robbie."

"I'm thankful to you both."

Mr. Wilson stuffed the crimson cloth into his satchel and took out another small bottle. "My own mixture for treating wounds." Putting some on yet another bit of cloth, he dabbed at the wound. The gash, now clearly visible, went from the end of Robbie's eyebrow to the edge of his hair and a bit beyond.

When the surgeon was finished with the small bottle, he took out a roll of white linen. "In addition to a fresh bandage, I'll wrap his head to protect the wound. The bandages will need to be changed at least once a day." He handed Ailie another roll. "I know you can do this, Miss Stephen, but remember to first clean the wound with a bit of brandy until it scabs over. A coating of honey will help avoid infection."

Ailie had treated wounds before, dutifully following the physician's instructions.

Putting all back in his satchel, Mr. Wilson closed it and turned to Nash. "Come, let us get him back to my office. He'll freeze here. And put your coat back on, young man or you'll freeze, too."

In what appeared to Ailie a mindless manner, Nash shrugged into his bloodstained coat and the two men lifted Robbie to an erect position.

Ailie picked up the physician's satchel, heavy with his bottles and instruments. They began to retrace their steps, slowly and in an awkward manner, as Robbie, unable to walk on his own, was dragged between the two men.

Ailie's spirits rose when Robbie let out a groan.

"He is regaining consciousness," said the physician, "a good sign."

Robbie's eyes were still closed, and there was blood on the side of his face and a red stain on his cravat. Still, Ailie was heartened to see no bright stain of red coming through his bandage.

They had only gone a short way when Ailie spotted Will driving the wagon with the ladies down the street toward them. Hugh rode alongside.

Will pulled up next to Ailie and jumped down. "Good Lord, what has happened?"

"Afternoon, Mr. Stephen, ladies," said Mr. Wilson. His gaze met Will's. "It seems one of your guests has been shot."

"It's Robbie," said Nash in a grave tone.

"We're taking him to Mr. Wilson's office," explained Ailie.

Hugh dismounted and joined Will. Emily and the other ladies looked on, their faces lined with worry.

"Here, let me take him," said Will. The physician surrendered his hold on Robbie to Ailie's brother. "How bad is it?"

The physician reclaimed his satchel. "The ball grazed his temple leaving a nasty gash but, with care, he should recover."

Hugh asked, "Can we take him back to the shipyard?"

"Aye," said Mr. Wilson. "I can give you some laudanum for the pain. Ailie knows what to do and I have given her more bandages." Reaching into his satchel, he took out a bottle and handed it to Will. "If you need more, send a footman and you shall have it. I will pay you a call tomorrow to see how he's doing."

"Thank you," said Will. "We are most grateful."

Mr. Wilson tipped his hat to the ladies and wished them a good day as he headed back toward his office.

As the men moved Robbie toward the back of the wagon, the women continued to watch anxiously from the side. Hugh let down the tail of the wagon and Nash and Will lifted Robbie to a horizontal position, carefully sliding him onto the bed of the wagon. Without the baskets, there was sufficient room for him between the benches.

Ailie climbed in and sat beside Robbie, gently raising his head to her lap. Nash took a seat on the bench across from her, his eyes fixed on his twin.

"Here, take this," said Mary, offering her lap blanket to Nash, which he laid over Robbie's prone form.

Tara offered her scarf to Ailie. "For under his head."

After they'd gone a short way, Robbie opened his eyes. Dazed, he looked up at Ailie and blinked twice. "Where am I? Heaven? Must be Heaven as I'm looking at an angel. But my head hurts like Hell."

The other women laughed, shaking their heads at Robbie's attempt at humor.

Ailie looked into Robbie's hazel eyes, so like his brother's. "As my brother can tell you, I am no angel, but I vow to take good care of you, Robbie Powell."

"The rascal recovers," announced Muriel in a jovial manner but Ailie could see the countess, whose face had been lined with worry moments before, was much relieved to see Robbie awake and feeling well enough to joke.

Chapter 19

27 December

The next morning Nash was keeping vigil at Robbie's bedside, as he had the night before, when Ailie arrived to change the bandage.

"The wound looks raw and ugly but 'tis not festering," she said with a hopeful smile. Robbie winced as she applied some brandy to the gash.

"Waste of good brandy," Robbie muttered. He reached for the flask. "At least give me the remains." She obliged and he drank it down. "Ah, now that's better."

Nash watched as Ailie applied the clean bandage and then circled Robbie's head with fresh linen and tied it off. Sitting back in her chair, she folded her hands and looked at Nash.

"Now that we know Robbie will live, I'd have the truth of it. The others are eager to know as well. What happened?"

Nash exchanged a look with Robbie, who had suddenly gone silent. Letting out a sigh of resignation for the story he must tell, Nash said, "Robbie and I have been working for the government, Ailie. Not just now but before, in Manchester last August."

She shot him am incredulous look. "You were in Manchester when the massacre took place?"

"We were. When the invitation to come to Scotland presented itself, Lord Sidmouth, who fears rebellion above all, asked us to be on the lookout for George Kinloch, the man who stirred all of Dundee with his speech. Things being tense in Scotland, Sidmouth wanted the man back in Edinburgh for trial. It was believed Kinloch might have come to Arbroath."

"You are government *spies*?" She spewed out the last word as if the very notion was repugnant, which, to her, it probably was.

Nash lowered his gaze. "We are."

"So, you thought to capture him and turn him over to his gaolers?" This time, her voice was tinged with anger. Her color was high and her lips pressed together.

Nash tried to summon a defense even he did not believe in. He met her infuriated gaze, fearing what he saw in her beautiful eyes. "That was the initial plan, yes."

She rose from her chair and shot Nash a look of stunned outrage. "All this time! You have heard me defend the man as wanting only good for Scotland. None in our family—your hosts, I might remind you—ever argued for Kinloch's capture. Yet, behind our backs, you went to town to spy on him, didn't you? Now that I think of it, there were many times only one of you was around. I can scarce believe you capable of such duplicity, such deceit, *even* if you are English!"

She turned on her heels and bolted for the door, slamming it behind her.

"Well," said Robbie, "that wraps it up with a bow, doesn't it? Now the Mistress of the Setters will have neither of us."

"We are truly unmasked," said Nash with a look of deep regret. "I fear our deception has cost me Ailie's good opinion." *And her love.* "I did foresee this happening, you'll recall, and I argued against the mission."

Robbie nodded. "You did. I was a fool to think Kinloch's guards might behave as the gentleman they protected."

"That is not my point. We never should have tried to take Kinloch in the first place. He came back, you know. He didn't want to leave me alone with you bleeding onto the pavement. Even offered to fetch a physician."

"Did he? I seem to recall someone saying the good Mr. Wilson hurried to the scene when summoned."

"That was not Kinloch. Ailie arrived and offered to go for the physician, which was fortunate. I urged Kinloch to leave while he could."

"It wasn't he who shot me; it was that hot-headed Lachy character."

"I'm sure he is still in Arbroath somewhere with his companions, unless they hail from Dundee. Only two cabins were booked on the *Panmure*."

"Alas, we cannot pursue him, Nash, much as I'd like. The story would expose our work for Sidmouth."

"You are right, of course. 'Tis best you accept your scar as the only souvenir you will have from this escapade. At least I still have a twin brother."

"I regret my scar will not be under my hair, as is yours. It will, however, serve as a reminder of the day you rescued me, an ironic twist to the many times I have saved you from harm."

Nash ran his hand through his hair, feeling the scar left by the yeoman's saber. "Hadn't thought of it like that. Anyway, 'tis time you stopped coming to my rescue. Let me design and sail ships and, if you must, use your courage, which you have in spades, to go about the Crown's business."

"I might. Right now, the only thing that appeals is a night of cards in my club."

"Sidmouth will have to be told," said Nash, knowing it would be an unpleasant business at best.

"Leave that to me. Perhaps my new scar will assist the telling."

William had been working in his study, trying to get a few things done before they were to sail to Stonehaven, when Ailie arrived. Now that his workers were off for Hogmanay, the shipyard activity had ground to a halt, but the paperwork never ceased.

Ailie droned on, telling him some Banbury tale of how Robbie Powell had come to be shot the day before. William's attention was waning, diverted by the numbers on the page before him.

"They are spies, I tell you!" Ailie shouted, her cheeks red with fury.

William dropped his quill and looked up. He had assumed Robbie's misfortune was merely a chance encounter with a ruffian from one of the shorefront taverns, but his sister's words said different. "Surely that cannot be. Those two are sons of Simon Powell of Powell and Sons Shipping, respectable shipmasters the both of them. Besides, I cannot countenance such behavior on the part of Ormond's friends."

Realizing he would accomplish no more work today, William set aside his ledgers and rose. "I can see there is nothing for it but for me to ask Ormond if he has an inkling of such being true." He proceeded out of the room, saying over his shoulder. "I will see you at the noon meal."

He found Hugh in the stables rubbing down the chestnut gelding he had ridden that morning. Sunlight drifted through the open shutters to fall upon the fresh hay.

His friend must have sensed his presence, for he glanced up. "Hello, William. What brings you to my favorite haunt?" Hugh returned his attention to the horse, moving to its right flank facing away from William.

"It's my sister. Ailie has it in her head that the twin Powell brothers are government spies."

Hugh's dark head popped up from the other side of the horse. "What?"

"Aye, something to do with that dust up in Arbroath yesterday and Robbie's getting shot. Ailie says 'tis all bound up with some work the two were doing for Lord Sidmouth. Spying on George Kinloch, to be precise."

"The man from Dundee charged with sedition is *here?*"

"Was, according to Ailie. But aye, the very one. Know anything about it?"

"No." Hugh put the horse back in its stall and wiped his hands on a cloth. "How about a brandy, old chum?"

"I've some good cognac waiting in my study," Will offered. They began to walk back to the house together. "I was certain none of your friends would be spying for the Crown," said Will, feeling much better about the whole thing. After all, he'd given Nash his blessing to court Ailie.

"Well, now. Speaking generally, William, that ain't so."

"Whatever do you mean?"

"I suppose I have never told you." Shaking his head, Hugh said, "Truth be told, there was never a reason to do so and, really, we don't speak much of it."

"What exactly are you muttering about?" William demanded, as they approached the front of the house.

"What I am trying to say, my friend, is that we have all been agents for the Crown at one time or another. I was a spy in Paris stealing the plans meant for Napoleon's generals; Sir Martin was a spy in France during the war, working with me. And just two years ago, Prinny dispatched him to the Midlands for that rebellion in Pentridge. At the Prince Regent's request, Nick chased a pirate all over the Caribbean, one I might add who held Tara captive for a time. Why, even their father Simon Powell was a spy for the government in the American War. Did you never know?"

Will paused, near speechless. "I had no idea."

"So," Hugh continued on, speaking as if it were no large matter, "while I know nothing of this business in Arbroath and, if it's true, would chide them most soundly for assuming on your good graces, I would not be surprised. Like their older brothers and their father before them, I expect the Crown would feel free to call upon them whenever they are needed. The Powells have served the country well."

"Good Lord. Government spies the lot of you and beneath my very roof. Tell me, while I was rotting in a French prison, were you in France?"

Hugh grinned. "Have you never heard of *L'Engoulevent*, the Nighthawk?"

Will raised a brow. "*You?*"

Hugh bowed. "*À votre service.*"

"You are a famous hero, Ormond. A glass of my best cognac is definitely in order."

Hugh chuckled. "If it earns me some of your fine cognac, I accept the accolade."

Ailie arrived in the dining room just as luncheon was being served. A quick glance around the table told her Robbie had elected to remain in his room. He was still dizzy when he'd tried to stand so it was not beyond reason for him to take the noon meal in his chamber.

Or, he might be hiding from her wrath.

She darted a glance at Will, who returned her a slight nod, telling her he had matters in hand. Very well, she would trust him to deal with the Powell twins' betrayal.

From across the table, Nash gave her a look of regret. It was the first time they sat apart. She averted her gaze. He could hardly expect her to overlook his perfidy, engaging in a dangerous pursuit that might have brought those ruffians to their home or got both of them killed. As it was, Robbie lay wounded. And Kinloch, a hero to many Scots, might have been tossed into prison or worse.

How could she love a government spy who had lied to her?

As bowls of haddie stew were served, everyone set into their food, except for Nash, whose bowl was still full when the others were almost finished.

Will set aside his spoon and sat back, crossing his arms over his chest. "It appears we have been harboring spies in our midst."

The announcement brought dead silence to the table and guilty expressions on most of the faces. The only one whose expression indicated surprise was Emily. Beneath her ebony brows her heather eyes were frowning.

So the rest of them all knew.

"I only learned today," Will continued, "that my good friend, the Marquess of Ormond, has acted the spy for the Crown. In fact, Ormond is the stuff of legends, the one known as *L'Engoulevent*, the Nighthawk."

Emily gasped. "Oh, I just loved him! *You*, Hugh?"

At Hugh's nod, Emily beamed.

Ailie did not know the name but her sister-in-law obviously did. Her worshipful gaze aimed at Hugh was a bit too much. Mary reached over and gave her husband a kiss on the cheek, obviously proud of whatever he had been doing as the Nighthawk.

When the excitement over Hugh's achievement died down, Will said, "And it seems the Powell brothers have all been, as Hugh puts it, 'agents for the Crown'. Sir Martin earned his knighthood spying for the government in France, making use of his fluent French. Captain Nicholas Powell is famous for going against the notorious pirate Roberto Cofresi and besting him. And now, to bring you all to the current day, Nash and Robbie Powell have been spying for Lord Sidmouth in Arbroath before our very noses."

This drew frowns from all save Nash who lowered his gaze to his soup.

"Do tell," said Nick to his youngest brother. "Now that the family secret's out, what have you two been up to?"

Ailie watched as Nash raised his head and set his shoulders back as if bracing for a storm. "Sidmouth sent us north to Manchester in August to search out what he believed was a rebellion brewing among the factory workers. He was wrong, and I nearly lost my life in the bloodbath that followed."

"Dear Nash, do not speak of blood whilst we are eating," put in Muriel. "'Tis bad form."

"Forgive me, Muriel."

"Good God," said Martin. "Mother never told us."

"We asked her not to," replied Nash.

Emily turned to the countess. "Did you know they were *all* spies, Muriel?"

"Having my own connections at Whitehall, I knew much of it. But even I was not aware the twins had accepted an assignment from Sidmouth. I consider that man beyond the pale. Never did trust him."

Hugh directed a disapproving look at Nash. "You should have confided in me, Nash, and in our host. William had a right to know. Look where your secret has led. Your own brother lies wounded."

As disgusted as she was, Ailie could not allow them to unjustly point all the blame at Nash. "It was Robbie who fired on Kinloch and the men with him, wasn't it, Nash?"

"Robbie only meant to warn them."

"Well, there is one good thing come of it," said Muriel. With all eyes on her, the countess smiled, a very knowing smile, thought Ailie. "We'll be able to tell you and your twin apart from now on. And a scar looks good on a rogue."

Muriel sat by the Yule log fire in one of the comfy velvet wing chairs she favored, a glass of Madeira on the small table next to her, as she finished another chapter in the Waverley novel she was reading.

The Antiquary, set in the century past, took place in the fictional seaside town of Fairport, which she believed was actually Arbroath. She had come to this conclusion because it was an open secret in London that the author was Walter Scott even though the book had been published anonymously. Muriel knew that Scott had traveled to Arbroath more than once. As described in the book, the two places, including the ruined abbey, were too similar not to be the same.

She was just thinking how appropriate her reading choice was in light of the discussion during luncheon when Aileen Stephen traipsed into the parlor and claimed the other wing chair.

"Aileen, whatever has caused that despairing look on your lovely face?"

"How can I not despair, Muriel, when the man I cared for betrayed my trust? Lurking about Arbroath, spying on a Scottish gentleman I respect, all the time hiding the truth from me."

"Ah, secrets," said Muriel, shifting her gaze to the flames. Lifting her glass of Madeira, she sipped the rich wine, then quoted aloud a line from Walter Scott's poem, *Marmion*. "*Oh! What a tangled web we weave, when first we practice to deceive!*"

"Exactly."

Muriel returned her gaze to the distraught young woman. "Come now, is there no room in your heart to forgive the young man and his brother? When I last saw Nash, he appeared most miserable."

Aileen pursed her lips and fiddled with her hands, clearly uncomfortable with the stand she had taken.

Muriel fixed her gaze on Aileen. "I doubt Ormond and the elder Powell brothers confided all they were doing to the women who became their wives. As I recall, only Kit was married when her husband was acting the spy in Pentridge and he never told her. 'Tis worse in your case, of course, because Nash and his brother spied on one of your countrymen, a man you admire, with the intent to put him in prison. But didn't Nash come to dislike the task he was given?"

"Aye. I suppose he did, though he still went to town with Robbie to search out Kinloch." Aileen suddenly jumped up from her chair. "Is there more of the Madeira?"

Muriel smiled to herself. "Why, yes. Just there on the sideboard."

Aileen returned with a glass of the wine. "I will consider forgiving him, but whether I do or not, I have decided to accept your invitation to come to London. That is, if you will still have me."

"Oh yes, my dear. I would welcome your company in London. I dare say you would be quite the hit."

From where he reclined on his bed, Robbie looked out the window, watching tree branches whip about in the wind. The deep rumble of thunder and a crack of lightning shook the house, unmistakable signs a storm was battering the Forfarshire coast.

Nash left his book and went to the window. "No one's going anywhere in this."

"A good afternoon to stay inside," Robbie agreed. "Now that our secret's out, perhaps we should go down to dinner together. They aren't likely to scourge us." Unlike Nash, Ailie's earlier visit had not discouraged Robbie. He was not even feeling badly for having lost his prey. Nash might well have been correct in his thinking; Kinloch was not a bad sort and putting him in prison would serve no purpose except to rile the Scots.

Nash turned from the window. "We might be in for a verbal scourging. You would think so if you'd seen the scowl Ailie gave me when she arrived at luncheon."

"Worry not. I will speak our apology and the lass will forgive you. In my experience, they always do. Look at our brothers' wives and all they have forgiven them. Love makes even the veriest harridan most amenable."

"You say that like one who has taken advantage."

Robbie slung his legs over the edge of his bed, preparing to rise. He paused as the room spun. "Many times, Brother. Many times."

"Shameless, that's what you are."

"I'll not deny it." Robbie chuckled, or tried to, but his head pounded and the wound in his temple ached. He had refused more laudanum, hating the effect of the opiate, and sent Mr. Wilson away with his thanks when the physician had graciously braved the storm to check on his patient. "By the bye, did you know of Ormond's exploits in France?"

"Not until William revealed them. Just think, our new friend Hugh, the Marquess of Ormond, is an infamous hero of our time. I suppose he would have been knighted for his service in France, like our brother, Martin, if he weren't already heir to a dukedom."

Thankful the room had stopped spinning, Robbie checked his bandage to make sure it would not fall into his eyes as he descended the stairs. "A baronet is far beneath a duke. Moreover, Ormond has the courtesy title of marquess to toss about. I like him all the more that he does not."

"I agree. William has no title at all, yet Hugh calls him his chum."

"Come on, Nash. Help me up. I want to go down to dinner, but I'll need you to steady me else I'll arrive at the bottom of the stairs face first."

With Nash beside him, Robbie entered the dining room to looks of concern from the ladies and shakes of the head from the men. He subsided into a chair across from Nick and Tara and took up his napkin.

"You look like a soldier off the battlefield," said Tara.

Robbie intended to make light of his injury, not wishing to curry either condemnation or sympathy. After all, he had only himself to blame. "I rather think the bandage adds to my appeal, don't you?"

From Muriel, two seats away, came a muffled, "Humph."

"Oh, very well, yes," Robbie admitted, "I grant you it's a pathetic attempt to justify my altered appearance." He picked up his spoon as the soup was served, a rich broth replete with carrots, turnips, peas and other vegetables, one of which was decidedly dark green, to which had been added barley and lamb. "A hearty soup for a stormy day and most welcome."

"'Tis a Scottish dish called hotch potch," offered Ailie, who appeared too reserved to be her usual self. He assumed her dour countenance and her failure to greet Nash or him with her usual smile meant she had not yet forgiven them the morning's revelations.

"I like the soup," he replied, "as I have all the Scottish dishes to which you have introduced us." Then, addressing himself to William and Hugh, sitting at one end of the table, he changed the subject. "I know Nash and I have presumed upon your good graces in failing to tell you of our assignment from Lord Sidmouth, which," he said, glancing at the others, "I assume you are all now aware of. We ask your humble pardon."

Nash nodded. "We do."

"If it matters," added Robbie, "we failed in our mission. George Kinloch has safely sailed to France, just ahead of the storm."

Emily's eyes darted to Robbie and Nash. "On behalf of my husband and our other guests, we accept your apology. Hugh has explained that you are not alone in being drafted by the Crown for special assignments, and that Lord Ormond and your brothers have also served in such a capacity."

"Even I spied for the Crown in France," put in Mary.

"Not with my blessing," scolded Hugh.

"We were not wed then, my love," replied the fair-haired marchioness with a mischievous grin.

Robbie knew his brothers' wives were hoydens and apparently Lady Ormond followed in their footsteps.

William took that moment to raise his wine glass. "We are glad Mr. Kinloch escaped our shores. There are enough so-called enemies of the Crown rotting in prison. There need not be another from Scotland joining them. So, with that in mind, I propose a toast to a new day and the celebration of the New Year that awaits us in Stonehaven, that is if the weather allows."

Everyone, save Ailie, raised their glass. "To a new day!"

At the end of William's toast, Muriel said, "Emily, per chance is the dark green matter floating in the soup kale?"

To Robbie's eternal gratitude, everyone laughed, bringing much-needed merriment to the otherwise somber session of confession and pardon. Alas, Nash would have much work ahead of him if he were to win forgiveness from the Mistress of the Setters.

Emily indulged her friend. "No, dear Muriel, 'tis spinach."

"Ah," breathed the countess, "I am much relieved." With that, Muriel began to consume her soup.

Robbie breathed a sigh of relief. At least one storm had passed.

The storm beating against her window meant that Ailie would be denied her late night stroll to gaze at the stars. Instead, she retired to her chamber to sit by the fire and stare into the flames, contemplating her future. Her tartan shawl was draped over her nightclothes and Goodness and Mercy lay curled up at her feet, bringing her comfort after a disturbing day.

Before William had wed Emily and Ailie had come to love her sister-in-law, she would never have considered an Englishman as a prospective husband. But now, in accepting Muriel's invitation to come to London, she had placed the possibility squarely in her path.

Despite her anger at Nash for failing to disclose his spying, she had not forgotten all she loved about him, his gentle touch, his humor, his passionate kisses, his approval of her ship design work that would forever be a part of her life, and his easy acceptance of life in Arbroath. When she thought of a future husband, his face was the only one that appeared in her mind. But could that ever be after what he had done? The others, even William and Emily, had been quick to forgive. Why was it so hard for Ailie?

She reached down to scratch Goodness behind his ears. Content, he did not even stir. Getting to her feet, she went to her writing desk and took up her quill. Dipping it in the ink, she began to write.

27 December

How do I begin to speak of a day in which many secrets were revealed? Nash Powell is a government spy! Along with his brother, Robbie, he had planned to arrest George Kinloch, the laird from Dundee who spoke for all Scots in condemning the bloodbath at Manchester. Worse, Nash told me nothing of it. Yesterday, I saw the horror of it unfolding on the streets of Arbroath. I heard the pistols firing; I saw Robbie lying in a pool of blood; and I feared for his life.

My dreams now make perfect sense. They warned me of men in taverns, where, like as not, Nash and Robbie acted the spies, and told me one of the twins would be shot. I have to confess I was glad Nash was not the one wounded, but I am furious with him for sharing his kisses while hiding his deception. And now I learn that his older brothers and Lord Ormond have all been spies for the Crown. So many secrets…

I have told Muriel I will go to London with her. Perhaps I do need a diversion just now. Will I see Nash there? My heart breaks at the thought of losing him from my life, but forgiveness has not come easily. Yet the wise Countess of Claremont urges me to consider doing just that.

Chapter 20

29 December

Two days later, Nash woke from a restless night still wondering if Ailie would ever forgive him. She had remained polite but distant since discovering he was Sidmouth's spy. Forgiveness, he knew, was an important part of marriage. He had seen its soothing effect in his parents' marriage and knew how much it had been required in the marriages of his two eldest brothers.

If Ailie could not forgive him this deception which, to his mind, had been necessary and, to hers, a transgression, how could she forgive him in the future for others? After all, no man was perfect. Would she ever again be the woman he had held in his arms beneath the stars, the woman he wanted for his wife?

Last evening at dinner, she had announced she was accepting Muriel's invitation to come to London. Everyone, save him, seemed pleased. Nash imagined the reception she would receive with the favor of the Countess of Claremont. Every bachelor in the *ton* would be nipping at her heels, asking for her hand.

Rising from his bed, he walked to the window, pleased to see the sun rising in a clear blue sky for the first time in days. Late yesterday, the storm had moved off to the west, but a sudden drop in temperature and a new snowfall had covered everything in white.

Today they were to sail to Stonehaven.

Adding a log to the fire, he turned to see Robbie, still asleep, his head no longer wrapped in linen. Now only a small white patch covered the ugly wound on his left temple. Robbie never complained but Nash had seen him wince when he changed the bandage, which Robbie now insisted on doing himself.

Nash thought about their return to London, less than a week away. He felt as if he were coming to the end of an era. He had expected that he and Robbie would one day part ways. And it seemed that day would be soon. He would miss his twin, having only holidays to look forward to when they would gather together with their other brothers. But, for now, he would enjoy the rest of the holiday with him.

"Time to rise, Brother. Today we are for Stonehaven."

Robbie groaned and opened his eyes, squinting at the bright light spilling into their chamber. "The sun is shining?"

"Indeed, it is. Very pretty, too, on the new snow."

Throwing off the cover, Robbie slowly sat up. "I'm glad we're to sail. I miss being on a ship."

"I as well."

They joined the others for breakfast and, once their valises were loaded on the *Albatross*, Captain Anderson welcomed them aboard.

Nash followed William and Emily up the gangplank. At the top, the good captain saluted William and dipped his head to Emily. "Sir, Madam, 'tis a fine day to sail."

"Aye," William replied. "Should be beautiful, if chilly."

"Ye'll be staying for Hogmanay, sir?"

William nodded. "Through New Year's Day, I imagine. Will you remain in the harbor on the ship?"

"Aye, sir, I will. We've a full stock of provisions and a few of the crew will stay on board as the watch. The others are looking forward to the celebration in Stonehaven, but I've no doubt we'll be able see the Hogmanay fires from the ship."

Nash tipped his hat to the captain and climbed aboard, Robbie behind him. The sky above them was the color of a robin's egg with nary a cloud and the North Sea a dark blue beneath it. The sailing to Stonehaven, he'd been told, would be short as the town lay only twenty-one nautical miles to the north.

The wind blowing across the deck was biting, causing Nash to pull his scarf up to his ears. His fellow passengers had elected to stay on deck and now stood at the rail, bundled up in their woolens.

Once they were out of the harbor, Nash joined William and Emily at the rail where they watched the craggy terrain and cliffs go by off the port beam.

A large flock of seabirds flew overhead, catching his eye.

"That's Fowlsheugh," said Captain Anderson from amidships. "In the spring, thousands of kittiwakes, guillemots and razorbills will be nesting on those cliffs. When they take to the wing, 'tis quite a sight."

Nash tried to imagine what so many shorebirds would look like covering the jagged cliffs and was reminded of exotic ports to which he had sailed. After his time in Scotland, he planned to return to the family business. There would be more ship travel to distant ports, only this time, he wanted to sail with Ailie.

He shifted his gaze to where she stood at the rail next to Muriel. He hoped the looks Ailie gave him meant that while she was not ready to forgive him, he was not forgotten.

The countess appeared to be enjoying herself, her sea legs keeping her as steady as the rest of them.

On Nash's left side, Kit stood with Martin. "I must try and remember those cliffs. They are starkly beautiful covered in snow."

"You've some amazing sketches already, Kitten," said Martin.

"'Tis a good thing I brought several sketchbooks. I'll be needing them if we're to see more of such scenery."

After they had been sailing for a while, Nash pointed to what looked like a ruined medieval castle perched atop a headland, its foundations blanketed in snow. "What is that?"

"*That* is Dunnottar," said William on Nash's right. "If this weather holds, we intend to visit the castle tomorrow. It's only a few miles from the harbor where we'll be staying."

"Dunnottar has one of the bloodiest histories of any castle in Scotland," Ailie commented from the other side of William and Emily.

"'Tis ancient history," William gently scolded. He patted Emily's arm. Nash supposed William took pains not to disturb his pregnant wife with tales of blood and gore.

"Well, if we are going to see the castle, our guests might want to be aware of the history," Ailie replied. "And you know Grandfather will be expounding at dinner tonight on the ghosts that walk the castle grounds."

William laughed. "Oh, aye, he will, and I'll be joining him."

Beneath her plumed hat, Muriel's silver brows rose. "Ghosts? How delicious!"

Robbie gave her a long, studying look. "Why, Muriel, I had no idea you were enamored of ghosts."

"Their presence adds a certain mystical element to a place, don't you agree? I shall have to ask Angus Ramsay what he knows of them."

"You won't have to ask," said Ailie. "When Grandfather learns we are to travel there on the morrow, he will insist on giving you a tour, that is, if you are up for tramping about in the snow."

The countess smiled. "I shall dress appropriately and take my flask of Madeira. A sledge ride in the snow to explore a haunted castle sounds like great fun."

"Countess, you continue to surprise me," Robbie said with a grin, his bandage of white just showing beneath his beaver hat. No one had forgotten what took place on Boxing Day in Arbroath, but Nash and Robbie were nevertheless accepted back into the fold, Ailie being the one exception.

Nash was determined to be patient with the rebellious Scottish lass. And perhaps a ruined castle complete with wailing ghosts would gain him both her forgiveness and her affection.

"I wonder how one sketches a ghost," said Kit thoughtfully as she stared at the castle ruins.

"If I see any," said Nash, "I'll be sure and let you know… as I'm running away."

She swatted his arm. "You would never run away from anything, Nash."

Nash shot a look at Ailie, who met his gaze. "No, perhaps not."

"Looks like the harbor up ahead," shouted Nick.

"Aye," said Captain Anderson, "prettiest harbor in Kincardineshire."

Muriel slipped her arm through Aileen's as they followed the others from where the *Albatross* docked toward The Ship Inn in the distance. The three-story, whitewashed building overlooked the tranquil harbor.

Her gaze swept over the well-constructed buildings set around the crescent harbor, the fishing boats rocking with the waves slapping against the quay and the two ships tied up. Behind the buildings at the harbor's edge, the rest of the town and a church with a tall steeple sat nestled against the hills. "A very picturesque little seaport."

"I have always thought so," said Aileen, who was sensibly dressed today in a simple but becoming gown of mazarine blue and a darker blue cloak. Her tartan scarf, draped over her head on the ship, now rested on her shoulders. "I think you will like the inn. 'Tis quite comfortable."

"And the food?" Muriel was curious to know what they might serve, given the possibilities.

"Since this is a fishing town, there will be salmon and cod, some of it smoked. As I recall, the inn serves a tolerably good mutton stew and doubtless they'll have roast chicken. Breakfast will be oatmeal, girdle scones and eggs. Oh, and I believe they have a kaleyard and will have stored some greens for winter use."

Muriel fought the urge to frown.

Aileen chuckled. "There is always the inn's shortbread to look forward to. Their cook bakes some of the best in all of Kincardineshire." Leaning in to whisper, she added, "I say that because our cook in Arbroath claims her shortbread is the best in Forfarshire."

The girl laughed and her cheeks, red from the cold, made her lovely eyes appear bright.

"It is good to see you laugh again, Aileen. I feared your somber countenance of the past several days would become permanent."

"I must apologize for being so sullen."

"You had reason enough. I don't suppose you have forgiven your young man yet?"

"He is not *my* young man, Muriel, and no," she said, biting her lip and gazing toward the blue waters of the harbor, "I have not."

Perhaps, thought Muriel, she could accomplish more if she reminded Aileen of her humanity. "Have you never deceived someone for the sake of what you believed was a good purpose?"

The girl looked down at her feet. After a moment, she said, "… I deceived my parents into thinking I'd given up my desire to design ships, while I never did."

"And did they forgive you?"

Aileen looked up, her eyes smiling now. "Aye, they did, and today my father is glad for my persistence if not my deceit. But Nash's deception was not the same. I believed we had confided our hearts to each other, yet not once did he mention his spying. Worse, what he and Robbie did could have led to someone's death, including their own!"

"Indeed, it was despicable!" Muriel carefully observed the girl's face for any sign of agreement. When she didn't see it, she went on, hoping to get Aileen to defend the young man. "Not telling your brother and Emily was terribly wrong, but not to speak a word of it to you was outside of enough."

The girl chewed her bottom lip, fingering a long strand of her hair. "Maybe he couldn't say anything. Might they have been sworn to secrecy?"

"Very possibly." Muriel inwardly smiled, happy her plan to turn Aileen into Nash's defender was working. "Have you asked him about that?"

Aileen looked up with a guilty expression. "No..."

"I have discovered that it is best to settle disagreements early while there is still a chance to do so. Perhaps it would be best to put behind you the mischief Nash and his brother undertook for that rascal Sidmouth. You don't have to marry the man just because you allow him back into your good graces."

Aileen gave her a sharp glance. "He has said nothing to me of marriage."

"Perhaps not, but an old matchmaker like me can see from the way he looks at you, the subject is on his mind."

They arrived at the front door of the inn behind the rest of their company. William turned to face them. "The Ship Inn is entirely ours through New Year's, so make yourselves at home. I will introduce to you to Mr. Cruickshank, the proprietor, and he will see you are escorted to your chambers. There are no plans for today except for dinner but, tomorrow, the adventurers among us assail the castle!"

As she stepped through the door of the inn, the first thing Muriel noticed was the warm air on her chilled face. She inhaled the pleasant smell of wood burning in the large fireplace she glimpsed through the doorway on her right, which appeared to lead to a common room.

Two servants accepted their coats, cloaks, gloves and hats and one ushered them into the well-appointed room where the rest of their party had gathered before the fire. Muriel could see it was not a place to dine but almost a parlor with upholstered chairs, a sofa and small tables perfectly sized for a cup of tea. "How very nice this is," she remarked to her companion.

"I did tell you the inn would be comfortable," Aileen reminded her.

"So you did." Muriel glanced out the large windows that provided a splendid view of the cerulean blue bay where the *Albatross* floated, its sails neatly furled.

A tall pleasant-looking man of middle years with brown hair and spectacles entered the room. At his side the auburn-haired William Stephen. "Allow me to present Mr. Cruickshank, the inn's proprietor and our host for the time we are here."

Mr. Cruickshank inclined his head. "'Tis an honor to have you as our guests. I assure you the employees of the inn and I will do all we can to make your stay with us an enjoyable one."

An attractive young woman came to his side. The proprietor put his arm around her shoulder. "This is my daughter, Fiona. As a widower, I have come to rely upon her as hostess in all things concerning our guests. You will find her competent and willing to assist with your needs."

The girl, who could not have been over twenty, smiled at their company, but quickly diverted her gaze to the two Powell twins, the only unaccompanied men among them. Fiona had the same brown hair as her father but her eyes were blue and her lovely face featured a dimple in each cheek that showed themselves when she smiled.

Muriel instantly sensed Aileen had competition.

"We've some hot tea, brandy and mulled claret to warm you," Fiona offered. Her voice was the soothing, seductive kind men favored with just a hint of a Scottish accent.

Oh, my yes, definitely competition.

At Fiona's words and, to the great happiness of the assembled guests, two male servants glided into the room carrying trays bearing cups, fragrant steam rising from them.

Muriel accepted a cup of the mulled claret, which, upon tasting, she found to be quite good. "I begin to thaw," she muttered.

Aileen took a cup from the tray, but did not raise it to her lips. Instead, she held the cup between her hands, her attention fixed on the proprietor's daughter talking to the Powell twins. "I should have remembered sweet Fiona," Aileen said.

Muriel took another sip of the spicy wine. "My dear, it would appear you have a rival."

Later that day, having changed her gown and allowed Rhona, who had accompanied them north with a few of the other maids, to comb the tangles from her hair, Ailie ventured downstairs. The dining room was empty save for Will and Emily.

Will looked up from the sideboard where he was pouring a drink. The inn had set out bottles of sherry, wine and brandy with an array of glasses for them. "Come join us," he urged. "Can I pour you a glass of sherry?"

"Good eve to you both. Aye, that would be most welcome. I'll just warm myself by the fire." She stepped nearer to the blazing fire and stretched her hands toward the flames. Even with the fireplaces well tended, the rooms of the inn could be chilly.

She had always liked this room, a testimony to life at sea, decorated as it was with flags and pennants from various ships, a fancy carved transom with a unicorn, the heraldic symbol of Scotland, and various cutlasses and weapons of the past. Over the fireplace between two sconces was a painting of a seventeenth century sixty-gun warship, its sails billowing with wind and its stern flying a Scottish red ensign.

Like the inn's common room, this one looked out on the harbor. She turned from the fire to gaze beyond the windows to the waters of the small bay turned lavender blue by the setting sun. The sky above them glowed a pale salmon color, making the harbor altogether magical in appearance.

Emily carried two glasses of sherry to Ailie and handed one to her. "Wasn't it thoughtful of the proprietor to combine the tables into one long one for us?"

"Aye, it was. That way all of our guests can hear Grandfather's tales of the castle ghosts."

Muriel swept into the dining room just then, a white feather rising above the jeweled band around her head.

"You look refreshed, Muriel," remarked Emily.

Muriel accepted a glass of Madeira from Will. "Thank you. I had a bit of a lie down, which has left me feeling wonderful. All that sea air, I expect."

The others began filtering into the dining room. When Nash and Robbie appeared on the threshold, Ailie's gaze immediately darted to Nash. His eyes met hers in a questioning look. Her heart ached for want of him. She decided being at odds with the man you love is dreadful.

He headed straight for her. "Ailie—"

"Would you like something to drink?" Fiona purred, as she rushed to his side, her dimples on display.

"Thank you, brandy would be fine," he said, never taking his eyes off Ailie. When Fiona had gone, he began again. "Ailie, I need to speak to you, but not here."

Her heart was in her throat, afraid of what he might say. "If you must."

The conversations around them grew boisterous as Nash's green and gold eyes stared into hers. A longing to rush into his arms came over her but, reminded of his deception, she resisted.

Before he could reply, Fiona returned with Nash's brandy. "Is there anything else you might like, sir?"

Thankfully, Ailie's grandfather strode into the room at that moment to welcome everyone to Stonehaven. His appearance took her aback.

For the fancy attire he wore, he might have just stepped into her father's drawing room in Aberdeen. His blue velvet coat paired with Ramsay blue tartan trews made his blue eyes shine and gave him a distinguished bearing. Even his white cravat appeared expertly tied. Ailie felt certain he had dressed for Muriel and the thought made her smile.

Her grandfather bowed before Muriel. "Guid eve'nin' tae ye, Countess."

"Mr. Ramsey, how gallant you look," replied Muriel. "You must sit near me at dinner. I am anxious to hear your stories of the ghosts at the castle we're to see tomorrow."

"I can tell ye some tales." Her grandfather surveyed the table, appearing to count chairs. "Och! There be thirteen places. 'Tis nae lucky."

"Good sir," came Muriel's reply. "I would much prefer an odd number at dinner, even if it be thirteen, else I feel like I'm entering the ark."

Ailie's grandfather laughed. "Ye're a one, Muriel. Verra weel, I shall brave the bad fairies tae please ye."

Ailie glanced toward the windows to see the sky had darkened to a deep violet. With all the people gathered in the dining room, the air was warm enough to cause steam to appear on the windows, leaving little to see except for the few lights onboard the two ships in the harbor.

"Let's warm ourselves by the fire," Nash suggested. She followed him to the fire steadily burning above glowing coals. He drank his brandy and she sipped her sherry, more conscious of him than anyone else in the room.

"You may not have forgiven me, Ailie," Nash said in a low voice, "but I'll be keeping you close till you do."

"You'll have a long wait," she blurted. But even as she said the words, she could feel her resolve to stay angry with him ebbing away.

When the others began to take their seats, Nash motioned to two chairs across the table from where Muriel and Ailie's grandfather had just taken a seat. "Sit with me, Ailie."

She nodded and followed him.

Once everyone was seated, beneath the table, Nash took her hand, brushing his thumb over her knuckles, causing an enticing shiver to ripple through her. She recognized his gesture as an invitation to reconcile and, though she was tempted to decline, she did not withdraw her hand.

The dinner the inn served was a fine baked cod with mustard sauce and chicken roasted with sage and thyme. Even knowing it would all be splendidly cooked, Ailie had little appetite. Her disagreement with Nash had robbed her of an appetite. Still, she managed to appear as if she would eat, adroitly moving the chicken about her plate.

Nash hadn't eaten either. She inclined her head toward him. "You aren't hungry?"

"Not very. I've much on my mind."

Did he, too, hate the distance between them?

Toward the end of the meal, which Ailie only picked at, Fiona and two male servants entered carrying plates of warm shortbread. "We've tea and port for you if you like," said the pretty girl, as she set a plate of shortbread before Nash.

Muriel took a bite of the shortbread. "Oh my. This is quite wonderful."

Ailie glanced at Nash, wanting desperately to be close to him again. "Here's something we can agree upon," she said, picking up a piece of shortbread with her free hand. "It melts in the mouth."

In a low voice, discernable only to her, he said, "I'm happy to eat it with one hand."

In truth, Ailie would gladly forego dessert for the comfort of his touch. It wasn't like any other man's touch. And it wasn't just the powerful attraction she felt for him. Holding Nash's hand made her feel like a ship moored in home port.

Ailie's grandfather pushed aside his empty plate, took up his wine and, with Muriel's encouragement, began to speak of Dunnottar.

The conversations around them died as he recited the words of the poem by Mrs. Carnegie:

"High on a rock, half sea-girt, half on land,
The castle stood, and still its ruins stand
Wide o'er the German main the prospect bent,
Steep is the path and rugged the ascent:
There hung the huge portcullis—there the bar
Drawn on the iron gate defied the war."

Her grandfather took a swallow of his wine. "Many wars have come and gone an' still Dunnottar stands, a broodin' fortress, aye, but nae alone. Her ghosts are many and they dinna sleep. 'Tis guid ye willna be visitin' her at night when the witches burned at Dunnottar cry from the cliffs."

Kit looked up with a fearful glance at Ailie's grandfather. "Witches?"

Will nodded. "In the sixteenth century, several were seized in Aberdeen and burned at Dunnottar. Lord only knows the torture they endured before their deaths."

In a voice Ailie was certain was designed to add to the mood of the evening, her grandfather intoned, "The anshent ruins speik wi' a loud voice. Every turret ha' a tongue. Ye may nae see a spectre, still, ye'll hear their screams. 'Tis as if the verra walls remember."

Will leaned in, the flickering candle casting shadows on his face and his auburn hair. "A woman is said to wander about in a green tartan dress. No one knows who she is."

Emily, who Ailie knew had never visited the castle, drew close to her husband, a frightened expression on her lovely face. "So many ghosts?"

Will wrapped his arm around his wife's shoulders. "Aye, *Leannan*, and there's more of the wee ghosties. The spectre of a young deerhound runs about the castle grounds, looking, they say, for his master. A Norseman frequents the guardroom at the main entrance yet if you were to follow him, he would vanish. And near the cave entrance leading from the sea, a soldier, dressed in military regalia from some past era, stares out to sea as if watching for a ship."

Grandfather Ramsay turned to Muriel. "Ye still be wantin' tae see it, Countess?"

"Oh yes," she said. "You'll not frighten me away so easily!"

Ailie's grandfather laughed. "Then I shall take ye meself an' we'll see if we can find a ghostie or two."

Ailie glanced out the large windows. Outside, night had descended and inside, the fire had burned to smoldering remnants, the candles now mere stubs. Shadows lurked around the room, calling up images of the ghosts they had spoken of. It was not difficult to believe that not far away stood an ancient castle where those same ghosts still roamed. In her mind, she could imagine them; she could hear their wails.

Nash must have sensed her disquiet, for he squeezed her hand. Her heart, which had been beating rapidly as Angus and William had spoken of ghosts, calmed as Nash's warmth and strength flowed into her. He was her anchor to all that was real. But could she forgive his deception?

Into the eerie silence, Robbie uttered the words that made everyone laugh. "Well, ain't it fortunate they're all dead?"

Chapter 21

30 December, Stonehaven

After a sleepless night, Nash had come to the dining room early, grateful for the hot coffee Fiona handed him. He did not feel up to returning her smile. Instead, he idly pushed his eggs about his plate, all desire for food having deserted him as he considered how to handle his stubborn Scottish lass.

Ailie was *his* or would be when he sorted all this out. She could not deny the passion between them. The fire was there, smoldering beneath all that had happened. He had only to rekindle it.

She might have decided to go to London but, if he were successful, she would greet the *ton* on his arm.

Robbie and the rest of their company filed in a short while later, complaining of dreams haunted by Dunnottar's ghosts. Angus had come for breakfast and claimed the chair next to Muriel.

Ailie had yet to appear.

Nash knew he had taken a risk when he reached for her hand the evening before, but she had not pulled away. It had taken all his resolve to keep from dragging her outside and reminding her of the passion and the love that lay between them.

"Says here tensions are running high in Glasgow," said William, poring over the *Stonehaven Journal*, the newspaper Angus had brought with him. "The weavers are none too happy."

Angus paused in the act of his lathing butter on a scone. "'Tis nae over yet."

Muriel looked up from her chocolate. "I do hope they do nothing foolish."

"If they do, they'll be in for it," predicted William. "The yeomanry is still camped around the city."

"Can I see that?" Robbie asked. William handed him the paper and returned to his omelet.

Nash glance at his brother as Robbie pulled his spectacles from his pocket and, careful not to scrape his healing wound, put them on. He still wore the small bandage. Nash had the impression he did so not because it was necessary but to hide the ugly scar forming on his temple.

Robbie bent his head to the paper. "Good Lord, according to this, it's getting worse. Won't be pretty if Sidmouth decides to make an example of Glasgow's weavers."

Hugh shook his head. "Parliament doesn't see the need for reform."

Nash agreed, doubting reform would come anytime soon. The Six Acts, robbing men of freedoms they had long held, discouraged him beyond hope.

Angus finished his haddies, wiping his mouth with his napkin. "A nod's as guid as a wink tae a blind horse."

Eyebrows rose around the table, including Nash's, but it was Muriel who spoke. "Whatever does that mean?"

"It means," said Ailie, entering the dining room, "if a horse is blind, it matters little if you nod your head or wink your eye, he still cannot see, just as the government is blind to what is happening in Scotland."

"Oh," said Muriel. "Yes, I quite understand."

Ailie turned to the sideboard, adding small bits of food to her plate.

Nash remembered she had not eaten much at dinner, so perhaps she was hungry. Since they'd been at odds, neither of them had much of an appetite.

She took a seat across from Nash. Her expression disclosed nothing until she glanced up at Robbie and a look of surprise crossed her face. "You wear spectacles?"

Robbie peered over his spectacles to look at her. "I do. Nash and I are the only ones in our family unlucky enough to require them to read."

Why did she ask? Then he remembered the day he had gone to town and Robbie took his place in the library. Had Robbie been wearing spectacles when she found him? He wondered again what kind of a kiss his twin had given her.

"Do you read horticulture books like Nash?" she asked.

Robbie paused, flicking a glance at Nash before returning to Ailie. Nash was certain each read the other's thoughts. Finally, Robbie said, "Rarely."

Ailie looked up from her plate and shook her head. "Robbie Powell, you *are* a rogue. Worse than I'd imagined."

"Likely so," Robbie admitted.

Nash believed the only one at the table who understood something had been left unsaid was Muriel, whose eyes bore into him and then moved to stare at Robbie.

"As soon as you've finished your breakfast," announced William, "we'll be off to the castle. We've two large sledges to accommodate us. That's a sleigh to you, Tara."

"I can hardly wait!" said Nick's wife.

A half-hour later, Nash had donned his hat, gloves and greatcoat and assisted Ailie into the sledge carrying Emily, Muriel and Angus. William took the seat next to the driver as he did the day they had gone in search of the Yule log.

With a nod to Nash, Robbie climbed into the second sledge with their two older brothers, their wives, and the Ormonds.

It was much like their earlier trip into the woods near Arbroath, the runners on the large vehicles easily traversing the road leading south to Dunnottar.

The brisk air chilled their faces even though the sun was shining. Only a few white clouds drifted in the blue sky. The inn had supplied them with lap blankets and beneath the one Nash shared with Ailie, he took her hand. Their gloves did not allow him the warm touch of her skin, but he was encouraged she did not resist the gesture.

In no time at all, they arrived at the approach to the castle and the sledges came to an abrupt halt, the horses snorting after their run. At this point, they were level with the top of the rocky snow-covered precipice on which the castle ruins stood, defying time. Behind the immense rock, the vast expanse of the blue sea stretched to the horizon.

Nash tried to envision Dunnottar as the castle it might have been, its battlements bright with colorful banners, the walls bristling with cannon and weapons, its practice yard crowded with men-at-arms, not the unroofed and untenanted sepulcher it had become. "It must have been magnificent."

"Aye," said Angus on a sigh. "She were a braw stronghold once." Nash wondered if the old Scot longed for the former times when the castles of Scotland were the bastions of powerful lairds.

"What happened to the roofs?" Nash asked.

"When the castle was forfeited after the rising in 1715," said Ailie, "the roofs were removed and sold. A travesty, as some might have survived to this day."

William shouted, "Hold on, everyone!"

At the driver's command, the horses plunged down the snow-covered slope. Nash gripped Ailie's hand and braced himself against the side of the sledge as the horses, seemingly unafraid, lunged forward and then veered to the left bringing them to the bottom of a valley in front of the castle's rocky foundation.

Ailie laughed. "A much wilder ride than in the summer when we walk."

"Indeed," said Muriel, hand over her heart. "But I quite enjoyed it."

Angus gave her a huge grin. "Ye're a grand lady, Countess."

"Nonsense."

William turned to Emily. "Are you all right, *Leannan*?"

"I am fine," she said. "It's the ghosts that have me worried."

Nash tilted his head back to look up at the formidable mound of rock looming hundreds of feet in the air. He could no longer see the ruins atop the massive rock. Looking behind him, he glimpsed the second sledge, smiles on everyone's faces.

"Your brother has a sense of the dramatic," he said to Ailie.

"He does. I suspect he wanted you to be surprised."

"When do we get to set our feet on the ground?" asked Muriel turning in her seat to look up at William who sat above her with the driver. "I'm anxious to see the castle."

"You can alight here," he replied. "The path leading up to the castle's entrance is too narrow to take the sledges farther. They will remain here until we are ready to return. If some of you want to go back early, just let the drivers know. They will take you to the inn and return for the rest of us."

They climbed down and trudged up the long steep path. At the top, stood a tall opening, carved into the rock, as if beckoning them to enter.

Beside him, Ailie stared at the entrance.

"You don't fear the ghosts, do you?"

She shook her head. "No, it's just that I've not seen Dunnottar in winter. 'Tis different with all the snow, colder and more forbidding than in summer."

They entered an arched stone passage, musty with age. Nash had the sense the tunnel slanting upward was taking them to another time. At the end of the passage, they encountered another gate that opened to the castle area where a dozen stone buildings, or parts of them, still remained.

At that point, the group broke apart, heading in different directions.

Nash paused to take in the breathtaking sight. At his side, Ailie said, "'Tis as if we have been lifted into the air, suspended high above the sea."

He took her hand. "Come, let's find a building to explore." He had in mind more than exploration of an ancient ruin but, for his purposes, they needed to be alone and more protected from the wind.

"The tower house?" she suggested, pointing to a multi-storied building, or at least the skeleton of one.

"Fine, let's go there." As they set out toward the looming keep, above them storm petrels took to flight, the small birds' shrill cry echoing off the stone walls.

"Just think," she said, as he tugged her along, "Mary Queen of Scots walked this same ground."

He gave her a lopsided grin. "Considering what happened to her and many of the castle's 'guests', I am none too eager to follow in their steps."

They stepped inside the ancient tower house. Roofless, it provided no warmth, but its thick stone walls sheltered them from the wind. For the moment, they were alone and Nash planned to take full advantage. "Ailie, we must talk." He'd rather kiss her but talking had to come first.

"Aye." She dropped the hood of her cloak to fall to her shoulders, giving Nash a splendid view of her glorious copper hair. Then, as if to delay what she knew was coming, she said, "Some of Dunnottar's buildings are not yet two hundred years old while others, like this one built by the Keiths are from many centuries ago."

Nash drew her to the window, an open portal to the castle's grounds. He could see no reason to delay. "Are you going to forgive me or not?"

She bit her full lower lip. "Would you ever do it again?"

"Do what?"

Her sherry eyes flashed. "Spy... lie. All of it!"

He stepped closer, placed his hands on her waist inside her cloak and gazed deeply into her eyes, wanting her to see the sincerity of his words. "My days of acting the spy are over, Ailie. As for lying, I did not lie to you. Well, not exactly. I just didn't—couldn't—tell you all I was about. The nature of the work required our silence and, at times, the assumption of a disguise."

A frown creased her forehead.

He glanced out the window, seeing only the ruins, the snow-covered ground and the sea beyond. "Once I learned how unjust it would be to return Kinloch for trial, I thought to let him escape. And when you spoke of him as wanting only good for Scotland, I knew you would feel betrayed if I did not let him go."

"Robbie was against it?"

Nash turned to face her. "He was, but I do not fault him. We had agreed to do the job for Sidmouth. I thought to persuade Robbie to let Kinloch escape, but I was not successful. In the end, Robbie paid a terrible price for being more constant than I." He touched his forehead to hers. "I've been miserable thinking you have rejected me, but last night you gave me hope. Forgive me, Ailie."

She brought her hands up and draped them around his neck.

"I suppose I shall have to forgive you since I love you."

Their eyes met. "You do?" He felt a silly grin spreading on his face.

She nodded. "Aye, for quite some time."

"Just as well," he said, more casually that he felt, "because it so happens I love you, too. Might have done since the first time I saw you waiting to meet us on the dock. Or perhaps it was that first morning you taught me about haddies. Or when I followed you into the woods to gather greenery and kissed you. You have a mind of your own, Ailie Stephen, and are not afraid to stand up for what you believe. How could I not love you?"

Nash bent his head to kiss her. "I love your freckles, Aileen Stephen, every one." He kissed the sprinkling of freckles on the top of her cheeks and then he took her mouth in a kiss he had waited too long to bestow. At first, their lips were cool from the chilled air around them but, soon, the kiss became one of passion and the blood running through his veins heated as his body melted into hers.

She welcomed his kiss and, when he slipped his tongue inside the sweet recesses of her mouth, she pulled him closer. He reached inside her cloak to fill his hand with a warm breast, drawing a moan from her throat.

The sound of a man clearing his throat caused Nash to lift his head. Turning, he saw the Ormonds standing just inside the entrance, smiling.

Peeling his body from Ailie's, Nash said, "Time we saw another part of the castle."

She nodded and he took her hand and led her toward the door.

"May I recommend the chapel?" offered Hugh. "I believe it's one of the oldest buildings and, I daresay, has been host to many a wedding."

Ailie felt her face flush with heat despite the cold as Nash took her hand and led her across the castle grounds to the quadrangle where the palace and chapel were located. Even though the buildings themselves were free of snow, a thin carpet of white still covered the ground.

Nash gave her a wide grin. "The chapel is the perfect place for what I have in mind." Now that all had been forgiven and they had confessed their love, the whole world had come right for Ailie. "Wherever you like."

The chapel, at one end of the quadrangle, was not hard to spot with its arched doorway and window. Unlike the tower house, most of one side of the chapel was missing. She stepped into the ancient church and followed Nash to the far wall, away from the windows and doorway. Sweeping his greatcoat behind him, he took her hands and dropped to one knee. Her heart rose in her throat and tears welled in her eyes as she anticipated his words.

"Aileen Stephen, I will never be the man I could be without you. You complete me. My heart is yours; I willingly lay it at your feet. Make me the happiest man in all of Britain and marry me."

She gave him an impudent smile. "Will you let me design ships?"

He nodded. "Even better, we will design them together."

Her spirits soared yet one question remained. "Must we always live in London?" She had to know if she would be asked to leave her beloved Scotland forever. She loved him enough to do it but perhaps he wouldn't mind a bit of negotiation.

Nash grinned up at her. "I can see this is to be the first of many compromises, but hopefully not all will be made with me on bent knee in cold rocky soil. To answer your question, I expect we will live in London for part of the year, but not all. The *Ossian* will be built in Arbroath, yes? So, we'll be there, too."

"Oh, Nash." Tears spilled down her cheeks. He could not have pleased her more. "You have made me very happy. You're the only man I ever desired for my husband. The only man I will ever love. Aye, I will marry you and gladly."

He got to his feet, dusted off his knees and took her into his arms. His kiss left her heart racing.

"Now, my love, all we need is a minister."

He led her from the church into the cold wind blowing across the quadrangle's inner yard, toward the well that was twenty feet across.

"Nash, I am old enough to marry without my parents' consent, but I would have Will approve of our marriage."

"William is not ignorant of my intentions toward you, Ailie. The night of the avalanche, I requested his permission to court you."

"You wanted me for your wife even then?"

"I did, but I wanted to be sure my suit would be welcomed before I confessed my conversation with your brother. He gave his approval once I convinced him I would always protect and love you, yet never seek to change the woman you are."

"Another secret, I see. But I heartily forgive you this one. Did Will question you most thoroughly?"

"Oh yes, and quite directly. Your brother loves you very much, Ailie. He would never approve of a man who did not desire your happiness above all."

"Are there any more secrets that I should know about?"

He gave her a puzzling look. "None that I can think of."

"Will you say nothing of that day in the library when I mistook Robbie for you? I almost died of embarrassment when I realized 'twas not you I had kissed but your brother!"

Nash had a sinking feeling Robbie had not disclosed all. "Robbie told me there was nothing to be concerned about. I assumed the kiss a mere peck on the cheek."

Her sherry-colored eyes shot daggers. "It was not a peck on the cheek, I assure you."

"He lied! If he wasn't already wounded, I would beat him about the head." Nash thought of how Robbie had behaved when he'd learned of Nash's feelings for Ailie. He had changed. "I am sorry, Ailie. You see, at the beginning, Robbie thought to win you. Not until he witnessed my anger that day for what I believed was a simple stolen kiss did he realize how much I cared for you. He promised to act circumspectly thereafter."

"Really, the two of you make a fine pair when you set out to deceive someone. I just wish it hadn't been me. At least now I can tell you apart. And, while we are at it, I have another question. What caused that scar beneath your hair? I felt the ridge when my fingers were in your thick curls that night when you kissed me under the stars."

"A souvenir from the yeomanry in Manchester. If Robbie had not come to my rescue, I would have been killed that day on St Peter's Field."

She reached her gloved hand to his cheek. "Then I owe him much." Had they not been in the courtyard where others might see them, she would have kissed him. "That day in Arbroath when it was Robbie whose head dripped blood, I felt guilty for my joy at discovering the man who lay wounded was not you."

"'Tis the first time I've rescued Robbie. With your help, of course."

"Come," she urged, "let us get out of the wind and see the palace." As they crossed the quadrangle, she wondered if she were bold enough to act upon her thoughts concerning their marriage. "You know," she began, "in Scotland, there is more than one way to wed."

"You mean we have a choice between an Anglican church and a Presbyterian kirk? It matters not to me where we are wed as long as our marriage is blessed by God."

"Actually, I was thinking of something else. In Scotland, we need not post banns or even summon a minister. We can marry by exchanging vows before witnesses as long as we live thereafter as man and wife."

He stopped and turned to face her. "As I am eager to begin living as man and wife, the idea appeals." The seductive gleam in his eyes brought heat to her cheeks. "But what of your family and mine?"

She looked down at the snow beneath her feet. "We could always be wed again in London."

Just then, Muriel and Angus emerged from one of the buildings on the right side of the quadrangle and hurried toward Ailie and Nash. "A ghost! We have seen a ghost!" shouted Muriel.

"Which one? Ailie asked.

"We was in the vault 'neath that one," said her grandfather, gesturing. "Where the puir Covenanters were left tae die. It were a woman I ne'er heard tell about afore."

"She wailed most pitifully," added Muriel, hand over her chest.

"Are you all right?" Nash asked the countess, who looked terribly pale.

"Oh yes. Just winded. I never thought to encounter one, you see. It was as if I had stepped into the past. How horrible it must have been for them, trapped beneath the stones and left to die."

"'Twas in winter tae," said Ailie's grandfather, "more 'an a hundred years ago."

"She disappeared before my very eyes," said Muriel, "her white Covenanters' cap and dark cloak suddenly vanishing. It quite took my breath away. The shock was almost as frightening as when she appeared."

Ailie shivered, both from the cold and from Muriel's tale.

"Do you wish to view more of the ruins?" asked Nash, "or might we return?"

Ailie was grateful for his suggestion. "Let's go back. All I want now is a fire and a warm drink."

"Here," said Muriel, thrusting a silver flask into Ailie's hand. "Have a drink of Madeira to tide you over."

"We want to get married!" Nash exclaimed when their fellow travelers returned to the inn. They had gathered in the common room with Muriel and her grandfather, warming themselves in front of the fire.

Only a few shocked faces greeted Nash's announcement. William, Muriel and the Ormonds—who had witnessed his kissing Ailie at Dunnottar—appeared unsurprised. Robbie just smiled.

William said, "Finally!"

Muriel followed this with a doleful, "So soon? I had hoped for some time with Aileen in London."

Nash couldn't resist a smile. He raised Ailie's hand and pressed a kiss to her knuckles. "You'll have time with both of us in London, Countess."

Hugh's face took on a puzzled expression. "I'm all for the marriage, but shouldn't the banns be read first?"

"No banns, Hugh." Again, Nash smiled. "Don't need 'em here. Brilliant of the Scots to make it so easy to wed."

Ailie explained, "We just announce our intention to marry before witnesses—as we have done—and then live as man and wife."

Robbie let out a whistle. "Good show, Brother. My felicitations to you both."

"You know," said Nick, "having been cheated out of a wedding, Mother will want a large reception."

Muriel's face brightened. "I daresay one can be arranged. A soiree in the ballroom at my London house would be just the thing."

Emily fixed her husband with a suspicious look. "You don't seem at all surprised."

William gave his wife a sheepish grin. "Nash asked to court Ailie some time ago and I gave my consent. He didn't want anyone to know until the lass looked upon his suit with favor. Still, 'tis not out of the question to arrange a wedding and I'd prefer it be done properly. Grandfather Ramsay knows the minister at the Dunnottar Parish Kirk in Stonehaven. He might be willing to read the banns all at once."

Angus pursed his lips. "Aye, I 'spect so."

"There you have it," said William. And to Nash, "Wedding tomorrow soon enough?"

Nash shifted his gaze to Ailie, who nodded.

"Tomorrow's fine," he told her brother.

"Hogmanay be the time tae hav' a weddin'," said Angus, his fingers rubbing across his jaw in what appeared to Nash to be a growing interest in the idea.

"Tomorrow it is!" enthused William. Facing Nash, he said, "I do believe your brothers, Ormond and I will require your attention for the afternoon. There are details to discuss, my sister's dowry, for one."

Content he would have the woman he loved in his arms tomorrow, Nash allowed himself to be pulled away.

Chapter 22

31 December

Ailie stood before the mirror in her room in the inn, admiring the gown Rhona had helped her to put on. Behind her, Muriel raised her quizzing glass to study the gown's fabric. But Ailie had no doubt the pale gold muslin with sprigs of heather embroidered in gold thread had been the right one for her Scottish wedding.

Her maid's eyes filled with unshed tears. "I canna believe this is yer wedding day."

"I expect you thought never to see it," Ailie teased.

"Enough of that, Aileen," Muriel protested. "The gown suits you. I do believe you made a fine choice. The man as well."

The afternoon before, Muriel and all the wives had hurried Ailie from the inn's dining room to immerse her in a flurry of gowns, petticoats and ribbons in search of the gown that would transform her into a bride. They had insisted Ailie try on every gown they had brought with them that might qualify. The whole affair reminded her of the time they had gathered in the parlor in Arbroath to decorate baskets. That auspicious day seemed like ages ago and now she was to be wed the man she had come to love, spy though he be.

In the end, she had decided to wear the gown Rhona had suggested Ailie bring with her to Stonehaven.

"Ye can wear it for Hogmanay," Rhona had said. She could not have known how fitting the choice would prove to be.

When the wives asked her why she chose that gown, Ailie explained, "Heather is the flower of good fortune for a Scottish bride."

This morning, Muriel asked to come to Ailie's room to help her dress for her wedding. Since Ailie had been nervous the day before, she believed Muriel had come more for encouragement, which endeared the countess to her.

Muriel sat watching Rhona brush out Ailie's thick hair that she would wear long. In the mirror, Ailie caught the wistful look on Muriel's face. "What are you thinking, Countess?"

"Just the memory of another bride long ago."

Ailie imagined the countess as a young woman, beautiful and spirited. Even in her sixties, she was still beautiful. "You are remembering when you were a bride?"

She smiled. "It was a day much like today when two impetuous people wed in a precipitous manner and loved very well."

"Oh, Muriel." She went to the countess and kissed her cheek. "Thank you. It means much to have your blessing."

When Ailie's hair had been brushed till it shone, Rhona took a sash of Ramsay tartan and fixed it over Ailie's right shoulder, securing it with a brooch at her waist. "This is the plaid of yer mother's clan. With the sash, yer bridegroom will have no doubt he's marrying a Scot."

"Humph," Muriel muttered. "I believe Nash Powell is well aware of that. More's to his credit that he prefers Aileen to the ladies in London who would jump at the chance to have him."

Last night after dinner, Nash had walked with Ailie along the harbor, sharing his vision of their future together. "You will never have to worry about my fidelity," he assured her. "There will be no other for me." Ailie believed him and the knowledge she could trust his love had calmed her bride's fears.

When Rhona left Ailie and the countess alone, Muriel came to kiss her cheek. "I'll see you downstairs, Aileen. Don't be long. I'm certain Nash is champing at the bit to get you to the church."

Alone in her chamber, Ailie went to the window to gaze out at the harbor. How appropriate she would marry on Hogmanay, the end of one year and the beginning of another. It would be a new year and a new life for her.

In the hall outside her door, she heard Emily say, "Everyone is ready, Ailie!"

Before she went to join the others, she scratched a few lines in her diary.

31 December

They are calling for me so I must go, but I had to record this day. I am to be wed to Nash Etienne Powell in Dunnottar's Parish Kirk. Yes, I know he's English, but so is Emily. After all, love recognizes no borders and considers no obstacles insurmountable. I have forgiven him for not telling me what he was sworn to keep secret. Doubtless, there will be many more occasions when each of us must forgive the other.

A new life awaits me and I am excited for it to begin.

Nash turned away from his brothers' teasing and fixed his gaze on the top of the stairs, impatient to see his bride. A moment later, she appeared, a golden goddess with a blue tartan sash across her shimmering gown. Behind him, the conversations ceased.

Ailie descended the stairs and he held out his hand, his heart swelling in his chest. "My love, you are truly the most beautiful bride."

She blushed. "And you are ever so handsome." He had worn the gold brocade waistcoat and dark blue tailcoat with velvet collar over his buff trousers because Muriel had insisted. Now he understood why. He and Ailie complemented each other in dress, a matched pair for their wedding, as he believed they would be in life.

William had arranged for carriages to transport them to the Dunnottar Parish Kirk in Dunnottar Woods a half-mile south of Stonehaven, and he had persuaded the minister to call the banns yesterday to allow them to wed today.

They entered the small country church, constructed of stone blocks, with its arched roof of oak, and made their way down the aisle to the chancel where he and Ailie took their place between Robbie and Emily. They were married there in the simple setting with light from the one window falling onto Ailie's copper hair like a halo around her.

The ceremony was blissfully short. Nash answered at the proper time but his thoughts were all for his bride, the gift the Good Lord had seen fit to give him. He slid the gold ring he had procured the afternoon before onto her finger, as they repeated the words that made them man and wife.

And then he kissed her. Not wishing to embarrass her, he did not allow himself a long kiss but he put his heart into it. Lifting his lips from hers, he told her, "You're mine now, Aileen Stephen Powell."

Her smile in reply was winning. "So I am."

They left the church hand in hand and were greeted by the women, who circled around Ailie wishing her well, and the men, who teased Nash about marrying above his station.

"I am only too aware of that fact," he admitted.

"Congratulations, Brother," said Robbie. "You have won the heart of The Mistress of the Setters."

Angus Ramsay came to Nash's side. "Treat 'er weel, Sassenach, or I'll be seein' ye. An' consider namin' yer first bairn Angus."

The smile on the old fisherman's face belied the warning and the request, but Nash did not take either lightly. "I intend to love her well, Angus. And if God gives us a male child, we shall find a way to add

Angus to his names."

Nash tucked her hand in his arm and they walked out of the church and passed through the gravestones toward the carriages.

Suddenly, Muriel said, "Why, that's amazing!"

Everyone came to see what had drawn the countess' attention. "What is it?" asked William.

The countess bent over a stone marker, her quizzing glass held in front of her as she read the carved words. "It's a memorial stone to mark the Covenanters who died prisoners in Dunnottar Castle in 1685. Look," she said, pointing to the stone, "it speaks of two women whose names they didn't know. I wonder…"

Angus glanced at her. "Be ye thinkin' o' the ghost?"

Muriel lifted her head from reading the stone. "I am."

Ailie tugged Nash closer to the stone. "The inscription reads 'for their adherence to the word of God and Scotland's covenanted work of reformation'."

Nash watched Ailie's face, wondering what her thoughts might be. "Heroes of the faith?"

She squeezed his arm. "I'm glad they'll be remembered."

"Time for the wedding feast, said William, "and, since it's Hogmanay, we might as well indoctrinate the groom into proper food."

Nash laughed. "Why not?" Today he would eat most anything.

"'Tis haggis," Ailie told her new husband when Nash inquired about the "strange" dish the servant had just placed before him. "Remember, I described it for you. 'Tis sheep's intestine, oatmeal and spices cooked in a sheep's stomach."

"Right," he said, his face contorting into an expression of pain. "Perhaps I'll begin with the soup. But what's that floating with the chicken and leeks?"

"Prunes. 'Tis the traditional way it's made." She could tell by the look on his face, Nash did not favor prunes, though they added much to what was essentially chicken soup.

"Well then," he said, "I'll have some salmon and potatoes."

"Tatties," she corrected, trying hard not to laugh. Glancing around the table, she noticed the others had declined the haggis, too. All except her grandfather, Captain Anderson, who'd been invited to the wedding, and Robbie.

Angus lifted a large bite of haggis onto his fork. "Food fer warriors."

"I'm for trying it all," quipped Robbie. "Else how can I describe the taste when asked?"

"Brave lad," said the eldest Powell brother. "I might have a go at the other dishes, but I'll be leaving the haggis to you."

"Personally," put in Tara, "I try to stay with what I recognize. Roast game, fish, steak pies and almost any dessert."

Ailie remembered Hugh's family had an estate in Scotland and wondered what foods he may have eaten. "Hugh, might you have tried some of our food while you were in Scotland?"

"Ah... once or twice. The fish is always fresh and the shortbread tasty."

Will shot him a side-glance. "Very diplomatic."

Emily leaned in to the countess. "And you, dear Muriel, what say you to the Scottish dishes? Will you have some?"

"Possibly," the countess replied. Through her quizzing glass, she gave the haggis a skeptical look. "I don't suppose there is kale in that mixture of things? That would be a bit much, I would think."

Chuckles ringed the table.

"No kale," said Will. "I urge you all to remember that dessert will follow shortly. We've some fine Scottish specialties: Dundee cake, clootie dumpling and shortbread. All go well with champagne." Lifting his glass, he said, "A toast to the bride and groom!"

Fourteen glasses were raised into the air. "To the bride and groom!"

Nash brushed her temple with his lips. "They are toasting us, my love."

She turned to gaze into his hazel eyes seeing only love and hoped it would always be so. "Aye, my husband, they are."

"For this night," William said, "Captain Anderson has taken a room in town to give Ailie and Nash his great cabin on the *Albatross*. Having slept there myself on one trip, I can assure you the bed is most comfortable."

Ailie's cheeks flamed at the thought of sharing a bed with Nash. She wanted to be his wife in all ways, but they had not talked about the wedding night. Thinking about it gave her anxious thoughts because she knew so little. Her mother in Aberdeen had given up on her rebellious daughter ever marrying. Emily had told Ailie not to worry, that she would find pleasure in the marriage bed.

"Very kind of you to make those arrangements for us, Will," said Nash. Then he lifted his glass to Captain Anderson, sitting farther down the table. "And very generous of you, Captain, to give up your cabin."

Captain Anderson smiled. "I'd do that and more for Miss Stephen, the young woman I have seen grow into womanhood to become Mrs. Powell."

Ailie was very fond of the often dour captain who, today, appeared quite jolly. "Thank you, Captain."

"You will have your privacy," said William, "and from the deck you will be able to see, and doubtless hear, the Hogmanay celebrations in town."

Having been assured by Ailie's brother that all aboard the *Albatross* had been made ready, Nash walked with Ailie to the ship. The sun was just setting behind the hills, casting a lavender blanket over the waters of the bay and turning the sky over the North Sea a stunning violet.

She gripped her tartan shawl tightly around her. "A beautiful night, aye?"

The nervous tremor in her voice was unmistakable. "Not so beautiful as my bride." Before she could reply, he slipped his arm around her shoulder and cuddled her against his side. "You have nothing to fear, Ailie. It's our first time together, that's all. Trust me, you will like our joining."

"I will?"

He smiled. "I know what I'm about, my love, and I promise to be gentle. Remember that I love you. Of all the women in the world, and I have seen many in my travels, I chose you for my wife."

She let out a deep sigh, her breath coming out in a cloud. He hoped her sigh meant she found comfort in his words. Only once had he taken a virgin. Both he and the girl were too young to know what they were about, much less did he know about loving a woman. Since then, all his partners had been experienced women. He was glad, for what he had learned from them would allow him to treat his bride as a precious gift.

"Tonight we begin what we have a lifetime to enjoy."

She tucked her head into his shoulder. "I know. Muriel said you'd explain everything to me."

He chuckled. "Did she now?"

They walked up the gangplank and were greeted by the junior officer. "Welcome aboard, Mr. and Mrs. Powell. Your chamber awaits you. Unless you call for service, you will not be disturbed."

With that, he left them and headed for the forward hatch. Nash escorted Ailie to the aft hatch and down the ladder.

At the end of the companionway, the captain's door stood ajar. He pushed it open and stepped over the threshold bringing her with him. A lantern cast its subtle light over the large interior. Because of the raised overhead, the cabin had windows on both sides, covered now with dark blue curtains.

Ailie took off her gloves and he helped her to shed her cloak, hanging it and his own on the pegs near the door. She went to stand before the stove where coals burned brightly, warming her hands. The ship rose and fell beneath them like the breathing of a sleeping sea.

Her gaze drifted toward the round pedestal table where a bottle of champagne and two glasses rested beside a tray of fruit, cheese and bread. "They went to a lot of trouble for us, didn't they?"

He took her hands in his, raising them to his lips. "As I would expect from those who love us." He pressed a kiss to her knuckles. "We only have one wedding night, Ailie. It should be a special event."

"I'm a bit shy about it, I know, but I do want you, Nash. I mean not just for my husband, but for the marriage bed." Her cheeks flushed. She let go of his hands and glanced toward the shelf bed, where the cover had been turned down and someone had laid out her nightclothes. She quickly looked back, biting her lower lip.

He took off his tailcoat and hung it over the back of a chair. His waistcoat and cravat followed. Ailie had seen him wearing only his shirt when she had come to change Robbie's bandage so he didn't think it would startle her.

He joined her in front of the stove and drew her into his arms, kissing her forehead, breathing in her sweet smell of lily of the valley. "One of our friends has a sense of humor, I think."

Her beautiful eyes met his. "What do you mean?"

"If I do this right, Ailie, you won't be needing those nightclothes."

"Oh."

They had dined earlier and drunk their fill of champagne, yet perhaps she needed more time. "Would you like something to drink? To eat?"

She shook her head and pressed her lips together. He had to try and calm her fears.

"Remember the woods, Ailie, when I first kissed you?" She nodded. "And the night we shared the stars together and I kissed you again?" She nodded. "And the kiss I gave you at Dunnottar?" Again she nodded.

"This is yet another time when I will kiss you, showing you my heart and, I hope, raising your passion. Only this time, we will become one."

He kissed her then, a teasing kiss. He wanted her eager for more before they moved to the bed. Knowing the woman he had desired for weeks was finally his and that, tonight, they would join together made him impatient to begin but, for her sake and that of their marriage, he planned to go slowly.

He kissed her until her breath came faster and she reached her hands to his nape, exploring his mouth as he explored hers. His body responded, his groin swelling in anticipation of what was to follow. Did she realize the entwining of their tongues foreshadowed what would come next?

He slid his hand to one of her warm breasts, touching for the second time what he'd only imagined before. Slowly, he stroked the sensitive peak through the silk and the thin fabric beneath it. In his mind, he pictured her naked. It was impossible not to.

Wanting to taste her, he pulled down one of her sleeves and the shift underneath it, exposing one silken shoulder. Brushing his lips over her warm skin he kissed her from her shoulder to her neck, gently nibbling along the way until he felt her shiver.

Raising his head, he looked into her eyes. "Do you like how that makes you feel?"

"Aye, I like it."

"Good. There is more to come. You can kiss me, too, Ailie, any-where you like. I *want* you to touch me." He loosened his shirt from his trousers and pulled it over his head until his chest was naked before her.

He let her look her fill. His chest was well-muscled from a combina-tion of his work on ships and his sporting activities with Robbie in London.

With innocent fingers, she raised her hand and tentatively ran her fingers over the dark curls sprinkled over his chest and glided her fingers across his nipple, sending a shiver to his core. She raised her head to meet his fevered gaze. "You're beautiful."

He resisted the desire to fling her onto the bed and take her. "Not beautiful," he said with a husky voice, as he opened his eyes, "but I'll take that as meaning you like the body of the man you married."

She smiled, then bit her bottom lip as if embarrassed. "I do."

"You must know how much I enjoy your touch, Ailie. There is no shame between us in the marriage bed. God gave it to us to enjoy." This time when he kissed her, he ended the kiss by taking her hand and leading her toward the bed. He removed her tartan sash and turned her around, unbuttoning her gown. It dropped to the floor and he laid it on the chest at the foot of the shelf bed. With her back to him, he kissed her neck and her shoulders, taking both her breasts in his hands. She bent her head to the side as he kissed her neck. "I think it's time we dispensed with all pretense of clothing." He unlaced her corset and let it drop, along with her shift.

She turned in his arms and no longer did he have to imagine what she looked like underneath the female frippery. His bride was everything he'd hoped for. And more. Intelligent, full of wonder and dreams and more beautiful than she knew. "You are perfect, Ailie."

She covered her breasts with one arm and the fiery hair at the apex of her thighs with the other. "Nay."

He pulled her hands away. "I say you are perfect. Your breasts like ripe fruit, your belly like a smooth sea and your legs. Ah, your legs are long and shapely and there's fire where they join." He lifted her onto the edge of the bed and removed her stockings, slowly rolling them down.

Even in the lantern light, he could see the blush rising from her chest to her face.

"Oh, Ailie, don't you know I would love you if you were not so beautiful? But I say again, you are perfect."

He held the cover for her so she could crawl beneath it. Then shedding the rest of his clothing, he joined her in the bed, pressing his body to hers. Heat seared his blood, so ready he was for the lovemaking that would follow. Forcing himself to go slow, he said. "I left the lantern to burn, so I can see you and you me."

Her eyes spoke of the trust she placed in him. "All right."

"And now, we begin."

Ailie woke sometime later, hearing the sounds of the revelry that always accompanied Hogmanay. Nash had draped his arm possessively around her, his body turned into hers as it had been when he had fallen asleep. One of her legs was caught between his.

She smiled, so happy she could not help it. He had loved her well, teaching her to love their joining. By the time they had coupled, she was desperate to have him inside her. The pain was brief and he had warned her. Once it had diminished, she had moved with him, delighting in his body, as he whispered words of love, and took them to that place she had never been.

That was the first time, but there had been a second time, which had been even better, for he had made love to her slowly, driving her mad.

More shouts sounded from the town's streets. She pictured the revelers swinging their fireballs. Wanting to see them before they were cast into the water of the harbor, she carefully extricated herself from Nash, kissing him on his forehead, and rose. She remembered seeing her blue velvet wrapper on the end of the bed and felt for it in the dim light. The lantern no longer gave its light, though the coals in the stove stilled glowed.

Donning her wrapper, she padded the short distance from the bed to the window that faced the harbor. Opening the curtains, she glimpsed the town, bright with flaming torches. Down the center of the main street, men marched, swinging the flaming balls they would have earlier steeped in paraffin, wrapped in sacking and tied with netting wire.

The fireballs that marked the Winter Solstice celebration lighted the snow-covered street, turning it into a river of glowing fire. Since she was a young girl, each year she and Will, and sometimes her parents and younger brothers, had sailed to Stonehaven to spend New Year's with her grandparents to witness the ceremony.

"The bed is cold without you, my love," said Nash, coming up behind her and crossing his arms over her chest. She leaned back into his warmth and turned her head to accept his kiss. He smelled of sandalwood and their joining.

She brought her hands up to cover his arms, loving the feel of the soft hair on his forearms, the same dark hair on his chest. "Don't you want to see the fireballs?"

"It seems appropriate our wedding night should be marked by fire, don't you think?"

Her skin flushed with heat. "Aye."

The men began to toss their fireballs into the harbor where they hissed as the flames were doused. She turned and laid her head on his warm chest. He was hers as she belonged to him now.

A chorus of Auld Lang Syne rose from the harbor. She looked back to see people standing together singing. Ailie joined them, singing softly,

"Should auld acquaintance be forgot and never brought to mind?
Should auld acquaintance be forgot and auld lang syne
For auld lang syne, my dear, for auld lang syne,
We'll take a cup o kindness yet, for auld lang syne."

He nuzzled her neck. "Another of Burns' poems?"

"Aye and no. 'Tis an ancient poem Burns committed to paper. We sing the song after midnight at year's end to remember happy days from the past, the days that followed after and coming back together."

He held her tightly and kissed her temple. "A little like us, eh?"

She nodded and raised her head to kiss him.

"Come to bed, my love."

Some hours later, Nash opened his eyes. The only light was from the dying coals in the stove that cast deep shadows around the cabin. He had no desire to leave his bride's bed, but he remembered another tradition Will advised him to keep. "If you happen to think of it, that is. 'Tis your wedding night, after all."

When he'd asked, Will told him of the Scots' tradition of "first-footing" whereby if a man of dark hair bearing a gift was the first to cross the threshold after midnight on New Year's Day, he would bring good luck to the household.

Nash tucked the cover around his bride and pulled on his breeches. Lifting from his coat pocket the gift he had acquired when he'd bought her wedding ring, he crept from the cabin. Once outside, standing in the cold passageway, he knocked loudly on the cabin door. When no sound came, he knocked again. She needed sleep after their night of lovemaking, but he thought she'd not mind rising for one of her traditions.

Finally, he heard her sleepy voice through the cabin door. "Nash?"

"Yes, love, it is I."

The door opened and he entered, closing it behind him.

She peered at him in the dim light of the cabin. "Where did you go? The door was unlocked, you know."

Rising to his full height, he grinned widely. "Behold, it is I, the first-footer!"

She laughed "Oh, Nash, you are, aren't you?" She kissed him on the cheek. "Clever man. Did you bring me a lump of coal? We could add it to the stove. It's freezing in here."

"I will stir the coals and gladly add wood to the fire, but first I have a gift for you." He pulled the brooch from his pocket and placed it in her palm. "I know a lump of coal is the usual gift but I thought you'd like this better. Come, you'll be able to see it better as I light the fire."

He went to the stove, stirred the coals to life and added two chunks of wood. When the flames caught, Ailie exclaimed, "Oh, Nash. 'Tis magnificent, a gift for a queen."

"So it is. *My* queen." He returned to her side and studied the brooch, a large sherry-colored oval stone surrounded by a wreath of silver, carved with thistle flowers and leaves. The gem seemed to be alive as it caught the light of the fire. "It's a Madeira citrine. When I saw it, I knew it had to be yours. It's the color of your eyes, Ailie."

When she finally looked up, her eyes were full of tears. "I shall wear it always."

"Here," he said, taking it from her. "I'll pin it to your wrapper for tonight."

They returned to their bed and did not wake till the sun's rays spilled into the cabin.

Chapter 23

New Year's Day

The day was fair but the wind off the sea biting as Muriel waved goodbye to Angus from the deck of the *Albatross*. Behind her, the ship's crew was preparing to set sail. Aileen and her new husband waved to the man who Muriel now called friend.

"He will miss you, I think," said Aileen.

"And I him. Do bring your grandfather to London for a visit, won't you?"

"I will at least suggest it," she replied, "but Grandfather's life is here on Scotland's coast with his fishermen friends and his business. Still, for you, he might come." A moment ago the young woman had been radiantly happy from her wedding night, but now she was wistful at having to say goodbye to her grandfather.

For herself, Muriel hated partings and always felt melancholy when they were forced upon her. There had been too many in her life. She had only to turn around and someone was departing, if not this life then England. She did not envy Aileen being the wife of a man who went to sea, but she would have the other Powell wives for company when that happened.

The pale winter sun hung low in the sky when the *Albatross* docked in Arbroath that afternoon. Muriel had come up on deck to see the butler Lamont, his head held high, Mrs. Platt, smiling broadly, and the housekeeper Mrs. Banks waiting to meet the ship. The three servants stood at the edge of the dock, Aileen's watchful setters sitting patiently at their feet.

William and Emily descended the gangplank first with Muriel just behind them on the arm of Robbie Powell. The setters rose and whimpered until their mistress, just behind Muriel, affectionately greeted them.

As the others filed off the ship, Muriel turned to Aileen. "Will you take the dogs to London?"

Aileen exchanged a glance with her husband before answering. "Aye. Nash has agreed Goodness and Mercy may come as long as Captain Anderson doesn't mind their presence on the *Albatross*."

Nash glanced at his bride and then faced Muriel. "Can't you picture us walking the setters in Hyde Park?"

Muriel could well imagine the sight. "A fine-looking young couple and their dashing black setters? Why, I expect all of London will speak of it."

"And every man will envy my brother," said Robbie, "including me."

Nash's face bore a victor's smug smile.

Muriel looked at Robbie askance. "Just remember, Robbie Powell, you are next."

Nash made a noise that Muriel could only describe as a snort, but Aileen smiled. "I look forward to seeing the rogue fall. Already I like my future sister-in-law."

"I wonder who she'll be," said Nash, turning to his brother. "Perhaps Muriel will find you some quiet, biddable girl for you to charm."

"I shall be looking, you can be certain of it," said Muriel, "but I do not promise biddable." She glanced again at the brooch Nash had given his bride, pinned to Aileen's cloak. "I do love that brooch, Aileen. Your new husband has excellent taste."

"Aye, he does, doesn't he?" Aileen gave her husband of one day a look that spoke of their wedding night. "I would expect you to admire it, Muriel. Nash told me the stone is a Madeira citrine."

"No wonder it caught my eye," Though many years past her own wedding, Muriel felt a blush coming on as she remembered her first night with the Earl of Claremont, the first time she had glimpsed the pearls he gave her.

They strolled up to the estate and William invited them into the parlor where drinks awaited them. "Since you sail tomorrow, we'll have an early dinner tonight."

Muriel was glad for the Madeira that fortified her for the sad parting she knew was coming. While she would be glad to see her friends in London, she would miss her dear friend Emily and the new friends she had made in Scotland. But what wonderful new memories she had.

William came to her side. "Have you quite enjoyed yourself these past weeks, Muriel?"

"Indeed, I have." She sipped her Madeira. "Can't recall a holiday I have enjoyed so much in years. You and Emily have been wonderful hosts."

"And, of course, there was Angus," said Robbie, tossing her a smirk.

"Shameless rogue," said Muriel.

Once she had rested and Rhona helped her pack for the sail to London, Muriel went downstairs early, hoping to see Emily before dinner. In the parlor, she found Kit sitting on one of the sofas setting her sketchbooks on the table in front of her, Muriel's charges gathered around the artist.

Her dark red hair neatly tied back at her nape, a pencil resting over one ear, Kit looked up when Muriel entered. "Oh good, you're here. Come sit next to me."

Muriel took the seat next to Kit and everyone pulled up a chair around the table. Emily claimed the other end of the sofa, William sitting on the arm above her.

Glancing from her sketchbook to William and Emily, Kit said, "I did these for you as a reminder of our time together and everyone cooperated."

"I knew you were making sketches," replied Emily, "but I had no idea they were for us. How thoughtful!" She looked up at her husband. "Won't these make wonderful keepsakes?"

"Aye, they will, *Leannan*. We thank you, Kit."

Kit directed her attention to her sketches, opening the first of the two large books. "I want to show you the couples first, beginning with the one of Martin and me."

Martin laughed when he saw it. The picture showed Kit sketching and Martin sitting in a chair watching her, affection in his eyes. "You have the right of it, sweetheart. And I expect our hosts appreciate all those hours I gazed with longing at my beautiful wife with other things in mind."

Kit regarded her husband with mild disapproval. "And didn't I make up for it?"

"You did."

Flipping the page, Kit said, "Here are Mary and Hugh as we might all think of them."

Muriel inclined her head to see the drawing of Hugh and Mary riding two of William's fine horses.

"Hasn't she captured us well, Hugh?" asked Mary.

"Indeed, she has."

"The next one," Kit went on, "is of Nick and Tara, together on the *Albatross*. It's how I remember them as we sailed from London to Arbroath."

"A good likeness," remarked Muriel. "The shipmaster and his lady aboard a ship." Kit had captured the essence of Nick's love of the sea and his wife. "A great talent."

Nick and Tara studied the sketch, nodding their approval.

Turning the page, Kit revealed a sketch of Aileen, Nash staring at her with adoring eyes.

"You sketched us together?" asked Ailie. "We have been so busy since the wedding, when did you find the time?"

"I didn't do this one after the wedding, but long before. It was the day we went deer stalking. I had begun one of Nash in the library one morning and finished it the night we all talked about the avalanche, adding you, Ailie. Not until that day did I know how things might turn out between you."

Nash, whose arm was around his bride, kissed her. "Told you."

Robbie raised a brow. It occurred to Muriel that he must not know of his twin's valiant act saving Ailie from the avalanche.

"And this one is of Robbie," said Kit, "though he's in others as well." Muriel thought the sketch a good likeness of him before he'd been shot. Now he had a scar that would forever distinguish him from his twin brother. In the bottom corners were drawings of an otter and a lion as they had discussed that afternoon in the parlor.

Robbie gave Kit a surprised look. "You added the animals you envisioned when you were drawing my face?"

"Of course. Those are the two sides of you," said Kit. "The playful rogue and the dangerous spy, though at the time, I did not know of your work for the Crown."

Muriel recognized her own image in the next drawing. It depicted that day in the library when she had puzzled over her cards while fiddling with her pearls. The sketch even captured the feather rising from her head into the air. "Our card game, I presume."

Emily laughed. "Yes, I believe that was the moment when I fetched you the Madeira, giving you time to consider your next move."

Muriel lifted her chin. She would not apologize for her small deception. "I did not even win that round. As I recall, that one went to Robbie."

Kit turned another page. "The last one of the couples is of William and Emily under the kissing bough."

"Oh my," said Emily, bringing her hand over her heart. "You caught us kissing."

William put his hand on his wife's shoulder. "Just as I would want to remember us this holiday. The first kissing bough at our home in Arbroath being christened. Something to tell the bairn about."

"This next one," explained Kit, turning the page, "is twice as large as the others, taking up two pages. It's my sketch of our time when you skated on the frozen pond. You're all in it, save Muriel and myself. We were sitting on the bench. And there are smaller drawings of some whose actions caught my eye."

"That would be me taking a fall," put in Robbie. "Nash is the one gliding around the ice with Ailie."

Muriel recalled the afternoon with great fondness. The others did as well, speaking of their time on the ice as a day they would long remember. As for Muriel, she would always think of the memory the day had brought to her mind when she and the earl had skated on another pond.

Turning the page, Kit said, "Here is Angus Ramsay dining with us. I am so glad I got to know him. Isn't he a distinguished-looking fellow?"

"That he is," said Ailie, "and a wonderful man."

Muriel studied the weathered face Kit had captured with her pencil. In the many lines and hearty smile, she saw a friend she hoped to see again. "A fine gentleman."

"Those of you who went deer stalking will remember this scene," offered Kit.

Muriel leaned over to see a glen between two hills and the hunters with their guns over their shoulders, waiting it seemed. Ailie stood to one side with Nash and the setters.

"What were you waiting for?" asked Emily.

"The hinds to appear," said William. "More particularly, the right kind of hind for the culling."

Muriel pointed to a small sketch in the bottom corner. "What's this?"

"That is the aftermath of the avalanche," replied Kit. "You can see the snow piled up and one deer's legs sticking out of the snow."

"Oh my," said Muriel. She had heard them describe it at dinner that night but to see it, even in miniature, was quite another matter.

Kit flipped to the next drawing. "This is the happy day we brought in the Yule log."

"Happy for those of you who did not have to drag the beast inside," said Nick.

"We did it together," William corrected.

"So we did," agreed Nick.

Turning the page, Kit announced, "The day everyone decorated the house for Christmas. I thought to capture the kitchen, a room you never see. Here are Emily and Muriel adding green boughs to the shelves with the help of Mrs. Platt and Martha."

"How thoughtful of you to draw this," said Emily. "Martha will be ever so pleased to see she was remembered as a part of your holiday."

"Mrs. Platt must see this as well," Muriel chimed in.

Kit turned the page to reveal a sketch of all the ladies, even Muriel. "Christmas Eve. You all looked so pretty, I just had to try and record it. I do hope I got the gowns right."

"You managed to get mine just right," said Muriel. "What a memory you have, Kit."

"Well, I did ask to see some of the gowns later to get a bit of our frippery correctly drawn."

Standing behind his wife, Martin leaned down and kissed the side of her head. "You did very well, Kitten."

"Since we were always eating it seems, I thought one of the sketches had to be a meal. This is Christmas dinner, roast goose and all the trimmings."

Many oohs and aahs resounded. Muriel remembered the dishes, especially the desserts. "Won't Mrs. Platt be pleased to see this?"

"You're making me hungry," said Hugh.

"And now for Dunnottar," announced Kit, who was well into the second sketchbook. "The brooding ruins, but without the ghosts. I really wouldn't know how to draw one."

Muriel scrutinized the drawing, seeing the massive dark rock and the ruins resting upon it, reminders of troublesome days in Scotland's past. In the corners of the drawing were smaller vignettes, the craggy coast as seen from the sea, a storm petrel in flight, and a few of the buildings. One was the chapel.

"I remember well the chapel," said Nash. "It was there Ailie accepted my proposal of marriage."

Ailie remembered it well, too, judging by the look she bestowed on Nash.

"And the final three sketches," said Kit, "are from Stonehaven: The Ship Inn, Nash and Ailie in the church being married and the Hogmanay feast after."

The others pored over the drawings, some asking to examine the first sketchbook. Muriel herself was more than a little impressed.

Emily kissed the artist on her cheek. "You have given us a wonderful gift, Kit. One we will treasure always. Now that you will all be returning to London, even taking our dear Ailie for a while, this will remind William and me of our time together."

"Thank you, Kit," said William. Rising, he added, "When everyone is finished here, dinner awaits."

The next morning, Ailie woke in the same chamber she had slept in for the last five years, only it was not the same. Now, a naked man lay beside her, a very attractive man, whose lovemaking brought heat to her cheeks just to think of it. He had taught her to love their bodies and the marriage bed.

She stared up at the ceiling as dawn crept into their chamber. "Nash, I've been thinking…"

He rolled toward her, brushing her breasts with his fingers, causing her nipples to draw into tight buds, sending a twinge of anticipation to her woman's center. "Yes, my love?"

"Where will we live when we are in London?"

He captured her hands in his and pressed them into the pillow above her head, as he trailed kisses down her neck. Her thoughts scattered. In between kisses, he said, "With my parents until we find our own house. I've had my eye on another one at Adelphi Terrace coming up for sale." He nibbled on her breasts. "Now I have a reason to buy it, that is, if you like it. We won't need a very large house, not at first anyway." He raised his head to give her a wicked smile. "And if we are close to my parents, they can keep an eye on our house while we're away in Arbroath. Would that suit?"

She gazed into his hazel eyes, glistening with desire. "Aye, it suits me fine. And since Rhona has agreed to come along, I feel better facing the gentry in London. She'll see that I am properly attired."

"You have nothing to worry about on that score. Muriel has agreed to help and she is an expert in the *ton*." He resumed kissing her neck, dropping his mouth to her breasts. "I can smell bread baking, my love, but we might have a bit of time for us if we don't dawdle."

But she and Nash did dawdle, as he put it. When they finally made their appearance downstairs, no one seemed surprised. Honeymooning couples, they were told, were not expected to watch the clock.

Ailie had taken the setters for a good long walk before stowing them belowdecks where special arrangements had been made for them.

From the deck of the *Albatross*, the passengers waved goodbye to Will and Emily. Ailie knew they were all sad to be leaving, but the parents among them were also eager to return to their children and their homes.

A lump formed in Ailie's throat and her eyes filled with tears as she waved goodbye to her brother and sister-in-law.

His arm around her, Nash shouted from the rail, "I'll bring her back in the spring to see the babe!"

The ship's sails billowed with wind as the *Albatross* left the coast heading south.

"Wherever you are is my home now, Nash."

"'Tis the same for me, Ailie."

"I don't suppose anyone knows if Captain Anderson carries Madeira on this ship," said Muriel as she turned toward the aft hatch.

Robbie offered Muriel his arm. "As to that, I've no intelligence, but he stocks a damn fine brandy."

Ailie laughed, grateful the two of them had lightened her mood.

Nash took her hand. "Come, my love. Since we failed to appear at breakfast, I've a hunger for some of that haddie stew."

"Cullen Skink," she said, returning his smile, secure in the knowledge she had found the right man and none too soon.

See the Pinterest Board for *A Secret Scottish Christmas*
pinterest.com/reganwalker123/a-secret-scottish-christmas-by-regan-walker

Author's Note

It may surprise you to know that Christmas was not celebrated as a festival in Scotland for about four hundred years. This dates back to the Protestant Reformation when the Scottish Kirk proclaimed Christmas a Catholic feast. While the actual prohibition, passed by Scotland's Parliament in 1640, didn't last long, the Church of Scotland, which is Presbyterian, discouraged Yule celebrations beginning as early as 1583 and this continued into the 1950s. Many Scots worked over Christmas and celebrated the Winter Solstice at the New Year, which celebration came to be known as Hogmanay.

It was not until 1958 that Christmas Day became a public holiday in Scotland; Boxing Day followed in 1974.

William Stephen. Should you be wondering, William Stephen's character is based on a real person, as is his family in Aberdeen and their business, Alexander Stephen & Sons. Alexander Stephen founded his shipbuilding enterprise on the Moray Firth in 1750. In 1793, William Stephen, a descendent of his, established a firm of shipbuilders in Aberdeen. In 1813, another member of the family, again named William, began another shipbuilding enterprise in Arbroath.

The real William Stephen did, indeed, fight in France where he was taken prisoner and, upon his release, opened a shipyard in Arbroath in 1814. You first met him and Emily in *The Holly & The Thistle*. His sister Aileen, however, is entirely fictional.

As of 1817, Arbroath was Scotland's biggest sailcloth producer. At the time of my story, it was a thriving harbor town with at least three shipbuilders.

Ailie's Setters. Yes, Goodness and Mercy were Gordon Setters. Alexander, the Duke of Gordon (1743-1827), established his famous kennel of working setters at Gordon Castle in Scotland, but at the time of my story, he was just perfecting the breed and they had not yet come to be known by his title. Nor were they just black with tan markings. In the early days, they also had white markings. You can see them on the Pinterest storyboard for the book.

The Ships. All the ships in the story were real and built in Arbroath. The *Albatross* was a ship built by William Stephen. The *Panmure*, a fully rigged schooner, was built by Alex Fernie. It was named after the Earl of Panmure, who lost his title after the Rising of 1715. The *Ossian* was a schooner built in Arbroath in 1820, though I doubt it was of the advanced design Ailie envisioned in my story. Those ships came a bit later.

The Peterloo Massacre. The Peterloo massacre that took place at St Peter's Field in Manchester in August 1819 happened as I have presented it, relying upon journals of individuals who were there that fateful day. The slaughter sparked protests in both England and Scotland. There was rioting in both Glasgow and Paisley. Unlike many workers in England, the weavers in Scotland were a skilled and literate group that traditionally worked on commission, choosing their own hours. They were proud, independent and, not surprisingly, more radical in their outlook than the English.

From the autumn of 1819, a "general rising" had been expected, hence the rumors that made their way to Arbroath that December. And perhaps that is one reason for the government's harsh treatment of George Kinloch. All these events culminated in what became known as the "Radical War" of April 1820.

George Kinloch, you will be pleased to know, safely reached Brittany, France and wrote to his wife at the end of December that he was in perfect health and good spirits. (He was a great correspondent and we know much of his thoughts from his letters to his wife Helen.) I took some poetic license with his point of departure; he sailed from Dover not Arbroath. The prior year, when he had gone to France with his two sons, he sailed from Dundee. But, to me, Arbroath seemed like such a reasonable place for him to sail from on this occasion. Don't you agree?

Henry Hunt was finally released from prison in 1822, wearing an elegant tartan courtesy of the Greenock Radicals. George Kinloch was pardoned in 1823 and, in December 1832, after passage of the Reform Bill, he was made the first representative in Parliament for the people of Dundee. Ailie was right. He was, indeed, a hero.

Inns, Taverns, Churches, Streets and Newspapers. All these were real. My readers know that the research to make my stories authentic is important to me. The Ship Inn and the taverns mentioned were actual establishments. Some are open to this day but others are historical. The churches were actual places of worship, open at the time. (The Covenanters' Stone in the Dunnottar churchyard did exist at the time and today.) The streets named were real streets. And the newspapers referenced were journals read at the time.

The Language of the Scots. As you might imagine, Scots living on the Northeast coast of Scotland spoke a unique dialect, as they do today, except in prominent families such as the Stephens, who spoke the King's English. (Their journals read like ones written by English men and women). They might have spoken with an accent, of course. Most of the common people would have spoken the Doric dialect. Since Doric would be hard for readers to understand, I used it sparingly and sprinkled the book with a few Scottish expressions to give you a flavor for the local speech, particularly in the taverns and for Ailie's grandfather.

Scot, Scotsman, Scotch or Scottish... how to refer to the Scots? The terminology can be confusing. Robert Burns, Scotland's poet, referred to the people of Scotland as "Scots". As you know from reading my stories set in Medieval Scotland, the people have always been "Scots" and their kings were never Kings of Scotland, but Kings of the Scots, the people being of first importance, not the land, as in England. The Scots themselves refer to their stories and language as "Scottish", but in past times they used the word "Scotch" in place of "Scottish" or "Scot", something not done today.

In *Reminiscences of Scottish Life and Character* by Edward Bannerman Ramsay, first published in 1857, the author looks back "forty years" (which would be to the Regency era) and describes the unique "Scottish dialect". In one place, he says, "I recollect old Scottish ladies and gentlemen who really spoke Scotch." He also refers to "the Scotch" as a people and describes himself as "an out and out Scotchman". So there you have it.

Clans, Septs and Tartans. In 1815, the Highland Society of London asked all the clan chiefs to authenticate their tartans. Thus, by the time of my story, many tartans had been recorded. The Stephens were a sept, or a part of, Clan MacDuff; and Angus Ramsay was of Clan Ramsay. Each had its own tartan.

Horticulture in Scotland and Orangeries. An orangery (or orangerie) was a room or a building on the grounds of fashionable estates from the 17th to the 19th centuries where orange and other fruit trees were protected during the winter, similar to a greenhouse or conservatory. Pineapples were grown in Scotland's orangeries (sometimes called the pinery) from the early 18th century, most often in pits filled with a source of heat. Oak bark in water was often used. When the oak chips fermented, they released heat at a slow and steady rate.

It was not until the 19th century that orangeries were able to develop into efficient glass houses for plants. By 1816, piped hot water had been introduced into Britain, making it possible to locate stoves outside the orangery.

Food and Drink. In the late 18th century, Georgian hostesses entertained in grand style in their new dining rooms. Instead of the usual two large courses of food at dinner, wealthy families in Scotland offered guests several smaller courses including soup, fish, game, roast meat, pudding and dessert. Food was richer with more complicated recipes and there was a greater emphasis on cream and sugar in desserts.

Kale. THE Scots national vegetable was the green kale, particularly among Lowlanders. Nettles, leeks, onions, sorrel, carrots, and turnips were all considered inadequate rivals. The cotter's garden is still called "the kaleyard", and the time-honored vegetable still holds a place of honor in the nation's esteem.

The Absence of Whisky. Some of you might wonder why my Scottish characters weren't drinking whisky. While distillation of whisky had been going on for a long time, most of the distilleries were illicit. The invention of the column still by Scotsman Robert Stein in 1828 revolutionized whisky making in Scotland. Then in 1831, Aeneas Coffey invented the Coffey or Patent Still, which enabled a continuous process of distillation leading to the production of grain whisky, a less intense spirit than the malt whisky produced in the copper pot stills. Andrew Usher & Co improved upon this invention in 1860, blending malt and grain whisky together to produce a lighter flavored whisky.

In the early days, Scotch whisky was mostly considered the equivalent of moonshine—a drink enjoyed by unrefined Highlanders, aged in sheep bladders and filtered through tartan. Men of William Stephen's stature would be drinking the finest European wines, along with sherry, port, brandy and cognac.

Shipmasters, like the Powells, sailing to France, would have brought back such drinks. In *To Tame the Wind*, we learned that Claire Powell was the daughter of Jean Donet, comte de Saintonge, who owned cognac-producing vineyards in France. From *The Holly & The Thistle* you might recall that Muriel's favorite drink is Madeira, the wine from Portugal popular in the Regency era.

Auld Lang Syne. A version of the song existed decades before Robert Burns wrote it down. It's said an old man dictated the words to him. Before Burns wrote it down, the ancient song had been passed on by word of mouth. The melody we know today that accompanies the lyrics didn't appear until after Burns' death in 1796.

The phrase "Auld Lang Syne" means "old long ago", which can be translated as "days gone by" or "back in the day". Thomas Keith, a Burns scholar, says the song symbolizes reunion, not parting, as some mistakenly believe. The song looks back over happy days from the past, a separation and then coming back together.

Author Bio

Regan Walker is an award-winning, Amazon bestselling author of Regency, Georgian and Medieval romances. A lawyer turned full-time writer, she has seven times been featured in USA TODAY's HEA column and nominated six times for the prestigious RONE award. (Her novels, *The Red Wolf's Prize* and *King's Knight*, won Best Historical Novel in the medieval category for 2015 and 2017, respectively.) In 2017, her novel *The Refuge: An Inspirational Novel of Scotland* won the Gold Medal in the Illumination Awards, and *To Tame the Wind* won the International Book Award for Romance Fiction.

Years of serving clients in private practice and several stints in high levels of government have given Regan a love of international travel and a feel for the demands of the "Crown". Hence her stories often feature a demanding sovereign who taps his subjects for special assignments. Each of her novels includes real history and real historical figures as characters. And, of course, adventure and love.

Follow Regan on Amazon and BookBub.
amazon.com/Regan-Walker/e/B008OUWC5Y
bookbub.com/profile/regan-walker

Keep in touch with her on Facebook, where you can join Regan Walker's Readers. You can sign up for her newsletter on her website.
facebook.com/regan.walker.104
facebook.com/groups/ReganWalkersReaders
www.reganwalkerauthor.com

Robbie's story, *Rogue's Holiday*, is coming in Fall 2018. Watch for it!

Books by Regan Walker

The Agents of the Crown series:

To Tame the Wind (prequel)
Racing with the Wind
Against the Wind
Wind Raven
A Secret Scottish Christmas
Rogue's Holiday (coming in 2018)

The Donet Trilogy:

To Tame the Wind
Echo in the Wind
A Fierce Wind (coming in 2018)

Holiday Novellas (related to the Agents of the Crown):

The Shamrock & The Rose
The Twelfth Night Wager
The Holly & The Thistle

The Medieval Warriors series:

The Red Wolf's Prize
Rogue Knight
Rebel Warrior
King's Knight

Inspirational

The Refuge: An Inspirational Novel of Scotland

www.ReganWalkerAuthor.com

Made in the USA
San Bernardino, CA
17 November 2017